C

MEMORY I

CHAPTER ONE
Eight months earlier, Fort Howard Neuro Clinic

The next few minutes would change the direction of Renee's life completely.

She was just a nurse after all, *just a nurse*, she thought. Yet she had worked so hard to be where she was. Countless hours of school, doing all the same subjects as the doctors without the promised payday. And she was going to throw it all away.

She palmed the syringe in her hand, wondering if she could really do it. She could administer the sedative easily enough – she'd done that for plenty of patients before.

But Memory II... tested only on a few patients, it had proven to be a finicky drug. It had worked before, for a few patients, but how was she to be sure it would work *this* time?

Renee had witnessed the doctor performing the procedure on seven or eight occasions. First, he injected the sedative in the small needle into the base of the neck. Once the patient was unconscious, he would insert the big one – the scary needle that held a revolutionary medicine colloquially referred to as Memory II. Most patients died immediately, and some had to be induced in a deep coma, but a rare few survived.

She pushed the thought from her mind, thumbing the syringe. It was almost shift change for the security guards.

Renee wiggled the computer mouse to wake the screen, confirming the time. 5:51. Dr. Ingels was still on vacation, and would be for another two days. The guards were scheduled to switch in 3 minutes.

Just a few feet from where Renee stood, the glazed guard in khakis slumped in his chair, unenthusiastically glowering at the hallway clock. Renee closed out of her calendar and shut down the computer.

She placed both needles onto a medical tray and tucked it underneath the nurses' computer, resting on top of the keyboard. She walked easily into Cornelia's room, where Renee had spent hours, professionally and non-, just chatting. Cornelia was a special soul.

"Are you ready?" Renee whispered as she came around to Cornelia's side.

She nodded, using a tissue to wipe a tear from her eye. She had been crying for days. As unethical as their plan felt, Renee jumped at the chance to end Cornelia's suffering.

"I can't do this anymore, I have to get out," Cornelia sniffled. She pushed her unevenly cut ash brown hair out of her face, revealing a puffy scar that buffered the top half of her ear.

Renee had dealt with her share of emotional patients, but Cornelia she truly *felt* for.

"There are other ways," Renee reminded her. She squeezed her patient's shoulder.

Cornelia shook her head. "I don't want to remember this. I don't want to know the life I had here. I don't want to remember Nate... like that," Cornelia said, bursting into tears again.

"Hey," Renee said, sitting down on the bed and pulling her in for a quick hug. "Stop your crying. You're going to be okay."

Cornelia nodded as Renee pulled away, wiping her tears. "Is it time yet?"

Renee glanced at the clock on the wall to see the minute hand hit the 12 o'clock position. The guard's footsteps echoed down the hallway.

"It's time," Renee said.

"Did you finish the chart?"

Renee nodded. "Do you want to look at it?"

Cornelia shook her head. "You're confident I'll never know what happened?"

Renee nodded. "As far as you or anyone will know, you were in a coma for 226 days."

Cornelia nodded, sniffling. "Good."

Renee sat on the edge of the bed and pulled Cornelia in for a hug. "I'm really going to miss you."

"Me too," she said, squeezing her close.

She was so used to following orders, it felt strange to have the power of directing, even if she was only directing herself. At least her stolen power could lead to the happiness of *one* patient. That would make it all worthwhile.

Renee stood and, realizing their window of opportunity was short, whisked into the hallway, checking that each direction was clear. She slipped the medical tray out from her keyboard drawer and brought it back to Cornelia's room, centering it on the stand by the bed.

Renee took a deep breath, looking for any sign of fear from Cornelia. If she thought Cornelia was second guessing, Renee knew she wouldn't be able to go through with this.

"Last chance," Renee said, praying she would change her mind.

"Do it," Cornelia said, brushing her hair away so the sedative could be injected into her neck.

Renee nodded and uncapped the first, smaller needle. Before it could puncture skin, Cornelia stiffened. "Wait."

Renee pulled back, hoping Cornelia had changed her mind.

Instead, Cornelia pulled off her wedding ring and handed it to Renee.

Renee faltered, a lump in her throat rising. She took the ring and placed it on Cornelia's bookshelf, out of their way.

Renee injected the sedative, and Cornelia rolled onto her side. Within 30 seconds, she was unconscious.

Renee breathed deeply, reminding herself how important it was to remain calm. She found the top bony part of Cornelia's neck, where the skull meets the spine, and tucked the horror-movie-sized needle into the skin.

She discarded the needles and her gloves, and unlocked Cornelia's bed. Grabbing the frame by Cornelia's feet, she swiveled the bed toward the door and pushed as fast as she could without losing control. She forgot how heavy those things were with people in them – normally the guards did all the moving.

She maneuvered the bed down the hall, out the front doors, and down the ramp to the narrow road out front, where an ambulance waited. The back opened as they approached, and her best friend from nursing school popped out.

Renee had, for the most part, gone dark after she started working at Fort Howard Veterans Hospital. Rumors had circulated that she was there, but Dan was the only one promised an inside scoop in return for his help. As far as anyone else knew, the hospital had been shut down for over a year for "ongoing renovations." The construction equipment was there, but no work ever seemed to get done.

"Thanks again Dan," she said, as they heaved Cornelia onto his stretcher, abandoning her bed in the parking lot.

As soon as the doors closed, Dan hopped in front and got the ambulance moving. They were on their way to Johns Hopkins Bayview.

Nestled next to a medical kit was a bag of clothes for Renee to change into. She did so quickly, a pair of jeans and a sweater much less conspicuous than scrubs and a medical ID belonging to the elusive hospital no one was sure even existed. Dan would drop her off a few blocks from the hospital, and she would walk in separately, searching for a family member – someone she had heard was recently transferred.

And she would make sure that Cornelia arrived alright, and that the "correct" chart hung at the bottom of the bed. She would say goodbye, and wish her sleeping friend luck, and flee to Philadelphia to start a new life where Dr. Liam Ingels could never find her.

And if their plan worked, so would Cornelia.

Cornelia would wake up the next day, a little groggy and sore, but otherwise alright.

Then again, maybe she wouldn't.

CHAPTER TWO
Seven months and 29 days earlier, Johns Hopkins Bayview

Cornelia recognized the feel of a lumpy bed and the glare of fluorescent lights. She heard a faint beeping, and the murmurings of people a room or two away.

She adjusted slowly to the light transuding her eyelids. Each photon stung as she forced her watering eyes wider. Sleep weighed on her eyes and shoulders, yet she felt she had already been asleep for far too long.

She wiggled her fingers and felt the blood slowly returning. Why were her fingers so weak? She glanced down at them, the strain in her neck profound. Her index finger had a blood pressure monitor attached to it, but the others were bare.

Cornelia's muscles tensed and ached. She was certain that at least something, but probably everything, had exploded or torn apart. Her eyes burst open and her chest heaved as she struggled to untangle her limbs from tightly tucked hospital sheets. The room was bright, but it bothered her less as she adjusted to her surroundings. She lifted her left hand, searching for her engagement ring. Nothing.

Her mind raced with possibilities. Was it all just a dream? No, she couldn't have dreamt up the last two years of her life. Where was Nathan? He had to be close by, somewhere... he had to. And where was her engagement ring?

Cornelia tried to shout, "help" as a nurse walked by her room, but no sound left her mouth. Her throat was dry and all she could manage was a breathy grunt. She tried to relax and remember that she was in a hospital, with help nearby for the most minor of incidents. She breathed deep, coaching herself, trying not to draw any premature conclusions.

Through a window to her left that looked out on the hallway, she could see no one coming her way. Why weren't they coming to help her? The beeping grew faster, mirroring her heartbeat, and she knew she would have to move while she could.

She took a gasping breath and pushed herself up. Her body felt heavy, muscles screaming in resistance. She didn't know what any of her wires did, other than the IV, so she pulled them all out. Droplets of blood dotted her skin.

She leaned against her bed. Black lines cut through her vision, and she blinked hard, hoping to erase them, but when she opened her eyes again the room was tilted. She overcorrected, and suddenly she was falling, her vision gone completely. She felt a swooshing motion in her stomach.

"Cornelia," he said.

She blinked, the lights behind his head too bright to make out the face looking down on her, creating a halo around his face.

"Cornelia," he prodded, brushing her hair out of her face.

"Nathan?" she asked, the face blurry but becoming sharper. Her heartbeat quickened, but as the face in front of her became clearer, she realized it wasn't him. Deflated, she felt a lump rising in her throat.

Something wasn't right, but she couldn't pinpoint what it was. Something happened – something tragic – but she didn't know what. She had no memory, no understanding of the pain she felt, but the physical pangs she experienced upon waking up were nothing compared to the heartache that was slowly clamping around her.

"No, my name is Dr. Malek. You took a little spill," he explained. "Let's get you back into bed and we can talk a little, okay?"

She nodded, determined not to cry in front of a stranger.

"Alright, I'm going to help you up," he warned. He looped one arm underneath her neck and the other beneath her knees, scooping her up in one swift motion and moving her back to bed.

"Alright Cornelia," he said, pulling her blanket over her legs. "I'll let you settle in for a few minutes, and then we can discuss your treatment. First off, can I ask you the last thing you remember?"

She gripped the edge of her blanket, returning to last weekend with her family.

Every year, Cornelia's family would go up to her father's mountain house, where they would cuddle up on the couch and read in front of the fire, or whoever was interested would go out hunting. Usually mid-November, just cold enough for a nip, but not cold enough that a hike should be passed up. That year was different for several reasons.

Cornelia's little sister, Heather, had invited her fiancé. It was the first time a significant other had come along on a cabin weekend, and her parents insisted she bring Nate along, too. They had been dating for two years, and she had never been happier.

They had just moved in together, a small white house just outside the city with black shutters and a bright red door. She had her own parking spot right next to his.

Their mountain weekend was filled with laughter, everyone getting along so well that the girls felt comfortable enough to sneak out for a few hours to grab drinks at a bar down the street while her parents and the guys cooked a hearty dinner of venison and various greens (at the insistence of her vegetarian sister). They came back warmed by spiked apple cider, and filled up on food until their pants unbuttoned themselves.

After dinner, they sat down by the fire with their books and board games and crossword puzzles, and spent the night in happy, quiet company. As the frequency of yawns increased

11

and Heather nodded off next to her fiancé, Cornelia put her book down on the side table and rested her head on Nathan's shoulder. She caught her mom smiling over the edge of an old James Patterson book.

A few beats of silence passed, crickets bleating outside, an owl hooting in the distance. "Cornelia, I have something to ask you," Nathan said softly, pulling away from the weight of her head. She sat up straight and watched as he slid off the couch and got down on one knee. She felt all of the breath leave her body.

She'll never forget the way his face lit up, the grin that spread around the room in a matter of seconds. The seconds melted as she waited, staring into those calming brown eyes.

"Cornelia, will you marry me?"

She recited her memory to Dr. Malek.

"May I ask you what date Nathan proposed?" he asked her.

"June 3rd, 2016," she said. It was seared into her memory.

The doctor nodded. "It's January 16th," he said. She couldn't breathe. "2018."

She was in a car accident, she heard.
There were no survivors, they said.
They don't know where she was.
They don't know how she got here.
You're safe now, she heard.
Safe now.
Amnesia.
Partial charts.
No survivors.
Safe now.

CHAPTER THREE
One month ago, Rittenhouse Square

The man she met on Thursdays came from Manayunk. It had taken a few weeks to find him, and Dr. Liam Ingels would have *preferred* to just find Cornelia's apartment, but he would take what he could get. He had been in Philadelphia over a month – if he hadn't found her yet, he needed to reevaluate his strategy.

He stumbled upon their meeting once, and only after the two walked in separate directions did he realize what the purpose of the meeting was. He gave her money - a small yellow package that she hid in her coat before they parted, walking briskly away from each other. He had been wondering why he couldn't trace her back accounts.

The second meeting he was prepared for. He waited every night in the park, and finally, the third Thursday of the month, he showed up again. He and Cornelia sat on a bench and talked for a few minutes, and when they got up, they hugged quickly. That's when the transfer took place.

At first he thought she might be buying drugs. Hospital drugs were fantastic; he wouldn't blame her for wanting more - but he didn't think Cornelia was the type to develop a habit. She never had before, even when all the drugs she could ever want were right at her fingertips. All she had had to do was ask.

He followed the man she met on Thursdays, on a comfortable September night. He hailed a cab that took him most of the way up Kelly Dr., to the border of Manayunk. From there, he walked along the water.

Liam parked across the street and got out, sitting on a bench a few yards away. He wasn't sure yet how he wanted to broach the subject. He had called in a security guard from the hospital who was still looking for work, just in case he was able to find Cornelia that night. She was so close he could *taste* her.

Mike sat on the bench next to Liam, and although wearing the clinic's uniform was a gross overestimation of his importance that night, Liam did appreciate the forethought. You never know when a uniform will make the difference in getting what you want. Mike was young and naive but planned ahead when he could. Though he tried significantly harder than any other employee, Liam couldn't help but feel he would go absolutely nowhere.

On that brisk September night, they waited for the man to reappear around the corner. Liam wasn't sure exactly where he had been going, but directed his taxi several blocks ahead once he saw the direction in which the man walked. This was his best bet to intercept him.

Dusk had fallen, and with the darkness came a fall chill. The strangers enjoying the night around them headed home. Liam craned his neck to see over the slight hill, scanning the walkways parallel to the river. With the impending darkness, it was harder and harder to make out faces. Instead, he looked for the man's loping, protective walk. He had been wearing a hat that night, as well as a fresh peacoat.

After a few minutes, Liam spotted him.

He walked nonchalantly in Liam's direction, and after another twenty or so paces, paused to face the water. He shuffled over to an empty bench and sat down, breathing into the wood. He watched over the water.

After a few minutes, he stood again and began walking down the Schyukhill Trail in the opposite direction he had come. Odd. Was it possible he suspected their trail?

Liam directed Mike to follow him.

Dr. Ingels waited as the two disappeared down the trail, Mike kicking up loose dirt with the back of his sneakers as he ran. Liam wondered, as his vision became obscured, what Mike might do to stop the man. Feign an injury? Borrow a phone? Liam hadn't given him any direction.

Before he could panic fully, Mike called him.

"He turned around as I was following him. I wasn't sure if you wanted me to give us away. He should be back in about four minutes, I can loop around the next block and make my way back if you want me to intercept him that way," he offered.

Liam nodded. "Make your way back," he directed. "I'll keep an eye out while you do."

Liam stood, leaning against the back of the bench, searching, searching, searching.

A few moments later, the man reappeared, rushing in Liam's direction. He looked over his shoulder as if he thought he was being followed. Liam let him pass, hoping Mike would reappear to do the dirty work of actually intercepting him, but he was nowhere to be found. He let a few seconds pass, hoping, and came to the conclusion he needed to seize the opportunity himself.

"Excuse me," Liam said, jogging to catch up.

"Yes?" he asked. He had an accent, maybe Italian. He was noticeably disheveled, a trail of blood running down his cheek.

"I think you know my patient, Cornelia Winthorp. I am her doctor, and I really need a way to get in contact with her," he explained. Maybe some version of the truth would suffice. "She may be in danger."

The man nodded. "If I had a friend named Cornelia I might be able to tell you, but I apologize, sir. I know no one by that name." He pushed past Liam and continued walking, never missing a beat.

"I know you know her," Liam insisted, grabbing the man's arm.

"I know no one by that name," he repeated, pulling away.

"A phone number would do," Liam insisted. He was shouting, desperate. He hated the airy hope in his voice.

"I don't know her," he insisted. Liam pulled on his arm,

and was shoved away. "Don't touch me."

"Call her from your phone. I just need to talk to her," Liam said.

"No." The man's eyes were a piercing green as he stared into Liam's. He wasn't going to budge.

Anger flooded through the doctor's veins.

He shoved the man as hard as he could, and he stumbled backwards over a low brick wall. Liam didn't realize that low brick wall was the only thing separating the trail from the river until he heard the splash a second or two later.

Liam stepped forward, peering out over the river, and in the dimness of the night, saw nothing in the water beneath him. He glanced around, searching for eyes, and saw none.

He retreated, stuck his hands in his pockets, and walked back to his car.

CHAPTER FOUR
Present Day, Rittenhouse Square

Petyr was never late.

Cornelia walked around Rittenhouse Square one last time before accepting he wasn't coming. She picked a bench and sat, watching the upper class exit the park and the homeless listlessly enter, picking from the benches their beds for the night.

A group of early twenty-something girls walked past, heels dangling from their knuckles, happily oblivious to the racket their laughter made. Hands clasped easily behind her back, an elderly woman in black meandered in the opposite direction with a small white poof of a dog. A young jogger swept by, the back of his shirt slick with sweat.

Cornelia scanned the crowd for Petyr's dark brown hair, listening for that slight accent.

She hoped she was just missing something – maybe he was late and forgot to text. Or maybe she had the wrong day? Cornelia checked her phone again. No dice. October 19th, 2018. It was the third Thursday of the month, nine PM. Petyr had never missed before.

Cornelia rose from her bench and did one more loop around the park before beginning her walk home. It was considerably colder this week than it had been before. More people wore long puffy jackets and hats, creating an anonymous hub of marshmallow strangers.

Meandering around to the south side of the park, she followed the woman dressed in black. Cornelia stuffed her hands into her pockets, thumbing her phone on the off chance that Petyr might call. She didn't have his phone number; *he* only ever called *her.*

She had always assumed someone would try to contact

her in the event of Petyr's absence. Apparently not.

Her eyes darted side to side, down alleyways and around sudden corners, searching, searching, searching for Petyr.

After a few minutes, the woman in black hung a sharp right, leaving Cornelia alone in the coming darkness. She had grown attached to the woman like you would grow attached to the person who tests your food before you.

A half block ahead, a couple walked with arms snaked around each other, the woman's head resting easily on the man's shoulder. Cornelia quickened her pace, coming up about ten feet behind them. She followed the couple for three blocks, until she turned right down her street and faced the familiar row homes she knew so well.

Once more, Cornelia glanced behind before turning. All *seemed* well.

CHAPTER FIVE
Present Day, Rittenhouse Square

Renee untucked her now-blonde hair from behind her ear. A soft breeze blew across the square, tangling the wavy strands. She zipped her jacket up to her chin and leaned against the hard wooden bench, waiting for Cornelia to appear. She met the same man every third Thursday of the month, nine PM. Renee had observed the last four.

Renee kept tabs on Cornelia as best she could. Assuming the Memory II injection worked properly, Cornelia had no clue who the (now) blonde woman was. Cornelia's memory was *gone*. In order to watch over her, Renee had to stay in the shadows. She skulked around after Cornelia when she left the apartment, and kept security cameras in the halls and entryway to make sure Dr. Ingels hadn't found them.

Renee wasn't sure what he would do if or when he found Cornelia, but she knew he was trying. When he found Cornelia missing from the hospital, he went into a rage, the likes of which Renee had never seen off a TV screen. Renee never returned to the hospital, but before she totally cut contact with the staff, she heard through the grapevine that he had gone off the deep end. In that moment, she was sure she had done the right thing for herself and Cornelia both.

She knew his feelings toward Cornelia were inappropriate at best, but she wasn't sure whether he was motivated by a false love interest or because Cornelia was the only one of his patients that had survived his trial.

Either way, Cornelia was his prize, and Renee was committed to making sure he lost.

One day, when Cornelia was ready, Renee would tell her all of this. But that day hadn't come yet.

But keeping this secret made Renee felt just as slimy

as she perceived Dr. Ingels to be. She manipulated Cornelia's world in a way that made her think she was making her own choices. She kept watch constantly, always reimagining their plan so Cornelia could live a happy, doctor-free life.

Of course, Cornelia seemed to do that well enough on her own. Sure, Renee controlled the security cameras and their apartment building (which was enough of a catfish to pull off), but Cornelia took care of herself, otherwise. She didn't talk to strangers and rarely left the building. When she did, she went to a MMA gym where she beat the ever loving shit out of a poor old punching bag. Most times, Renee felt she couldn't help Cornelia anymore than she already had, and if she tried, she'd probably only get in her way.

Renee had been blessed with a backup job managing her uncle's building. She disappeared from the hospital that fateful day, and after several death threats, ditched her phone and everything else that tied her to Maryland *or* Cornelia.

Thankfully, the one thing she kept was her final game plan with Cornelia - that's how she was able to craft the perfect Craigslist ad for the spare studio next door to hers. There were plenty of side effects that could be expected from Memory II, but Cornelia's biggest difficulty stemmed from the double whammy of anxiety and paranoia. Cornelia correctly expected that once she woke up from the "226-day coma," she would still be dealing with those side effects, and planned accordingly.

Before the final injection of Memory II, Renee and Cornelia sat together, going over what she would do when it came time to find an apartment and take care of herself. She expected a certain amount of recovery time, likely in her aunt's care thanks to a lack of housing or personal items, and then she would probably move to the city to hide in plain sight, and find a small, nondescript studio that accepts cash and doesn't ask questions. That's exactly how Renee phrased it.

Of course, Cornelia's response originated from somewhere in South Africa, likely as a cover up for any personal identification, but the signature "Thanks -C." was so unmistakably Cornelia, Renee laughed when she finally read it.

After all this time apart, Renee constantly wondered what was happening in Cornelia's brain.

Her treatment was one rarity after another: a previous injury in exactly the right place to damage the area that would repair the parts they wanted broken; a tendency toward anger and strategy; an extraordinary amount of self-control that ultimately led to her release.

Yet after everything Cornelia had gone through, all she seemed to care about was cyber security.

Sure, Renee doubted anyone could find her through credit cards or Facebook. Yet Cornelia found a ridiculously cheap 1-bedroom apartment in Rittenhouse Square set up as a cash deal on Craigslist, and found nothing curious about moving in right away. Renee shook her head. Sometimes she wondered if Cornelia was always a bit off, even before they met.

Renee glanced down - the time on her Blackberry read 9:05, and Cornelia sat on a bench about 50 feet away. Normally she wouldn't get so close, but she was almost certain at this point that Cornelia wouldn't recognize her even as the *building manager* if the two ran into each other. She opened up Solitaire and pretended to play, but watched Cornelia out of the corner of her eye. Usually the man she met would have shown up by then.

Cornelia obsessively checked her phone – pulling the little silver shit of a phone out of her pocket and pressing the little side button to check the time. She kept glancing around the park like he might magically appear. Her foot tapped, her eyes darted. She pulled her jacket tighter.

Eventually she got up and began walking through the park. Renee pressed buttons randomly.

It looked like she was about to head home when Renee noticed someone else watching her too. He was tall and broad chested, bulkily covered up with a large jacket and a baseball cap. She couldn't see his face, but she knew who he was. She scoured the crowd for Cornelia, and spotted her toward the edge of the park, about to cross the street and lead him directly to their building. Renee's heart thumped. She saw the outline of a smile under the shadow of his cap.

She thumbed the stack of rent money she had collected earlier that day - $800 in cash from a resident that she could trust to be at least a week late each month. That month, he was two weeks late. But she didn't care - it wasn't her money, anyways.

She scanned the park for a shady-looking teenager - anyone who would be a jackass for cash, really.

She eyed two skateboarders screwing around by the fountain. One wiggled back and forth on his board, while the other ate a candy bar, his leaning up against the cement side of the fountain. She approached them quickly, keeping an eye on Cornelia, who was quickly retreating, and Dr. Ingels, whose eyes saw no one but her.

"Hey! If I give you some money will you go distract that guy in the black coat and baseball cap?" she asked them. She leaned in close and spoke quietly. They glanced at each other, eyebrows raised.

"How much money?" He had pimples and frizzy hair.

"$400 between the two of you if you go right now and stop him in his tracks for at least 30 seconds," she said. The two boys looked at each other, eyes wide. She gave one two hundreds, feeling out the bills from within her pocket. "*Go! Now!* Meet me back here when you're done and I'll give you the rest. Go!"

She turned before she could be seen talking to them. They shot off on their skateboards, reaching the doctor just before Cornelia crossed the street. She looked both ways and behind her, as if she had been expecting it.

Instead, 20 feet behind her, a stupid kid on a skateboard rolled in front of a stranger in a baseball cap and an oversized jacket, trying to do a trick, and fell right in his path.

The skateboard shot out in front of him, colliding with

the man's shin just below the knee. He fell to the ground and the two skateboarders stopped to make sure he was alright and help him up. He graciously accepted their apology and peered around them, scanning the crowd.

After a few seconds, he gave up and headed in the opposite direction, his eyes pulling to the spot where Cornelia had disappeared. They followed, touching his knee and peppering him with questions about his serious injury.

Renee finally exhaled, lightheaded, and reminded herself that this was only the beginning. She would have to find out what happened to the man Cornelia met on Thursdays. Then, she would have to find a way to get her out of Philadelphia, to somewhere they would never be found.

But most of all, she had to figure out why Dr. Ingels was following Cornelia *now,* after eight months of silence, and how on earth *he* knew about the man who comes on Thursdays.

CHAPTER SIX
Present Day, Cornelia's apartment

Cornelia ducked behind the large evergreen that hid the entrance to her building. She unlocked the flimsy gate that barred the inside stairs from the rest of the world, locked it behind her, slipping down the cement stairs that led to the entrance. Blind without a light in the entryway, she shuffled her feet forward until they hit the lip of the door, and then fumbled around until she found the small deadbolt. Unlike the rest of the majestic old house, this door was small and unfinished, installed much later than the house was built – and since no one could see it from the outside, no one ever bothered to make it look nice.

The lock had to be turned twice clockwise and the door hip-checked. A blast of warm air breathed over her face as the door scuffed open. She stepped over the threshold as the fluorescent lights of the entranceway flickered on, the motion detector catching her movements. She fell back into the door until the handle clicked into place, and switched the deadbolt back into a locked position. Most of the basement tenants complained about the fight to get into their own front door, but Cornelia found it reassuring.

Although the paint chipped in places and the carpet had been replaced with something much less elegant than it once was, the high ceiling and lion statues at the end of the entry hallway hinted at the elegant time period in which the building was constructed. Beginning a foot or so from the door, a majestic staircase wound up around the foyer, ending at a spackled ceiling, the boarded up entrance of what had once been a drawing room. Or so Cornelia imagined.

As times changed, the building had transformed from the mansion of a rich Philadelphian family, to a duplex, and eventually to a smattering of awkwardly sized econo-apartments. Each floor was further separated – the basement accessed furtively underneath the main entrance, the second and third floors from what looked like a fire escape in the alleyway behind the building. The main floor, accessed by a wide staircase and tall wooden doors with symmetrical knockers, still emulated old Philadelphian wealth.

Five apartments branched off from the basement hallway. Number 14, the first on the right, constantly smelled of weed. If Cornelia hadn't known better, she would search for the stream of smoke coming from underneath the door. The woman who lived there, Amy, left her apartment every day at eight and came back around five, always dressed in a suit. Cornelia had a feeling she wasn't going to a typical 9-5 job, though. With cash rent and an obscure entryway, she assumed no one on her floor did.

But no one asked questions either.

Number 16 housed the building manager, but she was rarely ever home. Cornelia had heard other tenants complaining in passing, but Cornelia found it difficult to sympathize when her rent was about 50% of market value.

Apartment 17 housed a young college student who had asked to grab a drink a few times, but Cornelia always turned her down. The girl seemed sweet - naïve, almost - but Cornelia wasn't up for the college scene.

The door just before hers, 18, housed a younger man that Cornelia rarely saw. He wasn't inviting like the girl in 17 was, and he always asked too many questions. Cornelia restricted her answers to "fine," "it's okay," and "yes, have a great day." People like that freaked her out.

An amalgamation of her past lives, Cornelia's key chain was heavy with unnecessary metal – old car keys and house keys clumped together as if still relevant. She pushed past the last mounted lion statue, jingling through her extraneous mementos until she finally fought her way home, into apartment #19.

Once upon a time, Cornelia had a backlog of things, old furniture inherited from generations past. Her and Nate had pooled their stuff together, creating a household of mismatching items full of quirk and sentimental value. After the car accident, their stuff was redistributed and auctioned off to help pay for medical bills. Cornelia's Aunt Tanya stored for her a few odd and ends that were once a part of the couple's joined life, but they never again held the same value.

She had few pieces of furniture, mismatched pieces that accumulated over years of yard sales and moving around. She channeled her twenty-something-year-old self, fresh from college, when thrift stores and DIY were her bread and butter. She reupholstered her own couch and refinished a rocking chair, and all of her shelving, including her coffee table, she made from hand. A few pieces of art were scattered haphazardly around the room, mostly remnants of art projects she had tried and failed at.

Poking through the restored and neglected were the items she had bought since the accident and subsequent settlement. A "real" crystal ball she bought from a gypsy sat on the shelf above her computer, a $800 investment she was still trying to sell for a nice $50. A bottle of Johnny Walker Blue Label sat next to it, an ill-conceived gift for someone she didn't know yet, and - who was she kidding - it was mostly water at this point. Next to that, a collection of cashmere scarves from Macy's that she had bought at full price because she thought a little bit of soft fabric might help fill that hole in her heart.

She had one photograph framed and hung on the wall, of the people she had loved most in her life – her once-fiancé, parents, sister, and brother-in-law. It was taken just days before they had died, on a day when they had all independently decided to wear plaid, so *of course* Cornelia's mom needed to document the moment. It ended up being the last real memory she had of them. She was just glad they were laughing.

It hung on the wall by her desk, a reminder of *then* when

how became too much. For a long time it sat in plain view next to her bed, but she moved it once she realized the rabbit hole of depression is took her down if she stared too long.

She sat down in front of her computer and navigated to Weather Underground in preparation for their agreed upon security check. The car accident and subsequent recovery left Cornelia in quite a state - she dealt with extreme anxiety and paranoia that anyone normal would be taking high doses for, but thanks to the paranoia and anxiety, she didn't trust any doctors to prescribe it.

The phone rang once before she heard Luca's familiar Italian accent.

"Luca Hotchkin," he barked into the phone.

"Luca," she said.

"Who is this?" he asked, still shouting.

"It's Cornelia."

He softened, realizing who was calling. "Corey, Corey. How is the weather in... Denmark?"

She knew Luca was just humoring her in playing along with her security check. She was small potatoes compared to the billionaires he usually dealt with.

Regardless, she searched for Denmark.

"It's a very pleasant 70 degrees today. Clear and beautiful, but it looks like rain is coming this weekend."

"Good. Good to hear from you Corey. What can I do for you?" he asked. She could hear the shuffling of papers in the background, then silence.

It sounded like he had spent another night at the office – almost every time she called he was either in his office catching up or doing the same at home. She was never sure exactly what it was Luca did, but she knew he took discreet care of the assets of Italy's most affluent citizens.

Shortly after Cornelia woke from her coma, she expressed to Luca how out of control she felt of her spending. She had received a two million dollar settlement, and nearly fifty grand had disappeared within the first three weeks she moved out of her aunt's house, simply because she couldn't tell herself no. Luca suggested giving him the reigns, and Petyr could take care of distribution. It wasn't necessarily "by the books," but it worked for her.

"Petyr never showed up tonight. I waited for about half an hour. I guess I just wanted to make sure everything is okay?" she asked. He was quiet for a moment, and then started grumbling and shuffling through some more papers.

"I haven't heard from my nephew in a few days, that's odd for him. I'll look into it, but I am not sure what to tell you right now," he explained, his thick Italian accent coating each of his words. He sounded concerned.

Petyr and Luca's family was plagued with misfortune. Luca's three brothers had died young, one from cancer as a child, another from swimming drunk in riptide prone water, and the third, Nathan's father, from suicide after his wife had abandoned her husband and newborn son. Petyr, an unknown son of his second brother, turned up around the time Nathan graduated high school. Luca, working to the brim to keep his clients happy, loved him from afar as much as he could, while providing him a job and money when possible. Nathan, in a much better position to create family ties, loved him like the older brother he never got to have.

Cornelia had been hoping for a mix up, but now she was only concerned. If - god forbid - something had happened to Petyr, Luca would be losing his last bit of family, and Cornelia would be losing her last connection to Nathan.

She took a deep breath. "So what are our next steps? What do you need me to do?" Cornelia asked, her chest tight.

He paused. "Do you have an emergency fund?"

"I do, but it'll probably only last a few months."

Luca made a few noises of consideration.

"Well right now it seems everything depends on Petyr. As much as I hate to say it, I'm inclined to think something has happened. I'll see if I can get in contact with him, but in the meantime I'm not sure I have anyone in the US I can trust with your disbursements. We can transfer your money back into the US, but that would require some in-person paperwork. And as much as I might like to, I don't think I can pass as a dainty brunette," Luca said, and laughed gently, but Cornelia could hear the worry in his voice.

"Thank you Luca. Yes, please let me know as soon as you hear anything."

Cornelia considered her options. Almost the entire settlement from her car accident was stashed in the bank account Luca oversaw, and she had about a month's worth of expenses saved in the empty guts of her malfunctioning printer. Luca's custodial duties were supposed to be short term, just until she hit the savings goal Nate had set for their retirement – 3.24 million - and she could start withdrawing from it in the same way.

She audited her bills in her head. If she stretched herself thin enough she could probably make her emergency fund last two and a half, maybe three months. Beyond that, she would have to search for a job that paid cash, and she probably couldn't afford to procrastinate.

Cornelia signed out of her accounts and shut down her computer. She felt the familiar strings pulling her shoulders into her jawbone, and took a deep breath. She had no patience for stress.

She threw her jacket over the back of her couch, discarded her boots by the front door, and shuffled into her bedroom, stripping as she went. She had accidentally knocked over her laundry bin a few nights before, and on it she threw the black yoga pants she wore, an old soccer sweatshirt from high school with holes in the cuffs, a plain white v-neck t-shirt, a dark gray sports bra, and a small black thong with an embarrassing amount of pulled threads. The underwear was the straw that broke the camel's back, her clothes tumbling to the floor.

Cornelia pulled on one of Nate's old t-shirts and a pair of striped underwear. She hit the lights, climbed in bed, and watched the streetlight through her window.

CHAPTER SEVEN
Present Day, somewhere inside Cornelia's head

Cornelia sat at a small cafe off of Walnut St, the hem of her dress swaying peacefully in the mild summer breeze. It was mustard yellow - the pretty kind that goes well with flowers and white wine - and she hadn't worn it since high school, but there was something about *that one dress* that always made her feel like a million bucks.

She sat across from... someone. Who was it? She wore blue scrubs, and as she moved, gesticulating as she spoke, she nearly blended right into the clear blue sky. Cornelia stared, struggling, trying to put a name with the face.

Brown hair, heart-shaped face, easy brown eyes and the hint of a Spanish tint to her skin. Cornelia stared, unable to put what felt like an obvious equation together. $2 + 2 = ...$?

The woman spoke, laughing as she told some story that Cornelia couldn't hear. She turned her ear to her, but it was like there was a pane of soundproof glass between them. She could hear a mumble, read a few words from her lips, but she couldn't fit enough of the pieces together to create a cohesive picture.

They were interrupted by the waiter bringing over their dessert, something that smelled baked and rotten. Looking down, Cornelia realized it was some sort of fish.

She felt queasy, like she had already eaten it and their lunch date was suddenly moving in reverse. This isn't dessert.

She put her head in her hands, pain radiating from the base of her neck to the crown of her head, in circles around her temples. She felt her hairline sinking into her brain, as if the outside of her head was shrinking, her brain swelling.

She excused herself and ran into the restaurant's bathroom.

She locked the door behind her and turned to the mirror. Normal. She looked normal.

She exhaled, relieved, and pulled her hair back into a ponytail.

Just behind her hairline, she suddenly felt where her skin had sunken down.

She pulled harder on her hair, daring it to snap back to where it should be, and watched as her hairline moved further backwards. Her skin tore, revealing a ring of puss and blood like a headband one inch thick.

She stepped back from the mirror, her consciousness faltering.

Cornelia startled awake, eyes wide and staring at the peeling ceiling of her apartment. Her heart beat fast and hard as she sat up, her body stiff and unrested. Her shirt clung to her back, her legs to the sheets on her bed. The silence mocked her as she felt around for the light switch.

Light bathed the room as Cornelia scanned her surroundings. Everything looked menacing in the harsh light. Whenever she woke from a bad dream, it felt as though her whole apartment was different, everything taking on that medical, fluorescent tone.

She slid out of bed and padded into her bathroom. She pulled her hair back and felt around her hairline. Normal. She breathed.

Wide awake, she sat down at her desk, hoping for a distraction.

Her accident left her with frequent anxiety attacks and paranoia, like someone was always watching - and the feeling was strong at the moment. Cornelia glanced out of her windows, her eyes wide in an effort to combat the darkness outside. She thought she saw the beady black eyes of a crow perched on her windowsill, but reminded herself that chances were the crows had already migrated south. It was just a reflection.

Cornelia forced the thought from her mind. She booted up her machine, signed in, and searched Craigslist for an easy temp job.

On the first page, she found seven people hiring for waitressing positions. She scripted a quick email and carbon copied it to each address. That should do for tonight. If she had no responses in the morning, rinse and repeat.

Before she went back to bed, Cornelia checked the locks on each of her windows and doors a few extra times, just to be safe. Every reflection she saw was a pair of eyes waiting for a moment of weakness.

CHAPTER EIGHT
Present Day, some cigar bar off Walnut St.

Cornelia had two prospects.

The first was a waitressing position at a diner on the shady side of South Philly. They wanted her to come in for training for a week before she'd be able to collect her own tips. She had a feeling that meant they wanted her to work for a week at $2.83/hour.

The second was a cocktail waitressing position at a cigar club a few blocks away. Even more than she hated the smell of cigars, she hated the idea of being a cocktail waitress again. She had worked at one of the nicer campus bars in college, but like most things that made up her past lives, she had no strong inclination to return, despite enjoying it at the time. She didn't want too spoil a good memory with what had happened in between.

But beggars can't be choosers.

Cornelia's third day of work was uneventful. She observed one night and trained the next, witnessing a compilation of pseudo-pornographic interactions between the waitresses and business suit clientele.

She was given an official uniform her second night of work, a short black skirt and an apron to dangle over it. They didn't spoil their employees with a shirt, instead stipulating only that it must be a white button-up. The fit and style were the employee's choice, and judging from the other waitresses, the lesser the better.

While it was branded a cigar club, Cornelia had the nagging feeling the owner would have much preferred to be running a strip club. He had a general manager run the show while he hung out in the back corner, commandeering the full attention of two "cocktail waitresses."

She was stoked at the prospect of making rent, but she kicked herself for taking a "high class" (as described by the ad) job over the shitty diner job. At least there she could wear all of her clothes.

She donned her little black skirt with an elbow-length button-down shirt she tied playfully at her belly button. She wasn't out of place.

She tried to focus by counting prime numbers in her head, a practice she picked up when counting backwards from ten no longer worked, but the bustle and noise of the club threw her off.

She felt drained, subdued. She could feel unfamiliar eyes on her. Her migraine grew stronger every second she forced herself to smile.

Six hours into her eight-hour shift, she had been groped 6 times. Of those 6 times, she considered four interactions harmless - an arm around the waist, or a touch on the shoulder. Two of those times, someone (same drunk guy both times) had tried to pull out the tie of her shirt, and when that was unsuccessful, dove right into her shirt to grab her breast. He received a swift kick of a stiletto and a firm slap to the face. His friends seemed to enjoy her "feist," and suggested he back off, but one complained to the manager.

Thus ended Cornelia's brief career in waitressing.

Half a month's rent in her pocket, she ditched the apron in the locker room and didn't bother saying goodbye.

CHAPTER NINE
Present Day, Philly MMA

A month without seeing Petyr left Cornelia jittery. Luca put her account on hold, leaving her with nothing but her thoughts and a small wad of cash that smelled like cigars and degradation.

She kicked herself for not keeping a larger emergency fund before transferring everything overseas. Then again, she *did* originally have two million dollars in her account... $50k of which she spent within weeks. It was safer to store it behind a barrier, guarded by someone who would double-check her should her spending habits become erratic again.

She began her day with an early morning workout at the MMA school a few blocks north of her apartment in an effort to quell her money-related anxieties.

She knew that by traditional standards, you were supposed to cut out all unnecessary expenditures until you were financially stable, but it was one of the few things that made her feel alive again after the accident.

She made a pact with herself that if it came down to the gym or her apartment, the apartment would have to win, but that was one hit that would be tough to bear.

There was a point in her life where she had worked at Philly MMA. She was never an amazing practitioner of martial arts, but she used to be a feminist with a capital Fist, and that led her to become one of the most sought after self-defense teachers in the Philadelphia area. She led hundreds of classes that gave women the knowledge and confidence that they could get out of a sticky situation. She lost the feist that she used to bring to the gym, but she wouldn't lose the fight.

She still possessed the skills – as some things your body just doesn't forget – but she barely remembered the logic behind it. A few weeks prior, she thought a man she walked by in a narrow alleyway was about to hit her. Without thinking, she raised her arm to block. She had no idea why her logic was ten seconds behind, but her impulses seemed to have things under control. She was scared that if she had to stop going to the gym all together, she would lose those last few impulses her body had retained.

But she had saved a few hundred dollars so far, setting herself up to make her two months' emergency fund stretch to three, but that emergency fund now required a complimentary emergency *plan*. She'd have to find steady work somewhere... or move back in with her aunt. Neither option appealed to her.

Aunt Tanya had taken care of her when she first came home from the hospital. Cornelia underwent physical and mental therapy for six months before she could no longer bear Tanya's constant questions and concern, and ultimately quit her own recovery. She moved out and finally got a moment alone, no more questions. Yet the feeling of being observed never left.

She was drained and paranoid, so she took the opportunity to seclude herself. She sold her neglected car and moved to a small apartment in the middle of the city. No registered car, a cash apartment, and two million people to blend in with wasn't what the doctor ordered, but it was exactly what Cornelia needed.

But without her investment account, and ipso facto, her gigantic settlement check, she was unsure of herself again. She felt the anxiety creeping up through her bones, the what-if's clawing, disaster looming just over her shoulder. Only a few months earlier she had grasped the opportunity with both hands, and ran for her peace of mind until she found herself alone in Philadelphia.

Now, she could feel that peace slipping away.

Philly MMA was small. The main floor housed lifetime-warrantied, mismatched gym equipment sourced from older, failed gyms. They looked a bit ragged on the outside, but Cornelia was certain they gave twice the workout of the trendy matchy-matchy machines at any chain gym.

A thin, long desk ran along the wall to the right of the entrance, where there were usually one or two employees greeting or doing deskwork. She nodded to the person behind the desk and flashed her member card.

Over the years Cornelia had taught there, ownership changed hands several times, and again during her absence. She wasn't sure who the current owners were, but she was always happy to note the lack of change in their equipment or policies. It was the one place she counted on silent friends, from both before the accident and after. No one asked about the scar down her leg or the one that was just barely visible at her hairline when she had it tied up. The unspoken rules were strong at Philly MMA – don't ask, don't push, and don't be an asshole.

She squeezed her fingers around her hand wraps and took a deep breath. She pulled her phone out of her armband and adjusted the volume up, 21 Pilots blistering in her ears. She could sense other people around her, but she could no longer hear or see them. She stared at the insipid bag of grains hanging in front of her, and let her mounting anxiety have full control.

By the time she fatigued, her shirt was soaked in sweat. She stopped, wondering if that would be enough to clear her head for the rest of the day. She wandered away and sat on the bench a few feet away, reaching underneath to grab her water from her bag. She rested her elbows on her knees and focused on her breathing. Distressed workouts were always a good challenge.

When she looked up, a man wearing the gym's official insignia smiled down at her. He had a clean haircut that looked a little too perfect, and a strong jawline with what looked like a chinstrap of stubble but could also have been crumbs from his power bar. He was stocky, with legs the size of tree trunks and broad shoulders.

His mouth opened and closed a few times before she realized he was saying more than "good morning." Cornelia pulled her headphones out of her ears and waited for him to repeat himself. The gym was eerily quiet.

"Sorry, I should have noticed the headphones," he said, motioning to his ears and laughing.

Cornelia waited for him to explain. Philly MMA wasn't really the place for small talk.

"Sorry," he repeated, rubbing his hands together. "You're Cornelia, right?"

She stood up, along with the hairs on the back of her neck. She was cornered, but the two machines to her right had flat seats that lined up, creating a clear running path to the door if she needed it. She would just have to knock him out first. Good thing she still had her gloves on.

"What's it to you?" she asked.

"Well, you used to work here, right?" he asked.

She raised her eyebrows. "Yeah, why?"

"Well uh, we're short on instructors this month. Your name came up in our employee files. We were looking for past instructors who might be able to sub a few upcoming classes. You were a self-defense teacher, right?" he asked.

"Oh," she said, the tension in her shoulders slowly melting. "Yeah, I was." He had too much of a baby face to be harmful; she should have seen that. She felt silly for considering him a threat.

"So uh, I don't know if you met the new manager. Her name is Leanne, this is her business card," he said, handing over a beaten up card that showed only a name and number. "If you're interested, give her a call. You might also be able to catch her before she leaves – she's roaming around here somewhere but usually leaves around this time for school drop off."

Cornelia nodded, processing the information. "Thanks."

He looked like he was going to say something else, but decided against it and walked back to the front desk.

Awkward, but he seemed nice. Maybe she should have been nicer to him.

Cornelia put her headphones back in, grabbed her bag, and spread out on the stretching mats. She wiped it down with a Lysol towel from a nearby dispenser, and sat with her back to the wall. She let her eyes wander across the gym and folded into herself, her chin to her knees and her fingers wrapping easily around her toes.

A man with messy hair held back by what looked like a headband made from a ripped t-shirt had commandeered her punching bag seconds after she left, and kicked with a fully extended leg. Across the gym, someone else aimed for his opponent's neck rather than a body point of contact.

Sure, Cornelia had taught self defense before, but she could barely remember any of it. And might working there sour her experience when she just wanted to let loose on a punching bag? It never had before, but... well, some things had changed.

Cornelia switched positions, crossing one leg over the other and twisting. She had a direct view into one of the classrooms, and saw two of the teachers chatting happily next to a rolling shelf of papers. One woman was dressed in black yoga pants, a purple crop top, and a hot pink sports bra that poked out from her shirt. She looked straight out of the eighties.

Switching to the other side, she tried to remember what she used to teach. It was all basic stuff, the kind of thing that seems like common sense but because no one takes the time to think about it, you have to actually *explain* it. She did remember her number one rule for her classes: never look for the fight. Distract and run, and hope that your bark is bigger than your bite.

She had considered teaching again while she was regaining her strength, but at the time, all she could think of was when she used to come home after a class and Nate would make fun of her for "fighting like a girl." It was all a ruse to spar with her, just a way for them to be close, lightheartedly enjoying each other. But it hurt to think about now.

She thought her class notes might be hidden somewhere in her apartment. She wasn't a huge fan of holding onto stuff she didn't need, but that seemed like the kind of reference material that never really expires. If she could brush up a bit, she could at least teach an intro class. Right?

Cornelia wasn't fantastic with people, as evidenced by her brief career in waitressing. Could this be different? She enjoyed waitressing earlier in life, just like she enjoyed teaching classes. It felt like such a thin line between taking a chance and ruining the one place she felt safe.

Then again, she needed money, and beggars can't be choosers.

Cornelia unwound her limbs and stood. She pulled her ankle up to her butt, giving a good tug.

She pulled on her sweatshirt and swung her gym bag over her shoulder as she walked to the front desk. Chinstrap glanced at her, shuffled some papers behind the desk, and delivered an urgent message to the teachers chatting in the classroom.

Cornelia pulled her headphones out of her ears as she approached, her music fading back to the grunting and thumping of a well-used gym.

"Hi," she said to remaining desk attendant. She had long brown hair tied up into a ponytail, and a large toothy smile. She turned to greet Cornelia.

"Hi, what can I do for ya?" she asked easily. Her voice was peppy like her mascara.

"That guy who just left asked if I wanted to start teaching classes again? I used to work here a few years ago," Cornelia said, motioning to where Chin Strap had run to.

"Oh yes, he mentioned a former teacher came in. Let's go into the office so we can talk a little more," she said, walking out from behind the counter and waving Cornelia along behind her.

They walked past the classroom and the woman shouted at Eric, previously known only as Chin Strap, that he needed to be up front. Without the desk impeding Cornelia's view, she realized the woman she was talking to was significantly pregnant, seven to eight months by Cornelia's unprofessional estimate. She chattered mindlessly as they walked, filling Cornelia in on every last detail about the gym that might have changed since the last time she had taught.

"I don't think we've met before. I'm Leanne, I've been teaching here on and off for the past few years. We probably *just* missed each other," she explained, smiling.

She walked into a small office just beyond the counter and shut the door.

It was small and cramped, boxes of paperwork and forgotten gym equipment strewn about like a toddler's toys. Leanne bustled around the office, pulling papers out of cabinets and placing them in front of Cornelia without any discernible order. Just the stack of paperwork was overwhelming.

"Right now we really need a teacher for Tuesday nights. We can pay cash for the ones you work. If you like it, there'll be more slots opening in a few months – one of our instructors has a bun in the oven," she quipped, rubbing her stomach and turning to give Cornelia a side view. She grabbed a t-shirt from a lopsided pile on top of a filing cabinet. That was new - Cornelia had never gotten a shirt before. It was a black womens' v-neck, and had a simple logo, Philly MMA in red on the left breast floating on a barbell.

"I'll have you meet with one of our current instructors, Connor, who also happens to be the new owner. He likes to have final say on who teaches and you'll probably do a couple training sessions with him to get you back up to speed," she explained as she tidied up the pile on the desk.

"Now I don't know what your timeline is like, but if you're looking to do this long term, you'll probably need to get your certifications renewed?" She looked to Cornelia for confirmation and she nodded. "For now just look over everything and give us a call when you're ready to come in. If all goes well, we can have you start within a couple weeks! We'll worry about getting your certs up to date then."

"Yeah I'll check on the dates but I'm sure they're coming close to expiring if they haven't already," Cornelia said, trying to remember her last continuing education class. She was always on top of her credits before her accident, but afterwards it just wasn't a priority.

Leanne smiled. "I know this is a little out of the blue, but if you have any questions feel free to call me or text me, whatever works for you," she said, reaching forward to squeeze Cornelia's elbow. Oddly affectionate, and somewhat endearing after Leanne's lightning speed monologue.

"Thanks," Cornelia said. She stuffed her bulging folder of papers and t-shirt into her gym bag and turned to the door.

"Sure thing, hun. We're just happy to have someone interested in helping out, it's been a rough couple of months finding adequate coverage, but you know what they say: the best things in life are unexpected," she said, rubbing her stomach.

"Yeah, I know what you mean," Cornelia said, but the words felt contrived.

"That's Connor," Leanne said, motioning to a man closing one of the supply doors in the far corner of the gym. He had short, wavy hair, deep brown flecked with grays, and moved with intention. He carried a box of something - weights, or equipment - into the closest classroom, dropping the box with a thud by the door.

He turned toward Leanne and Cornelia, smiling when he saw them looking, and made his way over.

"How are we doing ladies?" he asked. The way he asked made Cornelia think he already knew Leanne wasn't just chatting up a customer - there was a glisten of intuition in his eyes, like he knew what Leanne was going to say before she did.

"Cornelia used to be a teacher here. Remember how we told Eric to let us know if any old teachers came in? Well, one did, and she has graciously agreed to help us out," Leanne filled him in.

"Fantastic," he said, and held out his hand to shake hers. It was warm and large, and she felt the rest of her body leeching the heat, a controlled fire spreading from one limb to the next. Before she knew it, her face was warm too, and she let her hair fall over her cheek in an attempt to hide it. "Very happy to meet you." He sounded sincere.

"Happy to be here," she said, focusing on each individual word as she said it. They felt jumbled and mismatched.

"Well, I have to finish setting up a classroom, but I look forward to working with you, Cornelia," he said, and as quickly as he had come, he was gone, and she was left saying her goodbyes to Leanne, slightly breathless and completely overwhelmed. Over the years, she had gone to the gym to browbeat many problems, but never had she left with a real, tangible solution.

Cornelia's phone vibrated as she stepped outside.

Sunlight pierced the still horizon, the Philadelphia air a chilly gray. Cornelia pulled her hood up and shuffled through the pockets of her duffel bag. She normally kept her phone in an outside pocket, but she couldn't pinpoint which one.

By the time she found it, the ringer stopped sounding, and the screen flashed 5 missed calls. She didn't have to look at caller ID to know it was Tanya.

Before she could press dial, Aunt Tanya's name popped up once again and this time, Cornelia answered. "Good morning Aunt Tanya," she said as she began her trek home.

"Well thank god you finally answered! I was worried you had *died!*" she said, her voice cracking as it stretched beyond the normal confines of a vocal range. It was eight in the morning, but Tanya sounded like about five shots of espresso.

"Tanya, I've told you before not to call before noon. I have stuff I do in the morning that requires concentration and I won't answer my phone anyways," she said. Blatant lie – she always went to the gym in the mornings, but beyond that she really just didn't feel like forced communication *ever*.

"I know, but I get worried. And either way you told me to specifically call before noon, not the other way around," she said. *Oops.*

"Sorry Tanya, I must have misspoke. Please only call me after noon."

"It's okay dear. Anyways, how are you doing? Where is it you're staying again? Can you give me an address? Have you been following up with your doctor's appointments? Your doctor has been calling me asking about you," she said.

"I'll give him a call today," Cornelia told her. There was silence on the other line.

"Well where are you staying?" Tanya pressed.

"I'm staying at a friend's house," she said. Cornelia looked both directions before crossing the street.

"Which friend? Do I know them?" Tanya asked.

Since her parents had died, Tanya treated Cornelia like what Cornelia guessed was Tanya's idea of a daughter: overbearing, intrusive, and a pain in the ass. She had once insisted that because she was Cornelia's godmother, it meant that she needed to adopt Cornelia, at *27 years old*. Cornelia not-so-gently reminded her that you can only legally adopt someone who is under 18. Silently she thanked her lucky stars for that one.

"No, Tanya, she's a friend from high school. You've never met her and I'm only staying there a little while longer, okay? I'll let you know when I get a permanent place," Cornelia insisted. She had been telling Tanya the same story since moving to Philadelphia.

It wasn't that she didn't trust her. She just wanted some time alone, time to decompress after losing so much. Time to feel sad.

Sometimes Cornelia wondered if Tanya needed a care-giver of her own. She had a history of falling for scams involving vacations, extravagant gift cards and outrageous presents like laptops, for the low, low price of one identity. She once tried to win her sister (Cornelia's mom) a vacation to the Caribbean, leading to about four years and seven months fighting the debt that a scammer had racked up under her social security number.

Cornelia knew much worse could happen from someone giving away her information, so she kept it all to herself. "Well what's this girl's name at least?" Tanya pushed.

Cornelia floundered. She glanced at the stores and people around her. What's a generic girl's name? A homeless man shouted at her, something about Jameson and Jack.

"Jamie. I'm staying with my friend Jamie," Cornelia said. She made a mental note to write down that name when she got home. She had always been terrible at remembering names, especially of people that didn't exist.

Although, technically a Jamie did exist, as evidenced by the yearbook picture in which the two finalized the layout for the 50th anniversary of their school newspaper. She was a friend by convenience in high school, but over time they drifted apart. Cornelia hadn't thought of her in years - she probably wouldn't even recognize her anymore.

"Oh okay, good!" Tanya said. "You know, sometimes I really worry about you, Cornelia. You're so reclusive! But I'm glad you're getting to know old friends again and building your life. This last year has been so hard and I'm so proud of your resilience," Tanya said.

Cornelia wanted to give her phone to the homeless man to sell for that whiskey he was asking for. Maybe he'd share.

But Cornelia knew better. Throwing her phone would lead to a nationwide manhunt spearheaded by her aunt, and it's always easier to remain unseen when no one is looking for you.

Tanya was quiet for a few seconds, and Cornelia prematurely thought she might get away with a quick phone call.

"So tell me about this girl. What's she like? Were you close in high school?" Tanya asked.

"Yeah, we were friends in high school."

She heard Tanya take a long breath in, like she was preparing to spout a mouthful. "Oh you know what Tanya? I'm so sorry, I promised a friend I would help them move today for a couple extra bucks and a case of beer. I really don't want to be late so I'll talk to you later!"

"Oh okay honey, say hi to your friends for me! And give me a call when you're done. You're so busy, I feel like we really never get to talk like we should. You know, your mother was always a talker and if we went a day without speaking we would have to spend an hour catching up the next night. You're so quiet compared to her, but I guess that's your father coming out in you a little bit. He was always very reserved but he was one of those men, when he talked, everyone listened. I can see that in you Cornelia," Tanya said. Give her an inch and she'd take a mile.

"Uh, I guess. Thanks Tanya. I'll call you later," Cornelia said.

When she got back to her apartment, she made herself a cup of tea and signed into her computer, then her bank account. Still locked.

She browsed a few news websites for any major updates, and discovered the world was a boring, boring place.

She felt restless. Normally she spent her days reading or sleeping, sometimes with a crossword or journaling, but she felt she needed to *do* something – she just didn't know what. Knowing that she might have a job was great, but it wasn't enough.

After a quick shower, she continued her Craigslist hunt

for any odd job she could find that would pay a quick $50 under the table. She scrolled through hundreds, sent emails to a few, and hoped a couple hundred dollars would magically fall into her lap.

Cornelia had a bachelor's degree in public relations that she hadn't used in three years, and although she wasn't searching for a long-term desk position with a 401k and fringe benefits, she thought it worthwhile to explore opportunities using her degree again. Teaching classes at the gym was a start, but she didn't expect it to pay the bills.

Pre-accident Cornelia had bent her skills to include copywriting, and managed to build up a solid freelance portfolio. She could easily make $50 a day doing what she did best: communicating. She could write up a press release in ten minutes if she was hard-pressed, or a fabulous one if given twice that time.

But now there were more freelancers than ever before, willing to do work for a fraction of the price she would have asked. They were just as talented as she was, and begging to give you a full day's work for twenty bucks. How could she compete with that?

CHAPTER TEN
Present Day, Cornelia's apartment

A month had passed by the time Cornelia heard back from Luca. She began to wonder if she would ever see her money again.

"Luca," she said.

"Cornelia," Luca said, his tone in shadows. She scrolled to Weather Underground. "How is the weather in Egypt?"

Cornelia found the keys quickly. "It is 53 degrees today and partly cloudy," she told him, reciting her findings.

"Cornelia, I have some grave news," he said. Her heart caught in her throat.

"What is it?"

"Petyr is dead."

The words hung between them.

She felt ashamed, assigning so much weight to her own situation when Petyr, a man who actually cared about her, was dead. He was her last connection to Nate, and she never bothered to get to know him the way she should have.

He knew so much of her life, even if it consisted of secondhand information from Nathan and miniscule snippets from their Thursday meetings.

"Cornelia?"

"Yes. I'm sorry," she sputtered. "How did he die?"

"We have not received the autopsy yet, but he was found in the Schyukhill River. I suspect he was killed," Luca explained.

"What do you think happened?"

He didn't say anything for a few seconds, but Cornelia could hear him breathing.

"I think that Petyr did not deserve to die, and whoever is responsible will pay for what they have done," he growled through the phone.

"So you don't think this was an accident," she clarified.

"I'm *sure* this was not an accident," he sniffled. "Petyr had good instincts. There was a reason I trusted him, and I'm *sure* there is a reason he's now dead. I don't have the details I need yet, but when I do... well, my dear Cornelia, you shall hear nothing more of it."

Cornelia felt a little chill run down her spine.

"Luca, I..."

"If you hear or remember anything that you think may be important to the investigation, please pass it along. Otherwise, please remember the delicate nature of our business when speaking with anyone else," he reminded her.

She remembered when she first met Luca, a meeting arranged by Petyr shortly after she was released from the hospital. Petyr was sympathetic, heartbroken from Nate's death, and willing to help Cornelia in any way he could. That help was Luca.

By all technicalities, the Italy account was completely legal.

Cornelia wasn't sure exactly how, but Luca assured her she wouldn't be breaking any laws, and him she trusted. That was all she needed to hear.

Regardless, communication was kept to a minimum as plenty of perfectly legal things are scrutinized unnecessarily. Luca treated her with the utmost kindness, but behind the smile lines and soft blue eyes, she could see another, darker man that he was careful to conceal. She again wondered what other "clients" he dealt with.

"Luca," she said, but could find no other words.

Luca cleared his throat. "Petyr was a good man, and I'm sure the police will find what they need to bring his attacker to justice. In the meantime, I'm sure you're concerned what will happen to your accounts here."

"Uh, yes, yes I am," she said, thrown by his easy transition.

"Well we can do one of several things. Right now we can wire you your money in small increments so nothing gets flagged. Keep in mind that if, for any reason, they do get flagged, our business does not exist, so you must have explanations prepared. We can also wire your money to an account of your choice that is not your own; a family member or trust," Luca suggested.

"I really don't want to do anything electronic. It needs to be cash," she said. She'd be damned if she was going to start leaving a paper trail now.

"I understand. In that case, we can have Petyr's replacement continue your cash disbursements, beginning with a large lump sum to cover the missed payments or replace what was used in your emergency fund, whatever you need. However, as I said before, it might take me some time before I find someone I can trust like Petyr," Luca explained. He knew what the weight of trust meant to Cornelia, and he knew that no matter what, her top priority was her privacy.

"Okay," she pandered. "Are these my only options?" she asked. She hated the way her voice sounded, desperate and needy and under the control of someone half a world away. She felt like a little kid begging a parent for just a *little* more allowance.

She stood from her desk chair and paced her apartment. In only underwear and Nathan's old t-shirt, she felt a wave of heat hit her legs as she passed the radiator, and a blast of cool air as she passed her crooked window. She huddled by the warmth.

"Can you come to Italy? We could give you cash from our office and you can take it back to the United States with you. We will of course pay for your plane ticket. Again, however, large amounts of cash are prohibited on international flights. This is a risk you must be willing to take," Luca said.

Cornelia rarely sat in a taxi, hadn't driven since her accident, and flew just once, only when she found enough Xanax to get her from the gate to Italy with little to no memory. She worried she wouldn't be so lucky this time.

"I don't think I can do that," she said. She worried he could hear the lump building in her throat.

"You must face your fears some time or another, Corey. Until you can get on a plane, I'm afraid our options are limited," Luca said, his voice stern but soft. He waited for Cornelia to respond, and when he realized she wouldn't, said, "Let me know when you are able to come visit. I will be happy to provide you with a plane ticket, whenever. Until then, Cornelia, I will continue to update you and do my best to get you whatever money I can. I'm sorry it has come to this."

"Thank you Luca," Cornelia said.

The line went dead, and a little piece of her went with it.

CHAPTER ELEVEN
Present Day, Cornelia's hometown

Dr. Liam Ingels flipped through the pages of Cornelia's yearbook. There was only one person in the entire book with the name Jamie, and she was pictured with Cornelia, working on some newspaper or another. She was blonde, pretty in a very conventional way. After some internet sleuthing, Liam discovered she was a waitress at American Star Diner.

Liam had called her twice already, and she was no help. The first time he called, she hung up on him. She told him she hadn't talked to Cornelia in years, and she had no idea where she was now. Her Aunt Tanya had said something similar, that they hadn't spoken in days and she had no idea where she was now.

The entire thing felt scripted.

But he got a name. Jamie was all he needed to make the necessary connections. He found her, and soon, he would find Cornelia too.

Jamie bustled around the diner, shutting off lights and powering down. He watched her from his car, his lights off, his breathing the only sound.

She pulled her apron off and grabbed her purse from behind the counter. She paused before leaving, as if she knew he was waiting there for her, and scanned the diner. Then, she pushed through the door, locked it from the outside, and continued to her car. She didn't notice the coupe idling across the parking lot.

Liam got out of his car, quietly, stealthily, and stole into the night. They reached her car at the same time, but she didn't notice him until he was only a few paces away.

"Can I help you?" she asked, her keys sprouting like thorns between her fingers.

"Yes, I'm looking for Cornelia Winthorp. She said she was staying with you," he said.

Jamie shook her head. "I haven't seen her since high school, best check with her parents," she suggested, and moved to get in the car.

Liam sidestepped her. "I know you know where she is," he said.

"I don't know where she is, I haven't talked to her in years. Now if you would please move, I need to get home to my kids," she said.

"Your kids," he said, licking his lips. "Let me see... Andrew and Elena? Those are their names, right?"

She paused. "No," she said. She pushed past him and got in her car. She locked the doors, and whipped out of the parking lot. Liam had her exactly where he wanted her.

He hopped out of the way when her tires came within inches of his toes.

He ran back to his car, turned the engine over, and flew out of the parking lot behind her. He followed her from a distance, and just as he predicted she would, she drove right into the police station. He drove past, content with scaring her a bit. People talked more when they had something to fear.

CHAPTER TWELVE
Present Day, Cornelia's apartment

Cornelia sat in silence. She flipped her phone shut and sank onto the floor in front of her radiator, the wood floor creaking under her weight as she leaned back. She let the heat burn through her t-shirt.

She had trouble determining whether her response to the news of Petyr's death was truly in mourning of the dead man she had grown so fond of, or the fear of what might come next for her.

She knew that putting money across seas came with some risk, but she never thought it would be because her line of supply was rearranged, or worse, annihilated.

She felt unnecessarily scared, like there was something more to this she was missing. Was karma finally coming for her? Looking back, she was mostly an okay person, aside from a few oversights. At least, no oversights that would warrant this kind of retaliation.

Besides, she only ever felt this way since her accident. If she had done something regrettable enough that another person wanted to do her harm, wouldn't she have felt this unease before? Aside from one or two jerky men she blew off, she couldn't even think of the last person she might have offended.

A bottle of 30-year Glenfiddich sat, dusty, to the side of the radiator. Cornelia rarely drank, but this felt like an appropriate occasion. That bottle of whiskey had been meant for Cornelia's wedding night, but had long ago been turned into her and Nate's special kind of "champagne."

When Nate was promoted to regional director, they agreed it was just as worthy a reason to have a taste. When they got through the graduation party thrown by Cornelia's mother and co-hosted by Aunt Tanya, they had another taste. When Cornelia was a week late and ended up ruining her favorite pair of jeans, they had one more.

She uncapped the bottle and took a sniff. The smell made her stomach flip and her mouth water. Memories, good and bad, resurfaced.

Climbing up from the floor, she rummaged through her clean dishes for a mug. Most of her glassware had disappeared while she was in a coma, sold off or given away to save space and money, but luckily her affinity for funny mugs preceded her. Her extensive collection was saved, and although she had no glasses or tumblers, she had learned an important lesson: red wine tastes just fine slurped from a Snoopy mug.

She poured herself a generous serving of whiskey in a FUCK CARDIO mug, Nate's loving gift when she first started teaching, and glanced at the picture on her wall. She held up her cup, toasting not only Petyr, but Nathan, too, and every part of the family she had lost.

The alcohol slid warm and tingly down her throat. She leaned against the wall and let the radiator warm her from the outside while the whiskey took care of her insides.

The taste was familiar and brought back things she didn't know she had forgotten: the smell of rain and soil after a surprise rainstorm cut an afternoon of gardening short; the friction of denim against denim under a fuzzy blanket; the creak of an office chair after a midnight work call disturbed the silence.

It was so easy to fall into the deep end. She took one sip, and another.

She poured herself another mug and sat down at her computer, hoping to distract herself by searching for any information that might have been released about Petyr's death. At least one article a year surfaced about someone washing up at the south end of the Schyukhill, but until now, she rarely paid attention to the details.

CHAPTER THIRTEEN
Present Day, Cornelia's hometown

Liam waited in his car in the parking lot, knowing that Jamie would have to show up any minute for her breakfast shift. Last time he visited the diner, he had "accidentally" taken a wrong turn and ended up in front of next week's schedule instead of the bathrooms. He was giddy, knowing that she could drive up at any moment. It was only a matter of time.

She looked tired when she arrived. Her eyes were dark, and her uniform dirty, unwashed from the day before. She had her hair up, and he suspected the stain on her shoulder was baby spit up.

He walked into the diner with the morning rush and requested a table by the window.

He sat and had a coffee, watching the traffic fly by on the highway outside. A family sat in the booth next to him, the kids kicking the seat into his back. He ordered a fruit salad, and glanced around the diner, searching for Jamie.

She stood with her back to him, a phone tucked under her ear. She was frantic, trying to count change while talking to someone. She hung up the phone and glanced to Liam. They locked eyes. He waved; she scowled.

She turned back to the change she was counting and called one of the bussers over to her. They had a quick conversation, and he helped her finish counting. He stayed with her until Liam had had his fill of coffee, tipped generously, and left.

He cruised by her house on his way home, searching for any sign of Cornelia. He saw Jamie's husband carrying a toddler in through the front door, but no sign anyone else was home.

But this was the only Jamie she knew. Cornelia was

there. Somewhere.

CHAPTER FOURTEEN
Three years earlier, greater Philadelphia area

Every fall, the Philly Fringe Festival took over the city, unique acts comprised of small, under-advertised performers in back rooms and on small, crowded stages.

It rained as Nate and Cornelia exited the Arts Conservatory, where they had just seen a 45-minute production detailing one woman's lifelong love for Billy Joel. The performance culminated with the solo actress shaving her head.

Cornelia waited in the arched doorway, in the one tiny, dry spot. She hugged her jacket around her, waiting for Nathan to finish his impromptu call. She wasn't sure what it was about, but he seemed excited, light on his feet.

He slipped his cell phone into his jacket pocket as he ran back to her, and held out his hand.

"Come on, let's go get some dinner," he said. He grinned as she took it.

They dashed down one street and across another, arriving in front of a diner most frequented by drunks at closing time. Regardless, about three quarters of the tables were full, mostly with damp tourists looking for reprieve from the rain.

"Wait," Nate said, pulling her back as she was about to open the door. He was still grinning.

"Nate it's pouring, can we go inside?" she asked.

He pulled her out of the doorway, wrapping his arms tight around her. He kissed her, dipping her halfway to the ground.

She could feel her cheeks turning a rosy red as he stood her up straight again.

"You're such a sap," she said, turning back to the diner, but she couldn't prevent the smile coming to her lips.

They hung their jackets on the coat rack by the door,

and sat at a rainy window booth.

With two coffees on the way and half a slice of pie to share, Nate sprang, "I have someone I want you to meet."

He had been looking out the window a lot, but she had attributed that to their mutual affinity for rainstorms and people watching. She had been absentmindedly staring, too.

A few moments later, Nate got up to greet an older gentleman who walked through the door. He pulled off his rain jacket and hung it next to theirs, smiling as Nate said hello. They shook hands, and pulled each other in for a hug - one too long for a business colleague.

"Corey, this is my Uncle Petyr," he said, one hand resting on the man's shoulder as they walked back to their table.

"Oh," she said, surprised. They shook hands as Nate slid into the diner booth across from her, his uncle just after him. "It's so nice to meet you," she said. "I've heard a lot about you."

Petyr, the mysterious uncle who popped out of the woodwork while Nate was still in school. Cornelia had heard the story, but she never had a face to match the name.

From a closer vantage point, Cornelia could see that he had the mannerisms of an older man, but the face of a younger one. She guessed Petyr could only be 10 or 15 years older than Nate.

He smiled, squeezing Nate's shoulder. Petyr continued, "we don't talk often, but from what I hear, he's quite smitten with you."

Not one to be easily embarrassed, Nate grinned. "He's heard all about you."

The majority of dinner consisted of Nate and Petyr catching up, and Cornelia created a timeline in her head of Nate's stories to figure out the last time they had seen each other; it had been about a year. Cornelia had already heard Nate's stories and anecdotes but happily followed along - she could tell by the animated way Nate talked that this was someone important to him.

Petyr took every opportunity to ask about their relationship; how they met, where they were living, etc. He barely spoke a word about himself.

After they paid the bill, Nate ran outside with the umbrella to get the car from the garage down the street, and Cornelia waited with Petyr for his taxi, just inside the diner's front door. Nate and Cornelia offered to drive Petyr to his hotel, but he insisted he had other business to attend to first. Seemingly used to these explanations, Nate agreed and bounded out into the grey dusk.

Waiting under the protection of the diner's pavilion, Petyr sighed. "I don't see Nathan nearly as much as I would like to," he started, pulling on his jacket and hat. "But I always tell him, if he ever needs anything, and I mean anything, I will help him in any way that I can."

Cornelia nodded. "That's incredibly kind of you," she said. A rain-soaked passerby ducked into the diner, shaking out her umbrella as the door clambered shut.

"I want to extend that same promise to you," Petyr explained. "I care for Nate very much, and I can see that he cares for you in the same way. If you ever need anything-" He paused and smiled. "-and I mean *anything*... you ask me."

Nate pulled up to the curb in front of the diner, followed by the taxi Petyr had called.

He jumped out of the car to give Petyr another handshake and a hug before his taxi pulled away. Cornelia hopped in the front seat, high off of meeting Nate's one living relative.

That was the last time Petyr saw Nathan before he died.

CHAPTER FIFTEEN
Present day, somewhere inside Cornelia's head

Cornelia checked into the blood drive for her 3pm appointment. She was a few minutes early.

She waited as they cleaned the bed she would use. There were four squished into the conference room, the normal tables and chairs pushed up against the walls. Three of the beds were occupied, the patients subdued by the needles in their arms. Two flexed, pushing the blood out faster, while one simply rested, unmoving.

A nurse led her to the open bed in the furthest corner. The first patient was a middle-aged woman with frizzy hair, pumping out as much blood as she could. She played with her phone while she waited.

The second patient was a younger man, a little scrawny looking with short blonde hair, wearing a short-sleeved polo. He had tattoos down his arm, which was strange because Cornelia thought her company didn't allow visible tattoos. Then she realized it was probably because he was drawing blood and didn't want to ruin a nice shirt – the company would have made an exception for that.

The third blood giver was in his late twenties, with short dark hair and handsome, sharp features. He seemed a little pale, so as Cornelia walked by, she gently squeezed his shoulder. His eyes popped open and he smiled at her. Good.

She laid down as the nurse prepared her needle. She didn't love giving blood, but it was for a good cause. She closed her eyes as the nurse popped the needle in her arm, and listened to the spiel about squeezing her fist. She nodded and closed her eyes, hoping to fall into a quick nap before having to go back to work.

After a few minutes, the woman with the frizzy hair finished up and left. A few minutes after that, the man with short blonde hair was done too. Cornelia and the dark-haired man waited, unclenched, allowing their bodies to naturally bleed just a little blood at a time.

After quite a while, Cornelia felt light-headed, and flagged one of the nurse's down. The two beds remained empty for what could have been eons, and Cornelia's body felt light, white, bled dry.

"Am I done yet?" Cornelia asked.

The nurse smiled kindly. "Not just yet, sweetie. Lie back down."

Cornelia glanced to the other end of the tube running to her arm. She started when she realized it ran to a five-gallon bucket on the floor that was halfway full with blood. She panicked, pulling the needle from her arm.

The nurse grabbed her before the needle dislodged. "Honey, you have to lie back down."

Cornelia shook her head, sitting up. The world spun. "This isn't right," she said, looking to the man next to her. She realized with a shock that it was Nathan.

He was paler than before. She reached over to him as the nurse tried to hold her back. She grabbed his shoulder, shaking. He wasn't waking.

She glanced to the bucket by his side and saw it was nearly full. She punched the nurse and scrambled to him, shaking him as hard as she could. He wouldn't wake up.

A gang of nurses descended on her, an impossible number from all sides, forcing her back to the bed. She felt herself growing weaker, tears running down her cheeks. All she could see was the insignia on the nurse's uniform, green squiggly lines interconnected, flowing wide into a circle and tying again, neatly toward the bottom in the shape of a brainstem.

"Nate!" she screamed, trying to force the nurses away. "Nathan!"

The room shook, a deep hum piercing her body like an earthquake was coming.

◆ ◆ ◆

Cornelia jerked awake, her heart pounding. Her skin was slick with sweat, her bed sheets tangled around her legs. She shook involuntarily

Underneath her left shoulder, her phone buzzed.

Cornelia felt for her lamp and flipped open her phone as the room was bathed in light.

"Hello," she breathed.

"Cornelia!"

"Tanya. What's up?" Her heart gradually slowed.

"I just wanted to call and say Happy Thanksgiving! I'm bummed we weren't here for the holiday but we'll see you for Christmas, right?" she asked. She was shouting, fighting with a crowd to be heard.

Tanya and her new boyfriend were on a traveling spree. Tanya had been retired for a few years and spent most of her free time exploring new places. She had been thrilled to find someone with similar aspirations.

"Yeah, I'll be there," Cornelia muttered, closing her eyes.

"Oh good. How are you doing? How's the girl you're staying with? Jamie?" she asked.

"Tanya, why are you calling me right now? It's four in the morning," Cornelia asked.

"Oh is it? Wow, I forgot about that time difference! We're sitting down for a drink before dinner, we arrived in Thailand this afternoon! I tried calling your other phone but you didn't answer!" she shouted.

Cornelia's "other" phone was the barely working smartphone she had a year ago that she kept on silent in her desk drawer. Despite having had multiple new phones since the accident, she could never get rid of this one. There wasn't anything quite like reading the last few texts her mom sent her.

Tanya knew all of this, but nevertheless insisted on calling that phone 4-5 times before trying Cornelia's new number.

She was the main reason that phone was kept on silent, rather than turned off completely and stored in a box somewhere. Cornelia delved into the drawer to clear out Tanya's notifications once every month or so.

"I'm going to go back to bed," Cornelia said, flipping the light off. "Happy Thanksgiving Tanya."

"Happy Thanksgiving. Sleep well! See you at Christmas! Love you honey!" Tanya shouted.

"Love you too," Cornelia nodded into her pillow as she shut her phone and retreated further into her covers.

CHAPTER SIXTEEN
Present day, Cornelia's hometown

Liam waited around the corner while she closed the diner. The building had windows on three sides, so he could see right through to the side where she parked. She scurried out, got in her car, and gunned it out of the parking lot.

He followed, and as she merged onto the highway to go back home, he merged too. He got into the left lane and drove next to her.

She missed her exit, and as Liam glanced over, he saw the fear riddled over her face. She knew it was him.

He moved with her effortlessly, their cars slowing and speeding in a coordinated dance. They merged onto Kelly Dr., and just past the spot Petyr Hotchkin had last been seen, a convenient pullover lane jutted out from her side of the road. Liam sped up so Jamie's car was solidly in his blind spot, and switched lanes.

Now, he had just meant for her to pull over. He really didn't expect she would keep going.

But she kept going.

Into the pull over lane. Past the wooden fence posts. Across the Schyukhill Trail. Through the grassy commons. Over the shallow brick wall.

And deep, deep into the cold brown water.

For a moment he panicked, thinking Jamie was the last connection he had to wherever Cornelia might be. But then he realized: Cornelia's cash disbursements were disrupted with Petyr's death, and now her living situation would be rocked by Jamie's.

Now, it was only a matter of time before Cornelia would have to resurface.

Come out, come out wherever you are....

Liam slowed back to a regular speed and continued on.

CHAPTER SEVENTEEN
Present day, Manayunk

Cornelia started walking. She knew she'd still be out after dark, so she carried a switchblade tucked into her sock. Bundled joggers and families milked the last of the nice weather before winter hit.

On a normal day, she might have enjoyed this walk, but today she had a destination in mind that she wasn't particularly thrilled to visit. It was only right, to say goodbye to Petyr.

Petyr's last known whereabouts were along the river, near the main strip in Manayunk.

Cornelia followed the investigation as closely as she could from afar, and guessed that Petyr had been walking either to or from meeting with a client sometime that Thursday. She knew he had other "clients" but beyond the services he provided her, she had no clue what he might be doing for other people.

Judging by the number of people meandering about by the river, she guessed there had been an event going on earlier in the day, probably a race or one of those "healthy mom" fests that were suddenly so trendy. It wasn't exactly her crowd, but nothing she couldn't blend right into with a ponytail and her ratty old Northface jacket.

She walked along the trail, the brisk fall wind nipping at her nose and exposed ears. She was coming up on the half-mile portion of Kelly Drive that was relevant to the investigation.

She had wanted just a few minutes to stew in her loss, but with the sheer amount of people milling about - the tired kids screaming, the joggers huffing - she doubted the possibility.

And as much as she tried to fight it, there was a part of

her that had been hoping for a clue, anything that could tell her what had really happened that day.

Along the trail where Petyr was last seen alive, people crowded around each other, chatting, enjoying. They seemed to get denser the closer she got. She deflated - the only alone time she might get would consist solely of the thoughts in her head.

She wanted something to tell Luca, or something that would prove Petyr's death was at least fast. She wanted to know what he was doing in that last moment. What was the last thing he thought before he knew he would die? Did he ever even realize which breath would be his last?

There was a Rite Aid across the street from the river trail. Cornelia darted across.

She picked up a blank card, a teddy bear, and a pack of pens.

She had no idea what she would say, but maybe leaving a little something would give her a smidge of closure.

She walked slowly down that half mile, ignoring the people bustling around her and focusing instead on her surroundings. There were few buildings with cameras, and plenty of places to "accidentally" take a dip into the river. She had no clue which place was Petyr's.

By the time she finished scouting, she had no leads and no idea what to write in Petyr's card.

She sat on an empty bench with the card and a box full of pens.

What do you write to someone you barely knew but meant so, *so* much to you?

All of the things you should have already told them.

She wrote: *Miss you. RIP. Love, Cornelia.*

For a moment she wondered if she shouldn't have signed her name. But really, who would be looking?

She knew whatever she wrote wouldn't be enough. She settled the card within the teddy bear's arms, and looked around for the best place to keep it safe.

Just under the wall at the edge of the river, the concrete met at an angle, creating a grassy little nook. She set the teddy bear down in the corner and patted its fuzzy head. She wondered what happens to all the teddy bears when no one comes to take care of them.

"I take it you know the guy they found in the river."

A gruff voice brought her back to the present and she jumped, looking around. A man stood next to her, facing the river north. He was far enough away that she hadn't noticed him approach, his silhouette blending in with the distant trees and the hum of people around them.

"Yes I did," she conceded.

He nodded, turning toward her. "Yeah, I heard them fighting that night. Didn't seem physical though, just seemed like some drunk assholes yelling at each other, pretty usual around here," the man remarked.

"Did you see them?"

"Nope, but I live in that building on the corner," he said, nodding his head in that direction. It looked like a brand new development, a sharp contrast with the rest of the neighborhood. "Keep tellin' 'em to send in the security footage but they won't do it without a subpoena and Philly PD's got their thumbs up their asses, like usual."

"That's frustrating," Cornelia muttered, staring out over the water.

The man was silent for a few beats, also watching the water, and then nodded to Cornelia. "Have a good night," he said, and continued on his way. Cornelia took that as her cue too.

Night was falling and Manayunk was winding down, all the joggers bopping home and peeling off their sweat wicking Lululemon in favor of their mom and dad jammies. A few sparse groups lingered, chatting and laughing by the water while children slept soundly in their strollers.

Cornelia kept her head down and walked home. She didn't want to see any happiness at the moment.

She had been following the news closely, watching for developments relating to Petyr's murder. On air and in print, they spun the same threads they had been sewn since Petyr had washed up in the river.

Several "witnesses" heard a fight, but no one had seen it; someone with an accent versus a burly-sounding American. They theorized a drunken bar fight got too serious, and - whether intentional or not - Petyr ended up in the river, dead, floating toward his watery grave in the reserve behind the art museum.

The footpath along Kelly Drive had only a short, chunky wall no higher than two feet off the ground, some areas none at all. Forget death by bar fight – she was surprised more people didn't die from trying to take a piss over the ledge and falling in.

Cornelia scoured the media every morning. She wanted to see somewhere that additional footage had been found – that at the very least they later saw Petyr walking in the opposite direction. Let them cross reference the times and for the sake of Petyr's family, narrow the mileage in which Petyr was suspected to hit the water. It had been too long for there to be no new information.

She had taken to pacing the length of her small apartment.

One, two, three, four, five, six, turn. One, two, three, four, five, six, turn.

How many cameras got a view of the river in that area? How many of them had actually been checked out? She knew police could be inundated, but she had to believe they checked every tip.

Her coat was in a pile by the door, her phone rested on her desk.

Would they take an anonymous caller seriously? They

certainly hadn't thus far, if the man by the river had told her any truth. Why would they start now?

But she had to try.

She pulled on her sneakers and her jacket and tooled out of her apartment, slamming the doors as she went. *This will be fast,* she told herself. *And this will be painless.*

Other than as a passerby on the street, she had had very little interaction with police since her accident. Cornelia had been told by doctors that it was just her paranoia flaring up, a side effect of her brain damage. Ironically, she trusted her doctors even less than the police. Something about being in a coma for nine months while they watched and moved her skeeved her out.

She walked into the police station. On one side of the room was a small waiting area, the other a glass-shielded desk, behind which sat a grumpy, slightly overweight woman cop. She was focused on the computer when Cornelia came to the window. Cornelia waited silently.

"How can I help you?" the cop asked, pursing her lips. She didn't look at Cornelia.

"I uh, wanted to talk to a detective," Cornelia stammered. "About Petyr Hotchkin's death."

She grumbled about something and nodded. "I'll see if Detective Sturgess is in, wait here," she said, disappearing behind a door in the back of her office. Cornelia nodded.

She waited 15 minutes before she considered sitting down, but just as she crossed the room to the row of flimsy plastic chairs, the door to the right of the glass-shielded office opened and the woman cop reappeared.

"Right this way," she said, cocking her head toward the open door.

Cornelia followed her into a small, cramped office space. Desks were pushed together in clumps of four, some cluttered with manila folders, a few decorated with pictures and gifts from loved ones, some completely empty. The one Cornelia was led to was decorated sparsely, with one picture, and was manned by a tall, young, somewhat rough-looking detective. He rose to greet her, shaking her hand.

"Detective Sturgess," he said, and looked at her expectantly.

"Cornelia."

"Please, have a seat," the detective said, motioning to the chair propped against the side of desk. She sat down gingerly, pulling her coat tighter around herself. Office chatter filled her ears, several cops and detectives buzzing together in little pockets around the room.

"So Cornelia," he started, placing his intertwined hands on the desk between them. "We've been looking for you."

For me? No no no no no.

Cornelia's heart stopped. She assumed they were looking for her in connection with Petyr, but as an acquaintance or a suspect?

"No reason to panic," he said, smiling. She hated that he could read her. "We found the teddy bear you left by the Schyukhill. We've been having some trouble locating Petyr's next of kin, and we were hoping you might be able to help us. You're quite elusive though, I have to say. We just about gave up on finding you."

"Oh," Cornelia breathed. "Uh, I'm sorry, I didn't really know Petyr all that well. He was kind of a family friend – my ex-fiance would refer to him as an uncle, but I don't know if they were blood-related."

"Yes, we were looking for your ex-fiance as well. This would be Nathan Montgomery, correct?" the detective asked. He pulled a notebook out from one of his desk drawers and began to scribble.

"Um, yes. That's him. He's dead though," Cornelia explained.

The detective turned his attention back to her, his eyebrows raised. "I'm so sorry," he said. His eyebrows furrowed. "I'm sorry, we must have forgotten to check death records, I didn't mean to bring up a sore past."

"It's no problem, it's not the first time I've had to explain." She smiled, but her heart still ached a little bit. That happened anytime Nate came up.

The detective nodded.

"Alright, thanks for clearing that up for us, Cornelia," he said, his voice softer. He gave her a cursory smile and scribbled a few more notes.

"So we've been doing some investigation into Petyr's accounts, and we've found that he had some large wire transfers deposited into several different checking accounts all under his name and all within the past few months. Would you know anything about that? Do you know if he involved with any drug trafficking, immigration schemes, Italian mob?" he asked, smiling.

Cornelia's heart beat fast, blood rushing to her face. She realized why Petyr's death wasn't progressing; he was just another organized crime syndicate who ended up on the wrong end of a blunt object.

"That was just a joke," the detective cautioned, the smile slowly leaving his face. Cornelia forced a smile again, this time with a chuckle. It felt like crushing gravel. "Well, the Italian mob part at least."

"I don't think he was involved in anything illegal," she said. That would cover both their asses, wouldn't it? Just plead ignorance?

"How close would you say you were to Petyr?" the detective asked, putting the pen down. His eyes narrowed as he studied her face.

"Not very close. We saw each other once in a while but never for long. He gave very few personal details. Mostly we traded stories about Nate. He was everything, to both of us," she said.

The detective nodded. A cop whisked by, mumbling incoherent numbers into the radio on his shoulder.

"Alright," he said. He scribbled something else down in his notebook, punctuating expressively.

He turned back to Cornelia. "I apologize for the questions, just wanted to get them out of the way. "I understand you have some other information relating to Petyr Hotchkin?" he prompted. He leaned back in his chair, giving Cornelia his full attention.

"Uh, well, it seems silly now," she stuttered. "I uh, when I went to see where Petyr died, I ran into a man who said he lived in a building with a security camera that overlooks that area. He said the building hadn't handed anything over, so I guess I just wanted to make sure that you knew it was there," she said.

She felt outright foolish for putting herself in the line of fire and coming back with a shit tip. She should have called the tip line. Better yet, she should have just stayed home. She bit her lip, wondering why, oh why, couldn't Tanya call her *now?* Cornelia would have welcomed the disruption.

"Do you know the building's address?" he asked her, picking up his pen again.

"Uh, I'm sorry, no. It's at the corner across from East Falls Bridge, right behind Kelly Drive. The new one that looks really out of place," she said.

The detective smiled. "I know exactly which building you are referring to," he said. He scribbled down the note. "I'll make sure somebody goes out to double check we got all surveillance footage. That's a great tip, Cornelia, thanks for bringing it in."

Cornelia waited silently, increasingly aware of how dumb her tip had sounded.

Maybe she had just wanted to help too much. She smiled. Was a smile appropriate?

"If you wouldn't mind leaving your phone number and address, you can be on your way," he said, flipping his notebook to a new sheet and sliding it in front of her.

She stalled, wondering which number to leave. Should she leave a fake? Probably a bad idea. She left Tanya's address, considering that's where all her mail went anyways.

"Thank you," he said. He stood up and held out his hand. "We will let you know if we find any more information. In the meantime, thank you coming in."

He led her out of the offices, back to the pitiful plastic waiting area. She ducked her head and skittered out, thankful for the cool air on her flaming cheeks.

CHAPTER EIGHTEEN
Present day, Cornelia's hometown

Liam was frustrated. Tanya had been helpful at first, at least in updating him on Cornelia's condition, but it seemed she had nothing new to tell him when he called. He was certain she was hiding something.

She had always been protective of Cornelia, but she had never steered him so blatantly in the wrong direction before. Jamie's disappearance led him to no new clues as to Cornelia's whereabouts, and he was starting to regret all the time he had wasted strategizing on her.

He had a new question he needed answering: was it Tanya lying to him, or Cornelia lying to Tanya? He could see it going either way.

And if Cornelia wasn't staying with Jamie, where was she?

He waited outside Tanya's house. It was Thanksgiving, and according to Cornelia's stories, the entire family used to go to Tanya's for holidays. He had assumed that tradition wouldn't change after her accident.

It was a small, quiet cul-de-sac filled to the brim with townhouses of varying colors. He had watched as families left and arrived, food entering and leaving, consuming and decorating, all around the neighborhood.

But still, Tanya's remained dark. What was she doing?

He got out of his car and crossed the street. He rang the doorbell, and after waiting a few minutes, opened the screen door and knocked. Still, there was nothing.

"Cornelia!" he shouted. He heard a door slam shut and he whipped around the find the source of the noise – the neighbors four houses over heading out for Thanksgiving dinner. Liam waved. "Hihowyadoin?"

He knocked again, and after they drove away, re-arranged the flowerpots. He unlocked the front door when he found the key and pushed inside.

It was dark. And cluttered.

Liam used the flashlight on his phone to find a light switch. There were tchotchkes everywhere, in groups on the floor and covering every open surface. Multiple religious denominations were represented, Hinduism, Christianity, some Paganism, all living in harmony.

Cornelia once mentioned that her aunt kept a list of important information by her computer, in her office on the second floor. He located the stairs and chose the first of three rooms to explore. It was the only one with a computer and file storage.

He skimmed the stacks of papers on top of the filing cabinets and searched the areas immediately surrounding the computer, but was unable to find that sheet. Maybe Cornelia had finally gotten through to her. He stood and turned slowly, surveying the mess around him.

He caught a little bunny statue only inches from death after knocking it off the window sill with his elbow. He replaced it and continued his muddled search.

Some passwords might have been nice, but he felt like his search had reached a point where sleuthing round wouldn't work anymore. He knew she was somewhere in Philadelphia, somewhere around Rittenhouse Square, some-where secluded. He resigned himself to the search he didn't really want to do - a long, laborious walk through Rittenhouse until he finally found her.

Seeing that Cornelia was nowhere in sight, Liam sulked back downstairs and out to his car, flipping off the lights he turned on, and replacing the key under the planters as he went.

It was worth a try, and he could always come back later.

CHAPTER NINETEEN
Present day, Rittenhouse

Cornelia paced, the day's events leaving her restless and unfulfilled. She felt trapped in a state of in between – wanting to help, yet desperate to remain unseen.

She pulled on a pair of jeans and an old sweater, grabbed her wallet and keys from the step stool next to the front door, and walked into the brisk evening. She wasn't sure whether the fresh air would help or hinder, but she couldn't bear the sight of four white walls any longer. She needed to *get out.*

Cornelia walked along 19th street, scanning the converted storefronts for an attractive hole in the wall. A block or so from her apartment, she spotted Monk's. *Bingo*, she thought, and scrambled inside.

The door was heavier than most and a blast of wind hit her as she entered the small hallway leading to the dark brown ambiance inside. Small, cramped tables with deep red cloths crowded the entryway. A chestnut brown bar lined the wall to the left, bathed in a red glow.

She sat down at the middle of three open stools, a girl with a mousy ponytail and glasses to her right, and a man in an oversize sweater with a white ring of hair like a halo around his head to her left. Cornelia smiled as the bartender approached - a mid-30's guy in simple flannel.

"What can I get you?" he asked.

"Gin and tonic," Cornelia requested. He poured her drink and slid it in front of her. She took a dainty sip and thanked him.

A TV in the corner behind the bar played the news. They showed a cute blonde girl with waxed, curly hair and a bright white smile. She was listed as missing in the Philadelphia area. For any information on Jamie Larson, contact her parents, Jim and Mary.

"Hey," said the girl sitting two stools down from Cornelia, very suddenly.

Cornelia studied the girl's face, and recognized her as the student who lived two doors down from her. She kicked herself for coming to a place so close to home.

"You're number 19," the girl said.

Cornelia's heart hammered, annoyed her address was about to be proclaimed to the entire bar.

"You're number 17," Cornelia said. An eye for an eye. The pressure in her stomach settled.

"I take it you're not having a great night either," the girl said.

Cornelia wondered why the girl would assume that. According to recent trends, her ripped 90's jeans and hole-y white sweater were actually in style. The only things not current were her dark brown booties, which were so dark you couldn't see the braided detail anyways.

She ran a hand through her hair and found no leaves, twigs, or excessive grease. She wasn't wearing makeup, but she didn't think she looked homeless or anything. Of course, she couldn't remember the last time she showered, but wasn't the grunge look in again?

"Drinking alone," Number 17 explained, with a slight smile.

Cornelia blinked. She hadn't had someone to drink with in a long time. "Ah. Yeah, it's been one of those weeks," she explained, taking a sip of her own drink. She put the glass back down gently on the bar. "One of those months, actually."

"I hear that. I come here whenever I'm feeling a little bit down. Something about a big burger, a big drink, and a little bit of darkness always makes my problems a little bit harder to see. In a couple ways," she explained, laughing.

She sipped her drink again, focusing her attention on the TV in the corner. They were still showing pictures of the missing person.

They sat in silence for a few minutes, and Cornelia drank fast, planning to find somewhere a little more secluded.

Her head was fuzzy, the drink stronger than she expected. Cornelia disliked the feeling of being out of control of her own body, but found herself relaxing into it.

"Another?" the bartender asked, his smile toothy and cute.

Cornelia nodded and thanked him, her shoulders untensing. She watched the news with hazy eyes and stewed in her own silence while those around her did the same, carrying on their small, meaningless conversations about their small, menial problems.

She took a deep breath and another sip. And another and another, until her second drink was finished too. She felt woozy and drunk, and it was time to go home. The man sitting two stools down from her had already left, but Number 17 still sat quietly to her right. She noticed Cornelia noticing her.

"Are you heading back home?" the girl asked. Cornelia felt like she was back in college again, living in a dorm room with three other girls. She never knew what was supposed to be so home-y about such a living situation, but she had enjoyed it at one point in her life.

"Yeah, I'm a little toasted," she conceded.

"Me too. Let's walk together," said Number 17.

They asked for their checks.

"Taken care of, ladies," the bartender explained. He motioned to the recently vacated seat two down from her left. "He covered both of you."

"That was *so* nice of him," the girl said, holding a hand over her heart, drunken pleasure showing through her cheeks. She pulled a few dollars out of her purse and left them on the counter for the bartender. Cornelia did the same.

The girls walked in silence, Cornelia's gait faster than Number 17's. The cold sobered her, and though it was nice to be out of her own apartment, that little nagging feeling that she *just needed to be home* snuck into her gut.

"You know what we shoulddo?" the girl said. Cornelia was surprised by her volume. She slurred a little bit, but Cornelia couldn't tell whether she was also shouting or her own drinks were interfering with her hearing. Her voice distracted Cornelia from her thoughts, an effect she was both craving and fearful of.

Cornelia lived in constant strife with herself. She had dedicated the past eight months of her life solely to the purpose of recovery and once in a while, she would do something out of her comfort zone, and find a moment of peace far more powerful than the kind she got from locking herself inside. This was one of those moments.

She was reminded of her college days, when she'd be huddled in a group of other girls, just trying to get to the next party before the frostbite set in. The tug in her heart felt less like aversion to the idea, and more like excitement, like maybe the thought wasn't all that bad after all.

Her life was split into two timelines – that which happened before her accident, and that which happened after. Maybe this is what it felt like to return to the person she once was, despite everything that happened in between.

"What is that?" Cornelia asked. Her tongue slipped over her words.

"Let's continue our night. This isn't something I do often, and I don't think it's something you do either," she said, looking to Cornelia for confirmation.

"What were you thinking?" Cornelia asked.

Number 17 smiled.

"Come on, this way."

Cornelia followed a stumbling Number 17 to a bar in Rittenhouse Square called Rouge, a place known for expensive food and bank-breaking drinks. Her earlier drinks were beginning to wear off, and her heart thumped as she realized she was out with a strange girl and still a little out of her own head. Her defenses were down.

"I have to run to the bathroom," Cornelia said as they walked through the door, and Number 17 glanced up with concerned eyes.

"Are you alright? You look a little pale."

"Yeah I'm fine," Cornelia said, and scampered to the bathroom.

Cornelia locked the door and leaned against it, forcing calm, calculated breaths.

The bathroom was nicely decorated, with a silver soap dispenser and thick disposable towels. Smooth jazz echoed out of an overhead speaker. *What am I doing here?*

She had been to Rouge several times, the first as a celebration and the rest as an ironic way of making fun of everyone celebrating. It was Nate's way to feel fancy, but Cornelia could never tell if he was mocking everyone or truly enjoying it.

The clientele consisted mostly of suited businessmen, as well as some "rich by other means" folk. They came with their dogs over summer and sat outside, facing the square, and valeted their tiny sports cars in the winter. Nate enjoyed the people watching, but Cornelia had trouble even enjoying a glass of wine if she was supposed to breathe-swish-breathe before tasting what could have been Franzia, for all she knew.

Nate wasn't normally a huge spender, but something about pretending for a night made him come alive. He would buy her fruity drinks, always with an order of water because he knew how easily she got headaches when she was dehydrated. He would dress up in a sport jacket and call them an Uber to take them around the city, and held her hand as they explored.

She thumbed the engagement ring she now wore around her neck. After a frantic week spent searching her apartment for the lost ring, after already having spent three weeks tracking it down from the hospital she woke up in, she decided a necklace was the smarter move. After all, she was no longer engaged.

She splashed some water on her face and patted it dry with an abnormally thick paper towel.

She paused before going back into the bustling bar, the image of Nate sitting at one of those rounded corner tables suddenly stuck in her head. If she just never opened the door, the possibility would always exist that he was waiting at the table just outside.

When Cornelia finally exited, Nate was not waiting for her. Instead, Number 17 chatted up two guys by herself at the bar. She sat on a stool while one guy leaned heavily on the bar like the closer he was, the better a chance he had, while the other stood halfheartedly as the third point of their triangle. He was in Cornelia's way.

"Hi," she said.

"Hey," he said, turning slightly toward her but not letting her in the conversation.

"Oh good, you're back!" Number 17 exclaimed, elbowing them out of her way. "Gentlemen, this is my neighbor Cornelia. Oh and Cornelia, the bartender came by so I just ordered us both margaritas. I hope that's okay!"

"Nice to meet you Cornelia," the leaner said, reaching out to shake her hand. The other guy stuck with his previous "hey." Cornelia turned to the bar and sat down, rolling her eyes.

The guys discussed the stock market, Number 17 interjecting thoughtless hmm's as they pontificated. Cornelia's eyes wandered.

The margarita she was drinking was $14, entirely too much money to be spending to wish you were elsewhere. Entirely too much money to be spending when you don't have money to spend.

Behind her, Number 17 told a vivid, slurred story about something she did in college and the men ate it up. They, like so many others in that bar, wore business suits and looked to be in their early thirties, workaholics who didn't know how to talk to women unless they were throwing money at them.

Shamelessly, Cornelia smiled at the closest one. If nothing else, maybe he'd buy her drink.

Her own callousness disgusted her.

She let her eyes wander across the room, and someone in the lounge area caught her eye. He was tall, very proper-looking, and wore a sport coat just like the one Nate used to wear. He smiled at her and raised his drink, oblivious to the conversation around him. She looked away, already having held his gaze too long.

The moment was fleeting and she felt her face heat, a lightness in her stomach that concerned her. She did another scan of the bar, skipping faces until she found the one she was looking for. He was walking in her direction.

"Hi," he said, grinning as he approached her.

"Hi." He looked at her expectantly.

"Sorry," he said, shaking his head, and reached to shake her hand. "I'm Liam."

"Cornelia," she said.

"Cornelia." He repeated it slowly, enunciating every syllable.

It had been a long time since someone truly wanted to listen to her. Liam peppered her with questions about her life, what she loved, how she spent her time, how she felt about her family. All she had learned about him was that he was a doctor, in town for a medical conference.

Although Cornelia's margarita tasted like a little bit of tequila and a whole lot of ice, she found herself laughing at his jokes. They had similar humor. She introduced Liam to Number 17 and found out her name was Naomi. She realized she had seen the name on the mailboxes every time she walked by, but never put the two together.

When she finished her drink, she felt even woozier than she had before, and knew she needed to go home. It felt good to laugh again, but she had already lost enough memory. She wouldn't even consider losing control, too.

"Liam, it was so nice to meet you, but I really need to be getting home," she said. Her first training session with the self-defense instructor was tomorrow. Granted, it wasn't until 4 pm, but work was a universal excuse.

"But it's so early!" he said. He took three big gulps and drained the rest of his beer, waving down the bartender as he did so. Cornelia asked for separate checks, but he insisted on paying for hers too. She glimpsed a few hundreds hiding in his wallet.

She had once been averted to stealing – even the thought of it, as if just thinking about it was a crime.

Naomi was still immersed in conversation, so Cornelia tapped her on the shoulder and said a quick goodbye. The leaner leaned closer, and the other leaned further away, lazily scanning the bar.

Liam caught up to Cornelia at the door. "I have a proposition for you," he started, reaching the door just before she did and holding it open for her.

"What is that?" she asked wearily.

"Take a walk through the park with me before you go?" he said. He seemed unsure of himself, almost needy.

Normally she would never trust a stranger without a background check and three forms of ID, but he was *familiar*. Maybe it was just the sports jacket, the memory of Nate coming back into her head. Maybe the two had been friends at some point. College buddies or something. Maybe they knew each other in some past life.

"Just a quick walk," she agreed.

They crossed the street into the square, meandering amongst the late night dog walkers and runners. Cornelia felt a pang in her heart as they passed the bench on which Cornelia usually waited on Thursdays. A chill ran down her back, Petyr in the brisk December air. It was too cold for a walk.

"Cold?" Liam asked. In one swift movement, he slid his jacket off and around her shoulders. "You know, Rittenhouse Square gets a little creepy at night," he said.

"Homeless people?" she asked, eyeing a man sleeping uncomfortably on a park bench. He was so still Cornelia watched him an extra second to make sure he was breathing.

"That and the emptiness, the quiet. It seems almost hollow at this time of night, especially in winter. The fountains don't run and the homeless pile up. People think it's beautiful during the day, but they never see that gritty underside," he lamented. He grabbed her hand, pulling her alongside him. She sighed.

"Tired?" He thought it was a yawn.

"A little bit, it's getting late. Thank you for the drink by the way."

"You're always so polite – just take it. You deserve it," he said, wrapping an arm around her shoulder and kissing her lightly on the ear. She pulled away, alarmed.

That was... odd. *Always?* Something struck Cornelia when he said that. *Always.*

Neither of them realized Cornelia had stopped walking until they were ten feet apart. He turned and walked back to her.

"I'm sorry, I don't know why I just did... I don't know why I just said that. I just... I got out of a relationship recently and I guess I just miss the closeness. I'm sorry, I got a bit confused. I had too much to drink tonight I think," he sputtered, one hand on his hip and another running through his hair as he stared at the ground. He looked to Cornelia, puppy dog eyes wide, like he was scared she might run away.

"It's alright. It was just a little weird," she said, but she felt like she was missing something. "Just don't uh, say stuff like that."

He nodded and they continued walking in silence. He kept his hands to himself.

"So tell me about the girl," Cornelia said.

Liam looked at her, eyebrows raised.

He was silent for a few seconds. "I say we talk about you."

They did a loop around Rittenhouse Square and then diverted off the given paths, winding through the gridded streets of Philadelphia. His hotel was four blocks from her apartment, and though she was hesitant about being alone with a boy, *especially* one she just met, he seemed relatively innocent.

Could she have been existing in a constant state of paranoia for no reason? She knew it was related to her head injury, but it made her wonder... if she had been forced out of her comfort zone earlier, might she be two steps closer now to normal?

It helped that every once in a while Liam would do something that showed just how nervous *he* was, like tripping and trying to pretend he was just going for a short jog. He turned and grinned at her, and for a moment she wondered if it was all an act.

It was a calm night. Sirens blared in the distance, as was usual in Philadelphia, but the people around them were unexcited, quiet, unassuming.

He led her up a flight of stairs to the second floor of an old converted townhouse, the off-white façade punctuated by the freshly painted bright red door. An old mail slot was glued shut, replaced with a row of mailboxes next to the door. The stairs were carpeted, illuminated only by a dim yellow light from the ceiling upstairs. A small, unmanned reception table was squished right up against the wall and only allowed about a foot of space to pass over the threshold, into the main house.

Liam's room was small but well-decorated. The furniture matched, antique cherry wood from a sturdy old set. Two blankets laid half folded on a small couch. The room itself was homey, yet felt cold and uninhabited.

Cornelia waited in silence as Liam closed and locked the door, struggling with the latch.

He dumped his keys, wallet, a flash drive, a handful of spare change, and those other random things that end up in your pocket, in a tray by the door.

He turned to her, mouth wide like he was about to say something. He nervously rubbed his thighs, and with a confused expression said, "I have to run to the bathroom. I'll be right back."

"Okay," she said, his nervous energy quelling her own. He wound his way around the kitchenette to a bathroom on the other side of the wall. As she waited, Cornelia eyed the wallet in the key tray.

What were the chances he would miss a hundred dollars?

He probably didn't even count how much was in his wallet, and a hundred dollars would be just about enough to make rent.

But could she do it?

As a girl, she had held a glass of water in her hand, knowing that if she dropped it, it would shatter. She dared herself to do it, just to see the way it broke, to feel the intention behind an "accident," but she never could.

She knew how much trouble she would be in, how she might hurt herself.

Was stealing the same way? That split second decision would change her – she would go from civilian to thief, just like that. Would she feel any different?

Cornelia had never stolen anything in her life. Maybe a dollar or two from her mom's purse when she was little, but that's far from stealing a hundred from a guy you met at a bar. How far was she willing to sink? Then again, what other options did she have? There was no guarantee Philly MMA would work out, and even if it did, she'd still be struggling.

She shuffled over to the key tray and picked up Liam's wallet. She opened it, just browsing, just looking. It wasn't a crime to look.

A medical ID card was in the place normal people put their licenses. His picture was on the left, as well as the name of a medical group she hadn't heard of, Fort Howard Neuro, on the right, along with a symbol that looked like a giant squiggly green brainstem. She paused for a moment, looking at it. *Where have I seen that before?*

She opened the wallet from the top and thumbed through the paper money. Upon closer inspection, he had been carrying over a thousand dollars. She didn't think doctors made *that* much money, but it reassured her that he wouldn't miss any of it.

She took out one crisp hundred dollar bill, and slipped it into her shirt and underneath the cup of her bra.

I am a thief.

She placed the wallet carefully on the key tray and backed away slowly, careful not to jostle the keys or coins.

She paused as she came to the conclusion that if she was going to take on the title of thief, she might as well make it worthwhile. She grabbed another slimy $200 and left the wallet in the key tray, defiled.

She heard running water and double-checked the scene, ensuring everything was in place. Her heart pounded.

As she nonchalantly leaned against the kitchenette's counter, her eye caught the flash drive poking out from the short side the wallet. It had that same green brain on it as was on his medical badge had, and her curiosity overwhelmed her. She grabbed that too, and slipped it into the other cup.

Might as well be thorough.

The bathroom door clicked open. She stepped back and leaned on the counter, *nonchalant.* Would he see the guilt in her eyes?

Liam stepped back into the kitchenette, wiping damp hands on his pant legs. He looked at her wide-eyed, like he just realized he should have been using a towel. He smiled and ran a hand through his hair.

Cornelia, looking so hard for signs he would know he stole from her, instead saw deep oblivion, child's eyes on the body of a grown man. She had seen so much of Nate in him that she had started assigning Liam the same personality traits.

The brown belt with the black shoes, worn purposely and repeatedly just to annoy her. Always walking with his left hand pocketed. The two finger interlace that held their hands together. All of it was so... Nate.

From a more objective standpoint, and underneath the glare of the fluorescent lights, she realized he was older, likely in his mid-forties, a trusting doctor well into his career. The money suddenly made much more sense. And she realized she was alone with a stranger.

He stood in front of her, at that distance that's just too close for someone you don't know very well, but not quite close enough for someone you want to know better. Cornelia wasn't sure which way she wanted things to go.

He reached to her face and brushed her hair behind her ear. They locked eyes, and Cornelia got a strange feeling of impatience, weariness, fatigue. Like she had been waiting and waiting for this night to just *end* already. She wasn't sure what it was, but something here felt repetitive and... perverse.

The stubble that ran from his right ear down to his chin made her stomach churn. She felt her mind fogging, her vision going in and out. She blinked, hard, trying to regain control.

He stepped away, looking at her with furrowed eyebrows. "Are you okay?"

She nodded, but the feeling in her stomach was growing.

"I'm... yeah, I'm okay. I just have to go," she said, swallowing down vomit. She pushed past him, beelining for the door.

"Wait Corey, can I get you a glass of water?" he asked, following her closely. She sidestepped him as his fingers brushed her arm.

She shook her head. "I just have to go, I'm sorry," she said, feeling the acid rising. "Thank you," she squeaked, before slipping out.

She took the stairs two at a time, so quickly she nearly missed one and tumbled head over heels down the narrow hallway. She held on tight to the railing as she descended, and threw her entire body weight into the front door.

She stumbled out into the brisk night air, and made it to the flowerpot just outside the hotel's front door before spilling the contents of her stomach. Behind her, the front door slowly clicked shut.

She walked home slowly, winding through familiar back alleys, the fresh air and seclusion freeing and safe.

Cornelia reflected on the new low her morals hit that evening. Would this come back to bite her in the ass? She made plans to do something good to offset her karma.

She turned onto her street, the distance to her front door stretching for an eternity. She yearned for a nice warm bed, a fuzzy blanket, and a cup of tea. She wondered if Number 17 had made it home yet.

Now that home was in sight, she wished she could forget the whole night. However many showers she might take in her lifetime, she will never wash away the label of 'Thief.' Worst of all, even though she had become "normal" for a night, there was nothing she wanted more than to burrow within her apartment and never see the light of day again. How long would it take to lose that feeling?

She threw her shoes into the small sad pile next to the door and stripped down out of her old sweater and jeans, running her fingers down the long scar that ran the length of her right shin, like she did every time she caught an unwitting glance in the mirror.

She sat down at her computer, the $300 and the flash drive on the desk next to her. She booted up in safe mode, just in case, and plugged in the USB. The contents loaded on screen, rows and rows of pictures and videos titled CW, followed by date stamps.

Fearing the worst (some sort of weird porn that Liam felt necessary to carry with him) Cornelia started with a picture.

She clicked CW061515.jpg.

After a few seconds of loading, Cornelia found herself staring at a picture of what looked like a bruised, unshaven woman's leg, taken from about mid-thigh and down to include the foot. The bruise was large and covered the entire left knee, centered at the very top of her tibia. The top of the picture showed a white gown with blue polka dots. A hospital gown.

Creepy.

She hoped this wasn't a cadaver or anything equally gross, if only for the sake of her queasy stomach. She didn't know much about Liam, but she knew medical students did plenty with cadavers in school and continued learning. Maybe he had been presenting at his conference and these were his notes.

… Maybe she should find a way to return this….

She clicked on the file CW081115.mp4.

The video took longer to load. Cornelia steeled herself, unsure if her stomach was ready to handle seeing a real dead person. She turned partially away and squinted her eyes, hoping to create enough of a buffer that she wouldn't have everlasting nightmares if she couldn't exit quickly enough. Her fingers rested on Ctrl + F4.

When the video finally loaded, Cornelia was staring at a frowning, pale version of *herself*.

The camera recorded from the foot of the bed, steadily like it stood upon a tripod. The room was white, fluorescent, quiet. Cornelia clicked her volume up and the sounds of muffled movements off camera bled, grainy, through her speakers.

She watched an interaction between her and Liam. In the video, he was dressed as a typical doctor - lab coat and all - sweeping into the room with a flourish and conviction. He asked her questions about her recovery, how she was feeling, her family. She answered all of them without batting an eye. Toward the end, a kind nurse brought her a change of clothes.

Cornelia watched the video in frozen silence, looking for an indication that the woman being filmed was anyone else. She could see no identifying tattoos or birthmarks. The woman's hair was darker than Cornelia's, but that wasn't surprising if she hadn't been in direct sunlight a lot. It was short, barely covering her ears, and chopped at different lengths on each side, one side thin and prickly. It was the area on her scalp that had been stripped of skin during her car accident.

Cornelia subconsciously brushed her fingers along the smooth part of her scalp that ran in an arc over her right ear. Her hair was considerably longer now, falling down past her shoulders. She hardly ever thought about the scar under there, about as wide as a fingertip and as long as the distance between the tips of her thumb and index fingers. She could line it up with the arch of her hand perfectly.

She let the video play through its entirety, the contents sobering her. The whole video consisted of question after question – about herself, the current state of the world, what she did through the day... to Liam.

Her voice sounded scratchy and surreal – was that really her speaking?

Judging by the time stamps, this was during her time in the hospital after her accident... except she had been in a coma for several months, and if the date in the title of the video was correct, she should have been breathing deeply without a conscious thought in her mind.

For an hour she listened to herself explain the contents of a book she had read a few days before being filmed, and Cornelia recognized the plot line from Her Sister's Keeper, though she must have remembered the ending wrong – Cornelia had seen the movie before her accident, but her filmed account of the book did not match her memory of the movie.

Cornelia reality-checked herself as the video came to an end.

If her eyes were not deceiving her, Liam was one of her doctors, she had no recollection of him, and he was walking around with medical interviews of her on a USB disk.

None of this made sense.

If the numbers in the title of these pictures and videos were indeed dates, as she originally guessed, they all took place within six months – six of the nine months during which she was purportedly unconscious.

She watched the video again, ignoring the audio and paying attention to only the girl on screen. She had Cornelia's ticks. She had the same flat expression when being told to do something she didn't want to do. Growing up, her mom had yelled at her for that face. She said getting that face from Cornelia was worse than any sarcastic or fresh comment she ever made, because she knew the ensuing fight would be bloody.

It was her. The beaten up girl in that video was, without a doubt, Cornelia.

MEMORY II

CHAPTER TWENTY
11 months and fifteen days earlier, Fort Howard Neuro Clinic

Cornelia sat in a white room, a crooked, faded clock positioned right above the foot of her bed like a centerpiece. Scratchy blankets covered her legs, the ends scrunched in a pile at the crease of her hips. The room smelled faintly like a dentist's office, the lights similarly blinding.

The door to her room sat diagonally from her left foot and had a view of the nurse's station outside. She couldn't hear anyone, but she knew there was at least one nurse sitting idly by.

In the distance she heard the determined tap of loafers on the laminate flooring outside her room. The doctor was coming.

She adjusted the blankets over her lap and pulled the medical gown higher up her neck.

"Cornelia," he said, his grin showcasing the small smile lines that framed his mouth.

"Hello," she nodded.

He strolled into her room, flicking on a small camera that was set up underneath the clock.

He recorded everything – their conversations, his thoughts, observations ranging from coincidental to causal. Cornelia thought it was weird, but she wasn't about to take on the Scientific Method.

He walked to the other side of her bed and pulled an armchair toward her.

"How are we doing today?" he asked, flipping through the pages of his little black book. His pen hovered over the lines he had written in the past as he re-familiarized himself.

"I'm still fine. Nothing has really changed since this

morning," she explained.

In reality, she wanted to beg of him to leave her alone. She was exhausted, sore, drained of all motivation and desire to improve her life.

She had completed five hours of physical therapy that morning, as well as an achingly long hour and a half discussing her emotional wellbeing. It was nearing five in the evening, and although she had spent many days of her life working well past that time with the vigor and energy that only a 24-year-old could have, a day of walking, speaking, and thinking now left her exhausted.

"Good, I'm glad to hear that," he said. He nodded, waiting for her to continue.

She smiled, unsure what else he wanted to hear.

"Well if there's been no change, I don't want to keep you," he said, closing his book again. He seemed like he was waiting for an invitation to stay. "I just want to make sure we're checking in with each other. Let me know if you need anything, but otherwise, I guess I'll just see you bright and early tomorrow morning."

Cornelia nodded. "Sounds fine to me," she said.

The doctor moved toward the door, pausing as he passed the camera but neglecting to turn it off. "Wait," Cornelia said, just before he left. "Can I have something else to wear? Some scrubs would be good enough," she asked.

He stopped at the door, one hand on the frame and one foot out the door. "I think I can make that happen," he nodded, smiling like he granted her a huge favor. "See you tomorrow, Miracle Girl," he said, tapping the frame twice, and swept out of her room. She heard low voices outside her door, and the tip-tap of his loafers retreating down the hall and into his office.

Cornelia stretched out her limbs. She had never felt so heavy, so weak. She closed her eyes, sinking further into her bed as she dreamed of landing a roundhouse into the cheekbone of the drunk driver who put her into this position. One act of stupidity had forever changed her life.

She didn't realize she had fallen asleep until a gentle rapping on the door startled her awake. She had dreamt of strength, the ability to move across an empty training room or gym mat like it was nothing, like she was lighter than a feather, faster than a fox. She was disappointed to wake up in the same weak body.

"Hey," the soft voice cooed.

Cornelia opened her eyes but didn't dare move her limbs.

Nurse Renee Cavallero rounded her bed, her white sneakers moving noiselessly across the floor.

She was a small woman, softly spoken and easygoing, with a round face and dark colored hair that fell in waves over her shoulders and down her back. She and Cornelia had made fast friends during her rehab session that day. "Hi," Cornelia choked.

The nurse held up a plastic bag. "I brought you some jammies," she said. She dumped the bag gently onto Cornelia's lap, and held the clothes up for her to see. "Old Navy's kind of the only place to shop around here, but this weekend I'm going to stop by somewhere that sells some really comfy yoga pants," she said, smiling. She held up a t-shirt, fleece pants, a sports bra and several different kinds of underwear for Cornelia to look through.

"Wow, you really didn't have to do that," Cornelia said. "Thank you so much, that's so kind of you."

"Happy to do it. It's not often I have such talkative patients to help," Renee said. She paused, noticing Cornelia staring at the clothes but making no moves to put them on. "Would you like some help getting into these?"

"I most certainly would not, but I think I'm going to need it regardless," Cornelia said, smiling. She hated needing people to do things for her that were so simple as changing her clothes.

"Alright, let's get you up," she said, helping Cornelia

move forward and stacking her pillows so she could sit up-right.

"Uh wait," Cornelia said, the red light on the camera catching her eye. "Can you turn the camera off?"

"Did he leave that on?" she asked. "Wow, he's usually so anal about that sort of thing," she remarked. She whisked around the bed to shut it off. "Much better," she muttered, returning to Cornelia. She had wrangled her way out of her hospital gown, but even that movement triggered a layer of sweat across her forehead.

Together, they swung Cornelia's legs over the side of her bed so she could step into her brand new underwear and comfy pants, and once she sat back down, the nurse helped pull her t-shirt over her head.

Cornelia relaxed back into her bed.

"Does that feel a little better?" the nurse asked.

"Much better," Cornelia said.

"Let me know if you need anything else," she said, squeezing Cornelia's shoulder, and slipped swiftly out of the room and back into the quiet hallway.

CHAPTER TWENTY ONE
Present Day, Philly MMA

Cornelia had not figured out her plan of action by the time she was supposed to leave for instructor training.

She had spent her night watching videos of herself, most relatively innocuous, aside from the fact that she remembered none of them and she had supposedly been in a coma at the time. Many of them involved a simple a recount of her day, which she gave begrudgingly. She couldn't remember the interviews, but she recognized the way her jaw jutted out just a millimeter as she answered questions the way the doctor wanted to hear.

Each interview lasted roughly an hour, aside from a few outliers. There was one for every day, except for a skipped few that looked like weekends or holidays, and the entire collection spanned from July 17th to January 15th, 2016. Assuming they weren't modified in any way, it proved she had been awake and functioning for six months prior to waking from her coma.

Even then, she couldn't really remember waking up – her memory began several hours later, when she began to process what had happened.

A few of the interviews she watched included snippets of books she had apparently read. Many she had only heard of, but some she had read when she was younger. She searched for a reading list somewhere on the flash drive, but found nothing aside from more pictures and videos.

She had come up with a few more theories as to what could have caused her to have no memory of those interviews.

The most plausible explanation was that she had or got amnesia at some point. If her accident caused temporary anterograde amnesia, it's possible she just didn't remember waking up the first time, her memory from the hospital never properly recording.

But in that case, why would the doctors tell her she was in a coma for nine months? She had heard of doctors letting patients recover their own memories but this seemed awfully unprofessional. Why wouldn't they at least tell her she had amnesia?

It was possible she was part of a medical trial. She was sure Tanya would have done anything to wake her up – including experimental therapies.

Only, she had no paperwork from this Fort Howard Neuro – she had discharge papers and some recommended mental and physical exercises from the nearby Johns Hopkins hospital, but nothing related to Fort Howard Neuro.

According to Cornelia's google research, the Fort Howard medical campus itself was closed down several months prior to her accident, due to a mold problem in the main hospital. There was no information on what sort of practices were done before then – not even a body part it was related to. The only information Cornelia could find was that the hospital existed, and according to her flash drive, at some point it was operational. None of that helped her understand why or how she was there in the first place.

The theory Cornelia clung to was based on the elementary knowledge she had regarding the brain damage she sustained in her accident. She knew brains worked in mysterious ways – maybe her memory had decided to delete itself, erasing a difficult time in her life? She hadn't heard of whole months getting erased, as her only experience with lost memory was getting a concussion during field hockey in high school, but there's a first time for everything. Right?

But where was Fort Howard in her records? Shouldn't she have heard of it if she spent time there, at least in passing from one of her doctors when she woke up? She recognized the symbol on the flash drive, for some odd reason that she couldn't pinpoint, but the name of the clinic was foreign to her.

Cornelia dodged phone calls from doctors for months, and Tanya in general when she could. She previously attributed the bad feeling she got to the paranoia from brain damage, but now she wondered if she had been picking up on something else, something invisible in the air that told her she was being watched.

But she couldn't shake the feeling that her brain was making things up where it shouldn't have been. Paranoia was enough to deal with, but what if her *eyes* were deceiving her? What if her own brain was creating the life that she wanted to see, and unbeknownst to her, she was living in an entirely separate reality from herself, bound between two separate halves of her own head?

Is this what it felt like to realize you've gone crazy? For months she had felt... off, in some way. She was starting to think Crazy was the only logical explanation.

Some of the pictures she scrolled through looked like they were taken right after the accident – injuries, bruises and cuts the main subject. There were a few medical diagrams that outlined different areas of the brain, several of them personalized and scribbled over, her initials scrawled in the upper right hand corner.

She found no clues as to what had happened over those six lost months, and no solace in diagrams that could only further prove she was crazy.

Cornelia hadn't slept, afraid of her own unconsciousness. Who's to say she wasn't transporting herself elsewhere in her sleep? What if these videos were the flipside of her consciousness, some sort of fully responsive state of unconsciousness?

Her heart beat faster.

The timer on her phone dinged, and Cornelia jumped.

Time to go.

She changed into gym clothes, grabbed her duffel bag, and ducked out of her apartment building.

She walked down the hallway, making an excruciating effort to clear her mind. She counted prime numbers; that might be enough to keep her mind occupied. Maybe she would even be able to relax for a second without her thoughts sneaking up on her. Maybe she would be able to actually learn something during her session.

It was dusk, the street lights just flickering on. Cars crowded the street, distant honks composing the discordant song of rush hour. People strolled down the sidewalks, their dogs popping squats in the rare patches of Philadelphian grass.

She felt eyes on her from every direction. She studied faces as they walked by, searching for one that held her gaze too long, or eyes she recognized. She wondered what Liam's role was in all of this – did he make it all happen or was he just an unwitting player in some larger scheme?

Cornelia thumbed the phone in her pocket, and against her better judgment, called Aunt Tanya.

"Corey!" Tanya shouted into the phone. She could hear the TV playing the news in the background.

"Corey, I have been trying to get a hold of you! I know you're an adult now and you need your space, but after everything that's happened with our family, it would be so nice to updated on your life!" Tanya toed the border between whiny and playful.

Cornelia heard a squeak in the background, Tanya lifting herself from her recliner. She was an average sized woman who liked working out when it was convenient, but enjoyed lounging around with a beer much more. Walking to the fridge was as good a work out as any.

Despite her general laziness and generous alcohol consumption, Tanya was fit. She drank strange green juices and touted the benefits of homeopathic medicines, yet neglected to admit that her favorite health food usually came with a six pack and bag of chips.

"Tanya, just wanted to confirm, how long was I in a coma?" she asked, jumping right into it.

"226 days, and it was the longest 226 days of my life. You have no idea how scared I was!" She took a breath and continued on. "Corey, you have to come visit me soon. Life is too short to live without family, and I haven't seen you in ages! If I didn't know any better I would say you were in a coma all over again! Knock on wood." Cornelia heard another squeak and a rap of Tanya's knuckles on the coffee table.

"And they didn't like, wake me up, and put me back in a coma because of brain damage or something like that, right?" Cornelia clarified.

"No honey. You were knocked out as soon as they scraped you off the asphalt, right up to January 15th," Tanya explained.

"And did you come to see me while I was in a coma?" Cornelia asked.

"When I could, of course! But after a month or so they transferred you to this high tech place for severe cases and I wasn't allowed in - they said there were a lot of really sensitive cases there and outside germs could interfere with treatment. Sounded like some sort of ICU for coma patients," Tanya said. She paused for a moment, and Cornelia could hear something clatter in the background. "And you know what? It worked! They brought you back to life and now you're healthier than I ever could have hoped for. Terrifying at the time, but worth it in my eyes."

Cornelia nodded, going over the other possibilities again. ICU for coma patients? She had never heard of such a thing. She didn't disregard the possibility that Tanya could be remembering something incorrectly, but she did hold onto one thing: Tanya wasn't allowed to see her while she was... wherever she was. That had to mean something.

"And how long was I there?" Cornelia asked.

"Hmm. Maybe five months? Something like that?" Tanya said.

Five months. Five whole months.

That retroactive fear kicked in, the kind that grabs

ahold of your chest when a car narrowly misses you on the highway, or when someone you love says they almost died doing something silly like climbing a ladder without a spotter or cliff jumping off season. Ultimately, she knew the specifics didn't matter anymore, but the thought still nagged her, especially considering she didn't know how she got there in the first place - how would she ever know what to avoid?

She crossed to the other side of the street when the light turned green. She nearly forgot she was on the phone, the weight of the videos clouding her concentration.

"Your doctor's office has been calling, Corey. You should give them a call back," Tanya said softly. "They said something about a hospital visit and some follow-up tests to make sure everything is still okay."

"I know. I'll make an appointment. I think I might actually be switching doctors," she explained.

Her doctors had been hounding Tanya, and Tanya Cornelia, since she woke up. She was under the impression it was the same doctor she had woken up to, but it dawned on her that any of the incessant calls could have been Liam, or at least motivated by him. How long had he been watching her? A chill ran down her back.

"Is that wise? Shouldn't you stay with a doctor who already knows your medical history?" Tanya asked.

That was exactly why she *should* switch doctors.

"Should or shouldn't, I'm switching. I'll let you know how it turns out. Next time they call you can tell them that and let them know there's no point in calling anymore," Cornelia said. It came out harsher than she intended. Tanya was not the person to bite.

"Alright, I'll let them know. Who are you switching to? I'm assuming you'll still be seeing a neurologist," Tanya said, her voice soft still. Tanya knew something was up.

"I don't know yet," Corey said, turning sideways to walk between another woman on her cell phone and a younger man walking his dog.

"Will you let me know when you do?"

She nodded. "Yeah I will."

Tanya was silent for a moment, and Cornelia again heard the chatter of the news through the phone.

"Isn't it a pity about that girl?" she asked.

"What girl?" Cornelia asked, taken off guard.

"That Jamie girl. Cute little blonde girl who went missing a few weeks ago? Jamie Larson? They were saying on the news that she grew up around here. Did you know her? Didn't you say you were staying with someone named Jamie? Not the same girl, was it?"

Cornelia's mouth felt dry. Someone brushed past her left shoulder and she jumped - she had stopped walking without realizing.

"Looks like she washed up in the Delaware River actually," Tanya said.

Cornelia's mind worked frantically as connections formed. She didn't intend to draw premature conclusions, but this conversation was painfully familiar. She couldn't help but feel like the common link.

"What a pity," Tanya muttered. She made a clicking sound with her tongue. "She seemed like such a nice young woman. Two young kids, *wow!* And what a handsome husband!"

She kept her head down and walked quickly, her mind and body begging for a run, to hit a speed faster than that of thought.

She pushed through the doors of Philly MMA and came face-to-face with Chin Strap. His smile dropped briefly, but he recovered quickly.

"Hey Eric, I'm here to meet with Connor before his class begins," Cornelia said.

He nodded, craning his neck to look into the classrooms

behind her. "I think he's in a lesson right now, but I'll go check for you," he said, and turned on his heel toward the back of the building, weaving fluidly through equipment until he reached the classroom door. He poked his head in, nodded a few times, and then bounced back to Cornelia.

"He's finishing up a private lesson but you're welcome to go back and watch if you want," he said, nodding toward the classroom.

"Thanks."

He smiled that big grin of his as she walked to the classroom. Liam's face popped into her head again and she whacked her hip off a piece of equipment that was sticking out. She cursed under her breath.

The classroom was warmer than the rest of the gym and smelled of old socks. A thin film of sweat developed over her forehead.

There were four men in the room – two wrestled on a mat in the center of the room with one spectator, and Connor, with his back to her, watching from the sidelines but clearly running the show. It was silent aside from the occasional grunt and the dribble of the gym's music leaking in through the closing door. They didn't notice her come in.

Cornelia settled her bag on the bench that lined one side of the room and dropped her sweatshirt on top. She felt a mild breeze over her skin from the rotating fan above the doorway. She tied up her hair and sat, waiting.

The men on the floor wiggled around a bit and eventually Connor bent down, counted to three, and whacked the mat twice with his hand. The wrestlers broke apart and got to their feet, chatting quickly and easily, stretching and wandering toward their stash of bags on the other side of Cornelia's bench. They chatted lazily about a girl named Liz who may or may not become famous.

"Cornelia," he said, smiling. He wore a plain grey t-shirt and red gym shorts that stopped a few inches above his kneecaps.

"How are you?" she asked, standing up to shake his hand.

"Fantastic, you?" he asked, taking a seat on the bench Cornelia had been sitting on.

"Doing alright."

Her words sank into nothingness for a second while he took a sip of his water. "So what did Leanne explain to you?"

"She said I'd be shadowing a couple classes and once you deem me fit to take over, I'll start with the beginner self-defense classes," she said.

Connor shrugged. "That's the basic gist of it. What's your skill level?" he asked.

"I used to teach the beginner classes," she quickly explained. "I briefly considered trying to teach some higher level stuff but the beginners seemed to be my forte."

He wandered back to the mats and stacked them up against the wall. "That's great, I'm glad we were able to pull you in again. Obviously take your time getting back up and running, but I'm sure you'll snap right back into it. The point of self-defense is really so that you'll never forget it, right?"

She smiled, nervous. She had planned to re-familiarize herself with her old notes the night before, but thanks to those videos, she totally forgot. Her mind blanked repeatedly as she struggled to remember the scenarios she used to teach. It was like they had been wiped clean from her memory.

"I can't promise anything, but I sure hope so," she said.

"Take your time, really," he said, smiling. "But if you don't mind, could I use you as my attackee for demonstrations tonight? Usually I pick a lucky member from the audience but it might help you kick into gear a little," he suggested, smiling. He nudged her elbow, a quick gesture that made her stomach flip.

"Of course," she said, nodding and praying to whatever gods might listen that she would remember even half of what she used to teach.

"Hold tight after class, we can meet up and go over some more stuff. This is the last class I teach tonight so we'll have time and space to go over anything we need to afterwards," he said.

"Yeah, of course."

He turned towards the front of the room, where a few girls had walked in. They chatted quietly as their eyes wandered about, scoping for an indication of how class was set up. Cornelia, just as clueless as they were, stayed on her bench until class started, observing. Then she followed Connor to the front of the room by the mirrors, and stood off to the side while he gave his opening speech.

There were twelve people in class, all women of various sizes. Cornelia noted each one as she watched them enter. One was a group of what looked like sorority girls, a couple of roommates who walked from a few blocks away, and a handful of stragglers without conversation for Cornelia to eavesdrop on.

He emphasized the things that Cornelia remembered. The best fight to be in is none at all. Running is the smartest thing you can do. Listen to your gut.

Cornelia knew Connor was speaking specifically about physical fights and stranger danger, but something about his speech felt relevant on a few different levels.

"I'm going to ask my helper Cornelia to join me," he said, beckoning her over.

"So first of all," he said, holding up his hand to stop her. He turned to the rest of the class. "What do you do if a strange man tells you to 'come here'?"

"Do you want me to demonstrate running away?" she asked, laughing, and a few giggles resounded from their students. The room felt lighter.

"No," he said smiling. "No, but if we didn't already know each other and we were out on the street somewhere, and I told you to come here, you would first and foremost go the opposite direction. Never be ashamed of running."

He had a way with the students. As he joked, they loosened up.

"Okay, now come here," he said, beckoning her over again.

He positioned her a few feet to his right.

"Alright, let's start with a wrist grab. Cornelia, I'm going to come up to you and grab your wrist," he said, looking to her for confirmation.

She nodded, standing still and pretending to mind her own business. In the classes she taught, she made it a point to show that these things will never happen when you're ready for it. She smiled, the first nugget of knowledge returning. *Yes.*

He walked briskly up to her, and grabbed her arm firmly but nothing like she would expect from a stranger with mal intent. She twisted her arm in an outward circle around his, breaking his grasp. He nodded and grinned. "Good."

They repositioned. Connor gave another quick monologue and they demonstrated a second way to get out of a wrist grab. Then they had the students line up so they could each try it. Since Cornelia didn't have her certifications renewed yet, she watched and commented, but didn't participate further than in demonstrations. Connor stayed mostly silent, acting as the attacker and letting her do the teaching.

For the next exercise, Connor placed Cornelia so she was facing away from him. She didn't bother listening to his spiel – it was all coming back to her. He was either going to put her into a chokehold or a bear hug. She wanted to test herself, to see if, in the moment, she could still choose the best method of defense.

He went for the chokehold. She felt his body heat before his skin, and automatically ducked her chin into the pouch of his elbow, ensuring she couldn't be put out. She held an arm up over his hand and her ear, stepped and spun out. Granted, he wasn't holding her very hard.

They went through a series of exercises, Cornelia serving as the teacher and Connor as the attacker. She glanced to him a few times, sure that some teaching methods had changed since he took over, but he just smiled and indicated she should keep going. He thought she was on a roll, too.

Cornelia hung back while the rest of the class left. She took a drink of her water and watched the crowd dwindle until there were only two students left in the room. She pulled a pair of sweatpants over her leggings. Connor disconnected his phone from the stereo and joined her on the bench.

"So what did you think?" he asked.

"It was fun. I didn't realize how much I missed teaching," she said. She could barely stop herself from smiling.

"Good. I'm glad you enjoyed it," he said, chuckling. "You seemed a little weary at the beginning there, but you really snapped into it."

"Honestly, I was blanking before class. I couldn't remember a thing I used to teach. Thank god that stuff was ingrained in my brain," she said. "I think I just needed to be thrown into the fire."

He slapped his thighs and stood up, walking over to the wrestling mats. "Well come on then, let's do some more advanced stuff. You're past the beginner classes, I wanna see where you get challenged."

"What, you want me to fight you?" she asked, incredulous.

"Gentle sparring - no fighting," he said.

"I kinda have to be angry," she said.

He caught her eye and smiled. "Well, get angry," he said. He tipped a mat that was leaning against the wall so it landed on the floor with a muffled thump.

"So?" he asked, grinning, daring her.

The last time she sparred with someone was in that very room, many years ago, when she was training for the intermediate classes, which were a little less self-defense and more Intro to Fighting Your Siblings.

As she approached the mat, he ducked into a loose sparring position, his fists just below and in front of his chin.

"No headshots, no crotch shots," he said, as she raised her fists. She waited for him to move toward her, but he never did. She didn't want to punch first.

"Your move," he said. So much for that.

She reached out and hit his right shoulder lightly. She realized as her fist grazed his arm that this was not seventh grade and she was supposed to actually put some force into it.

He stood up straight, letting his fists down for a second. "Come on, you can do better than that," he scoffed. He shook his head and returned to position.

This time Cornelia jabbed with her right hand to his left shoulder, and he deflected seamlessly, moving his left forearm in front of her fist. He smiled.

"We just went over that in class," he said, not breaking his stance. "Again."

Keeping eye contact, she threw a quick jab to his left shoulder, his stomach, and then pulled her leg up to kick him in the gut. He blocked each jab but wasn't expecting the kick until it hit him. He caught her foot and held it. She hopped to keep from falling over.

"Thought you were being clever, huh?" he asked her, two hands with a death grip on her right foot. She could feel each of his fingers individually through her shoe. "If this were a real fight, you just gave me a ton of options.

"Option one: I could dig an elbow into your leg," he explained, holding her foot with one hand and spinning along the length of her leg. He rested his elbow on her thigh where he would have planted it.

"Option two," he said, spinning back out. "I can pretty easily pull you straight into a punch with one hand," he said. He pulled her leg to his side and propelled her forward, her face grazing his fist before she could steady herself.

"And option three," he said, lifting her leg higher. She hopped around a few times before she could steady herself. She expected a punch or a kick, but all he did was swiftly push her foot back toward her. It was enough force that she fell to the ground.

"I would suggest you work on your balance a bit. If your kick gets caught, keep your knee bent, so much that feels like you're squatting. You could have controlled your fall, landed on your butt, and rolled away, so even if your attacker is in a power position, he wouldn't have you pinned," he said.

He reached down, extending a hand to her. For a moment, she was reminded of when Heather and her would play fight, and a hand of armistice only resulted in both kids back on the ground. She had a feeling martial arts instructors had much better ways of laying you out on your ass than a prank.

He lifted her up easily, even though every second she expected him to drop her like Heather would have. She stumbled over her two left feet as she stood, Connor immediately stepping to steady her.

"Again, work on the balance thing," he said, the skin at the corners of his eyes just barely crinkling as he smiled.

His hands were warm, one on her hip, the other still holding her hand. She felt a shiver run down her spine.

"I will work on that," she said.

They hovered for a moment, stuck in a mutual state of caution. She noticed he had bright blue eyes and a hooked nose, and when he smiled one corner of his mouth lifted up ever so slightly more than the other. He smelled of something crisp yet musky, like fresh linens and summertime grilling.

He cleared his throat. "So what kind of supplemental training did you do last time you taught here?" he asked. He started cleaning up the mats, balancing them up against the wall.

She struggled to find her words. "Uh, not much. I was going to start teaching kickboxing, so one of the old instructors was giving me some lessons on the side. I think she quit a while back though," Cornelia said.

He nodded. "Yeah there was a hefty amount of turnover before I bought the place," he said, grabbing a crate of bands and walking them into the corner closet. "Hopefully that will change."

"I bet it will," she said, getting the hint that it was time to go home.

She gathered her stuff and slung her bag over her shoulder, Connor meeting her at the classroom door.

"That was a fun session," she said, unsure if that was the right thing to say. Her mind raced. Was this something she should repeat? Not repeat? Find a job elsewhere?

"It was," he said. "Now you can go home and show your brother what he's worth," Connor joked.

"What?" She was sure she misheard.

"Sister?" he countered.

"What do you mean?" she asked, feeling her heart sinking.

"You fight defensively. You can tell when someone got picked on by an older sibling," he said, smiling.

"Oh," she said. While she was so focused on remembering everything she had forgotten about self-defense, Connor came up and attacked her from behind with the memory of her sister. Her head moved in two different directions, and she deflated. "Uh, younger, actually."

"Either way. You're stronger than you think," he said, leading the way out to the front desk.

"Thanks," she mumbled.

"Probably couldn't take down a team, but I think you hold your own very well," he said. He was smiling, trying to build her up.

"I guess that's all I can hope for," she said. They reached the front doors. "I'll see you next time."

She was halfway down the block when Connor popped out the door behind her.

"I usually get a cup of coffee at the shop over there-" he said, motioning to a cafe across the street. "-before coming in to train in the mornings. You're welcome to join me next time."

She nodded, but didn't stop walking. "Sure, that sounds nice," she called over her shoulder.

CHAPTER TWENTY TWO
Present Day, Philly MMA

Connor sat at the front desk, conflicted. That was definitely entirely inappropriate. He would apologize next time she came in, *if* she came back.

The gym was quiet, the lull between classes filled with only the occasional drop and grunt. He was waiting on Leanne to come in and relieve him, but due to her increasingly swollen pregnant belly, the woman was constantly late. It was his own fault for keeping her on schedule during her eighth month, but he was not about to tell Leanne what she was or was not allowed to do - she insisted she was fine to work, and he knew when to pick his battles.

"Shit," he muttered, throwing his pen down on the desk. Cornelia was the only person with previous experience who agreed to come in, and he had to go and ruin it by asking her on a date. That's what he was trying to do right? It had been so long since he had been a proper date - he didn't even know how to anymore. It certainly felt like he asked her on a date.

But he just didn't have the time or resources to train someone brand new - he needed her for her knowledge, not her... anything else.

His phone rang. He glanced at the caller ID. Kate. He ignored it.

He grabbed the old personnel files from the shelf underneath the desk. They were scattered and random at best.

Connor overestimated the competence of the previous owners, but he blamed himself for trusting distant relatives with complicated business transactions. They were his cousins married-into cousins on the other side, who inherited a great amount of wealth from a grand-whoever that Connor never had the pleasure of knowing, and when they got bored with their gym, let it rot until they got bored paying taxes on it. They listed it for sale just as Connor's divorce was complete, and he couldn't think of a better celebration than buying some very expensive metal and making something beautiful out of it.

He thumbed through old job applications, performance reviews (some without names), schedules. He had trouble deciphering between teachers. Before Connor owned it, they had much higher turnover, and if he was reading correctly, seven Becca's on staff.

His phone rang again. Kate. He ignored it.

He shut the personnel files with an angry flourish and leaned back in his chair, surveying his gym.

He wanted nothing more to do with Kate. What he wanted was a new teacher, and naturally, he had shot himself in the foot on that one. Cornelia wouldn't come back after that. She probably felt creeped out, and if she heeded his own advice when the strange man said 'come here,' she'd never show her face in Philly MMA again.

His phone buzzed again. Against his better judgment, he answered. Out of concern or masochism, he didn't know.

"What's up, Kate?"

"Connor!" She didn't continue.

"What's up, Kate?" he repeated, slower.

"How are you?" she asked.

"Fine. What's up Kate?"

Leanne powered through the door, wrapped in extra layers, her belly bulging out like an extra layer itself. She waved to him as she waddled by, rounding the desk and dropping her bag by the other chair.

"Not much..."

"Oookay," he said. "Guess I'll talk to you later then."

"Oh wait!" she shouted.

"Kate. What do you want?" He had spent ten years pulling teeth getting her to talk to him.

He glanced at Leanne, who had stopped bustling when

he said Kate's name. Her eyes were wide, and she mouthed, "hang up."

"Well I was hoping you could do me a super tiny little favor?" she asked, her voice lilting up.

"What is it?" he asked. He wouldn't do it. He would say no.

"My headlight went out and normally I would take it to a garage but last time you did that thing that fixed it really quick, so I was hoping you could just do that again," she said.

"You want me to change the light bulb in your headlight?" he clarified.

"Yeah. I mean, normally I wouldn't ask but I have to go somewhere tonight," she explained.

"Take it to the shop, they're probably still open if you go now," he told her.

"But I don't have time!" she said. "I got a job interview, isn't that great? But I have to go like, now."

Connor glanced at the clock, confirming the time he thought it was. Job interview at 6pm? He had a feeling this was a play – she had gotten him before with the "job interview" excuse. Despite the hundreds of job interviews she had gone on while they were married, she never seemed to land that dream job of hers she kept applying to.

"When's the last time you drove your car?" he asked.

"A couple nights ago I think," she said.

"Was the light out then?"

She paused. "Well it was, but I didn't know I would have to go somewhere tonight so I was just going to do it later," she said. "Look, please can you help me just this once? I swear I'll never ask for anything again."

He hated himself for it. He had heard it all before, like a script he was forced to listen to on repeat, every few months. Leanne begged him not to go, but he insisted. This would be the last time.

He wasn't sure what it was that made him feel obligated to Kate. Maybe it was the fact that there was a time when he did truly love her, or maybe it was just that he always kept his promises. Either way, he felt compelled to help, if only to say he was one lightbulb change better than her.

He almost turned back twice on his walk over. It's not about Kate, he told himself, but following through on promises made.

And this would be the last time. That, he promised himself.

The car was ten blocks away, in a parking lot he had begrudgingly paid for before they split up. Kate met him by the entrance, wearing a tight black dress with a slit that reached mid-thigh.

"You're wearing that to a job interview?" he asked. He already knew she wasn't, but the masochistic side of him wanted to see what story she might spin.

Her eyes shifted back and forth. "Well, yes," she said.

He didn't bother.

"Where's the car?" he asked.

"It's kinda toward the back," she said, motioning vaguely toward the entire parking lot. He didn't wait for her to finish before he started walking – he'd be able to pick out the behemoth assuming there was a smudge of light in the sky. It was usually freshly washed, white paint clear as a mirror. He heard her heels clicking behind him as she struggled to catch up.

"Oh but Connor, I actually got a ride!"

He turned. "You couldn't have called to tell me that?"

"Well I just got a ride, like right now. But I was hoping that since you're already here, you wouldn't mind changing the bulb for me? It's the right one that's out."

He hated himself. She unlocked the car and Connor rifled through the glove compartment while she clicked off to catch her ride. Connor watched her go, her tiny purse bouncing off her hip as she went. It occurred to him that she probably didn't want to burden her date with her car problems. He felt sick.

He grabbed the spare light bulb he had previously stashed in the glove compartment and left the trash on her front seat. Ha. Take that, Kate.

He went around back and pulled a pair of gloves from the emergency car box he put together for her (which was untouched), and went about replacing the bulb. Yet another five minutes of his life controlled by Kate.

He left the burnt out bulb on the seat, and sat for a moment in the monstrosity that had cost him a year of his pay. He told her repeatedly how unnecessary that car was, how it would be more of a pain than an asset.

But again and again, he caved.

As he closed the glove compartment up, he glanced at the registration: Connor McPherson.

Transfer papers for the car has been included in their divorce settlement. All she had had to do was show up at the DMV and pay the fee. Yet again, if Kate screwed up and got in an accident or did something stupid, it would get blamed on Connor. It was his car, after all.

He crumpled up the registration and slammed the glove box shut.

He got out of the car, slammed the door, and took off back to the gym.

He noticed a luxury car idling just up the alleyway between the parking lot and Kate's apartment. Curiosity propelled him forward, thinking he saw a glint of blonde through the window, and... was that the sparkle of the engagement ring he gave her?

He glanced inside as he passed, and saw his ex-wife liplocked with some corporate guy in a suit with slicked back hair and a fancy wristwatch - no engagement ring there. Classy. He rolled his eyes and continued down the alley, popping out onto 20th street at the far side and redirecting home.

He took off his jacket, heat rising up his neck. *This is the last damn time.*

He was nearly back to the gym when his anger took over

for a split second. He rang up Kate, who of course, didn't answer. He left a succinct voicemail for her. "Change your fucking registration."

He blasted into the gym and Leanne glanced up at him, wide-eyed.

"Are you okay?" she asked, her eyebrows crinkled together.

"I need a board," he said.

She scrambled over to one of the supply closets, moving with all the speed and agility of a non-pregnant martial arts instructor. She was back within a few seconds, poised with a board ready for breaking.

He waited by the door, unwilling to go behind the desk until he was in a better mindset.

This is it. If this is what she does to me, I have to be done.

He broke the board, and with it, any remaining thoughts of Kate.

CHAPTER TWENTY THREE
11 months and seven days earlier, Fort Howard Neuro Clinic

Cornelia's life pre-accident was a series of adventures. She taught self-defense, went on citywide scavenger hunts for the best spicy Thai this side of the Schyukhill River, hiked sporadically and never with the right equipment....

And Nate was a big kid, always on the lookout for the next fun thing to do, and it lit a small fire within Cornelia that made her search, too. She was never sure what for, but she knew there was always something worth seeing right around the corner.

Despite all of the adventures she had, and the seemingly boundless energy she used to carry with her, Cornelia was stoked just to *walk*. She walked without assistance, without a walker, a cane, or someone right next to her waiting to catch her. She was fully mobile, and finally able to get into the trouble she had been missing.

She was used to pushing herself. Once she started teaching self-defense, she became invested in being as strong and knowledgeable as possible. She spent at least ten hours in the gym each week, taking classes, lifting weights, pushing herself until she felt weak and slept like a baby. That was the best sleep after all – the kind that came on strong and unencumbered.

She gathered every ounce of strength she had and put it into physical therapy. She noticeably outpaced the expected progression of exercises, to the surprise and delight of her nurses and the doctor alike. That was *exactly* what she was aiming for.

Everyday, she felt a little stronger, a little closer to where she had been Before.

So the day when, after all of her therapy, she still had some energy to take a walk by *herself*, she recorded her biggest milestone yet. After the doctor had gone home for the day, she slipped out of bed and laced up her little white sneakers. She pulled her sweatshirt over her head, the movement still a little awkward, and trekked out of her little room, into the quiet hallway outside.

Renee stood behind her computer. Her eyes darted up to match Cornelia's as her sneakers scuffed across the floor. Cornelia couldn't help but smile mischievously, her expression mirrored on the nurse's face. "Miss Cornelia," she scolded. "What do you think you're up to?"

"Catch me if you can!" she shouted, and scuffed down the hallway toward the rec room. She didn't know where she was going – she just wanted to move.

Renee's footsteps accelerated and easily matched hers. Normally during therapy, Cornelia leaned on something, be it a walker or a person, but Renee made no move to support her. Instead, she walked leisurely beside Cornelia as she made her way down the hall.

"You're making some fast progress," she commented.

"Thanks," Cornelia said. "I'd kind of like to get out of here soon."

"What do you plan on doing once you're out?"

Cornelia had thought about it often. She considered traveling for a while until she figured out what she actually wanted to do. She couldn't imagine going back to her old job, if they were even willing to have her. But what else would she *do*?

Assuming her medical bills hadn't wiped out her savings accounts, she had enough to spend some time soul searching. Without anyone left to worry about, that seemed like her only worthwhile option.

She wouldn't be hurting if she took a year off, but would she know any better what she wanted to do with her life at the end of it? All of the things she loved were gone – what was the point of working for a house, a family, the future, if she had none?

"I'm not sure yet," Cornelia answered. "I'm just feeling cooped up. I'm ready to get out of here."

Renee nodded. "I understand."

"Do you know when I'll be able to leave?"

She shook her head. "You've made significant progress. I can't imagine it will be much longer," she said. "I'm sure you'll leave any day now."

Cornelia sighed. "I know, I'm just a little impatient."

They walked in silence for a few moments. "You know what? In my opinion, I think you're more than ready to go home with some exercises to perform on your own time. I'll draw up your discharge papers tomorrow and start hounding the doctor. I'm sure he'll take some convincing, but we'll put the idea in his head. How does that sound?" she asked.

Cornelia smiled. "That sounds great," she said. "The sooner, the better."

They walked around a corner, down a hallway nearly identical to the one they just left.

"You're doing so well," Renee said. "The progress you've made really *is* incredible."

"Thank you."

Cornelia glanced into patients' rooms as they passed. A few beds were empty, a square of folded linens collecting dust at the foot of the beds, but some were occupied by still, silent patients who not only slept through the night, but the day too. Not too long ago, Cornelia had been one of them.

"Will they ever wake up?" she wondered aloud.

"No one knows."

Cornelia nodded. She had a feeling that would be her answer.

The nurse glanced at her watch. "I have to clock out before I go too far past my shift," she said. "Will you be okay for five minutes? I'll hear if you shout."

Cornelia nodded enthusiastically. She had been hoping

for a few minutes of peace anyways. She hadn't been to this side of the hospital yet, and it was exciting to be able to explore on her own.

Renee darted back the same way they had come, and Cornelia continued walking. She glanced into another patient room, one of a man with short, dark hair. The room was dark, but a thin stream of light from the hallway fell across his face.

And Cornelia would recognize that face anywhere.

Her heart beat fast in her chest. She had been thrilled just to walk only seconds before, but now she felt frozen to the spot, unable to take a step forward or back.

She stared into the room. He was so thin, gaunt, a ghost of who he had once been.

She moved toward the room and pushed the door open, slowly and quietly as was her custom when he used to fall asleep early on the couch. She stood by his side, looking down at him as he slept.

She rested her hand on his shoulder, a shoulder that had once been strong, rounded, her perfect pillow. He was warm, so familiar.

She leaned against the bed, the weight of her body and the discovery zapping the energy right out of her. She squeezed his hand, hoping he might wake up and say her name, the way he used to on Saturday mornings when she wanted to get up early for the gym and he wanted *just ten more minutes.*

"Cornelia?" Renee called. She was on her way back.

She squeezed Nate's hand again, and this time, his eyes opened. Her heart stopped and her breath caught in her throat. He was looking right at her.

"Cornelia, where are you?" Renee called.

"He's-" she stammered. He stared right into her eyes. "He's awake!" she shouted, as Renee rounded the corner into his room.

She jogged in, coming up behind Cornelia and resting a hand on her arm. She shook her head. "He's not awake, honey. Coma patients do that sometimes," she explained.

Cornelia turned back to Nate. His eyes were closed, and he slept peacefully on. "Nate," she urged, squeezing his hand again. She knew she could make his eyes open again, and if she could do *that*, there was no doubt in her mind she could wake him up for good.

"Wait," the nurse said. "Is this Nate, as in your Nate?" she asked.

"Yes," Cornelia said. "Yes, this is Nate. Why the *hell* did you tell me he was dead?" she spun around, eyes shooting daggers.

The nurse held up her hands. "I-I had no idea, the doctor told me he was dead and he came in a while after you did, by several weeks," she explained. "I really didn't know this was *your* Nate, I wouldn't have kept this from you if I did."

Cornelia bit her lip. "Why should I believe you?"

"Why would I let you wander around the hospital if there was any chance you might wander right into your dead fiancé's room?" she countered.

Cornelia blinked. She had a point.

"Look, Corey. I don't know what happened here, but Nate isn't going anywhere," she said. "Why don't we get you in bed so you can get some sleep, and tomorrow we'll confront the doctor? And maybe you can come talk to Nate some tomorrow."

Cornelia nodded. Renee wasn't her enemy here.

CHAPTER TWENTY FOUR
Present Day, Renee's apartment

A long time had passed without any sign of Liam. Renee was surprised he hadn't been walking up and down the streets of Rittenhouse in an attempt to flesh out Cornelia's exact location, considering how close he had been. Once he knew where she was, Renee doubted she could do anything else to stop him.

Her nose wrinkled at the thought. She made herself a Cup o' Ramen and sat down in front of the TV. She had prepared an insulin shot with her dinner, a complimentary side dish she had been taking since she was a little girl.

She stuck herself in the hip while she waited for her ramen to moisten.

She paused. "Goddamnit," she cursed, remembering she was supposed to change her injection site. She would have to wait another thirty minutes to eat her Ramen – her hip was all scar tissue at that point.

You can't teach an old dog new tricks, especially if that old dog was a nurse for nine years and a Type 1 for 30.

She begrudgingly set aside her Ramen and thumbed through the entry screen of her security system. She selected four security tapes from the past few days and hit fast forward. She didn't need details, just reassurance.

Renee sat down on her ratty brown couch and absent-mindedly stirred her Ramen, half watching the tapes as they played through. The only motion they saw was the swaying of the pine tree next to the door, until Cornelia came barreling through with a duffel bag slung over her shoulder.

She looked flustered, like usual, and sped off down the street. Renee sniffed her Ramen, her stomach groaning in anticipation.

About a minute after her tapes started, a pair of men's dress shoes stopped in front of the door. He was about a foot away and more toward the street, like he was waiting or looking for someone. Renee slowed the tapes to 1x replay.

He took a step closer, craning his neck to see between the bars of the metal gate. Renee recognized Dr. Ingels immediately.

He was just as she remembered, aside from the scruffy beard, which was unusual for him, considering the anal-retentive freak he was. The first time she met Dr. Ingels, he was scolding another doctor on staff for having a beard, apparently because they carry a lot of germs, and a type of insect whose name Renee couldn't remember, but she lovingly referred to as Beard Mites.

He stepped closer to the gate, and put his hands around two of the iron bars. He shook the gate hard, as if just shaking it would allow him entry, and if Renee had been home at the time she was sure she would have heard the sound.

He glanced around, squinting in the darkening dusk light. His eyes darted back and forth, taking stock of the small area between the gate and the front door of the building. He paused to look down the street, and a second or so later, ducked back into the entryway and pulled a piece of paper and pen from his pocket. He scribbled something quickly, and tucked it into an area of the door that couldn't be seen from the camera.

Renee stood so fast she spilled hot noodles all over her lap. She slammed the styrofoam cup onto her coffee table, ignoring the splatters, and moved closer to her TV. She was hyper alert, the running toilet the next floor up suddenly a *nuisance*. Dr. Ingels looked right into her eyes.

Just as Renee started to wonder if he actually *could* see her, he swept out of the frame and disappeared.

She waited to see if he would come back, but instead, she saw *herself* approach the door, unlock it and bust in. She was reading something on her cell phone, totally oblivious.

Her heart sank.

He was right there in front of her. She had probably given them away, just because she *needed* to check something on her phone before coming inside. She couldn't even remember what it was, it was so unimportant.

She shut the TV off and abandoned her measly dinner, no longer hungry. She paused the feeds and slunk out of her apartment door, feeling weary. She didn't have a backup plan if this one didn't work out, and if Cornelia had devised another plan since most recently regaining consciousness, Renee had no idea what it was.

At least Cornelia had her settlement money – Renee didn't even get severance. Working as a building manager for her uncle was the best outcome she could have hoped for. Free housing and a small monthly allowance was enough that she could get by, however modestly that might be.

She left her door open as she went outside to inspect the gate. She used the flashlight on her phone to illuminate the area, and found the note pretty fast, the bright white paper reflective in the yellow glow of the street lights.

Renee - I didn't think you were capable.

She could hear it in her own mother's voice. The surprise that suggested, 'wow, you exceeded expectations!' which is great, until you realize how low the expectations were to begin with. She shouldn't have expected anything else.

Renee read through the note several times and then crumpled it in her fist.

She slunk back into her apartment and sat down at her desk, pulling a notebook from the drawer and ripping a page out.

She scribbled a note she hoped would get through to Cornelia. She wouldn't risk talking to her in person, for fear of triggering any random memories. Not to mention, ominous warnings from strangers never turned out well in the movies.

Renee slipped the note into a pre-stamped envelope,

the only kind she had, and wrote out Cornelia's address. She tiptoed into the hall and dropped the envelope into the pile of mail waiting to be sorted. For a moment, she was concerned that Cornelia might not see the note in time to take appropriate action. But then she remembered Cornelia *always* picked up her mail once a day, usually a within a few hours of delivery, though Renee noticed she used several different, ethnically diverse names.

She spent a few minutes sorting, stacking each resident's pile neatly on the hall table. The far left pile was for Cornelia, and on top was the letter Renee had written, a note from not-a-stranger, a note for the girl in apartment 19.

CHAPTER TWENTY FIVE
Present Day, Cornelia's apartment

Cornelia bundled up in bed, her laptop open in front of her. It was unusually cold that week, temperatures dipping to lows normally seen only in February. She hadn't turned the heat on in an effort to save money, so instead she wore layers upon layers of pants and shirts, sweats and blankets, hoping to retain as much heat as she could. Using the bathroom felt like sticking her ass in an ice bucket.

She crawled under the covers and made a little cocoon in which she could share the heat from her laptop.

CW091017.mp4

Cornelia and Liam exchanged their pleasantries, a series of hums and haws that ultimately led to no one getting the information they wanted. They were both trying to play each other, questioning and pushing and dancing around what they really wanted.

Cornelia smoothed down the crossword she had been working on. She had fully turned her attention away from the doctor, leading to an array of increasingly incendiary remarks from him. Cornelia's nostrils flared, but she never lost her temper.

She bit her lip, staring at the half-solved puzzle, and then looked up at Liam. "With all due respect, *doctor*, I would like to go home, and I will, whether you like it or not. My asking is merely a courtesy," she warned, her voice low, velvety soft.

The doctor's nostrils flared ever so slightly in response.

"Cornelia, it is ill-advised that you take treatment into

your own hands. I will let you know when you are viable for release. Until then, your patience and cooperation is most appreciated," he explained, his script. As he talked, the pen came to rest on the page. Cornelia followed it with her eyes as he began gently tapping pen on paper, repetitively, the theme song to her captivity.

"Again, I wasn't asking," she said, pursing her lips as she picked up the crossword. She ignored the doctor as he stared at her, his pen tapping in rhythm like the even cut heartbeat of a metronome.

He stood and whisked by the camera. For a count of two seconds, his lab coat filled a third of the screen. He had stopped, presumably watching Cornelia, and then continued out of the room.

When he was gone, Cornelia locked eyes with herself.

CHAPTER TWENTY SIX
Present Day, a no-name coffee shop somewhere near
Philly MMA

Cornelia's alarm clock blared at 5:45 and she bounded out of bed.

She pulled on her gym clothes, brushed her teeth, and checked the time on her phone. 5:49. Gotta go.

She slipped a cold water bottle into her gym bag and ran. She swung one door shut, then another, and finally her clangy gate. As she turned to run toward the gym, she ran face first into Liam.

She felt the panic rising, the fear that he knew where she lived coming to a crescendo. They were in the middle of the street, sunlight streaming over red brick houses as early morning joggers swept by, commuters on cell phones marched, and tiny loved dogs relieved themselves.

And there, Cornelia sank into herself, her heartbeat tangible, her eyes scanning her surroundings for every possible scenario. How could she get away, how did he find her, how could she explain this away, make him think this wasn't her apartment after all?

He stood tall in front of her, with red eyes and ragged facial hair. She pushed past him, mustering up the speed with which she had completed her morning routine.

"I'm not here to hurt you. Please, let me explain," he said.

"I'll believe you're not here to hurt me when you leave me alone. Otherwise, get out of my way," she said. She power walked away from him.

Before she got more than a few feet, Liam grabbed her elbow. She twisted quickly, pulling away from him. "And let me be clear: don't ever fucking touch me again. I don't know what kind of weird, twisted, fucked up world you come from, but I don't want anything to do with *you* or *it*. Leave me alone."

She turned away again. He grabbed her hand forcefully this time and she stumbled back toward him. She used the momentum to land a fist in his nose.

"What about leaving me alone don't you understand?" A thin stream of blood trickled from his nose.

She refused to be afraid of him, but she wouldn't hesitate to knock him out if necessary.

She looked him in the eye, and then began her walk to the gym again, this time slowly, daring him to grab her again. She was determined to show no fear. If he came up behind her, she would know, and she would be ready.

"Don't you want your memory back?" he shouted.

Against her better judgment, Cornelia paused and turned to Liam. He held his nose closed with two fingers, tipping his head back.

"What do you mean?" she asked him. It hadn't occurred to her that there might be one big easy fix to her dilemma. Was her memory stored in a jar somewhere? Backed up in the cloud?

"There's a drug. It's the third drug in the series of treatments you were a part of. If it works, you'll have back all of your memories like you never lost them in the first place," he explained.

Cornelia studied his face. Was this someone she could trust?

"And what if it doesn't?"

His eyes darted side to side. "It *will*," he assured her.

She deemed him untrustworthy. She shook her head and continued walking toward the gym.

"Your memories are all in your head," he shouted after her. "They just need to be activated. I can do that for you!"

She wanted her memory back, sure, but for what price? Was Liam the only way? If there was only a way to retrieve her memory without entrusting her safety to him, she might finally understand what actually happened to her, and *why*.

Cornelia pulled her phone out of the side pocket of her duffel bag and checked the time. 5:52. Eight minutes to go six blocks. She could make it.

She slung her duffel bag over her shoulder, tightened the strap so it clung to her body, and ran those six blocks faster than she ever had before, the steps falling easily. She slowed her pace fifty feet from the coffee shop and fell into step with Connor. With a smile, he opened the door for her, and they continued to the counter.

Connor ordered something that sounded like a Christmas dessert, Cornelia a latte. She followed him to a table against the window.

He studied her face as they sat, his eyebrows furrowed. "Are you alright?"

She nodded. "Yeah, I'm fine, just a little tired," she said, the high note in her voice at a stark contrast to her demeanor.

She smiled, and absently glanced out the window. In the dim morning light, the street outside was barely visible, a glare commandeering most of her view. With the little visibility she had, she saw someone lurking across the street, a dark shadow against the opposite building, staring, unmoving. After a few seconds, the person turned and walked away, disappearing into the morning dew.

"Cornelia?"

She whipped her head back to Connor, whose eyebrows were still scrunched. She realized she had forgotten to breathe.

"I'm sorry?" she said. He looked like he was expecting an answer to something.

"Did you hear me?"

"Um, no, I'm sorry. Could you repeat that?" she asked. She felt like a dick.

"I just asked what you wanted to learn and hopefully, eventually teach. Self-defense or otherwise, so I can try to tailor our lessons to what you'd eventually like to do," he said. He glanced out the window to where Cornelia's eyes gravitated.

She struggled to regain control of her thoughts. *Get your shit together, Cornelia*, she told herself.

"I guess my first goal is to learn intermediate self-defense. Beyond that, I would want to learn whatever you think would be useful," she said. The truth was, she hadn't thought about what she wanted to learn – she just needed a job. She never thought about the other benefits she might see.

Connor nodded, again following her eyes. It took all of Cornelia's self-control to keep them focused in front of her.

CHAPTER TWENTY SEVEN
10 months and seventeen days earlier, Fort Howard Neuro Clinic

Cornelia had taken her recovery into her own hands. She still went through the recommended exercises with her nurses, but she also supplemented with her own before they even entered the building. The only person privy to her routine was Renee.

Cornelia had decided to keep her knowledge of Nate a secret, testing the doctor for some time to see if he might come clean. Meanwhile, she snuck into Nate's room nightly and sat with him.

The first four nights she did so, Nate's eyes opened, and he stared into her own like he was searching for something deep down inside of her. On the fifth night, he said her name. It was a little mangled, but it was her name – she was sure of it.

When he finally woke for good, Nate had a much more difficult recovery than Cornelia did. While she regained her strength and improved her mental faculties, he was still bedridden, performing exercises as simple as raising his arms slightly further off the bed than the day before.

He was as exhausted as she had been during her first few weeks of recovery, but regardless, she snuck into his room every night to spend what little time she could with him. Some nights she read to him, or told him about her own progress. She told him excitedly that soon they'd be doing physical therapy together, once he caught up. Little did she know, their separation had been intentional.

As Cornelia progressed, she gained more energy – something the doctor had been excitedly expecting. He stayed progressively later, asking her questions and theorizing about her recovery.

She arrived in Nate's room later and later, and although he tried to wait for her, many nights she found him already sleeping peacefully. Rather than wake him, she would sit in the armchair by his bed and read silently to herself, or work on one of the crosswords Renee had brought her. It was good enough just to hold his hand.

Over time, the color returned to his face and the muscles to his shoulders. She no longer felt so scared, as she knew they'd both be going home soon.

Cornelia sat in bed, wearing an old Warped Tour t-shirt Renee had brought her. She had been awake for quite some time, having already gone through her morning exercises and showered for the day.

The doctor whisked into her room. "Good morning," he said. He no longer knocked before coming in, opting instead to bluster through like he had an open invitation. Cornelia learned to listen for the tapping of his loafers on the floor.

"Morning," she said.

"How are we today?" he asked.

"Doing fine."

"Good, good," he said, turning on the camera and sitting in the armchair next to her bed. He flipped through his little black book, skimming his notes. He settled on a blank page and scribbled something, presumably the date.

"When do I get to go home?" she asked.

"When we're sure you've recovered." He smiled.

"I think I'm sure I'm recovered. I think it's time for me to go home," she said. She took a deep breath, and eyed the doctor as she continued. "Nate too."

The doctor glanced up from his book.

"Nate?" he asked her.

"Nate, my fiancé?" she clarified. "The one you told me was dead."

The doctor sighed, closing the book. He pressed his fingers to his temples. "Look, we only told you that because we didn't want to further upset you coming out of such a traumatic experience. How do you know Nate is here anyways?"

"Does it matter how I know?" she asked. She pulled a clipboard from underneath her blankets. "I'd like you to sign these discharge papers please."

The doctor bit his lip, looking from her to the papers and back. "Look Cornelia, I understand that you'd like to leave. But we need to be sure you'll be healthy and safe before you do, and we're just not there yet."

"Then I will check myself out against medical advice. That's what it's called right? This is me trying to work with you. If *you* don't want to work with *me*, then I will do it myself," she said.

"Cornelia, this isn't a regular hospital," he said.

He stood, pushing the armchair back to its place on the wall. He took the clipboard from her and separated the pages. He handed the clipboard back, and ripped the discharge papers vertically, horizontally, diagonally, and then let the scraps fall pitifully to her lap. "You will be here as long as I say, as will Nate."

The doctor walked out, leaving Cornelia open-mouthed, staring at the battlezone of pink and yellow limbs strewn across her bedsheets. The doctor didn't come back for two days.

CHAPTER TWENTY EIGHT
Present Day, Philly MMA

It was a familiar feeling, the way her body arced. She fielded the familiar questions, how do I do this, and what if that. She had been gone for so long, and she was so concerned she had forgotten it all, but all she really needed was to be thrown into the fire.

Connor attacked, she defended. He let her lead the class as if she had never taken a break at all, and that, she was thankful for, because for the first time in months, she felt competent.

The students filed out after class, smiling and laughing and Cornelia couldn't help but smile and laugh too. She felt strong, in control, ready to take on the world.

She stood next to Connor and said goodbye as everyone wandered out.

"You did great today," he said, as the last couple of students filtered out.

"I did, didn't I?" She couldn't help the grin.

"And I barely had to teach you anything," he said. He nudged her elbow. "I'm proud of you."

She felt her face reddening.

"Are we training tonight?" she asked.

They had gotten into a nice rhythm of teaching a class followed by a quick workout, sometimes together and sometimes apart, but always checking in either each other for that extra push. Sometimes they would spar, Connor teaching Cornelia how to best take out a man who was twice her size.

With everyday they trained together, she grew more comfortable in her own ability to fight someone off. Of course, Liam's absence the past few days didn't hurt, either.

The first time her and Connor were alone together, her

stomach knotted up, her hands clammy. Over time she realized he was just someone trying to navigate a world that had beaten him up once or twice already. Yet he was still kind.

Despite her slightly more optimistic outlook on life, she couldn't help but backslide into thinking about those videos. Was the first person version of those scenes of herself stored somewhere in her memory, inaccessible to her conscious mind, yet influencing her every thought and move? How was she supposed to fight a trauma she couldn't remember?

She knew she had become a homebody, but she was beginning to wonder if the penultimate factor of her recovery was finding someone who would accept her for the paranoid, unstable person she had become. Not that Connor knew the half of it.

What would have happened if she had been spurred to re-enter the real world sooner? Would she have bounced back in the same way? She was reluctant to admit the potential loss of her small fortune might have been the best thing that could have happened to her.

"I think we're good for tonight," Connor said, checking his phone. He seemed distracted. Cornelia deflated, but tried not to let it show. "How about we meet up tomorrow morning? Grab some coffee?"

"Yeah, sure," she said, nodding. She grabbed her bag and followed him out of the gym. A few blocks later, they parted ways and headed in their respective directions.

CHAPTER TWENTY NINE
Present Day, Philly PD

As Cornelia hip-checked her way into her building, her phone rang. It was a number she didn't recognize.

"Hi, I'm looking for Cornelia?"

"Detective," she said wearily. "What can I do for you?"

"Well I'm happy to report that your tip led us to some footage that might be of use in our investigation," he said.

"Oh," she said, relieved that he wasn't calling to siphon information out of her about Petyr's financial habits. "Well that's great."

"Mostly, yes. The only thing is: we still have no idea who it is that got into a fight with Mr. Hotchkin that night," he said. Cornelia grabbed her mail as she walked by the table in the entranceway. "We were hoping you might be able to come to the station and see if you recognize him or his accomplice."

"Accomplice? I thought there was just one other man," Cornelia said. She jingled through her keys for the one that would open her apartment.

"We thought so too. The witnesses who heard the fight only heard two voices, but from the video, it appears that there was more than one man with Petyr that night," the detective explained. "But we can go over all of that in person. Can you come in tomorrow morning?"

Cornelia agreed, unsure if she had a choice in the matter anyways.

Cornelia sat in the waiting area of the police station, doing her best to breathe through her mouth as a crusty homeless man checked out. His belongings consisted of a pair of socks and a dirty magazine, and his stench preceded him. She cringed, trying to block the image from her mind.

Cornelia waited for about 20 minutes before Detective Sturgess popped his head into the waiting area to greet her. He led her through the office area, into a small room with a couch and a coffee table. A short Indian man in glasses and a button-down shirt sat in a chair across from the couch, his laptop open on the table.

"This is Rafi," the detective said. The man stood to shake her hand. "He'll be playing you the surveillance footage we found."

"Alright, nice to meet you," Cornelia said, nodding to the man.

She sat down on the couch across from Rafi, and Detective Sturgess perched next to her, leaning on the table.

"Can I get you anything before we get started?" the detective asked. "This should be quick," he added.

"No, thank you."

"Alright then," he nodded to Rafi, who swiveled the laptop around so Cornelia could see the screen. "We're going to show you two clips. This first was taken at 11:17pm from a business that looks over Kelly Drive. Petyr is seen walking along the river alone. We'd like it if you could tell us anything about the video that feels different, out of the ordinary, or if you recognize where he might be going. Anything that you think could help us find this man."

"Okay," she agreed.

Rafi hit the space bar and the video clip played through. There was no sound – just 16 seconds of Petyr moving across the screen. The Schyukhill River in the background, Petyr walked north, hands tucked into his jacket pocket and his fedora balanced delicately on his head. He looked like normal Petyr.

They played the video twice more for Cornelia before they asked her what she thought.

"I don't know where he was going but that's how he

dressed, that's how he walked. It looks like a normal night for him," she said.

"That's what we expected. From what we can tell, this footage is from before he met the person who killed him."

Rafi turned the laptop toward himself, clicked around a few times, and spun the computer back toward Cornelia. Detective Sturgess nodded, and Rafi clicked play.

"This next video shows him walking down another part of Kelly Drive. I do want to warn you that he is noticeably disheveled. If you need to turn the video off, just hit the space bar and we will give you a moment. We would like you to focus on the man following Petyr," the detective explained.

Cornelia's breath caught in her chest. She had never seen Petyr "disheveled." He was a static character in her life, the same gentleman who always met her on Thursdays, dressed in his nice suit with his little fedora on top. She couldn't imagine seeing him any other way.

This video was 18 seconds and showed a different area of Kelly Drive. Cornelia couldn't tell exactly where it was, as it was quite a bit darker in this video. She could see no people other than Petyr and the man following him.

He didn't look as bad as Cornelia had expected. His hat was gone, revealing a bald spot and some wispy brown hair. At first that was the only difference she could find, until Petyr glanced in the direction of the camera. His right eye was noticeably darker, the beginnings of a black eye, and a small stream of blood trickled down from his cheekbone. Her heart swelled for him.

The man following Petyr wore some sort of uniform; a knit cap, a dark green polo shirt poking out from a plain black zip up jacket, and khaki pants. Cornelia pointed out that he had a key card attached by a retractable string to his pants pocket. She had never seen him before.

They played the video twice more, and Cornelia came to the same conclusion.

"I'm sorry," she said. "I don't know that man. And I don't

know where Petyr was going to or coming from."

The detective nodded. Rafi closed the laptop.

"Well either way, thank you for coming in," the detective said as Cornelia stood and zipped up her jacket. "And please, let us know if you think of anything else."

"Of course," she said.

He shook her hand and led her out again, depositing her into the waiting area. He gave her another copy of his card just in case.

CHAPTER THIRTY
10 months and ten days earlier, Fort Howard Neuro Clinic

Cornelia and the doctor existed in a limbo of thinly veiled mutual respect. After her attempt to leave, she did her best to be involved with Nathan's recovery, forcing herself into Nate's physical therapy sessions. The doctor said nothing, and she didn't bring up her discharge again.

At night, Cornelia wandered the halls. Renee didn't mind that she was up and moving about, but the other night nurses followed her, watching like a hawk as she passed any method of egress. The doctor appeased them by stationing armed guards around the building.

As Cornelia searched for her opportunity, she became increasingly aware that any move she made could put Nate in danger. Who's to say what might happen if she left? Since the doctor ripped up her discharge papers, she had the nagging feeling that her and Nate were in this together, and if she was leaving, he was coming with her.

Cornelia walked at Nate's side as he balanced between two ballet bars. One nurse walked ahead of him and another behind, ready to catch him if he lost his balance. It was his first day on his feet, and Cornelia had never seen him work so hard.

He reached the end of the bars and collapsed into a wheelchair, breathing a sigh of relief. Cornelia kissed him. "I'm so proud of you," she whispered.

The doctor entered the rehab room with a flourish, and stopped when he saw Nate and Cornelia together. "I'm going to need both of you to go back to your rooms," he said. They glanced at each other. "There's a leak in the upstairs hallway that needs to be inspected. For everyone's wellbeing, I'm cancelling any activities for today."

"Can we just finish up? We only have a few exercises

left," Cornelia said, her hands on Nate's shoulders.

"Back to your rooms," the doctor insisted. He turned on his heel and disappeared down the hall.

Nate shrugged. "Come on, I'm tired anyways," he said. "Let's just do what he says and maybe I'll see you later," he whispered, smirking mischievously at her.

She was reluctant, but agreed. She wheeled him back to his room and helped him into bed.

On her way back to her own room, she heard voices from down the hall. She stopped and listened.

"... upstairs hallway, toward the right. You can see mold covering the outer wall, I can lead you up there," the doctor said.

Cornelia glanced down the hall. He spoke with one man who was in a military uniform, and another who carried a toolbox and construction equipment. The doctor stepped toward the elevator and swiped his badge on the keypad. The three men filed in and went upstairs.

Cornelia had never been upstairs, thanks to the locked elevator and her own lack of confidence in taking the stairs. She had progressed significantly, but she wasn't sure she was up for stairs just yet.

Cornelia wound around to the nurse's station, where Renee was busy typing away on the computer. She had been demoted to desk duty when the doctor found out how Cornelia knew Nate was alive, so she no longer helped with rehab, and instead, just entered and pulled patient information. Cornelia was just happy she still worked nights, because at least that gave her the freedom to roam.

"What's with the construction guy?" she asked, nodding toward the entrance.

"Mold on the second floor. Looks like black mold, been there for ages, and they're finally getting it checked out. Military dude is the doctor's boss, Dr. Heltz," she said, murmuring quietly so the security guard down the hall couldn't hear.

"That's his boss?" Cornelia glanced down the hall, wondering if she'd be able to get a good look before he left.

"Yeah, he only shows up once in a blue moon. He seems reasonably nice, but then again, so does the doctor when you first meet him," she said.

"Can we talk to him?" Cornelia asked, a distant light appearing at the end of her tunnel.

"I don't know if you'll get anywhere, he's pretty strict," the nurse said. "More so than the doctor."

"Can *you* talk to him?" Cornelia pushed.

The nurse bit her lip. "Corey, I'm already on thin ice. I don't know if I should be sticking my neck out like that."

Cornelia nodded, agreeing it was too much to ask. She wandered back down the hallway to the front entrance, and waited.

It took about twenty minutes for the three men to return. The doctor was disgruntled, grumbling as the foreman described the type of work that would have to be done to the building. The costs they mentioned were executive level. They couldn't see her waiting just around the corner.

She heard snippets of the conversation, not wanting to move or get closer for fear of drawing attention to herself.

"It would be cheaper to tear the whole place down than to fix the mold problem," the foreman mentioned, and she could hear breath exhaling, a mumble or grumble that came from either the doctor or his boss.

"Maybe we should just call it a day then," Dr. Heltz mentioned.

"But where would we move to?" Dr. Ingels asked.

There was silence, and Cornelia silently urged someone to say *something.* Where might she end up? And more importantly, did it give her an opportunity to leave altogether?

"Thank you for coming out today," Dr. Heltz said, and Cornelia heard a series of goodbyes, some grumbles, a smattering of thank you's.

"Where would we move to?" Dr. Ingels repeated once the front door slammed shut.

"There are some projects that will likely take precedence over yours," Dr. Heltz stated.

"But what about my patients?"

"They'll be transferred."

"To... where?"

"Area hospitals most likely," Dr. Heltz said, and paused for a moment. "Liam, I don't think this study will be funded much longer. It's likely that when this hospital shuts down, so will your program."

Cornelia heard only silence and the thumping of her heart in her throat. Was this the end? How long would it take for the hospital to close down? She supposed it could be days, but probably months. It's not like anyone was walking around complaining about the state of it, and Cornelia couldn't even see the mold from her floor.

It would be months - months and months of the same four hallways.

She decided this news was not enough to keep her mouth shut and play at obedience for the next however many days, months, years it might be until the hospital was officially closed. Now was her opportunity.

"Hi, you must be Dr. Heltz," Cornelia said, popping out from behind the wall and immediately shaking his hand. He looked from her to Dr. Ingels and back. She must have looked straight out of the loony bin.

"I am," he said, smiling reservedly. "Who might you be?"

"Cornelia, I'm a patient here," she explained.

"Oh," he said, his tone softening.

"I know Dr. Ingels has a lot of responsibilities here, and I'm sure the wellbeing of his patients is top priority," she said, glancing to the doctor. His face was red, his lips pursed. "He has expressed concerns that I am not fit to be discharged, but I was wondering if there is a higher authority I might appeal to, to be released."

Both men were silent.

"That's really not my area of expertise," Dr. Heltz

hedged.

"What *is* your area of expertise?" she questioned.

"Cornelia, go back to your room," Dr. Ingels interjected, grabbing her arm and pushing her in that direction. She stumbled, but caught herself. She had gotten further than she expected, but not quite far enough.

Defeated, she shuffled on. Nurse Cavallero caught up with her as she crossed the threshold to her room. "That was awfully daring," she said, helping Cornelia into bed.

"In hindsight, that probably wasn't the most thought out plan I could have come up with, but I felt time was of the essence," she reasoned, leaning back into her pillows.

Renee smiled. "I know. And I'm doing all I can," she whispered, a reminder that they were on the same side.

Cornelia nodded. "I've never been one to sit around and wait for things to happen."

Renee returned to the nurse's station. The doctors' muffled voices carried from down the hall, and a few minutes later, the crash of the front door punctuated their conversation. Dr. Ingels's footsteps echoed, crescendoing as they reached Cornelia's room.

He swept into her room, the tails of his white coat swirling around him.

"What the *hell* do you think you're doing?" he spat, his fists curled together at his sides. He began pacing back and forth at the foot of her bed. Cornelia had never seen him so angry.

"I told you I wanted out," she said, honestly confused that he was so surprised.

"That could have cost me *my job*," he seethed. He stepped to the side of her bed, and her fight-or-flight reflexes started to kick in. She inched toward the far side of her bed.

"I'm sorry," she stammered, his outburst throwing her.

"So fucking entitled!" he shouted. "You do realize all I'm trying to do here is help you."

Cornelia shrugged. "Then let me go."

He stepped toward her again, and her heart caught in her throat.

A cough from the doorway caught their attention. "Doctor, I don't think she realized what she was doing. Remember, Cornelia had severe brain damage. Perhaps her indiscretion is related to her injury," Renee postulated. She held her hands in front of her and looked directly at the doctor, holding his gaze.

"You're on desk duty until further notice," he growled. "Go back to your station."

Renee nodded and sent Cornelia a sad smile before leaving the room.

The doctor turned back to Cornelia.

"I'm not happy about your behavior today," he said. He closed his eyes and breathed deeply. "But I understand your thought process is just a product of your injury," he quoted. "And I forgive you."

Cornelia's gut turned in on itself, but she felt it wasn't a good time to lash out. She clenched her teeth, determined now more than ever, to get out.

He took a step closer to her and took her hand. He looked into her eyes, and smiled as he tucked a stray hair behind her ear.

Her heart hammered.

He leaned forward and gently kissed her cheek. He paused there, his cologne assaulting her senses. Cornelia froze, her body tense.

He stood back, gently laying Cornelia's hand back on the bed, and walked out of the room.

Cornelia slipped out of bed and went into her bathroom. She knelt down in front of the toilet and spilled every last piece of food she had in her stomach. When there was nothing left to purge, she heaved over the bowl until she fell asleep, her cheek cold against the tile floor. She dreamt nightmares of men drenched in musk.

CHAPTER THIRTY ONE
Present Day, Cornelia and Renee's building

Cornelia moved through her dark apartment, restless.

She needed something to occupy her mind. Connor hadn't followed up with her about getting her officially on the schedule, she had heard nothing from Detective Sturgess about Petyr's investigation, and there was only silence from Luca.

She spotted her mail pile by the door, unopened and growing larger with every passing day. She figured now was as good a time as any to tackle it.

As Cornelia went through her mental checklist of all the things she might need, she noticed a flashing light from her desk drawer.

She flipped through her mail absentmindedly as she booted up her phone, looking for any that required attention. Most of her bills were paid by the landlord, her phone by her aunt. The pile was entirely spam.

Her old phone started buzzing, weeks of messages and missed calls (mostly Tanya) finding their way through. She turned it on once a month or so to wade through the crap, in case something important came in. It was as good a distraction as any.

She thumbed through her passcode and let it sit for a few minutes. It dinged and buzzed every few seconds as slowpoke voicemails and text messages registered. Cornelia watched the notifications come in while absentmindedly leafing through her spam mail for any coupons she could use on food.

She glanced at her phone. 67 new voicemails, 132 missed calls, 24 text messages.

She abandoned the mail and started in on the text messages first. Most were from Tanya – she had trouble remembering which number to call. She usually called the old number twice, left a voicemail, then a text, and finally remembered to call the new number.

She cleared out Tanya's repeats quickly, most of them something along the lines of: "Called you. Call me back."

She had two texts from another person – a Jamie she used to know in high school. The first read: "Corey, we have to talk. Call me back." A few days later, her second text read: "Cornelia, seriously call me back. This isn't funny. This guy is following me, asking about you. I filed a police report. I don't know how he knows who I am, but you need to call me back."

Cornelia felt the blood leave her face. Her ears rang in the silence of her apartment.

She scrolled through her missed calls. Mostly Tanya and a smattering of doctor's offices, except for five from Jamie. All within the span of a week. She left two voicemails.

"Hey Corey, it's Jamie from high school. I know we haven't talked in a while but someone came to my work asking about you today. I don't know who he is but it creeped me out a bit. Give me a call back."

The second was more forceful, an echo of her text message:

"Cornelia, call me back. This isn't funny. This guy is following me, asking about you, and it's really freaking me out. I don't know what you're involved in, but you need to talk to him or something. I filed a police report and a restraining order but he still showed up at my work this morning. Call me back."

After a quick google search, Cornelia learned that the second voicemail was left the same day that Jamie disappeared.

She sat at her desk, staring at the phone. She felt a level of guilt she hadn't known existed.

What were the chances that Jamie might still be alive if Cornelia had answered her phone?

Then again, what could Cornelia have done?

Cornelia didn't recognize the uniforms of the men that followed Petyr, but she had a sneaking suspicion they were somehow related to Liam. But this voicemail... whether or not Liam had anything to do with Petyr's death, she was certain he had something to do with Jamie's.

Liam knew where Jamie and Petyr worked. What did that mean for Cornelia, if he knew where she lived?

She glanced down at the pile of mail she still clutched. One letter wasn't postmarked, despite being stamped.

She ripped the envelope open. It was a folded up sheet of lined paper, ripped from a spiral bound notebook. The content was succinct: *Cornelia, stay far away from Dr. Liam Ingels. He does not have your best interests at heart.*

She read the letter over several times, searching for any alternative meaning she could find. After another listen to the anxious voicemail and a long, slow perusal of the matching text message, Cornelia came to only one conclusion: it was time to go.

Cornelia packed her two suitcases and a gym bag. Most of her belongings fit, as she never re-accumulated stuff after her coma. She left behind her secondhand furniture, and slipped her $700 for January rent in cash into the landlord's mail slot. She wasn't sure if or when she would be back, but a month should buy her time to figure it out.

She dialed her only ally in the city, one hand on her doorknob, ready to leave.

"Hey Corey," he said.

"Connor," she said, relieved that he picked up. "I have a really large favor to ask of you."

"Shoot."

She took a deep breath. "I have to leave my apartment for a little while. Could I stay with you for a couple days until I figure everything out?"

He paused. "Are you okay?"

"Yeah, I'm fine, just need to crash somewhere for a

couple days."

He cleared his throat. "Absolutely. Are you ready now? I can come get you."

She nodded. "Yes, thank you."

They agreed to meet at the northwest corner of her block in fifteen minutes.

Renee heard voices. She was groggy, her internal clock telling her to go back to bed. Her mind unraveled from her dreams as she digested the noises from outside her door and opened her eyes to the darkness settled around her. It was nighttime, just approaching dawn. She could see a little sliver of light blue sky through her tiny bedroom window.

Through the walls, she heard Naomi chatting happily with someone in the hallway.

She listened closer, the temptation to eavesdrop too strong to ignore. The male voice outside was familiar, and her blood immediately pulsed in high gear.

She heard them moving down the hall, murmured directives determining logistics.

"... easier to break in? ..."

"... come willingly if we did that..."

"... do it already, wasting time..."

Renee stood and sprinted to her door as quietly as she could. She peered out of her peephole, just in time to see Liam and one of the clinic guards walk by. Judging from the voices, there was someone else there that she couldn't see. They were already at Cornelia's door.

She did the only thing she could think of doing.

She ran to the wall she shared with Cornelia and threw her body weight into it as hard as she could. She did that twice more, hoping that if nothing else, Cornelia would wake up and prepare herself. Hopefully she would hear the voices and make a run for it.

The guards stammered.

"What was that noise?"

"Is she escaping?"

"Can you hear her?"

Since her cover was already blown, she shouted through the wall, "Cornelia! If you can hear me, you have to get out *now!*"

Renee waited and listened. Not only was Cornelia's side of the wall quiet, but so was the hallway. They were listening for Renee too.

Panic set in as she wondered what they might do.

She snuck back to her peephole and looked out again. Her view was obscured, completely blacked out.

"Fuck fuck fuck fuck fuck," she mouthed to herself. She didn't dare say anything out loud, though it probably wouldn't have mattered at that point.

After a few moments she heard a knocking, but not on her door – on Cornelia's. "Cornelia! It's Dr. Ingels. We need you to come with us for an evaluation," he shouted.

No answer.

"Cornelia," he called, knocking on the door again. "We need you to come out now or we'll have to break down the door," he warned in a sing-song voice like you might use to scold a toddler.

He talked to her like she was a child. Renee and Liam both knew just how ineffective that was. Even Renee, who was used to taking orders from arrogant, condescending doctors, felt her stomach churn in response to his coated tone.

Cornelia hid her disgust well the first few weeks they knew each other. Whenever someone talked down to her, she would simply say "ok," and nod. The "ok" she disguised perfectly, but the nod was what gave her away.

Liam claimed he just *knew* when Cornelia wasn't listening, but he was only right about half the time – if she said "ok" and maintained eye contact, you were on her shit list. If she nodded and dipped her eyes for a moment, she meant it sincerely. After all the time he spent observing her, Renee was surprised he hadn't noticed that little detail. It was obvious from an outsider's perspective.

So Renee kept the discovery to herself, allowing Liam to think whatever special connection he had with Cornelia was, in fact, special. Cornelia *was* an incredibly special patient, with or without a "connection" to the doctor. Renee, however, knew the doctor was likely to forget that if he ever lost interest. It was a short spiral from medical marvel to cadaver.

Liam banged on the door again, this time louder. In the stillness of the morning, Renee could feel the whole building shake. She shut her eyes tight and hoped, hoped, *hoped* that Cornelia wasn't there. Even better – maybe she never came home the night before. She was prone to disappearing randomly, at times Renee couldn't rationalize. Cornelia had always been a free spirit.

Renee breathed so heavily she could hardly hear what was going on outside. She took a deep breath and held it, listening for a footstep, a whisper. She heard nothing.

"Alright," she heard Liam's pinched voice.

She chanced another glance through the peephole, and found her vision suddenly un-obscured. She could see one security guard, from the side, and Liam standing next to him at a 45-degree angle to her door. They focused on something outside of Renee's view.

"Are you in?" Liam asked. Renee's heart stopped.

"No, just about though. I can feel it," the invisible person said. Something clanged to the ground.

Renee stiffened. It couldn't be that easy. She had spent months planning her life around someone she could only predict. She couldn't let it all go to waste. She paused, stumped. She had to do *something.*

She grabbed a fire extinguisher off the wall of her apartment with one hand and swung her apartment door open with the other. She charged for the closest security guard first.

Despite the buzz cut and stun gun on his hip, he was

knocked out with one blow, slumping to the ground against the opposite wall. With the same swing, Renee grazed Liam's head.

She swiveled for the second security guard, but she was too late. He expected the swing and ducked just in time, instead using his stun gun to knock her off her feet.

That, she expected. She was just glad she hit two of them before getting taken out. Pretty good odds for a retired nurse, she thought.

"What the... what the fuck Renee?" Liam shouted. He leaned against the wall next to the slumped security guard, delicately touching the bloody slit that ran across hit temple.

"Cornelia, run!" she shouted, with every ounce of strength she had left. Her body screamed in pain, muscles spasming. She couldn't even hear her own voice.

Fuck.

Cornelia watched from the end of the street as a black SUV pulled away from her building with two security guards, one injured and one dazed. Liam sported a split temple, and following him, a small blonde woman hobbled along. Cornelia recognized her as the elusive building manager. They had only met once or twice in passing, both content having their own private, unadulterated space.

She wasn't sure if the security guard was the same one she had seen in the video at the police station, but she was certain he was dressed the same.

She didn't want to believe it, but it all made sense. It was all connected somehow - Petyr, Jamie, her... and Liam, right at the center.

It was as if nothing surprised her anymore. All the strange things she was experiencing had a common denominator.

At least she had an update for Luca.

She opened the note in her hand and read it again. It wasn't postmarked, but it had a stamp on it. Whomever it was from must have slipped it into the mail slot after the regular delivery, hoping it would blend in with the regular mail. Who else knew she lived there?

"Come on," Connor said, nudging her elbow and pulling her in the direction of his apartment by her sleeve. He threw one of her duffel bags over one shoulder, the hood of his sweat-shirt pulled up over his head.

Cornelia paused, wondering if she should be concerned. Why would the building manager go with them? Was she help-ing them?

"Should we help her?" Cornelia asked, hoping to get an idea of what Connor thought of the situation. Was she crazy in his eyes?

Connor glanced toward the van. "It looked like she went willingly. Do you know her?" he asked.

She couldn't tell whether the woman went willingly or not. Was she helping them?

She stuffed the note in her pocket, the folds rubbing against her skin through the fabric, a constant reminder.

Cornelia shook her head. "Only in passing."

Could she have been the writer of the note?

Connor nodded. "Let's get out of here," he said, and ducked in the direction of his apartment. Cornelia followed, keeping the SUV in sight as long as she could before they rounded the corner and everything returned to normal.

If she was the writer of the note, was she working with or against them? Double crossing?

She ran a hand through her hair as she walked, her sad old duffel bags smushing back and forth over her backside as she walked. She could still smell the dye she used to turn her hair that unfamiliar dark chestnut. She felt like she had added a new layer of invisibility.

But would Liam see right through it? Would he recog-nize the way she walked? Or maybe the same ratty gym shoes she wore everywhere? How much would she have to change before he didn't know her anymore?

How well did he really know her, anyways?

She wanted to comment on the beauty of the sun breaking over the horizon in slivers of orange-pink cotton candy, but the whole setting felt contrived, a beautiful backdrop to cover up the tragedy at hand.

CHAPTER THIRTY TWO
Present Day, Connor's apartment

Connor's apartment was on the second floor of a large building not unlike Cornelia's. Newer and larger, it was built as one cohesive apartment building rather than a mansion that was later converted.

As they walked, Connor explained to her the long journey that led him to his current dwellings. A long divorce, an even longer marriage, and a passion for martial arts taught him that life is too short to spend it with toxic people, and that dreams should be followed at all costs.

Any other day, Cornelia might have enjoyed his little speech – even found it motivational – but today she saw it for what it was: a way to justify a small and lightly furnished bachelor pad.

They came upon his doorstep and she was overwhelmed with beige. The exterior was a beige stucco, the inner hallway carpeted in beige and painted a slightly lighter shade of beige.

In his apartment, the beige continued, the flooring and walls joined by furniture made of bamboo and a beige couch, on top of which rested a folded, beige set of sheets.

"You like beige, huh?" she asked.

He scrunched his eyebrows. "Well everybody used to make fun of me for having mismatching stuff so I matched it all," he explained.

Cornelia smiled, scared she might have hit a nerve. "I'm just kidding. I like beige too," she said. "But I also think it's totally okay to live life a little mismatched." She thought fondly of the mismatched furniture littering her apartment. Would she ever see it again?

He smiled. "This will be your area. Sorry it's not much,

but it's a place to stay while..."

She got the feeling he was hoping for some kind of explanation, but she wasn't sure where to start.

A beige Ikea futon lined the wall adjacent to the door. On it was a pile of folded bed sheets and a pillow.

"Thanks again for letting me stay," she said.

"No problem. As long as you need," he said. They dropped her bags by the couch.

Connor pulled out the sofa and helped her put the sheets on.

She longed for her familiar old room, the darkness and solitude of her basement apartment where she could curl up and hide. Connor's apartment was in the front of the building, with huge old windows that showcased his living room. She bet herself she would wake up to blinding southern sunlight at seven in the morning. Her body might even adjust to a normal schedule if she stayed more than a few days.

Though she had to admit, she didn't hate the warmth. Going without heat had become a bit of a drag.

She sat on the edge of the makeshift bed and ran her hands over the fading sheets. Connor had two deadbolts and a chain, and despite the large windows, she was on the second floor and relatively inaccessible.

Out of all of the possible outcomes of this night, this was probably her luckiest break.

She sighed. "Thank you for letting me stay," she said.

He smiled and repeated, "Really, as long as you need," he repeated, sitting down next to her. He wrapped an arm around her, and she rested her head on his shoulder.

Connor watched a movie in his room, leaving Cornelia with some alone time. She snuck out the front door and sat on the stairs in the hallway, her laptop open next to her. She dialed Luca's number.

"Luca Hotchkin," he answered.

"Luca, it's Cornelia."

"Corey, how is the weather in Frankfurt?" he asked. She typed Frankfurt into her weather search.

"A brisk 43 degrees, clear skies," she said.

He launched right in. "I'm sorry, Corey, I don't have any updates for you yet. I'm still looking for a replacement though, and I will let you know as soon as I find one."

"That's fine, thanks. I actually called to give *you* an update," she said, playing with the hem of her sweatshirt.

"Oh really? Are you finally going to come visit us?" he asked her. She could hear the smile in his voice.

She laughed. "I don't think I'm quite there yet, however much I'd like to be," she started. "I actually might have a lead on what happened to Petyr. I'm not sure exactly what it means, but I found some connection. To me, actually."

"What do you mean?"

"The police showed me some footage from the night Petyr disappeared. It showed him walking down Kelly Dr., and a man following him in some sort of security uniform. I didn't recognize it at the time, but I later found out it's the uniform from a hospital in Maryland. Fort Howard Veterans, and... I was there for a time," she explained. She wasn't sure how to go on. "I think it might be my fault that he's dead."

Luca sighed. "Corey, did you send this man after Petyr?" Luca asked.

"No, but I think they were looking for me," she said. She sounded paranoid, delusional.

Luca's voice softened. "There is *no way* this is your fault," he paused, making sure his words landed. "Thank you for telling me, I'll have someone check out this hospital. Fort Howard... Veterans, did you say?"

She nodded. "Yes. Do you want me to tell the police too?"

He was silent for a few beats. "No, I think we have it covered."

CHAPTER THIRTY THREE
10 months and one day earlier, Fort Howard Neuro Clinic

Renee leaned against the rough brick exterior of the hospital, her phone tucked into the nook between her cheek and her shoulder.

She smoked a cigarette she had bummed from one of the security guards. She wasn't a smoker, but she needed an excuse to go outside and make her call.

"Baltimore PD," the voice on the other line said.

"Hi," she said, turning toward the parking lot in an attempt to keep the conversation private. "I was wondering if I could speak with a detective."

"What is this regarding?" the man barked.

Renee's mind blanked.

"Miss?"

"I'm doing a project for school, I was hoping to speak to a detective who could help me outline the process of solving a crime from beginning to end based on a specific scenario. Would that be possible?" she asked. If that didn't work, she'd have to call back with another more plausible scenario. She kicked herself for not thinking this through prior to dialing.

"Hold," he said, and the line clicked over to elevator jazz.

Her mother called her twice times while she waited, but she hit ignore, too worried she might screw up her conversation with the detective.

Renee burned through most of her cigarette before someone clicked on the line. She waited so long, she had forgotten what call she was on by the time someone picked up.

"Detective Miller," he said

"Hi," she said.

"You're the criminal justice student, right? You had a

question about a... crime scenario?" he asked. He wasn't as terse as the first person she had talked to, but she had the idea he wasn't up for any bullshit.

"Yes. The scenario is based on a patient being held in a hospital against her will. What would the protocol for that be? The doctor claims it is for her own safety, but she feels she is ready to leave," she explained. Her phone started beeping, and Renee held the phone up to decline another call from her mom. Her eyebrows crinkled - three calls in a row was unusual for her.

"Well in that case, we would probably just remind the doctor of the illegality. Most people are ready to cooperate when you send over a few blues," he said. "Very rarely do you have to go further than that."

Renee nodded, her cigarette barely burning freely between her fingers. "And what if the hospital is private, like on a military base or something with restricted access?"

The detective harrumphed. "Well, that makes things a little more complicated. If it's a military hospital, they likely have their own police and would have to go through an internal affairs type of investigation. Regular police departments would have a lot of trouble even getting permission."

She nodded. "What if the internal investigation showed no wrongdoing? Or if there was some sort of corruption that didn't allow the patient to prove she's fit for release?"

"Well I can't say I know much about this sort of investigation. This is really out of my jurisdiction, but I would imagine that the patient would have to keep escalating things until someone listens. Worse comes to worst, a little bit of publicity works wonders with cases like that."

"Mm, okay. So kind of trial by public opinion?" she clarified. Her phone buzzed again, and she hit decline once more, the worry for her mom starting to eclipse her concern for Cornelia.

"Kind of. That's an interesting case you're studying, definitely not something they go over in *our* training," he said.

She heard the squeak of what sounded like a chair hinging back. "Did you have any other questions?"

"No, that's it. Thank you very much for your time," she said.

"No problem."

The line clicked, and Renee navigated to her voicemail box to check the voicemails her mother had left. The multitude quickened her pulse - her mother wasn't one to press if Renee needed her space.

"Renee, Uncle Joe is in the hospital. He fell during lunch, just keeled over like a floppy banana peel. They think he had a heart attack. We need you home, *now,*" her mother's rushed voice spouted. The voicemail ended before she could process what she heard.

Renee's heart thumped in her chest. She had never known her dad, but her uncle more than made up for his absence. When she was young, he would take her to father's day breakfasts at school and fix her bike when the chain popped off.

She stomped out the cigarette stub she had taken a lonely drag of, and turned back toward the building. One of the security guards, whom she hadn't noticed come up behind her, leaned against the wall less than ten feet away. They locked eyes.

"I didn't notice you there," she said.

"Yeah," he mumbled, raising his eyebrows as he took a drag.

Renee nodded, and pushed past him into the building. She had other things to worry about.

CHAPTER THIRTY FOUR
Present Day, Connor's apartment

Cornelia held her phone in her hand, rapping her fingers along the edge. She sat outside the door to Connor's apartment, surrounded by eerie silence and *beige*.

She dialed the phone number again, her finger hovering over the call button for a moment before she cancelled. She took a deep breath. How crazy would she seem?

She pressed send before she could change her mind.

"Detective Sturgess," he announced.

"Hi, it's Cornelia Winthorp," she said.

A note of surprise in his voice, he said, "how can I help you?"

"I had a question," she started. "Unrelated to Petyr," she clarified.

"Okay."

"I was reading about someone who was held against her will. It was in kind of like a psychiatric hospital I guess, but she wasn't crazy. They just wanted to keep her," she paused, waiting for him to start laughing at her or hang up on her, but never did. "What sort of proof would you need to... uh, prove something like that?"

"Well you would need proof she wasn't crazy. Probably a medical examination by another doctor, and then you could go through the process of suing the original doctor for false imprisonment," he said. "Probably falsifying records, maybe a few other charges in there for good measure."

She nodded. "And what if the hospital requires some sort of security clearance?" she asked.

"You mean like a military hospital?" he asked.

She gulped. She had never said it aloud before. "Yes."

"They have separate police, you wouldn't go through a

regular department for that," he said.

"And how difficult is that to do?"

"Ideally it's supposed to be easy, but from what I've heard it can be a pain in the ass," he said. He was silent for a few moments. "Is there something else you'd like to ask? Or... tell me?"

"Uh, no, that's all. Just a question. Thanks for answering," she said.

"Let me know if you have any other questions," he said.

"Thank you, I will."

CHAPTER THIRTY FIVE
Present Day, Dr. Liam Ingels's Hotel Room

"When did you most recently see Cornelia?" the doctor prompted.

He had been asking her variations of the same question for hours. When they first sat down, she gave him the benefit of the doubt. She answered his questions to the best of her ability without giving Cornelia away, which turned out surprisingly easy considering she really had no idea where Cornelia might be or what her new plan was.

But about an hour into his questioning, she picked up an old copy of Pride and Prejudice off of the dusty bookshelf behind the kitchen table and focused on Jane Austen, Liam Ingels an annoying fly buzzing around her ears. He paced, sat down, alternated between staring out the window and staring at her. He was restless and desperate, and Renee had never been happier to see him agitated.

"She's not going to come after me," Renee reasoned, struggling to read her book as he peppered her with fast, leaping questions that didn't follow any discernible thought pattern. "She doesn't have a clue who I am or how we know each other. She doesn't care about me."

Liam hadn't expressly said so, but it was clear she wasn't "allowed" to leave just yet. She was just thankful she was allowed to use the bathroom alone, though she expected if there was any means of egress from that tiny room, she wouldn't be granted even that peace.

Liam looked more ragged than he had when Renee spotted him in her front door camera. He hadn't showered, and his patchy teenage-boy beard grew in spots, heavier on his left cheek than the right.

Renee sat on a stool by the window, reading. It wasn't a

new story by any means, but her only other choices consisted of medical journals or mass market thrillers about patriarchal misogynists with a penchant for kidnapping and murder.

Despite the entertainment value, those were hitting a little too close to home.

"She'll come," Liam insisted, his voice flat. He pored over one of his personal medical journals, no doubt Cornelia's, probably looking for some switch or cheat code that would make Cornelia behave the way he wanted her to. Unfortunately for him, brains were not as simple as he wanted them to be.

During the time they worked together, Renee had ample opportunities to observe Liam and the way he worked with his patients, as well as his true self when the patients weren't around.

He regarded his patients with a certain esteem that was lost on his colleagues. If you had no medical value to him, you were no better than dog shit on his loafers. Renee's saving grace had been her closeness to Cornelia. She was sure, even now, that the only reason he remembered her name at all was because he thought it might help him get through to Cornelia.

Renee had followed him from his Alzheimer's experiments to the Memory I trials, and later to the Memory II experiments, but she was smart enough to get out before being called into the Memory III. She counted herself stupid for not recognizing his true motivations sooner.

He was a gifted scientist – that was certain – but when it came to being a doctor, Renee still wondered if there was anyone with the authority to intercede in his practice. There were plenty of coworkers and patients who believed he should be stripped of his license, but when you are the director of your division, as well as the only doctor on staff... there's only so much your staff can do to displace you.

Renee had only met his boss a few times, but the effect Dr. Heltz had was priceless. He was unquestionably military – you could tell by the way he stood: feet shoulder width apart, shoulders wide, hands clasped behind his back. The doctor would stutter trying to explain things to him, and after he left, Dr. Ingels would mope around like a dog with his tail between his legs. Renee and Cornelia had tried to appeal to him on one of those days, hoping to hit a soft spot, but his stubbornness never faltered.

It was obvious to Renee that he cared unequivocally about his work, but she wondered how an award-winning doctor would lack the ability to connect with his patients on a deeper level, as bedside manner was heavily emphasized early on in medical school. Renee always thought the best diagnoses came from the heart. Then again, she was "just a nurse."

Even in her practicum at a young women's clinic, Renee could see the difference that comfort could have in a patient's treatment. The first 17-year-old girl she had seen about birth control, timid and quiet, asked for "just the pill." After a dirty joke and the tale of Renee's own first awkward adventure, they had an open discussion about safe sex and relationships. The girl left with a low dose pill and a promise to follow up in a few weeks for "deets."

Granted, Renee gave no shits about the actual act, but she cared that her patient was safe and educated. Renee, rather than the prescribing doctor, was the receiver of the girl's thank you call, and after that, Renee resolved to *always* be open with her patients.

Her heart broke when her practicum ended and there weren't any open positions at the clinic. After failing to find her perfect job, she landed in an Alzheimer's study, where she occasionally won a "thanks" from patients' families, but it never felt as good as that phone call from the 17-year-old girl.

And it all went downhill from there.

Dr. Ingels was friendly, caring, *enamored* with patients when they talked about their symptoms, but in the time during which most doctors and patients would build up a rapport, Dr. Ingels would grow more distant and stop responding with the same enthusiasm for their treatments. He had a fondness for symptoms, but felt very little for the people who experienced them.

"You can't just make someone listen to you because you want them to," Renee told him. She felt a brief rush of blood to her head. Dr. Ingels had always been her superior, the epitome of an authority figure, but now *Liam*, in this state, was undeserving of her respect. The outburst felt cathartic.

"Don't speak to me in that tone," Liam snapped, staring intently at his journal.

She sighed, her frustration reaching an apex. "Stop wasting everyone's time. I'm sure your *body guards* are itching to go back to work where they actually belong," she said. She looked to Liam, who was still staring at his book, jaw clenched. She had expected a retort - silence was odd for him.

She sat up straight in her chair, folding her book closed and clasping her hands over top of it. She glanced at the security guards, who were glancing at each other, eyebrows furrowed. She felt another burst of warmth tickling her ears.

She waited, silently baiting him. *Do anything*, she dared him. She wanted a reason to run her mouth, tell him exactly what she thought of him and his dirty practices. He was unraveling, and she wanted to pull at his strings.

And then a thought occurred to her.

"Wait," she said, trying to find a solution in her head before she asked the question.

"If you've been here for the past, what, month, two months-?" She looked to Liam and the guards for confirmation. Liam raised an eyebrow. "Who has been taking care of your patients?"

Liam slammed his book closed on the table in front of him.

"Look Renee, I've given you the benefit out of the doubt. I've given you leeway. I've done more for you than I've done for any other nurse. Do me a favor, and just *shut up*," he said. The words dripped like slime over the quiet room.

He wasn't always pleasant, but this was a different side

of him – a different animal that she could only guess secretly fueled his dangerous experiments in the first place.

It dawned on Renee that he might not be as contained as she thought. There was another beast in there that she hadn't truly met yet.

The silence was full, questions hanging between them, suffocating.

"I can't deal with being shut in here anymore, I need to go for a walk," Liam said. He stood from his chair with a screech of metal against wood, grabbed his jacket from the chair opposite, and swished out of the hotel room with grace and flourish.

"Watch her," he grunted, as he slammed the door.

Renee looked at the guards, standing still and silent along the wall between Renee and the kitchen table where Liam had been sitting. They glanced at her, and then each other. Renee wondered if either of them would say anything.

"I'm not going to tattle if you sit down on the job," she said, leaning back in her chair. They had been standing the entire time she was there, and she wondered if they had a new standing rule at the clinic after some of the guards had taken to falling asleep on the job.

After all, everyone else was sleeping too.

She recognized them both but hadn't worked closely with either, and had to pick up their names on the fly. She wasn't sure what their orders had been, but she was certain they were outside of regular job duties. She wondered how much they were being paid, and out of whose pocket.

Her curiosity was piqued.

They glanced at each other, and Josh – the shorter of the guards – pursed his lips, taking in a deep breath. He let his shoulders slump, and pulled a chair out from the kitchen table, sinking into it with a sigh.

"Oh man, does that feel good," he said, rolling his head around on his neck.

Renee glanced to the other guard, Mike, who looked a

little squirmy. He caught her gaze and broke character.

"I gotta piss so bad, you got this dude?" he asked. They nodded in agreement and the full bladdered guard traipsed to the bathroom at the other end of the suite.

She moved toward Josh, her socks sliding easily over the wood floor, and took her chance. "So seriously, who's looking over Dr. Ingels' patients?" she asked, easing gingerly into the chair across from him. She had a hunch, but she wanted confirmation.

Josh glanced toward the bathroom.

"I'm really not allowed to say," he said, shaking his head.

"Is it his boss?"

"I don't think so," he said. His eyes shifted, uncomfortable.

Renee waited for him to explain, but after a few seconds of silence, grew impatient.

"Well, who is it then?" she asked, forcefully. She imagined her words sliding, icky and sticky out of her mouth and taking hold around his neck.

Mike stepped out of the bathroom, looking relieved. Smile on his face, he took a seat across from Renee at the table, oblivious to their conversation.

"How long do you think he'll be gone for?" he asked, casual enough to make Renee roll her eyes. So intentional.

"Well, hopefully he won't come back," she said, standing up to shuffle back to her post by the window. She looked outside to the street, traffic dying down after rush hour. Fewer people walked the streets these days, the cold turning light jackets to puff. She wondered if anyone would even see her if she tried to signal a passerby. Would the guards care, without direction from their supreme leader?

Renee had botched every plan she had ever tried to close Fort Howard, but her shining accomplishment was getting Cornelia out. She wished she could have saved everyone, but Cornelia was the one that thrived, and if she was going to save anyone, it had to be her. She had the best chance of anyone to live a normal life. The rest were taken care of, and mostly in much less immediate danger, considering they were still in comas and thus, much less interesting to Dr. Ingels.

For many patients, it really was an okay place. The majority were simple coma patients, sent by families who had lost hope their loved ones would ever wake up. When one did, they were sent back to those families who touted the success of experimental trials everywhere. Little did they know, they were part of something much bigger.

Dr. Ingels started small, so many of his early patients were entirely unaware that part of their memory had been tampered with. But as time went on, he got greedy.

The doctor harbored a fondness for Cornelia from day one, her brain scans showing something perfectly broken for the Memory trials. One small area of her brain was misshapen, likely as a result of her accident, and it provided the perfect buffer for the drug to interact with all of the right parts of her brain and none of the wrong ones. At least, that's how Liam explained it to her.

Renee was never able to confirm if he ever acted inappropriately with Cornelia or if he stopped just shy of that point, but she always got a slimy feeling when he left her room. And Cornelia didn't want to talk about it - she just wanted out. Renee didn't have to ask why.

And now, after all of their work, it came back to the same game of learning your enemies when they're masked as the people who care about you most.

Renee had felt hopeless for years at that point. She regretted ever sending her resume to that military clinic, that she had ever seen Dr. Ingels as someone who just wanted to save the world. Because even when she was finally done, when she had saved *that one person* that she always said would be worth all of the deaths and the debts, she had to *keep* saving her. She might have done it once, but does it count as saving someone if all of your attempts result in their death in the end, anyways?

Renee hoped Cornelia knew to stay away. They had taken risks for each other before, but Cornelia wouldn't remember any of that, or the unlikely friendship that bloomed in that clinic. And that's what Renee counted on.

After all of the plans and the scheming to take home the one person she could, Renee couldn't help but wonder: would she still have to save Cornelia *now* if she had been able to save Nate, then?

CHAPTER THIRTY SIX
Present Day, Connor's apartment

CW010217.mp4

A shadow walked by the window to the right of the screen. The angle was too severe to see through it from the camera's vantage point, but video-Cornelia noticed, turned and smiled, lifting a hand to wave.

"You know patient interaction is strictly supervised," the doctor warned her.

She turned back toward him. "You're supervising me now, aren't you?"

Cornelia sighed, closing her crossword. She had the look of someone who knew she was in for a long night.

Cornelia slammed on the space bar, pausing the video, and zoomed in on her hands.

She was wearing her engagement ring, but there was a second ring around that finger she hadn't seen before. It looked like a wedding band.

Nothing fancy, just a run-of-the-mill wedding band – but it was on her finger. That had to mean something.

Frozen, Cornelia stared at her screen, considering every possibility that would lead to a wedding band around her finger. Is that why she was suddenly more pleasant? Did he convince her to trust him, marry him? Did he pump that many drugs through her veins?

Cornelia navigated to the Vital Records Department of Maryland, her breath caught in her throat.

She thumbed the engagement ring that hung around her neck, wondering where its partner was now.

She read through the application process for a marriage license. She had thought that two people were required to apply for a marriage license, but apparently Maryland is a one-party consent state. Only one person had to show up at that County Clerk for a marriage license to be issued, for her freedom to be irrevocably taken away.

How would she even remedy this? Marriages might only require one person, but she was fairly certain divorces required two.

Marriage records were split by county, so she did a quick Google search to determine which was home to Fort Howard Veterans. Baltimore.

The thought crossed her mind that he had forged her signature. How low was he willing to go?

Maybe he had something on her – something much worse than her white-walled jail.

Cornelia stood, her laptop falling to the sofa next to her. She took a deep breath and paced.

The walls came in closer and closer as she walked circles around the room. It was too repetitive, too close, too overwhelming. She ripped her coat off the hook, pulled it around her shoulders and barreled down the stairs and out the front door into the chilly December night.

CHAPTER THIRTY SEVEN
Present Day, Liam's Hotel Room

Renee perched by her window, watching the people walk by beneath her, bundled up in their winter scarves, hats, puffy jackets. She could feel the lightness in the air that preceded Christmas – the extra laughter, warm lattes, time off work and strange family members you only see once a year.

Renee used her time in Liam's apartment to observe. He was harmless, but prone to throwing tantrums, and she assumed that was why she hadn't been "cleared" to leave.

She considered throwing a punch and running for it, or even trying to just sneak away, but she had taken plenty of crisis intervention courses. The last thing she wanted to do was escalate things. The doctor would calm down eventually.

Or so she told herself.

His hotel room was sparse and uninhabited. He kept a few weeks of warm clothes in his closet, a box of trinkets under the bed that looked random at best, and boxes upon boxes of medical journals strewn across the room, many of which were actual journals describing the treatment for specific cases.

Renee dedicated a few hours to combing through them, hoping to find the one about Cornelia. She was sure he had one - she had seen him scribbling in it every time he visited her.

She read through the journal of another of her ex-patients, Marco. He was there prior to Nathan and Cornelia, and was one of the first to be given Memory II. Before Cornelia arrived, Marcus was Dr. Ingels's pet. Although the doctor didn't show quite the same inappropriate bedside manner with Marcus, he still doled out special attention that other patients craved. While the doctor could have saved multiple lives, he spent his time doting on one or two.

Marcus never woke up from his second coma. As his condition worsened, the notes became short and haphazard. They stopped abruptly on August 15th, 2017.

She placed the notebook back in the box where she found it and opened another, Allison's. She had never woken up at all, but Renee took a second to fondly remember the way she smiled in her sleep.

The doctor's notes on her were even terser, almost rude. His observations lasted no more than a few lines each day, and her story came to an end suddenly, on August 15th.

Renee paused, and then shuffled through the journals to find Marcus's again. They ended on the same date.

She took out another book from the same box and, rather than reading through all of his notes, flipped right to the end. Also August 15th, 2017.

What happened on August 15th?

Renee put the books back and sat by the window again, looking to the quiet streets for hidden answers. She racked her brain. August 15th, August 15th, August 15th....

Liam had run an errand with Mike, so her and Josh were left alone, meandering around the small space. Renee preferred it that way, as her and Josh seemed to have a budding rapport.

Of course, she worried that Liam and Mike were out harassing Cornelia, but she was starting to wonder if Cornelia even needed her help anymore. She seemed perfectly capable of taking care of herself, while Renee only got herself in deeper the more she tried to help.

"What are you staring at?" Josh asked. He was doing a crossword puzzle at the table while Renee gazed lazily out the window. She wandered over to the seat next to him.

"Oh nothing," she said, twisting her head over his shoulder to read the clues of his puzzle.

"Oreo," she said, pointing to the clue that read "popular cookie."

"How do you know it's oreo?" he asked her. He followed

her finger through the clues.

"It's always oreo," she explained. He looked at the words around that number, and apparently decided he agreed with Renee. He wrote in oreo.

"No more hints," he said, smiling just a little. He shook his pen at her, giving her a stern look before turning his gaze back to the puzzle.

"What about questions?" she asked, slipping into the chair across from him.

He put his pen down and leaned back in his chair, refocusing his attention on her. "What do you mean by questions?"

"Who's been looking after Dr. Ingels's patients for the past two months while he's been here stalking mine?" she asked.

"Cornelia's your patient now?" Josh asked, crossing his arms. Evasive. Typical.

Renee shrugged. "I guess not at this point, but I like to think I help her. It may not be official, but I'm the closest she's had to proper medical care in months, even if it's only to make sure she's still breathing," she explained.

"So tell me," she repeated. "Who's taking care of his patients?"

"Look, I'm really not at liberty to discuss," Josh explained, shaking his head and holding his hands up, surrendering. Renee was sick of asking the same thing anyways.

"Whose payroll are you on, his or the hospital's?" she pushed.

"Renee, come on." Josh rolled his eyes at her and turned his attention back to his crossword puzzle.

"I noticed that you're wearing hospital attire but I don't see your key swipe," she said.

"Well we're not at the hospital, are we?"

"No. But isn't the point of finding Cornelia to bring her back to the hospital? How would you get her back to the hospital if you can't get in?"

"The doctor has a key," Josh explained, attempting to turn his attention back to the crossword.

"No he doesn't," Renee said, watching Josh's face as closely as she could. She was bluffing, but Josh wouldn't look at her anyways.

"Mike has one," Josh said. Bingo.

"No," Renee said. That, she had checked for. "He definitely doesn't."

"Why are you so concerned with how we're going to get into the hospital? We'll get in just fine, you don't need to worry."

"I'm not worried at all," Renee said. She paused to gauge his reaction, but he remained fixated on his crossword. "Because I don't think we're going back to the hospital."

He looked at her again. "And what would make you think that? Where else would we go?"

"I don't know. But I *do* know there's no way you'll even get into that hospital without a swipe card, which none of you have."

Josh shook his head in annoyance, entranced by his crossword.

"So either the three of you decided to go on a two-month tracking expedition, without pay, for just the one patient, or something happened after we left," Renee fished. She wanted to hear him say it. *The hospital closed.* Those fateful words.

"Nothing happened," he said. He was defensive, crossing his arms like a teenager getting interrogated by his parents. She watched him like a hawk.

"Then why are you here?"

He looked her in the eye, anger flashing across his face. "I'm here because that job was my only hope to feed my family. It's almost Christmas, and I'm in fucking Philadelphia instead of spending time with them. I'm here because we need the money. Does that answer your question?" She let the weight of his words dissipate into silence before continuing.

He stared blankly at the crossword. "Who's paying you?" she asked, softer this time.

He huffed. "The doctor," he conceded.

"What happened after we left the hospital?" Same soothing tone she used with patients' families.

He paused. "It was shut down." Her heart quickened.

"Why?" she asked. Mold or… malpractice?

"Honestly, Renee, I would just stop asking questions. He's not the same person he used to be. I've seen him do some horrifying things," he said.

She was stunned, and morbidly curious. She could tell *something* in the doctor had changed, mutated. If his life's work was suddenly taken away from him, though… she bet that would have a significant effect.

"What happened to the patients?" she asked.

"Sent to local hospitals. General transfers, for all of them," he explained. She wasn't sure how they would do that without extreme diversionary tactics, but she had more pressing questions.

"What happened to Nate Montgomery?"

Josh stood from the table, smoothing down his khaki pants. "*That*, I don't have the answer to."

Renee nodded, thinking of all of her zombie patients. She hoped they all landed in better places, in this life or the next.

"I have to go to the bathroom," Josh said, scooping up his pen and crossword. "I might be a while."

Renee scrunched up her nose. *Why would you tell someone that?*

He nodded to her, and made his way around the kitchenette to the tiny hidden bathroom.

Then, she understood.

She was on her feet in seconds, slipping quietly out of the hotel door to the carpeted hallway, tip-toeing along until she reached the fire escape. She pushed the door open slowly, carefully, and thankfully, no alarm was triggered. Cigarette butts covered the landing and further down, the asphalt below.

She climbed down to the dirty old alleyway and glanced in each direction. She didn't expect to run into anyone on her way out, but she kept an eye out just in case. She walked gingerly, the harsh pavement poking through her socks. She turned the corner at the end of the street and ran.

CHAPTER THIRTY EIGHT
Nine months and twenty-eight days earlier, Fort Howard
Neuro Clinic

Renee spent four days with her family while Uncle Joe recovered. By the time she arrived, he had already been transferred to the Coronary Care Unit. He was smiling, as usual, with his two sisters on either side. Her cousins sat next to their mom, and Renee claimed the seat next to hers for herself.

During the next few days, they spent a long weekend together. Uncle Joe wasn't happy about it being in a hospital, but her family was always quick to turn a bad situation positive. It was like a breath of fresh air.

By the time she returned to her own hospital, the tall brick walls suffocated her before she even walked through the front doors. She told herself it was just because she hadn't been able to get away from *any* hospital within the last two weeks, but she knew in her heart that the work she once loved was starting to wither on her. It would be time to move on soon.

As gratifying as it was to feel like she could help those who couldn't be helped by anyone else, she couldn't subject herself to a life of dread for the sake of others. She would find another hospital job – maybe one with more patient interaction – and hopefully, she could do some good there. Maybe not *as* much good, but she would settle for some.

How long should she wait before quitting? How quickly might she find another job?

She loved working with the Alzheimer's patients, mostly because she could see the difference in their treatment. She could see someone whose brain had been deteriorating for so long, suddenly level off. It wasn't a miracle, but it was a start. Maybe she could find a nursing home to work at temporarily while she looked for a promising clinical study she could apply to.

Renee pushed through the front doors as the clock chimed 7pm. That was another thing; maybe she could find a nice eight to five. The overnights were killing her.

She clocked in and sat at the computer behind the nurse's station. All was quiet in the hospital, the patients sleeping, the guards screwing around bored, and the doctor at home, leaving his little toy soldiers to play.

She pulled her hair back, the stack of paperwork next to the computer daunting.

But if she was quitting anyways, did it really need to get done *right now*?

Renee shrugged and decided to visit Cornelia instead.

She had expected Cornelia to be visiting Nate, so she tried his room first, but to her surprise, Nate was awake (though it was quite near his bedtime), and Cornelia was no-where in sight.

"Hey Nate, how you doing?" she asked, as she passed by his room.

His eyebrows scrunched together. "Good, how are you?" he asked, glancing up from the book he was reading. He didn't wait for her answer before returning to his reading material, the same kind of greeting you give to a coworker as you pass them in the hall.

"I'm alright," she said, pausing before she continued. That was... odd. Nate was usually a little more chatty.

She rounded the corner and walked down the hall to Cornelia's room, her footsteps echoing her heartbeat.

"Hey you," she said, walking right in. Cornelia was focused on a crossword puzzle, but smiled politely as Renee came up to her bed and perched on the edge.

"Hi," she said, resting her pen in the book and closing it.

"How are you? How were the past few days?" she asked, patting Cornelia's leg over the blankets.

"I'm okay," she sighed. "The past few days have really sucked but I think I'll be okay. I'm just taking it one day at a time."

Renee nodded, unsure where Cornelia was going. It sounded like she was joking, but sarcastic Cornelia usually had a little eye twitch and a faint smile. She seemed genuine.

"Did something happen?" Renee asked, unsure if she was supposed to be in on the joke.

"Well, yeah," she said. She looked as confused as Nate had.

"Is everything okay?"

Cornelia shook her head, her eyes narrowing. "Aren't you guys briefed on your patients?" she asked, crossing her arms. "I just woke up from a coma, my family is dead, my fiancé is dead, and I'm stuck in a hospital. Everything is very much not okay." Renee could see the tears welling up in Cornelia's eyes, the defensive note in her tone that sagged and chopped as she tried to hold it in.

Renee didn't know what to say. She stood, paused to debate in her head what exactly she should tell Cornelia, and then left, deciding time was what she needed most right now.

She sat down behind the nurse's station, flabbergasted, and cried, because the one person who made her job worth it no longer knew who she was.

CHAPTER THIRTY NINE
Present Day, Connor's apartment

Cornelia was not particularly looking forward to the holiday, but her presence at Christmas Eve dinner was the only gift Tanya asked for each year. Even before the accident, the whole family would take a deep breath and walk into the bohemian den of crazy with smiles on their faces.

In her defense, Cornelia never thought Tanya was *that bad*, she just had some quirks that were hard to get used to, and she talked *a lot*. The nice thing about her was that you really didn't have to participate in conversation – if you didn't say anything, she would just make it up as she went.

But if Cornelia was being honest with herself, she really just wanted to raid the filing cabinets for her medical documents. Tanya was the only person who was involved with her extended hospital stay, and her house was the only place Cornelia thought she might find something - any clue, any trace - of what might have happened while she was in a coma.

She wore her favorite red sweater, one of the few items that had survived the various yard sales, donation and trash piles that her stuff had been sorted into while she was sleeping. It was well worn, conforming to her body in ways that only well-worn clothing can.

Staring into Connor's bathroom mirror, she smoothed down the wrinkles. She noticed a pulled thread at the hem and clipped it with a pair of nail cutters. If she didn't know any better, she'd say she was damn normal.

How had so much changed, yet she looked exactly the same?

She had dyed her hair plenty of strange colors in high school and college, but she had never tried a color so normal as dark brown. It brought out the greenish tint in her eyes, the miracle of hair dye turning her into a different person.

She didn't normally wear makeup, but the sudden change in her appearance had her feeling daring. An old mascara tube had been floating around her duffel bag for the past few years. No time like Christmas for some Bambi eyes.

She held the tube between her thumb and finger. The motion was so familiar, yet the sensation on her eyelashes made them water, just like the very first time she ever applied makeup. The smell throttled her into her distant past: the college girl, the young adult, the first-job-out-of-college, the young professional... and someone new, someone with a totally different life story - one she was still trying to unravel.

She blinked at herself in the mirror. For a moment, she forgot all about Liam and the year she had missed. She *was* normal, just a girl going to her crazy aunt's house.

She took a deep breath and exited the bathroom, to find Connor tidying up the area she had claimed as her bedroom, folding up the sheets and making the sofa again. Two lit candles sat on the end table. Her stuff had already been packed away.

"Oh, I can clean that up," she said, quickly rushing toward him to finish collecting the sheets. Her heart beat faster, wondering again if she was bothering him.

"Don't worry about it, this is your area," he said, the collected sheets in a pile in his arms. He moved them toward the side of the sofa. "I just wanted to watch a movie and didn't want to be sitting in your bed clothes."

She wondered what it was he would be doing in the morning if he was spending Christmas Eve watching a movie.

"Don't you have family to visit tonight?" she asked.

Their relationship consisted mostly of morning coffee and training sessions – nothing personal. Despite the little rush of fire that surged through her veins every time his skin brushed along hers, they maintained their professionalism.

He shook his head.

"No, I don't have much family. My dad died while I was

in high school, my mom about 7 years ago now. I used to spend Christmas with my ex's family, but this year I'm kind of looking forward to avoiding the train wreck," he explained, chuckling. "Going to start my own tradition of wine and bacon."

"Wine and bacon?"

"Don't knock it 'til you try it," he said, stuffing the sheets further into the basket. Cornelia smiled, a little jealous of his plan. "I just wanted to clear off a little space for me to sit. I'll throw the sheets in the laundry with my stuff though, it'll be just as you left it when you get back."

Cornelia paused. "Why don't you come with me?" She recognized the attraction of alone time on a holiday, but something her mom said to her when Cornelia didn't want to come home from college one Easter stuck with her: "Alone time is great, but the whole point of family is to get on your nerves once in awhile. It wouldn't be a holiday if you didn't come home second-guessing your life decisions. In three hours you'll be more sure of yourself than you ever were before."

Cornelia had a long history of trying to get out of going to Tanya's house growing up, but it was mostly because she hated the smell of incense.

"To your aunt's?" he asked.

She nodded. "Yeah, I could use the distraction. She can be a little much sometimes, and this time of year she usually has a new soul mate she wants me to meet. It can take a lot of energy," she explained. She didn't know if she was grasping at straws for her own benefit or for Connor's.

"I wouldn't want to impede on family," he said, holding his hands up.

"We could *really* go for an imposition."

CHAPTER FORTY
Present Day, Aunt Tanya's

Tanya's new soul mate, Rob, was just as Cornelia expected – a little bit hippie and a little bit insane. In other words, he was perfect for Tanya. He talked about the moon's discourse and its' effect on house plants, while Cornelia and Connor nodded politely. Connor played a much better listener than Cornelia did.

The whole meal was prepared by the time they arrived, a beautiful Christmas spread of ham, various veggies and breads, spread across a red and green tablecloth. Two tall candles lit the room, drawing attention away from the otherwise cluttered and kitschy house.

"I don't know how we planned it this way, but my ham timer went off just as you arrived," Tanya said, waving her arms in the air with a jangle.

She wore dozens of bracelets between her two wrists that clanged together with her grandiose motions, several necklaces, and loose, long garb in many colors. Rob was dressed a bit more inconspicuously in an old 80's-style knit sweater and classic Levi's.

Cornelia and Connor left their coats on the rack by the door and followed the couple into the dining room. Bottles of wine had already been opened, and Tanya poured everyone a glass.

"It must have been the electro magnetism in the air tonight. It was palpable, did you guys feel it? Everything came together for us perfectly, thank goodness we're on the same plane as the universe," Tanya said, squeezing her fists together like she could feel the energy running through her. Her and Rob shared a glance and giggled to themselves.

Cornelia glanced at Connor, shrugging with a closed

smile. She wondered if she should have warned him.

Some time and several bottles of wine later, Cornelia asked Tanya the question that had been plaguing her for several weeks.

"Tanya, do you have any of my medical records saved?" Cornelia asked, as the conversation came to a lull.

Connor glanced at her, his eyebrows furrowed. Cornelia had gotten the sense that Connor enjoyed the hippie company, asking Tanya follow up questions about the moon and birth planes. He even went as far as to ask which days, according to the stars, he shouldn't be practicing martial arts. Cornelia had tried her hardest not to roll her eyes - she couldn't tell if Connor was playing to Tanya or if he was seriously interested.

"Of course, all of them," she said, with a wave of her hand, motioning generally to the ceiling above them.

"Thanks, do you mind if I take a look?" Cornelia asked.

"Go ahead dear. They're upstairs in the office, second cabinet down. There are a couple folders regarding your treatment in the second drawer of the filing cabinet, has your name on it," she said. "We can keep Connor entertained." She smiled and turned back to him.

Cornelia padded up the stairs into Tanya's small office, murmurs of conversation growing quieter as she ascended.

The office had once doubled as Cornelia's room before she found her own apartment. A pull out couch lined one side of the room, adjacent to a ramshackle dresser that had been passed between family members for years before coming to die in Tanya's office/spare bedroom. Long light-blocking curtains hung from the window, the edges illuminated by the street lamps outside, a remnant of Cornelia's first few weeks out of the hospital.

Cornelia flicked on the light and fixed on the filing cabinet. Like the dresser, it had seen better days. She noticed the small Easter bunny that lived on the window sill had been moved to the other side. *Odd,* she thought. She could see the dust outline of where it sat before, the imprint of at least ten years of silent bunny servitude. She moved him back to his proper place.

Stacks of paper interspersed with file folders crowded the top of the filing cabinet. The drawer third from the bottom stuck out, papers strewn about in such a way that it was impossible to close.

She started with the stacks on top, pulling them all down to the adjacent desk. It was old, dark wood, and covered with cloth consisting of every color in the visible spectrum, woven together with rough gold string. Every time Cornelia tried to rearrange a stack, her papers got stuck between threads and she had to wiggle them free.

The stack on top of the filing cabinets turned out to be just a summary of Tanya's past year. One folder contained her phone bills – every single call she had made for the past twelve months - gas bill, and electric bills, including graphs of her monthly usage.

Cornelia pushed the pile of bills back on the top of the cabinet and started in on the third drawer. This one looked like a mix of school documents and Tanya's own medical records. Cornelia got excited, thinking maybe all familial medical records would be filed in the same place.

She read through what felt like hundreds of academic papers about holistic medicine and the benefits of shunning western medicine in favor of shamans and healers. Some of them detailed Tanya's own experience working with a shaman, as well as home remedies for some sort of skin rash and a variety of symptoms that could easily have been cured with some ibuprofen and the regular consumption of vegetables.

Another stack done, Cornelia stretched out her limbs and rolled her neck. She hadn't kept track of the time, but her body was starting to ache like it was time for another glass of wine.

She shook out her limbs and moved the third drawer out of the way.

The fourth looked promising when she opened it up. It was a little more organized, and although Cornelia would have killed for some labels, she could tell by the colors and tissue-thin paper that these were legitimate hospital records – not homeopathic crap for Tanya. She dumped the entire contents out onto the desk, and started at the top.

In true Tanya form, she had requested copies of every test and report she could get her hands on. Cornelia read through every ailment she was admitted with. Broken leg, broken ribs, collapsed lung, etc... patient admitted unresponsive....

She skipped through the earlier documents, searching for timestamps beginning about a month later.

As she came to the end of the stack, her heart sank, recognizing the good chance that there *was* no documentation.

The very last sliver of paper in the stack was a contract, signed by Tanya Winthorp and Dr. Liam Ingels.

Cornelia was not well versed in contract law, but as she read through, it became increasingly apparent that Tanya hadn't even read it. No sane person would sign it if they had.

The patient may receive any therapies that have a possibility of improving quality of life. The patient may receive other therapies that could or could not benefit quality of life but would contribute to research by Dr. Liam Ingels.

Cornelia's stomach flipped.

She read through, again and again. She didn't have to read between the lines to see that Liam had covered his ass all the way through. No privacy policy, no document that outlined context; nothing except for Tanya's signature on a piece of flimsy copy paper that signed her life away, to *him.*

The question popped into her mind of legality, but at this point, what could she really do?

She was out, she was safe, and regular police wouldn't touch her with a ten foot pole.

ALEXANDRA WILLIAMS

◆ ◆ ◆

Cornelia and Connor walked home in silence. Cornelia had disappeared for an hour upstairs, looking for medical records, and came down somber and removed. He couldn't find the right way to ask what happened.

He happily chatted with her family, and though he wasn't all that into holistic medicine, he found their kind of affliction endearing, an interesting concept at least. He liked passionate people, and though Cornelia probably didn't want to admit it, he saw the same sort of passion in her that he did in her aunt, albeit deployed quite differently.

He still wasn't sure what plagued Cornelia in her past and especially in their present, but he could see it weighing on her. She had an expressive demeanor – forward and abrupt when engaged, withdrawn and shrunken when bothered.

It was something he picked up on when they first met - she knew what she was doing, and she did it confidently, but as soon as she was taken out of that zone, she shrunk into a smaller person. Usually when she was bothered, it was fleeting, wiped away with a quick joke or fast jab to the gut, but this felt different.

He didn't know much about her. He didn't know where she worked before, or what became of the accident she was in. She knew she had dealt with death... but to what extent? Was it even appropriate to ask?

They came to his doorstep, cold air swishing Cornelia's hair around below her hat.

"Everything okay?" he asked her, nudging her elbow. She glanced up and smiled, seemingly surprised that he was even there.

"Yeah, just... have some stuff on my mind," she explained, shaking her head like that might make the worry fall out.

He unlocked the front door and pushed through.

"You know you can tell me," he said, shrugging. "If you want."

As much as he didn't want to bring the past up, he couldn't help but think of Kate. Whenever she was quiet like that it meant she was pouting. It took Connor the longest time to figure out that "something on my mind" meant he had done something wrong. Now he just couldn't shake that feeling.

"Yeah, I just… it's personal," she murmured.

The nail in the coffin. The end all, be all of "stop asking." He had been wondering where they stood. Now he knew.

He felt a wall go up, an insurmountable divide between them. He had thought the dinner invite was at least a friendly thing, but her tone confirmed it: it was just pity.

Not wanting to act any more unprofessionally, he had refrained from bringing it up, at least until they were done training. He didn't want to be *that guy*, anymore than he already was. He felt foolish the first time he asked her out, like a teenager under the influence of his own hormones. Now his foolishness was confirmed, solidified, impenetrable.

"I understand."

Some part of him thought that she called *him* of all people because she wanted him to help her – she wanted *him* to be the person she could rely on in whatever battle she was fighting. But she would have taken anyone, anyone at all with a spare couch and the desire to be a hero.

He should have learned the first time.

He walked up the stairs first, followed by Cornelia after she shut and locked the front door. He unlocked his apartment and barreled in, flipping on the lights as he went and dumping his jacket and hat on the rack by the door.

Now, if only he could escape his own thoughts. With Cornelia on his couch, he expected they would follow him.

"Hey," she said. She hadn't taken off her outerwear. He turned to her, raising his eyebrows. "I just meant that I have some stuff that I'm still working through in my head. It's not that it's personal, it's just that I want to work through them myself first. In time, I'll explain everything." She nudged his elbow, just like he had hers. She smiled, and despite himself, he felt assured Cornelia was nothing like Kate.

One day, she would explain it all to him. He trusted that.

"I get it," he said. "Take your time."

"Thank you," she said, smiling.

She turned to the coat rack to hang up her things, brushing through her static-y hair as she pulled her knit cap off. He didn't want the night to end.

It's A Wonderful Life sat on the TV stand, a relic of the night's thwarted plans.

"I propose a movie," he said, grabbing the flimsy case and wiggling it between his fingers. "What do you say?"

She nodded. "That sounds perfect," she said.

"If you pop the wine, I'll pop the popcorn," he offered.

"Also sounds perfect," she said, her gloom slowly fading. She padded over to the kitchen and took a look at the wine rack. Connor followed, pulling a bag of popcorn from a box in the cabinet above the fridge.

"Which wine?" she asked, peering at the dusty labels in the wine rack.

He came up behind her and glanced at the bottles. He wasn't a huge wine drinker, other than special occasions, so the majority of his bottles had been gifts. Most of the labels he recognized as cheap wines you could get at the supermarket, but one came from a particularly wealthy client at Philly MMA. He slid it from the rack and held it out to Cornelia, label up like at all the fancy restaurants.

"I've been saving this one for someone special," he said. He hadn't meant it the way it sounded – he just *didn't* drink wine by himself and it wasn't the sort of wine he wanted to throw around willy-nilly.

"Alright then," she said, and grabbed the magnetic corkscrew from the fridge. He couldn't gauge her reaction - charmed? Grossed out? Oblivious?

Connor threw the popcorn in the microwave, set it to two minutes, and turned to see Cornelia struggling to get the cork out of the bottle. The screw had gone in lopsided, skimming the side of the bottle rather than the heart of the cork.

He reached over her shoulders, screwed it in a little further than comfortable, and popped the cork right out.

"Show off," she said, turning around. She had a little smirk on her face that was cat-like, adorable but simultaneously incredibly sexy.

They were close, Cornelia leaning back against the counter. He couldn't help but lean down and kiss her, this strange little bird who tasted like sweet apples and cherry chapstick.

Their bodies pressed easily together, and he touched her.

Arms entangled, legs, fingers, hair, dancing clumsily away, knees, breath, sheets, bodies....

CHAPTER FORTY ONE
Nine months and twenty-four days earlier, Fort Howard
Neuro Clinic

When Renee had a chance to calm down and check on both Nate and Cornelia, their charts gave her the entire story.

The day Renee left to visit her uncle, both patients were administered Memory II, the drug that erases everything that Memory I tagged. It also showed a second dose of Memory I, meaning the doctor was beginning the process all over.

He told them they had just woken up from a long coma, that they were *both* the lone survivor.

He had also scheduled their therapies to be conducted in separate parts of the building. Cornelia was chauffeured up to the second floor, where she spent her day until she was exhausted, and then they sent her back downstairs to sleep. Nate still did his therapy in the rec room, which was just across the hall from his room. All other patients were still sleeping.

Renee had gone back and forth, back and forth - should she tell them or should she not? Was it healthier to let them heal or give them knowledge? In all the scenarios Renee had pictured coming back to, she had never considered this one before.

Her internal battle ended with a verdict of "tell them." Whether Cornelia remembered her or not, Renee knew her, and she knew without a doubt in her mind that Cornelia prioritized knowledge over comfort.

But Renee started with Nate first, also knowing that of the two, he was much more likely to react rationally.

"Hey Nate," she said, knocking on his doorframe. She had taken precaution over the past few days to treat Nate and Cornelia as if she had never met either of them. "Do you mind if we talk for a minute?" She held two clipboards – one with

Nate's chart, and one with Cornelia's.

"Sure," he said. He folded the newspaper he had been reading and rested it on the chair next to his bed. "What's up?"

"Have you gotten a chance to look at your chart at all?" she asked him, holding out the first clipboard to him.

"No," he said, his eyebrows scrunching together. He hesitantly took the clipboard and read through, lifting each page as he skimmed. He looked to her and shook his head. "I'm sorry, I don't really understand. What is it you want me to see?"

She perched on the side of his bed and flipped through to the summary page.

"Why don't you read through this?" she said.

He took a few moments to read through the page. He shook his head. "I really don't know what you want me to see, I don't understand any of this, it's all medical jargon." He handed the clipboard back to her.

"Did you notice you were given three Memory drugs?" she asked.

He nodded. "Yeah, I assume that's par for the course with a brain injury, right?" he asked her.

"It can be, but in this case, it's not," she said. She pointed to the page so Nate could follow her thought process. "You were given a variety of barbiturates when you first came in. You'll see that they were all given fairly regularly before July, and then they drop off. The last drug administered in that period was Memory I. Then you woke up," she explained, tracing the timeline in the chart.

He narrowed his eyes, scanning through the summary page again. "I don't understand, I only woke up a week ago, and I got one shot after that, not two," he said, lifting up the summary page as if looking for a replacement. "Is there an error?"

"Look at the dates."

"So I was given Memory I, Memory II, and Memory I again? I guess the combination finally got me going?" he asked, looking to her for clarification.

"You can only be given Memory I when you've been awake for some time," she said.

"So I was awake before I was... awake? Is that normal?" he asked.

"No. That's not the intention of these drugs," she said, and took the chart back from him, lying it on top of Cornelia's. "They have nothing to do with your wellbeing. They're experimental, a procedure Dr. Ingels has been working on for a very long time. Memory I tags your memory as it's created. Memory II erases it," she said, and then held her breath.

He was silent for a few breaths. "What?" he asked, sitting up straighter as his muscles allowed. "I'm sorry, what is this, are you fucking with me?"

"No, Nate," she said, and almost laughed, his sometimes callous nature endearing, once you got to know him. Then she remembered *he* didn't know *her*, and stopped herself. "I'm trying to explain to you that you were awake for a significant period of time, and then induced into another coma-like state by Memory II. The shot you remember getting was Memory I. Again."

"Is that... a common procedure?" he asked.

"No."

He blinked. "So what are you trying to tell me?"

She took a deep breath. "You're part of a medical trial that you didn't agree to. One of the treatments that was intended to wake up hopeless coma patients also has an effect on memory, and when combined with the next two drugs in the trial, it acts as an eraser. Unless we find a way to get you out of here, it's eventually going to happen again.

He was quiet, processing.

"Haven't you wondered how you're so strong after being in a coma for so long?" she asked softly.

He bit his lip, his eyes roaming.

"Do you have any proof?" he finally asked.

She stood and dismantled the camera facing his bed. She popped in the memory card she had stolen from the doctor's office and flipped through the gallery until she found a video from two weeks before. She played the video through for Nate.

"Okay," he said when he was finished, handing the camcorder back to her. "How do I know that's not doctored?"

"I thought you might ask that," she said, nodding. Par for the course - Nate was a skeptic. "And the only way I could think of proving this to you otherwise is through confirmation from someone you know and trust. Cornelia."

"Cornelia, my fiancée Cornelia?" he asked. His voice flattened, dark and stormy. "Cornelia. Really. Well, I guess that sucks then, because she's dead." He slunk down into his bed and turned away from her. "Go away, I don't care anyways. Fuck with my memory all you want."

"She's not dead. That's what the doctor told you. I can take you to her, but you'll need to wait until I can explain this all to her, too."

He turned back toward her, just a little. He was silent for what felt like a lifetime.

"Did they... do this to her too?" he asked. A wave of relief washed through her; he believed her.

Renee nodded. "Yes," she said.

When he said nothing else, Renee continued.

"I have a collection of her crosswords from when she first woke up. She'll be able to identify her own handwriting and confirm that she was at least awake."

Nate didn't move.

"Do you want to see the crosswords? Or her charts?" she asked. She hadn't planned on showing him Cornelia's charts, clinging to boundaries that had no place in her world anymore, but she was grasping at straws here. If anyone found out she was sharing patient information... well, she was already in enough trouble as it was.

Nate turned his head almost imperceptibly and held out his hand. "The crosswords."

She unclipped the stack from beneath Cornelia chart and handed them over.

"She started with the puzzles in the Baltimore Sun, but she got bored quickly so we got her a book. The doctor replaced it when he wiped her memory, but I don't think he realized I kept the ones from the newspaper.

He didn't say anything as he looked over them. Renee felt the need to explain herself further.

"They were fascinating to look over. You can see the strength returning in her motor skills, as well as her brainpower growing. If I didn't know any better, the first ten or so were filled out by a second grader, chicken scratch and obviously wrong answers," she said.

She could have gone on, detailing the way Cornelia attacked a puzzle like that. The doctor watched interactions, studied mannerisms, pored over brain waves, but Renee had the crosswords. Sometimes the most telling chart is the one the patient writes herself.

Nate sat up, reading through. He spread them across his lap, and Renee was happy to see that he was double checking they were in chronological order, just as she had expected.

"Oreo," he muttered, running his finger over the only filled line in one of her earlier puzzles.

"Oreo?"

When looking through Cornelia's crosswords, she did notice the word 'oreo' was scribbled frequently, but she figured it was a fascination with the treat. After all, everyone loves oreos, and you never know what's going to be important in someone's mind after such a traumatic injury.

Nate looked up at her. "Oreo," he repeated, and then started reading through the clues, jumping from one puzzle to the next. "Cream-filled cookie. Cookie. Black and white cookie. Cookie. Popular cookie. Two-toned cookie."

"Yeah, I guess they like using 'oreo' a lot. Is that significant to you?" she asked.

"Look here," he said, pulling the first few crosswords Cornelia had done. He pointed at the first crossword. "Oreo is the one word she fills in on every sheet, even in the beginning."

He paused, smiling. He looked into Renee's eyes. "That's the word she looks for first. Before trying to fill in anything else, she always looks for oreo."

"Why?" She couldn't imagine the word was that popular.

"When we lived in Philadelphia, the occurrence of 'oreo' in the daily crossword was something like 50%. It's for the vowels. That was her shortcut to always feel like she got a word in," he said. He looked through some of the more recent crosswords, his fingers trailing over every ink mark. "It looks like at first she filled in oreo wherever it would fit, it's the only word on the first few. The clue doesn't match, but... I don't think anyone other than Cornelia would have filled in a crossword like this."

Renee helped him gather up the papers and clipped them back under Cornelia's charts, a triumphant smile glued to her face.

"Well then," she said. "Shall we go see her?"

CHAPTER FORTY TWO
Present Day, Philly MMA

Connor had just finished his second morning class. The blonde moms that came in five days a week were on their game, but Connor kicked it up a notch, just to see how they would do. Most petered out within the last fifteen minutes.

He grabbed his stuff and watched as the ladies meandered out of the room. And one man.

On occasion, a random guy would come into a self-defense class, and although Connor promoted knowledge of self-defense for *anyone,* this was the first time he got such a... strange feeling.

The man seemed nice enough, courteous and willing to learn, but Connor *just didn't like him.* He moved with ease and confidence, and watched Connor like a hawk, a kind of gaze that lingers even after the gazer is gone.

Once everyone was out, he closed the door, locking the group room behind him.

Leanne was behind the front counter with her oldest kid, showing him something on the computer. He had been seeing her less and less, and whenever she was in the gym, she usually had her 12-year-old, Brian, with her. Leanne was a long time teacher at the gym, and as she moved toward a family life, she brought Brian in to help pick up her slack. He was shy at that age, but smart and more importantly, trustworthy. Connor was happy to have him, especially if he would help pick up the pace while his mom was out.

When he was Brian's age, Kate was everything he wanted – a hot blonde freak of a girlfriend who drank champagne in bubble baths and drove a new Range Rover every year. If they had been completely honest with each other from the beginning, they probably both could have avoided some heartbreak.

They met when she was 22 and he was 29. He always thought that she would grow up over time, but now that she was 27 and he was 34, he realized that her immaturity was something that wouldn't just go away. She still went running to daddy whenever she didn't get what she wanted, and thanks to daddy, Connor was taken for just about everything he owned. The house, the cars, every piece of furniture they bought together – all of it went to her.

Part of Connor was thankful for that. It was a clean break – if he had nothing left to give, there was nothing left for her to take. Let someone else deal with her.

With the little money he scraped together at the tender age of 35, he bought Philly MMA right when it went up for sale. It was perfect timing.

After a year of struggling to put himself back together, he regularly got up on time, cooked a mean steak and potatoes, and ran Philly MMA well enough that he was even starting to turn a profit.

And then Cornelia... this strange, ragged girl stumbled into his gym. He had known her from afar for years, and technically, she had some seniority over him. Years ago, she had overseen the birth of the self-defense program. She was half the reason all the blonde moms came to these classes – at least, according to Leanne's (undoubtedly embellished) history lesson. He wasn't sure he saw a revolution in her, but she was good.

She had been gone for a long time, no leave of absence or resignation; she just disappeared. And then, a year and a half later, she turned up again and started coming to the gym by herself, always wearing the same black hoodie, headphones audible from two feet away. She didn't talk to anyone, and Connor suspected if you got between her and the punching bag, she would show no hesitation.

She lost weight, maybe 15 pounds judging from her old ID picture. She still looked healthy, but she looked less like the blonde moms now, and more like one of their angry teenagers.

Connor never understood what it was that made her twitch when she heard noises in the night. She had nightmares and some odd compulsions. She checked the locks three times before going to bed and never sat by windows she couldn't see through. He asked time and time again, but she would go silent, preferring awkwardness over openness, something that made Connor weary.

He looped around to the other side of the counter next to Leanne and Brian. She was teaching him how to work the client check-in. In the past, Leanne made some theoretical comments about Brian helping out at the gym, and Connor was happy it was still a possibility.

A few minutes later, they finished their lesson and said a brief goodbye. A few guys in the free weight area could be heard dropping, but Connor ignored it since there was no one else there for the noise to bother. He was alone, silence descending quickly around him.

Cornelia was in the far corner with her punching bag, her headphones likely dangerously loud, just the way she liked it. It was one of the few times he saw her zone out, the rest of the world arbitrary scenery. He expected she was channeling a little unresolved anger, so he never bothered her while she was in the zone.

But he did keep tabs on her while she was there, curious what her typical routine was like, only to discover she didn't *have one.* She warmed up randomly, throwing in stretches on one side without always matching on the other, switching from jabs to hooks to hammers to chops. The first time he saw her throw out a roundhouse, he realized why she could surprise him sometimes – she didn't plan further than could be predicted.

Connor put his feet up on the desk and fiddled with his phone – something he wouldn't do on any normal day, but the only people there were Cornelia and the guys in free weights – buddies he had known for years. The gym was really only open for them.

Just then, the bell on the front door clanged and two men walked in, one wearing street clothes and the other wearing what looked like a security guard uniform. The man in street clothes strode confidently to the desk, and Connor recognized him from his class, the one who gave him such an odd feeling. Liam, was his name?

The other man made a beeline for the far corner of the gym, where Cornelia was deep in her workout.

"Can I help you?" Connor asked, standing to watch where the other man had gone.

"We're just here to pick someone up," he said, smiling.

Connor looked over his shoulder, and felt his gut kicking in. He had no doubt she could fend for herself, but that's a lot harder when you don't see the fight coming.

"Corey!" he shouted.

She didn't hear him. Liam was now following the security guard with a relaxed arrogance.

On one hand, he hated leaving the desk unattended. On the other hand, he had a gut feeling he was needed elsewhere.

Connor grabbed a tennis ball from the desk and chucked it across the gym, hitting Cornelia square in the center of her back. She whipped around, scowling, and took stock of her surroundings, her eyes growing wide as she took a step back.

The man in the security uniform was about ten feet from her when she turned, the tennis ball rolling sloppily away, bumping over the feet of equipment. He stopped short, hesitating.

Connor couldn't hear what he said as he held out a paper for Cornelia to read and she stepped back, shoving the paper away. He advanced.

Keeping his eyes on her the entire time, Connor hoisted himself up and over the desk. As Cornelia retreated, the guard reached to grab her arm, and without hesitation, she popped him in the nose. He stumbled, but reached out for her again.

Connor waited a moment, unsure what level of intervention was necessary. He had told Cornelia plenty of times that no matter how strong and experienced she gets, the first thing she needed to do is run. His curiosity was piqued; what was her next move?

The second man – Liam – took a step toward them and Connor pulled him back by the collar. He was easily unbalanced, stepping back and flailing like someone swiped the ground right out from under him. He gave the man a quick shove and table-topped him over a bench.

Cornelia made fist to jaw contact with the security guard, the sound of teeth clashing together audible. In the split second during which he closed his eyes and brought his hands to his face, Cornelia hit him with a roundhouse, toppling him over a bench and onto his buddy. He rolled away, struggling to get to his hands and knees while Liam pushed him off.

He rebounded back to her, and managed to land a jab to her right eye. Connor's heart kick-started. Why didn't he step in sooner? He moved forward, and while his attention was focused on Cornelia, Liam kicked his knees out. He caught himself before hitting the floor. Liam recoiled, using a bench to pull himself up, and with a newfound rage boiling in his veins, Connor landed a fist to his gut. He stumbled but stood.

Connor went for his face and he retreated, backing up to the wall.

"Okay, okay, it's not me you want, it's him!" Liam shouted, pointing to the security guard that Cornelia now straddled on the ground. She landed punch after punch as he struggled and failed to fight back.

Connor realized the sounds of weights dropping had stopped. The gym stood in eerie silence, something that didn't usually happen during waking hours. He glanced over his shoulder and saw the guys from the weight room had formed a haphazard semi-circle behind them, watching Cornelia.

For a fleeting moment, Connor's rage subsided and

reason returned. He realized Cornelia was on the verge of murder; she wasn't stopping.

"Corey!" he shouted, springing behind her and grabbing her by the upper arms. He pulled her off the guard, whose face by then looked like a patchy quilt of red. Connor breathed a sigh of relief, noticing he was still fully conscious. If someone a little stronger than Cornelia had gone to town on him the way she did, he wouldn't be so lucky. And they'd all be liable.

Cornelia was still throwing punches, even as Connor wrapped both arms around her.

"Corey you have to chill, you cannot kill someone," he said to her, hoping a calm voice might bring her back to reality.

"They tried to kill *me!*" she spat, even as the two men struggled to stand. They glanced around the gym at the ring around them – a body builder, two martial artists, and a guy who had just started at the gym but seemed very able.

"We'll get them another way," Connor told her, and felt her slowly relax in his arms. He held her a few more seconds, just in case she was bluffing.

The security guard stepped forward, grabbing the paper from where it fell next to a pull-up machine. He held it out to Connor.

"We have a warrant," he explained. "She's a danger to herself and those around her." Monotone. He wouldn't look either of them in the eye.

Connor looked at both men. Something about this was very, very wrong. He took the paper and ripped it, dropping the shreds on the ground in front of them.

"And I have confetti."

No one responded.

"I better never see either of you again," he said. The two men shuffled lamely out of the gym.

Connor loosened his grip on Cornelia, but she stayed where she was, leaning back into him. He kissed her cheek.

"Wow, that was awesome!" the new guy shouted as their

small circle dispersed, eyes wide with excitement.

Connor laughed despite himself, and he could feel the beginning shakes of a giggle in Cornelia. The body builder rolled his eyes and moved back to the free weights, the new guy following him while still shaking his head in wonder. The two martial artists went back to the mats they had set up in one of the classrooms.

"Does that happen all the time?" the new guy asked his body builder friend. The body builder slapped him gently on the shoulder, shaking his head.

Cornelia turned around in front of Connor, winding her arms around his torso. He held her tight.

CHAPTER FORTY THREE
Present Day, Connor's apartment

All she wanted was a shower, to wash the day's activity off of her body and down the drain.

She padded into the bathroom. She was exhausted, but after a hot shower she could go to bed and wake up a whole new person.

If only.

She turned the shower on, the cold water assaulting the delicate skin on her knuckles, and closed the shower door, letting it heat.

Cornelia braved a glance at herself in the mirror. She brushed her fingers over the dark circle forming underneath her eye and flinched, the skin tender.

In the moment, she barely noticed the fist collide with her eye. It felt no more harmful than the tennis ball that bounced off her back. *And I mean, you should have seen the other guy....*

She wasn't too concerned with her injuries – after all, it wasn't like anything was broken. She would have a black eye for a few days and she'd have to wear some loose pants over the bruise forming on her hip, but it was nothing she couldn't work with. She had seen much worse.

No, what she was most concerned with was that Liam had come back with reinforcements. Previously, he had insisted he just wanted to talk, but it seemed that ship had sailed.

If it weren't for a measly tennis ball, she might have indeed left with Liam. She shuddered at the thought.

She shook the idea from her head. No use getting caught up in what could have been.

"Are you sure you're okay?" Connor asked. He stripped

off his sweaty t-shirt as he came up behind her.

"I'm fine. Really," she said, turning to face him. Her eye felt hot, puffy. "I just don't understand why he would try something like that at an MMA gym. With you there, and I'm trained enough to hold my own at least. I just don't get *why*," she trailed off, staring at herself in the mirror. It seemed like pretty obvious logic, not to attack someone in a martial arts gym.

Connor rested his hands on her shoulders, warm and strong, calloused skin rubbing against hers. "I've known guys like him before," Connor sighed. "You can tell when they come in, overbearing and confident. It's just arrogance, Corey," he murmured into her neck.

"But what does that say about me? He has to know I'm a self-defense teacher. Why would you even try?" she asked. "Am I that weak, that unintimidating?"

"Hey," he said, pulling her around to face him. "This has nothing to do with *you.* You can't control how other people act, what they come up with in their own mind. Yeah, he might have thought little of you this morning, but you proved him wrong. That's what counts."

She hmmed, unsatisfied. "If you hadn't thrown that tennis ball at me, I wouldn't be here right now," she insisted.

"You don't know that, Corey. You underestimate yourself," he said, kissing the skin at the base of her neck. He lifted her chin, staring at the ring forming around her eye. Holding her cheek, he brushed his thumb lightly over the skin underneath the bruise. It sent shivers down her spine, such a contrast to the heat and tenderness. She closed her eyes as he kissed her.

"Did he get you anywhere else?" he asked.

She nodded. "I whacked my hip off one of the machines when he pushed me down," she said, running her fingertips over the bone and feeling the tenderness there, too.

He reached to the hem of her t-shirt and lifted it over her head. The bruise started just over the top of her leggings.

Careful not to hit the marbling skin, he pulled her leggings down over her ankles and into a pile on the floor. It was eight inches high and four wide, already dark black and blue.

"That must hurt," he said, lightly brushing the undisturbed skin around it.

She nodded. "It really fucking hurts."

He bent down and kissed the skin on her hip, just above the bruise.

"If you weren't there to help me, I probably wouldn't be here right now," she repeated, the thought running through her mind over and over again. As hard as she tried to need no one, she always felt like she was relying on someone else.

He smiled at her, his lips still grazing the skin above her hip. "You're stronger than you think," he mumbled, his words muffled in her belly button.

His lips moved to the center of her body, and she temporarily forgot about the pain as she slowly dissolved into a state of pure bliss.

CHAPTER FORTY FOUR
Nine months twenty-three days earlier, Fort Howard Neuro Clinic

Renee was surprised and entertained when Cornelia's thought process matched Nate's almost verbatim. She was skeptical until she saw the crosswords.

"This is my handwriting," she confirmed, resting the crosswords on her lap. A few moments passed in silence. "So... you're telling me, Nate's alive?" Her eyes weren't sad, per se, but Renee still couldn't get her to smile.

Renee nodded.

"And you and I were friends," she said. Renee hadn't expected that. "Before... all of this," she said, waving vaguely to the charts and crosswords.

"We were... friends, yes," she said.

"I'm sorry," Cornelia said.

Renee was taken aback. "For what?"

"I was an asshole to you. I saw the recognition in your face, you looked at me that way that you look at someone you know," she said, shaking her head. "I'm not explaining it well. You know, you look at someone and it's like everything you've done together or talked about is held within that look, even if it's just a smile to say hello."

Something in her eased, the confinement of their friendship no longer necessary. It would never again be like it was, but now there was *something*, even if it wasn't much.

Renee nodded. "I know what you mean."

"I saw it and I ignored it because I was angry at the world. And I'm sorry," she repeated. "I should have known, I should have put that together. This whole hospital stay has been weird. I've felt off since waking up," she said, and paused, thinking. "I wonder if I felt this weird the last time I woke up."

"Probably not," Renee said. She had no idea, but she hoped it would ease her mind nonetheless.

"So when do I get to see him?" Cornelia asked, her voice bubbly, her eyes brightening.

"Nate?" The sudden change of subject had thrown her.

"Of course."

Renee smiled. "What, am I not good enough for you anymore?"

"Oh, stop. Come on, where is he?" she asked, laughing.

She pushed the blankets off her legs and stood next to Renee, rocking onto her toes, biting her lip. She inched toward the door, and before Renee said anything, Nate swept in and hugged her. Renee couldn't help but smile.

"Corey," he said.

"Nate," she whispered.

Renee slipped out while they embraced, pulling the door shut quietly. She sat down at the nurse's station, and taking a satisfied breath, thought that maybe moments like that made all the shit slinging worth it.

Renee busied herself with paperwork, the shit slinging slightly less dirty that day.

An hour or so later, Nate stepped out of Cornelia's room and rounded the nurse's station to sit next to her.

"Everything okay?" she asked, happily ignoring her busywork.

"More than okay," he said, grinning. He spun in his chair and rolled over to her. He had more energy than she had ever seen him with before. His voice was low, nearly a whisper. "I wanted to talk to you. I need a really big favor, and I need you to not tell Cornelia."

CHAPTER FORTY FIVE
Present Day, Connor's apartment

CW011017.mp4

"Cornelia, you have let us know what's happening in your head right now," Dr. Ingels said. He pulled her armchair up to the side of the bed and sat, pen poised over his notebook.

She stared blankly. The doctor encouraged her to tell him anything and everything that popped into her head. "You *must* be having some extreme changes in your emotions right now," he insisted. "What are you feeling? What are you thinking?"

Cornelia ignored the questions.

"How does loss make you feel?"

She glanced down to the sheets bunched in her lap.

"This is very important in terms of monitoring your progress," the doctor pressed.

She glanced to him quickly. Her eye twitched and her jaw clenched.

"Have recent events affected your ability to process emotions? You seem very closed off today," the doctor remarked, scribbling in his book. Cornelia stared straight ahead. He waited another 30 seconds, watching.

"Well if that's how you're going to be, I'll just leave you to work through your emotions on your own," he said. He flashed briefly in front of the screen as he exited the room, Cornelia's eyes following him as he went. She took a visibly deep breath once he was gone.

She sniffled, leveling her gaze to the sheets covering her legs, and sank into her bed, turning on her side so all the camera could view was a shaking lump of sheets. Small sniffles, shaking blankets.

The video went on for another 45 minutes until a brunette nurse stole into the screen, her footsteps quiet as a mouse. She placed something on the bedside table that looked like a chocolate bar. In her other hand, she held a teddy bear.

"Cornelia?" she asked gently, putting a hand on the covers.

The covers parted, and a mess of brownish hair poked out.

"I'm so sorry," the nurse said, moving the teddy bear gently into Cornelia's arms.

She kicked off her shoes and scooted into bed next to Cornelia, pulling her in for a hug. The nurse rocked her as Cornelia's whimpers turned into sobs. They stayed that way for eight minutes and 47 seconds, until Cornelia asked her to check if the camera was off.

"I'm so sorry."

Cornelia didn't want to believe it at first, that anyone in that clinic wasn't absolutely evil, but she was starting to warm up to this nurse who brought her jammies and comforted her when she was so upset.

But why *was* she so upset? There were few things in life that could affect her so severely. She assumed she had just been told her family died. Maybe Nate.

But something didn't add up – the date on the video was closer to when she woke up than it was to her accident. Surely they wouldn't have waited that long to tell her the fate of her family.

And who was this nurse who came to her rescue? If the doctor was doing everything he could to find Cornelia, should she have been looking out for this little brunette woman too? She thought the nurse looked familiar, but so had the doctor.

Cornelia rewound the tape and focused on her. She had wispy brown hair, and a short, thin, stature. She wore plain blue scrubs and jogging shoes, and looked like half the nurses in Philadelphia.

She glanced into the camera for a second as she maneuvered around the bed, and Cornelia paused the video again to stare at the details of her face.

So familiar.

If it was the right date, something terrible happened, only weeks before she officially woke up.

She saw no reason why the filename might be wrong, unless Liam had intentionally thwarted a few timestamps for shits and giggles. And after Cornelia had picked it up, there was no way he could access it - she only ever looked through the USB disk while disconnected from the internet.

So assuming the timestamp was correct...

Something devastating happened, just after Christmas last year.

A thought in the back of her mind tingled, breaking the surface of her consciousness.

It was something she yearned for, hoped for, would give anything for, but would never ever let herself truly feel. It would be too painful.

When Detective Sturgess asked her about the current whereabouts of her fiance, his lack of death certificate surprised her. She assumed that was an institutional thing - shouldn't they be able to look that up?

She could understand why it might not have been filed with her immediate family's death certificates. They weren't technically married yet, despite Nate being just as part of their family as she was at that point.

The only other place it could have landed was in Luca's or Petyr's hands, but judging from Luca's silence, it was not in their possession.

What if Nate... wasn't dead?

Cornelia couldn't help a few tears escaping as she

watched through the video again. She didn't know why she was crying, then or now, but she felt an extreme sadness as she watched. It was a deep-seated sadness, one that made her entire body weep, the kind that never really gets better, just buried.

When the video ended, Cornelia shut down her laptop. She pushed it to the ground, grabbed a blanket, and buried herself in the couch.

"Corey, are you okay?"

She jumped. She had forgotten Connor was in the next room.

She sprang up, wiping the tears from her eyes and pushing the blanket away. "Yes, I'm fine," she blurted.

"Corey," he said, sighing. He sat down next to her on the couch and pulled her in for a hug. "I don't know what's going on, but I think we need to talk about it."

"It's nothing, really," she said, hoping to brush him off.

He sighed. "Whatever it is, it now involves me and my gym," he said sternly, softly.

How much she would have to tell him? A tid bit? Half the story? Or would she have to dredge up the whole dreadful thing and hang out her dirty laundry in the middle of Connor's living room?

She took a deep breath, nodding, understanding She was scared he would want nothing more to do with her. "What do you want to know?" she asked him.

"Who are you running from?"

She wasn't sure how to start.

"Is it an ex?" Connor asked, softly, as if it might cause Cornelia to spin out in a rage.

"It's the man I suspect killed him," she said. "He killed my fiancé."

The words felt strange in her mouth.

She had no explicit evidence that Liam had killed Nate, but she had enough evidence to point a finger at him for Petyr and now for Jamie, too. Cornelia felt the lump in her throat returning. She wasn't sure how many more times she could handle Nate's death. Every time she thought she was over it, he came roaring back to her.

"What happened?" Connor asked, letting her get through most of her tears before pressing.

"We were in a car accident that killed my entire family, except for me and... Nate. I think," she started.

She had refused to talk about him for months. Eventually, people stopped asking. Now the name felt homey and familiar, devastatingly beautiful. "I don't have any memory of this, it's just what I've been able to piece together."

"We were sent to another hospital that specializes in coma recovery," she said, thinking back on the contract she had read a few days earlier. "But something happened while we were there, and... and somehow I got out."

"Well what happened?" Connor asked.

"I don't know. That's the problem. It's not like things are just fuzzy - there were five months before I actually *remember* waking up that do not exist in my head," she said. She pulled her computer back into her lap. Hesitantly, she opened the folder that contained her videos. She wasn't sure what to expect.

"These videos are the only documentation I have so I'm trying to piece together what exactly happened from these – I don't even know what to call them – medical interviews? Just questions and observations and endless talking. No facts, no explanations."

He nodded, a wave of understanding passing over him. "*That's* why you're so secretive about it," he said. She hadn't realized she made it so obvious that she was hiding something.

She turned the computer toward him so he could see. He rested his hand on hers and closed the screen. "I don't understand. How did you come across those videos? I'm assuming they weren't just handed out to you."

Cornelia bit her lip.

THE GIRL IN APARTMENT 19

"I stole them."

He nodded. "From where?"

"The doctor's hotel room."

"Did he know you were there?" A delicate way to ask if she was adept at B&E.

"Yes."

"How?"

"He invited me."

Connor looked wearily at Cornelia.

"So it's your former doctor who's... after you? And he... tricked you-" he looked to Cornelia for confirmation. "-into his apartment and you... snooped?"

She nodded. She felt the other theft, that couple hundred dollars, wasn't an important part of the story. "That was him yesterday. Him and I guess a security guard from the hospital," she said, brushing her fingers over the tender skin on her hip.

"And that day we had coffee? He was watching us from outside, wasn't he?" Connor asked. He already knew the answer.

Cornelia bit her lip. "I think so. I couldn't really see him, but who else would stand outside in the cold just *watching*?"

Cornelia shivered, thinking of all the times she had felt the paranoia creeping up on her. So often she had felt eyes on her, but she could never tell where from. How long had Liam been looking for her, watching her? Could her paranoia have just been a side effect of a sixth sense, that little twinge in the back of your mind that tells you someone is watching?

Cornelia told Connor most of the story – that Liam wanted her for *something*. She guessed, having watched most of her medical interviews, that once he got it, she might not remember a thing. But that, she kept to herself.

Aside from her obvious predicament, Cornelia felt there was something uniquely predatory about the ability to influence memory, like gaslighting to the max. There's nothing in the world more personal – your deepest passions, your greatest loves, your fears and accomplishments. Sure, memories can be recreated with pictures and stories, but they never get to be yours again. Memory retold by someone else is always someone else's story.

CHAPTER FORTY SIX
Present Day, Rittenhouse

Connor wrung his hands as they walked. He was fond of Cornelia's strange quirks. They were endearing, like that of a baby bobcat.

But he struggled to understand Cornelia's story. It wasn't that it was *unbelievable*, per se, but he felt a nagging need to poke holes in it. He wanted to prove that it all wasn't true, that she...

That she what? Took him for a ride? Is a compulsive liar? He didn't know what better outcome he was searching for.

She was wearing one of his sweatshirts and a pair of jeans loose enough they didn't hit her bruise. She had to pull them up constantly.

The bar they were going to was only a few blocks away, and as they walked, Cornelia chatted about one of the classes she taught the day before. He half-listened, caught up in his own thoughts.

He looked at the bruise surrounding her right eye. Despite their best efforts to ease the swelling, it was still puffy and red. How could she laugh about her class with yesterday's events so fresh on her skin? How do you put that on the back burner?

"...talked to her about kickboxing classes too, because apparently that's my mantra now..."

He wanted to feel for her, but the whole situation was so strange. He wasn't sure what he was *supposed* to feel. He felt scared for her, a little angry, but most of all just confused out of his mind. How does this even *happen?*

They arrived at the bar. It was packed, naturally, because it was a Saturday night.

Cornelia walked in ahead of him, slithering easily

through the crowd of people by the doorway. She was slick and silent like a cat, popping up between chatting friends like a permanent fixture, invisible until she made herself known.

"...made of pineapples or apples...?"

Cornelia was cryptic about her past. Connor had tried to convince her he was trustworthy, but she was a closed book, stubborn, locked, defensive. He didn't know how to get through to her.

"...so good, like fuck me in the mouth good..."

She rolled up her sleeves as the heat of the bar sunk into their clothing and manifested as a layer of moisture over their skin. The red lights lining the counter made her skin glow light pink.

"...taste like pineapple?"

Connor recognized silence.

"I'm sorry?" he asked. She looked at him expectantly.

"Does your cider taste like pineapple?" she asked, nodding to the drink in his hand.

Connor looked at the label. He had ordered a pineapple cider. Weird. He took a sip of it.

"Not too pineapple-y. It's really good. Do you want to try?" he asked, holding the bottle out without waiting for an answer.

They moved easily into sharing things - drinks, laughs, food, thoughts, hands, beds....

Was this the catch? The fine print with strings attached?

She took a dainty sip. "Mm, that is surprisingly good," she said, nodding. She took another.

He was starting to wonder if their relationship was too good to be true. Her story was... well, quite a story. This whole time, he had just taken her word for everything.

"...such a filling drink, I don't know if I could..."

But assuming her story was true...

What else could have happened to her? What couldn't she vocalize? What couldn't she remember at all? A car accident didn't seem like the type of thing that would inspire obsessive tendencies about locked windows and doors and the proximity to the nearest exit. He was no expert on neurology, but he had never heard of a car accident creating paranoia. But some clinical trial that interfered with her memory? Well, he supposed that *would* probably do it.

"...thank you so much..." Had Cornelia been a nut job to begin with? Was her story just a collection of psychotic musings?

He looked at her, with those kind eyes and a gentle smile. "You're very welcome." He smiled.

"Shall we?" she asked, nudging his elbow. She certainly didn't seem crazy.

He nodded. "Let's go."

He checked his phone; three hours had passed. The receipt he stuffed in his wallet outlined four drinks each. He drank four pineapple ciders. But he didn't need the receipt to tell him that – he could feel the sugar causing uproar in his stomach.

They walked back toward the house, taking the same route home as they had come. They crossed into Rittenhouse Square and she grabbed his hand, their intertwined fingers swinging as they walked.

Maybe now wasn't the time for analyzing Cornelia's mental health, or postulating about her past. It was nicer not to worry about who may be lurking around the corner.

"...saxophone like there's no tomorrow..."

He glanced around the square, searching for lurkers. Every person they passed held the threat of unknown thoughts, desires that could hurt someone he cared for.

He held her hand a little tighter, deciding he liked her anyways, con woman or not.

She had been worried about telling Connor, but she didn't expect *this* sort of reaction. At first he was supportive, warm, but as it sunk in, he became distant, to the point of not talking at all.

He was distracted, twitchy in a way Cornelia hadn't seen in him before. Maybe she was becoming too much for him.

He held onto her hand, but mentally he was no more present than the homeless man asleep on the bench they just passed. He jumped as a pigeon flew by, diving for a lonely piece of bread on the sidewalk.

"Connor, what has gotten into you tonight?" she asked, stopping by the fountain and taking a seat. She didn't want to upset him even more than she already had, but she wasn't willing to wait around for a blow up that would leave her friendless. Not to mention homeless.

The night was warm, comfortable, and people still milled about, despite it being bedtime inside the park. A few kids screwed around on skateboards toward the other side of the fountain, and a group of college kids swayed drunkenly down the winding footpaths, attempting to pinpoint their next destination.

"I'm just a little paranoid," he explained. He didn't sit, instead pulling her to continue walking home. "This is too much." She resisted his pulls on her arm and maintained the eye contact she had been fighting for all night.

"Too much how?" she asked. "Talk to me."

"I feel like I have to be constantly vigilant in case this guy comes back. We have no idea what he might do. And you're right, obviously he's off his rocker if he tried to attack a self-defense teacher in the middle of a martial arts gym. What else might he try? What else might he try that will *work?*" he asked her.

She pulled on him until he sat down next to her. "Nothing. We'll keep evading him. Eventually he'll give up," she said. "You don't need to worry about me, I've been taking care of myself for a while now. Let the shock wear off and you'll realize this isn't a big deal."

She smiled, hoping that might calm him. He looked at her crossly. She could see the scenarios running through his mind, the preoccupation that plagued him all night. He still only knew half the story.

"Do you really think he'll give up? Just like that?" he asked her, incredulous.

"It's not 'just like that.' I don't doubt he'll try again – I doubt his ability to succeed," she said.

"I think I just need some time to understand all of this," he said, shaking his head. "Can we just go home?"

She nodded, and let him pull her up. They crossed to the south side of the park, Connor scanning the surrounding crowds enough for the both of them.

Just as they reached the edge of the park, Cornelia's ears pricked - yelling from the southwest corner of the square. Connor was oblivious, but Cornelia stopped and turned.

A black SUV had pulled up next to a small blonde girl, and someone was trying to drag her inside. It was the girl she heard screaming, her voice projected across the entire square. No one made a move to help her.

Cornelia zeroed in on them and recognized the security guard working with Liam. The same one that gave her the black eye she was sporting.

She debated for a moment. Should she? Maybe not. She beat him once already. But now she had the element of surprise. Revenge...? Tastes sweet.

She let go of Connor's hand and sprinted toward the altercation, using her speed to back the punch she landed to the side of his head. She knocked him into the van and he let go, tumbling onto his back.

Cornelia was poised for the doctor to pop out at any second, but the only movement from inside the van came from the security guard scrambling to his feet in a rush to slam the back doors.

Seconds later he sped away, tires screeching.

Connor had run up behind her, and as Cornelia focused

on the woman in front of her, he beckoned her back toward his apartment.

"Are you okay?" she asked the blonde girl.

She sat on the curb, her head in her hands. She nodded, and looked up at Cornelia from behind her hands. "Thank you," she said.

Cornelia froze. She knew that voice.

She looked closely at her face. The blonde hair threw her off, but Cornelia was certain. It *had* to be her.

"Renee," she said, the name foreign on her tongue.

Her eyebrows crinkled in confusion as she smiled. "You remember me?" she asked, standing. She had a cut along her cheek that looked fresh but not deep. If she had been older, it would have blended right into smile wrinkles.

"No not exactly. But you were my nurse," Cornelia said. "And... my neighbor," she continued, struggling to piece the connections together.

Renee nodded enthusiastically. "But... how did you find out?" she asked.

"I just-" Cornelia struggled to put it into words. "Luck?"

CHAPTER FORTY SEVEN
Present Day, Connor's apartment

Renee sat on Connor's beige armchair, her blonde hair tied back in a ponytail as she scanned the room. The blonde faded to a deep brown at her scalp, a color similar to the one Cornelia was now sporting. She wrapped her arms around herself, pulling her coat tight.

"Can I get you something to drink? Tea, coffee, water?" Cornelia asked.

"A cup of tea would be nice," Renee said, smiling wearily.

Cornelia moved toward the kitchen, but before she could start boiling water, Connor motioned for her to stop. He took the kettle out of her hand and cocked his head toward Renee. "Why don't you go sit? I'll bring in the tea when it's done."

She nodded, seeing how hard he was trying. "Thank you," she said, and slid onto the side of the couch closest to Renee.

Both women were silent, looking at each other. Neither knew where to start.

"So what all do you know?" Renee asked.

An innocent question, Cornelia thought. Yet so many considerations, nuances, maybes.... She wasn't sure where to begin, and she wasn't sure what she was supposed to know. Instead, she bent over the side of the couch and pulled the USB drive out of her computer. She held it up to the light, so Renee could see the large green brain on it.

"Is that what I think it is?" Renee asked.

"I think so," she said. "Medical interviews."

"How did you get it?"

"I was invited back Dr. Ingels' hotel room," Cornelia said. "Before I knew who he was." She glanced to the kitchen, and was relieved to see Connor was still fiddling away with their mugs and boiling the water.

Renee raised her eyebrows. "Really?"

Cornelia nodded. "We met at a bar. I thought it was pure chance that he seemed so familiar," Cornelia bit her lip, wondering if she should tell Renee the next part of her story. "I uh, kind of stole some money from his wallet, and while I was there, grabbed the USB too."

"Wow," Renee said, shaking her head. She sat back in silence for a moment. Connor clacked mugs together in the kitchen.

"So, Renee," she started. She wasn't sure how to phrase it. "What... happened?"

"There's a loaded question if I ever heard one," Renee said, smiling. She had seemed friendly the whole night, but this was the first time her smile reached her eyes. Cornelia couldn't help but smile back, like in some weird way their shared experience brought them closer.

Connor tiptoed out of the kitchen, balancing three steaming mugs on a cutting board, along with a sample of each flavor of tea he had in the cupboard. Cornelia waited until Renee had hers, a decaf vanilla chai, until she grabbed her favorite minty flavor. Connor absentmindedly picked one of the ones that were left, squishing down next to Cornelia on the couch.

Cornelia dunked the tea bag in the hot water and turned to Renee, waiting for the story.

Renee glanced from Cornelia to him and back again, raising her eyebrows.

"I think he should hear it too," Cornelia answered, taking the moment to squeeze his knee.

She could sense Connor's frustration, having only pieces of the story. Up to that point, she told him only what she needed to, to quell the part of him that needed to constantly press for one more piece of the puzzle.

Renee nodded, swishing her tea bag around in her mug.

"The doctor has feelers all across the country, neurologists in his pocket who let him know when an interesting case comes by related to his field. One of them let him know about a coma patient who recently came under his care who had sustained some unique injuries," Renee started.

"That patient was you. There was an area of your brain right near your amygdala that was damaged in the accident that seemed to show no effect on any of your EEGs, MRIs, PET scans, nothing. You could physically see that it was there – there was an area of your brain that had changed since your last MRI. I think your aunt brought it in, frizzy haired woman? She brought that in for comparison, and it had everyone intrigued.

"Now, that actually wasn't the reason Dr. Ingels was called. Everyone loves an interesting new case, but he was called because of his ability to seemingly snap his fingers and wake up hopeless patients. His practice was government funded and top secret, but he had previously run a clinic for Alzheimer's patients, and that's where he made a name for himself as a 'brain whisperer,' if you will," Renee said, with air quotes.

"But so many doctors had heard of what he could do, and they didn't stop using him as a guide when he began at Fort Howard. He didn't ever have to search for patients – they lined up to come to him," Renee said, blowing on her tea. "And it worked out really well for a while. They would come, stay for a few months, participate in some... *voluntary* tests and mental exercises, and then they would go home to their families, good as new."

Renee closed her eyes and shook her head. Her fingers shook as she placed her tea down on the coffee table in front of her.

Cornelia had so many questions, but wanted Renee to tell her story uninterrupted.

"Until he got greedy. He wanted to play with new medicines, faster. He stopped waiting for government approval and started fudging his documentation, and I didn't realize until it was too late. I noticed he was giving certain drugs more frequently and starting to disregard patient wishes. He got reckless, so I started questioning him, demanding every last piece of paperwork and insisting that everything was done by the books."

Renee shrugged. "It slowed him down a bit, I guess, but he just started asking one of the other nurses to do the things I wouldn't. I got stuck on paperwork, which I suppose is fitting considering that's all I asked for from him." Renee forced a smile.

"So anyway, I loosened my grip a bit so I could be patient-side again. I wanted to see what he was doing and try to document it. Because you were one of the few conscious patients we had, I spent a whole lot of time trying to make sure he didn't try anything too dangerous with you. Of course, I wasn't there the weekend he wiped your memory. He gave you two treatments back to back. My uncle was ill, and I couldn't have lived with myself if I didn't visit him," she explained, rushing through her words. "I'm so sorry I wasn't there," she said, reaching to squeeze Cornelia's hand.

"How does that even work?" Cornelia muttered, moving right past Renee's apology.

Renee nodded. "Memory I is given upon arrival. That's the milder treatment, all it really does is mark your memories as they're created. Memory II is a much more volatile experience," she said. "You were fine with Memory I, but over time you became more agitated, less cooperative. It was the only way he could think of to make you docile again, to repeat the process. He administered Memory II to inactivate the memory of your time there. You woke up in October, thinking you had been in a coma for four months."

Cornelia took a deep breath, connecting the dots. That lined up exactly with the second "first day" she had in the hospital. "That makes sense," she said, nodding. So it was her brain that wasn't going in chronological order.

"So we started the process all over again, only the doctor didn't think the patients would figure out what was happening to them. He thought wiping your memories would fix everything. But you and Nate figured it out."

"Me and Nate?" Cornelia blurted, her heart jumping into her throat. She sat up, putting her tea down on the coffee table with Renee's. Connor was silent, listening.

"You and Nate were given the same treatments that weekend, so you both woke up thinking you had been out for four months," Renee said, nodding. "He wasn't worried about you two getting a chance to talk, or even see each other - he had you on two separate sides of the hospital and on different schedules for that exact reason - but he didn't expect anyone else to tell you what happened," she said, cocking her head to the side. "Most people stayed quiet in that hospital, especially the staff, but I couldn't let you guys live in a repetitive cycle of constant memory loss."

Nate *was* there too. And their last few months together were forever gone from her memory.

"Naturally, you were furious. Your last few months there were spent coming up with various escape plans. We started by letting Dr. Ingels know what he was doing was illegal, then contacting a lawyer, then the American Medical Association, then anyone else we could think of who could possibly help. We even called your aunt, but thanks to a preventative call from the doctor, she had already been assured that you were perfectly safe where you were, just suffering from some minor brain damage.

"Eventually you gave up hope, as did Nate. So rather than focusing your energy on escaping, you planned a little wedding," Renee said, smiling.

"A wedding?" Cornelia asked, her eyebrows crinkling. Her mind raced.

She smiled. "You and Nate got married in the courtyard," Renee said, nodding as she took a sip of her tea.

Cornelia's body went fuzzy, like an allergic reaction or

the sudden need to puke. It was always Nate. She put her hand over her heart, to the place where her engagement ring rested.

"I got ordained for the occasion, and found you some white scrubs. I wore my pink scrubs because that's the color you always wanted for your bridesmaids," Renee said, giggling. "It was January 1ˢᵗ, so Dr. Ingels was away with his family and there were fewer guards than usual. We were basically on lock down inside the clinic, but I convinced one of them to let us outside to see fireworks in the distance.

"As you might expect, the doctor was furious when he found out. We didn't think he ever would, but apparently the other nurse on call that night had some loose lips. He acted like he was all happy for you, and we were so confused, wondering what had broken in *his* head. He went on like that for a week or so, and then he... well, he administered Memory III to Nate that Wednesday," Renee said, staring down into her tea.

"What is Memory III?" Cornelia asked.

"In theory, it's the third drug in the series. The first tags your memory, and the second wipes those strengthened neurons out, and the third reactivates the dormant memories, to put it simply," she explained. "If the drugs worked properly, it wouldn't be a big deal."

"But it kills you instead," Cornelia finished. The lump in her throat grew.

"It sent Nate into a deep coma. We weren't able to find any brain activity," Renee said softly.

"When did he pass?" she asked.

Renee's lips tightened. "I'm not completely sure, but when we left he was unresponsive. I'm guessing it would have been pretty soon after," Renee said. "Our priority was getting you out safe. Nate was... well, he was gone when the needle went in."

"I'm so sorry," she said.

"But you're sure he's... dead?"

Renee nodded. "No one could survive Memory III. I don't think Nate was the exception in this case," she said.

Cornelia nodded, unable to speak.

"So that was it, for both of us. We waited until Dr. Ingels was far enough from the hospital to enact emergency protocol – meaning if a patient codes without a doctor present, they get transported to the nearest public hospital.

"At your insistence, I administered Memory II, and then once I saw the appropriate reaction, a stimulant that induces seizures. I had a friend from a local hospital waiting outside with an ambulance, and he transported you as if you had just been in a car accident. You woke up to a different life outside the hospital."

Cornelia picked up her tea and sank back into the couch. "Wow," she said, breathlessly.

Connor squeezed her knee. "Are you okay?"

She nodded, processing.

"I wish I could have told you everything, but I had no idea how you would react. You might think I'm a crazy, or you might remember things in the wrong way. I did my best to let you live your life and only interfere if I had to," Renee said, studying Cornelia's face.

Cornelia nodded, thinking over her time spent living right next to each other. Her memory was truly obliterated – all the times she had seen Renee, she never recognized her. She was always just the girl next door.

But something else had been bothering her.

"How did you get me to rent the apartment?" Cornelia asked.

Renee smiled. "You told me to price the studio at seven hundred a month, cash preferred, and *you* would find *me*," she explained.

Cornelia nodded. "Wow, I guess I'm pretty predictable," she said. She tried to laugh as a tear dropped down her cheek.

"I think you just know yourself," Renee said, smiling sadly.

Cornelia sipped her tea, unsure what she really wanted to remember.

CHAPTER FORTY EIGHT
Present Day, Pete's Diner

The next day they got together again, this time as old friends rather than nurse and patient. Before Cornelia left for their brunch date, Connor handed her a key to his apartment.

"Just so you can get in," he clarified, and she laughed as she turned for the door.

"Oh and hey," he said, grabbing her by the waist and pulling her to face him. "Only if you're up for it... I was thinking we could go on a real date tonight?"

She raised her eyebrows. "What does a real date entail?"

"A nice dinner and no jeans," he said.

"So... underwear only. Got it," she said.

"You know what I mean. Let's do something nice," he said.

She smiled. "Absolutely," she said. "I'll be back in a few hours."

He gave her a sloppy kiss, and she slinked out the door, down the stairs, and into the frigid sunshine outside.

Knowing now that Renee had been next door all along, she wondered if she really had to leave in the first place. Maybe they could have fought off Liam and his lackeys, together.

She meandered down the street, a pair of Ray-bans she had borrowed from Connor shielding her eyes. Wind blew her hair in swirls around her head. She burrowed into her jacket, stuffing her hands inside the deep pockets.

She quickened her pace, hoping an increase in blood flow might warm her up. A couple gandered along in front of her, mittened hands melded together. A man jaywalked across the street, hurrying just like she was. A car horn honked at the light, annoyed with the stationary vehicle blocking its way. The world felt quiet.

Cornelia glanced around, getting the sudden feeling like she was being watched, but no one was looking at her.

She reached an intersection and waited for the light to turn green. She glanced to her right and saw a white van speeding toward her, slowing to a stop last minute in the shoulder just in front of her. Cornelia's heart kick-started itself. She turned back toward the intersection, stepped out to look, and in the split second before another car sped through, dashed to the other side of the street. The car leaned on its horn.

She turned back to check out the van, and realized it was a regular moving van. A man got out of the driver side with a clipboard, checked the signs at the intersection, and then started scanning street numbers. He wasn't interested in Cornelia at all.

She sighed in relief and continued walking. She urged her thumping heart to calm.

The café they met at was six blocks from Connor's apartment. It was quaint, tables so close that you got intimate with not only your date, but the other patrons around you too. Cornelia had been there many times, a few with Nate, once with Connor and many times with old friends. They had unlimited mimosas, after all.

Renee had a table toward the back, and stood to wave when Cornelia walked in.

"Glad you could make it," she said. She leaned over for a hesitant hug.

"Me too."

"I took the liberty of ordering the limitless mimosas," Renee said, pushing a glass toward Cornelia.

"How'd you know?" Cornelia asked jokingly.

"You told me," Renee said, smiling that sad smile again. Her recent past came roaring back.

Cornelia wondered how much Renee knew about her that, how much she had shared in those six months they spent together.

They drank mimosas as they waited for their food to arrive, and they drank mimosas as their plates were cleared, and they drank mimosas until they were the last people left in the café, the servers eyeing them wearily as they waited for their pre-dinner break.

"Maybe we should head out," Cornelia said, even though she didn't really want to.

"Yeah, probably."

They paid and thanked the staff, ambling toward the door.

"Oh, I almost forgot," Renee said, grabbing Cornelia by the elbow before she pushed through into the cold.

Renee reached into her bag and pulled out a CD case. "This is the video of your wedding," she said, pressing it into Cornelia's hand.

"Thank you," Cornelia said, holding the CD with both hands.

"And I wasn't sure if you would want it or not," she said, reaching into her bag and pulling out a USB drive that matched the one she had grown to hate. "This has all of Nate's videos on it. I thought you should have it."

Cornelia took the disk and held it on top of the CD case. She nodded. "Thank you."

CHAPTER FORTY NINE
Nine months and three days earlier, Fort Howard Neuro Clinic

Cornelia was satisfied with their plan. She wasn't sure it would work, but they didn't have many other options.

Dr. Ingels was planning on taking a long weekend over Martin Luther King Day.

Normally over the weekend, three or four security guards could be found anywhere around the hospital. One was stationed at the front entrance, another at the emergency exit - which doubled as the trash exit - and the last one or two would roam.

But on MLK Day, they were down to two guards. Sure, each would be stationed at an entrance, like usual, but there would be no one to cover internal emergencies. One of them would have to leave their post.

So Renee, in the middle of the building, would light a small fire underneath one of the sprinklers. Once the fire alarm went off, Nate and Cornelia would sneak around the corner of the nurse's station, determine which exit the guard had come from, and take off in that direction.

Renee could claim innocence, as she was otherwise occupied, and Nate and Cornelia had already somewhat made a name for themselves as troublemakers. Cornelia's lack of obedience was endearing to the doctor, cute, girly, mysterious. Nate's insolence, however, made that vein in the doctor's forehead pop. He certainly wasn't a favorite, but he was useful.

Renee would search high and low for the missing patients. She would call the doctor in a panic. She would call the police, claiming missing mental patients (and give wildly inaccurate descriptions on the down low). She would cry, beg forgiveness, (pretend to) do everything she possibly could to compensate for her oversight. If all went well, all three would be home free.

Renee had given them a thousand dollars to get home in a small envelope. Cornelia insisted that wasn't necessary, that all they needed was a window to freedom and they would crawl their way back. She had planned on begging for money at the bus stop, or hoping someone might drop their ticket. Maybe she could sneak on in the luggage compartment.

Cornelia suggested situation after situation, hoping to cover all of her bases before they left, but Nate willfully ignored all of them. She was a planner; he was a winger. Sometimes she liked that he forced her to live in the moment, but times like these, she just wanted agreement, time, and maybe consideration.

"Nate, can you please just think of the possibilities for a moment," she said. It was nearing midnight on a Saturday and Cornelia had been going over their plan for hours. She was stressing herself out, and Nate, fully opposed to any stressors originating from planning too soon, was frustrated.

"Have you considered there's a good chance any plan we make won't work? What do you think he'll do when we fail?" he asked. He sat in the armchair next to her bed while she paced. "He loves Princess Cornelia, but he won't hesitate to cut off the jester's head.

"Don't call me that."

"Alright. Queen Cornelia," he said. She fixed a pointed gaze on him and he grinned.

She ignored the jab. "That's the only possibility I'm not considering," she said.

"Well so much for being prepared!" he said, throwing his hands up.

"Nate. Humor me here," she insisted. She stopped walking, her hands gesticulating on without her.

He mocked her, throwing his hands around like he was conducting an orchestra of flying things. "Corey. Humor *me* here. We have time. Give me one night where we don't obsess over this," he insisted, standing up and taking her hands. He pulled them around his middle and wrapped her tight. He kissed her head. "Let's just be us, together."

Cornelia sighed. "Fine," she grumbled.

"What was that?" he asked, pulling away to look at her.

She rolled her eyes. "Fine," she said a little louder.

"Wow, Queen Cornelia bows to the jester. What a new age we live in!" he said, kissing her cheek. She hated how he could anger her and make her smile at the same time.

He glanced at the clock. "Hey, wait here a second, I have to run to the bathroom," he said, and ducked out of the room.

She sat at the foot of her bed, once again going over the scenarios, and a minute later Renee knocked on the door.

"Hey Corey," she said. She had fresh scrubs in her hand. "I'm sorry, I've been a little busy recently. I wanted to bring you some fresh clothes but I haven't gotten a chance to do any laundry yet, so I scrounged up some old scrubs for you. I can take your stuff home tonight and throw it in the laundry with mine though, I know you hate the hospital smell that you get with the washers here."

She handed over the scrubs and Cornelia changed. "Thanks Renee," she said, glancing down at bleached white scrubs. "Wow, I feel like a painter."

"Yeah, I know the white scrubs are a little tacky, but it's all I had. Sorry," she said, shrugging.

"Hey, I'm just stoked my ass is covered," she said.

"You and me both!" They laughed.

"Oh, and it turns out I have a secret admirer, someone sent me flowers," Renee said, running out to the nurse's station to grab a small bouquet. "But I suck at caring for plants, and I think they would really brighten up your room. Do you want to care for them for me?"

"Yeah, I'd love to. I miss my plants."

"I don't have a vase, but there might be one in the supply room. Do you want to take a walk and check with me?" Renee said, handing over a small bouquet of red roses.

"Wow, these are beautiful," she said, sniffing them. "Wow, it's been so long since I've smelled fresh roses." She couldn't stop breathing them in.

They walked down the quiet hallway. "Wow, I feel like I'm getting married. Or baptized," Cornelia joked, giggling.

"Oh, they might have something in here," Renee said, and veered off into the rec room.

Cornelia followed her. Through the windows she saw an unfamiliar glow. "Wow, the moon must be bright tonight," she commented, wandering toward the window.

"Let's take a look outside. It was supposed to be warm tonight anyways," Renee said, pushing through the door to the little outdoor area.

It was normally surrounded by a 20' high electric fence, a drab, sad place. Rotting picnic tables littered the yard, and through the electric fence you could see overgrown green grass, trees, an entire outside world that you could touch if you could just reach your fingers between the links.

But tonight, when Cornelia followed Renee through the door, she found herself in a small hallway, a clear night sky the ceiling. The picnic tables had been stood up on their sides, and little white lights hung from the tops. Flowers were woven into crisscrossed ropes, covering the divots and imperfections of the wood.

At the end of the makeshift hallway, Nate stood in black scrubs, with a red rose from her bouquet tucked into the breast pocket. He was beaming, his smile lit gently by the twinkly lights. He leaned on the cane he used for longer walks. When he saw them walk through the door, he switched on the small camera standing on a tripod to his left.

"What is this?" Cornelia breathed, momentarily frozen.

"Well, it's certainly not a baptism," Renee said. Renee poked her elbow out and motioned for Cornelia to take it.

They walked down the short aisle, and as soon as Nate was within arms length, he pulled her in for a kiss. Renee whacked his arm. "You're not allowed to do that yet," she scolded.

"My bad," he said, and instead held her hand.

"We're leaving in two weeks," Cornelia said. "I don't object but… why now?"

He took a deep breath. "You said I don't plan for the future, that I need to consider the possibilities," he started. "Well, this is me planning for the future. I love you Corey, and I trust that whatever happens to me, to you, or us, that we can now make the right decision for each other."

Cornelia's breath caught. She nodded. "Is this all legal?"

Nate glanced to Renee. She held out her hand to Cornelia. "Hi, my name is Cornelia Winthorp, born July 31st, 1992. I'm a Leo, I have a degree in Public Relations from Philadelphia University, and I love oreos," she said, the words rolling effortlessly off her tongue. "In Maryland only one person has to show up at the courthouse."

"Wow, you committed a felony for me. Renee, I'm touched," Cornelia said.

"It was worth every minute of potential jail time." She squeezed Cornelia's hand. "Well kids," she said, holding up her script. "Let's get married."

MEMORY III

CHAPTER FIFTY
Present day, Rittenhouse

Cornelia wondered whether Nate's USB disk might give her the answers she was looking for. Would watching her own wedding make her happy, or just devastate her all over again? Once again, she was faced with the question: was it better to know or forget?

Between knowledge and ignorance, Cornelia prided herself on always choosing knowledge. She wanted to know, to understand everything, but if she had already chosen to forget, could that mean whatever happened to her wasn't worth trying to understand?

She thumbed the drive as she sat on Connor's beige couch, waiting for him to get ready. He had misinterpreted her when she told him she would be twenty minutes; he had only just gotten dressed and was busy looking at himself in the bathroom mirror.

"Alright, are you ready yet?" Connor asked, adjusting the collar of his shirt as he emerged from the bathroom. He smiled at her, checking his watch as he crossed the room to the coat rack by the front door.

"Alright princess, let's go. Hopefully they held our table for us," Cornelia said with a smirk, as Connor helped her into her coat. It was a warm enough to get away with a dress, but not quite warm enough to go coat-less. She used the warm weather as an excuse to take a quick detour to a boutique she passed on the way home from brunch, and bought herself the first dress she had worn in a year.

It was small and red, and though she liked another dress better, she wasn't daring enough for the super tight look. She opted for something loose and flowy, girly yet classy. She put on blush and twirled her hair as it dried from her shower, giving it those loose waves that every girl on a date in the city wore. They were just like any other couple out on Friday night.

Connor shut and locked the front door, and as they walked down the street, he reached down and grabbed her hand. He smiled at her, their arms swinging as they walked. Cornelia felt light, the warm air coupling with that confidence that she had finally scared off Liam.

Yet as they walked, she felt a momentary panic creep up on her like she was being watched. She glanced around, searching, but didn't see anyone.

Was it just her mind playing tricks on her again?

They walked through the square to a small Italian restaurant with a fancy wine list and a sommelier on staff. Cornelia wasn't crazy about spending a ton of money on a fancy place, but Connor had wanted to treat her, and she was trying to be thankful instead of weary.

Despite the line that poured out of the door in a in a gaggle of brightly colored women and grey-scale men, they were seated immediately, at a small table in the back corner. A small votive sat in the middle of the white tablecloth, along with a single rose in a dainty vase.

Their server came by to ask if they would like a bottle of wine, or a consultation with the sommelier. Connor politely declined, and asked for a fancy sounding French wine. The server nodded, and scurried off to grab their bottle.

"I thought you didn't know anything about wine," Cornelia said.

"I don't. But I am an astute user of this thing called the Google," Connor said.

Cornelia couldn't help but laugh. Connor could be so serious while teaching, or even while just reading on the couch, and two seconds later, he would crack a joke and the tall brooding exterior broke down into someone full of kindness, uninterrupted compassion. She could feel the switch when it happened – a calm, easygoing silence that shattered into laughter.

Two glasses of water were dropped off at their table. Connor reached for her hand, and their fingers sat intertwined on the white tablecloth, right next to the lonely rose. The server returned with the bottle of wine and poured Connor a sip to taste. That calmness passed over them again, as he nodded and smiled and they both had two full red glasses in front of them.

"So what do you think so far?" he asked her, leaning in.

"It's perfect," she said. She wanted to qualify her assertion by saying she couldn't remember the last time she had felt so content to be anywhere, with anyone. Instead, she let the calm silence linger. He smiled. 'Perfect' was all she had needed to say.

"So I wanted to ask you something," he said, taking a sip of his wine.

"Go right ahead," she said, tasting hers. She kept an eye on him over the lip of her glass.

"What are you planning to do about... Liam? That's his name, right?" he asked.

Her heart sank. She didn't want to think about the things that plagued her in the dead of night, not now.

"Well I doubt he'll attack me again," she said, shrugging. "Renee says he's run out of money, so he can't pay his guy anymore, and he couldn't take me on his own if he tried."

He nodded. "I don't know, it just bothers me." He ran his finger in a circle around the base of his wine glass. "If it were me, I don't think I'd feel safe with him still out there. He doesn't seem totally right in the head. People like that can do crazy things."

She sighed. "Let's not talk about it tonight. I don't think we have to," she told him.

"I get it," he said, nodding. "I'm sorry I brought it up, but can we talk about it tomorrow?"

She nodded. "Let's talk tomorrow."

A momentary silence fell over them, Connor clicking

his fingernail on the base of his wine glass. "I just… from what I've heard, I wouldn't blame you if you wanted to do something about it," he said.

"What, you want me to kill him? You told me not to only a few days ago," she said offhandedly. He didn't laugh.

"That was before I knew the whole story. Maybe I shouldn't have stopped you," he said.

They sat in silence again, Cornelia unsure what to say. She decided to waltz right past it. "Tonight is for celebrating," she said, holding up her wine glass.

He smiled, and she felt that shattering feeling again. "What are we celebrating?"

She shrugged, unable to come up with a good answer. "Happiness without reason."

He raised his eyebrows. "Good enough for me," he said, and clinked his glass against hers.

Connor and Cornelia wandered home the long way, through the square, the noisy nightlife of the city keeping it noisy and alive. Connor enjoyed people watching, and although he knew Cornelia was more of a homebody, she seemed to be enjoying it too.

He was in awe of the transformation she made that night. She came home from brunch slightly drunk, though she adamantly refused she drank more than "a glass or two." She brought back a dress, something he had never seen her in before, and she seemed excited, relaxed, with an ease about the way she moved.

She walked in front of him a few paces as they wound their way through a group of artists and musicians staking out the pathways. She held his hand, leading the way as he watched her little red dress swing lightly underneath her coat. Her legs were bare, white and skinny, but toned in a way he usually only saw at Philly MMA.

They wound their way through a small crowded surrounding an acoustic guitarist and eased back into their wandering pace. He could still see a dark circle shadowing her eye, but she had done a good job covering it up.

He brushed her cheek with his fingers. "Does that still hurt?" he asked.

"Just a little," she said, smiling.

She wound her arm through his and rested her head on his shoulder. So easy.

Years of passive aggression and fighting had taught him to pick up on emotional movements as well as physical ones, and throughout all the time he had known Cornelia, she had never seemed so relaxed.

He thought back to the two men who attacked her in the gym, and how differently she acted afterwards. He didn't notice right away, but she hadn't been checking over her shoulder so much, or doing repetitive rounds in the apartment to make sure all the doors and windows were shut. That one tiny fight had given her confidence.

He was glad she felt more comfortable, but he couldn't shake the feeling that the doctor would come back. He didn't trust Liam to not try again.

But Cornelia had promised, that conversation would come in time. There was no need to spoil a good night with his (apparently) one-sided concern.

They stopped in front of a spray painter creating art using a variety of pots, pans and a torch. He wore a facemask as he worked, creating galaxies and meadows in seconds, his hands moving like lightning back and forth across the glossy pages.

"That's so cool," Cornelia murmured.

"Do you want one?" he asked.

"Totally but I wouldn't even know how to choose," she said in astonishment. "They're incredible."

"How about you take a minute to pick your favorite, while I run over and grab us a couple of coffees?" he asked, eyeing the small kiosk on the corner.

"Yeah that sounds good," she said, and took a step closer as Connor darted off toward the corner store.

He had gone there a few times before and was never disappointed. Maybe he would suggest to Cornelia that they get their morning coffee from there next time and bring it home, rather than their normal chain.

Home... it felt weird to include Cornelia in that.

He had been a little apprehensive at first, letting someone into his life who was obviously running from something, but he had come to really enjoy having her there.

He hoped she would stay for a while. She was a nice presence, never demanding of attention or leaving her stuff strewn about. She was simple, plain. He was too.

The little kiosk had no customers, the lonesome Russian husband and wife in quiet conversation by the heater in their little hut. The woman came up to the counter when she saw Connor.

"Two coffees please, black," he said. Their coffee was perfect as it was, no need for additives. He always appreciated that.

As the wife poured, Connor glanced back toward Cornelia. She was still leaning over the spray painter. It looked like she was asking him a question, listening animatedly as he motioned to his supplies and demonstrated something for her.

"Four dollars please," the woman said in a thick Russian accent.

Connor fished around his pants, forgetting which pocket he left his wallet in. Slacks always threw him off. He pulled out four dollars and handed them over, the woman nodding as he grabbed the coffees and turned back to find Cornelia.

She walked down the sidewalk toward him, one of the artist's paintings in her hand. She held it up so Connor could see, grinning from ear to ear.

They were almost within shouting range when a SUV

popped over the curb, screeching to a halt next to her.

Connor dropped the coffees.

"Corey!" he shouted, running toward her.

She turned to the sound of the screeching tires, but before she had a moment to fight back, the same guard she had fought off just days before had her in a headlock. He inserted a needle in her neck and popped back into the SUV, looping his arms under hers and hauling her up after him.

Connor ran as fast as he could, but they were gone by the time he reached the spot it had stopped. It made a left at the next intersection, disappearing into a sea of traffic.

He held his hands on his head, pacing.

"Hey man, you okay?" a passerby asked.

The gall. Connor ignored him.

The picture Cornelia bought laid on the ground, unperturbed.

He picked it up, staring at the two dimensional galaxy, a glowing red planet with two golden moons.

He didn't think she would have chosen one in the time it took for him to get coffee.

He should have told her explicitly that he wanted to buy it for her. If she had just *stayed* where she was, surrounded with people, they never would have had the opportunity to scoop her up like a poor fish who bit the wrong worm.

Defeated, he went straight to Renee.

CHAPTER FIFTY ONE
Present day, Renee's apartment

Renee was relieved. For a long time, she felt like she was fighting an impossible battle – how do you protect someone who doesn't even know they need protection?

But now... Cornelia knew everything, what to fear and why. She knew what happened to her, finally, and Renee could focus a little more on herself.

She knew it was selfish to pass the buck along like that, but there was really only so much she could do for Cornelia without her taking control. But Renee wasn't too worried – Cornelia could handle herself.

She heard someone in the hallway clicking their door shut, the sound of metal on metal as it locked. She guessed it was Naomi, the student who never slept. Renee heard her leaving at all hours of the night, unaware of the noise she made when she did. She heard voices as the front door opened and closed.

A loud banging erupted from the other side of her door. "RENEE!"

She double checked her door was locked, and stayed silent.

"Renee!" They banged again. "Renee, it's Connor, he's got Cornelia!"

She hopped over the back of her futon and clambered to the door, peering out the peephole to confirm. He leaned against the door with his head down, one arm disappearing upward into the warped glass.

She unlocked the door and let him in, standing aside as he blustered through.

"He got Cornelia," he said, coming in and immediately sitting down. He looked nice, dressy.

"Dr. Ingels?" she asked.

He nodded. "We were walking home from dinner, I went to get coffee and as I was walking back to her, he just drove up and plucked her off the street," he said, running a hand over his short hair. "God why did I leave her alone?"

"Shit," she said, sitting down next to him.

"Please tell me you know where he took her," Connor said, turning to Renee.

She thought about the possibilities. He would probably want to start Memory III in the morning. But where? Would his equipment have been moved to a new facility? There couldn't have been enough time. "I mean, I can only guess he took her back to the hospital," Renee said, the weight of it dawning on her.

Cornelia was his prize because she was the *only* patient who responded positively to both Memories I and II - he had just been waiting for the right time to administer Memory III.

What if *now* was the right time?

"What will he do to her once they're there?" Connor asked, glancing up at her. She could see the fear in his eyes.

"I don't know," she lied. "But we need to leave. *Now*."

As he walked, the weight of the night's events dawned on him. She had been a part of that clinic against her will for so long, and she finally fought off the people who put her there... only to be defeated by a needle. Pansies. Connor remembered the beating that guard took; she wasn't gentle. Yet she let them go.

Granted, he would have done the same. He had been involved in a few fights, several times in the gym and once or twice at a rowdy bar. He fought back enough that they realized what they were dealing with, and offered them a gracious out. Most took it. One guy didn't, but learned his lesson, and Connor hadn't seen him since. He always wondered why amateur street fighters would go to a martial arts gym and try to fight a teacher.

But if he had gone through what Cornelia had – held against her will, memory tampered with… he wasn't sure either man would have made it out alive. This was life or death for her, and she wasn't given the option to fight for it.

Connor had a difficult time believing some of the things Cornelia had told him, and she explained it like she knew that too. She offered him bite sizes pieces of information until he had enough to put only part of the picture together. His inability to believe never had anything to do with her, but his own past experiences. Kate had primed him for the worst.

He had been giving Dr. Ingels the benefit of the doubt. Obviously the car accident was traumatic whether or not Cornelia remembered the aftermath, but somewhere inside him, Connor thought there was a possibility that her memory loss was just that accidental. A military hospital using civilians to test new treatments without patient consent? That resonated with the Cold War.

Whether he believed her or not, he could tell from the look in her eye that she told her truth. However their worlds or version of events differed, she believed that Dr. Ingels used her as a dummy for his experiments.

And Connor, rather than trying to comfort her, looked for holes in her story.

What was I thinking…

Every second Cornelia was gone, the panic grew on his chest, his shoulders, as if he could feel her moving further and further away.

"Go home and grab clothes and food, we don't want to have to stop on the way. I'll get a bag packed for her and meet you there," Renee said, pulling on his arm until he stood.

And when he didn't move right away: "Go, be ready when I get there," she urged, and ushered him out toward the hallway.

He nodded, struggling to move even as she shut the door

on him.

Renee could hardly think. One second she was sure that Cornelia could take care of herself, and the next she was called into action. She was just thankful that Connor had come to her before trying to do something stupid. Then again, he probably didn't know where to start.

Renee waited until she heard the echo of Connor's retreating footsteps and the squeak of the front door as he wrestled it closed. Then, she rooted through her desk drawers until she found the spare set of keys to Cornelia's apartment. On a large ring much like the ones janitors shuffled around with, each key was labeled with the apartment number it corresponded to.

Normally she threw the ring to the maintenance guy or the handyman and let them figure it out. The keys jingled as she frantically searched for apartment 19, the numbers ascending until she found the one she wanted.

She ran into the hallway and stuck the key in Cornelia's door. She knew it stuck, thanks to the banging Renee would hear when Cornelia came in, so she jiggled the key a few times and threw her weight into the door. After a groan and a crunch, it swung open.

Cornelia's space was sparse, mismatched, the obvious byproduct of too many yard sales and discount outlets.

Cornelia's bed sat unmade in the corner, a dresser between the bed and the bathroom door. Renee hoped it wouldn't be too harsh an invasion of privacy considering the circumstances, and dove into the dresser, grabbing her a change of clothes.

As she ran back toward the front door, she grabbed the sweatshirt lying across the loveseat that separated the bedroom area from the kitchen. She kept thinking she was forgetting something. The first time she met Cornelia played in her head on repeat, asking for just a pair of scrubs, struggling to do a task so simple as getting dressed. In a world she couldn't control or make sense of, all Cornelia wanted was some comfortable clothing. Renee always loved that.

She stormed back into her own apartment now, struggling to hold back tears, and grabbed herself a change of clothes and the contents of her pantry. They had already taken so many risks to get Cornelia out safely. What if it was all for naught?

If Renee hadn't fudged the paperwork and administered some illegal medicine, she had no doubt Cornelia would be dead. She'd be damned if she allowed her to end up right back where she started.

She zipped everything into a duffel bag and threw it over her shoulder. She paused for a second, taking stock of her apartment, and dashed out the door. She made her way to Connor's house at a speed she hadn't hit since she ran track in high school, as she had already wasted too much time gathering things to take with her. It was time to go.

She arrived at Connor's just as he locked the front door of his building.

"Ready?" she asked, as he turned.

"Yeah, let's go," he said.

They looked at each other, each waiting for the other to make a move.

"How are we getting there?" Connor asked.

"Don't you have a car?"

"Don't you?" he asked, incredulous.

"Oh my god, I can't believe this," Renee said, her heart sinking.

Where do you get a rental car at 2 am?

They were silent for a few moments.

"I might have *access* to a car," Connor said, biting his lip. "Wait here."

Connor went back inside.

Renee grew agitated as she waited. How much would a

taxi would cost to go to Maryland at two in the morning on a Friday night? Would any taxi even take them there? And once they got there, what if they had to make a fast getaway? Renee's heart threatened to explode out of her chest.

Connor re-emerged from his apartment with a set of keys in his hand.

"It's in a parking lot four blocks away. Let's go."

CHAPTER FIFTY TWO
Eight months and twenty-three days earlier, Fort Howard
Neuro Clinic

Cornelia showered off the day's work. She was feeling like herself again, pre-accident. She felt stronger, abler, ready to finally get out.

Her ring caught in her hair as she shampooed, and she reminded herself to take it off when she got out. They didn't want to unnecessarily anger the doctor before it was time. Until they left, they would remain the perfect little patients, Nate especially, but Cornelia would limit the attitude too.

She toweled off, dressed, and got into bed, her wet hair leaving little spots on the shoulders of her t-shirt. She busied herself with a crossword while she waited for the doctor to show up.

He swept in only a few minutes later and took his usual seat in the armchair next to her bed. He flipped the camera on as he passed by.

"How are we doing today?" he asked her, black book open and pen poised.

"Fine," she said, smiling.

"You seem happy today," he remarked.

"I am," she said, and she really couldn't help but smile.

"What's making you so happy?"

"Just... had a good day, I suppose," she said, closing her crossword book. He looked at her hand and her breath caught. She knew she'd forget. She couldn't slip it underneath her book fast enough.

When she glanced to the doctor, his lips were pursed. He stood, and took a step closer to her. He picked up a strand of her wet hair and fixed her with a gaze so heavy she felt she needed to look away. He was close enough she could smell his gross, musky cologne. She could feel his breath. "Looks like you need a towel," he said.

He went into her bathroom and retrieved one of the smaller towels. For a moment, he just looked at her, unsmiling, and then moved as if he was going to place the towel around her shoulders. She sat up straighter, moving away from him, and he handed it to her.

Without another word, he stalked out of the room, and Cornelia felt her gut screaming.

CHAPTER FIFTY THREE
Present day, somewhere along I-95 S

She felt movement, as if she were on a boat. Or... in a car.

She remembered being grabbed, strong hands wrapping around her arms. She could still feel them. She opened her eyes, and saw she was in the back of a van, splayed out on a stretcher. She heard conversation, two people sitting above her head.

She patted herself down and flexed her muscles. Everything was in working order. She sat up, dizzy as both the car and the stretcher moved underneath her.

"How ya feeling?" the guard asked conversationally.

"Is she awake?" Liam.

"Yeah, she just sat up," the guard murmured. He sat on a padded bench seat, directly behind Liam as he drove.

"Cornelia, lie down. We don't want you getting hurt back there," Liam said loudly, condescendingly, while braking suddenly.

"Well that's fine with me. I'll just be going." The van slowed more, coming to a mild stop.

Cornelia stood and walked unsteadily toward the sliding door.

"Mike!" Liam barked, eyes flitting between the road and the rearview mirror.

"Really, I don't think she'll-"

Cornelia grabbed the handle and pulled the door open, only to find herself watching pavement and endless forest fly by at upwards of fifty miles an hour. Her hair flew into her eyes, the hem of her dress billowing in the wind. It barely felt like they were moving at all.

Should I?

The guard pushed her away from the door before

she could decide. She fell back against the stretcher as he slammed the door shut. She was unsteady, foggy in the brain.

"What the hell are you doing? Are you trying to get yourself killed?" Liam shouted from the front.

"Ironic *you* should ask such a thing," she said. She moved toward the front of the van, ready to go down in flames if it meant she was taking Liam with her.

"Put her out!" he shouted, as she approached. His eyes were wide in the rearview. "Put her out!"

She felt a pinprick in her shoulder. She reached for Liam over the headrest and managed to get her hands around his neck, but couldn't squeeze. Her muscles felt like jelly, floppy, unsupportive.

He fought like a pansy. She promised to tell him so. As soon as she could.

CHAPTER FIFTY FOUR
Present day, the parking lot underneath 30th street station

The parking lot was situated underneath the rail bridges that connected center city to the terminals at 30th Street. It was full of potholes and badly lit, but it was significantly cheaper than some of the other options Kate had floated him when he first bought her the car.

He was so smug when she finally agreed to that parking lot. Where to put the fancy car had been a point of contention, as Kate wanted it as close as possible. Connor, already feeling conned out of fifty grand, said that if he bought her the car, she'd have to keep it in the cheaper parking lot and walk to it. Huffing, she agreed.

Yes, Connor *finally won.* He shook his head at himself, the resentment resurfacing.

He clicked the panic button, but heard nothing. *Oh, no.*

They walked further into the parking lot, to the shadowed places where street lamps couldn't find them. They relied on the lights from the train tracks reflecting off the shiny pampered cars to guide their way. He hit the panic button again, and this time, five rows over, the car alarm went off.

"That's it!" Connor shouted, and they ran in that direction. He thanked his lucky stars the battery hadn't died.

They clambered inside and threw their bags into the backseat. Renee moved the packaging from Kate's new light bulb to the ground.

"Wow, this is really nice," Renee said, rubbing her hands over the leather seats.

"My ex-wife says thanks," Connor remarked, scathingly.

"Oops, sorry. I mean this car is shit," Renee said.

"Where am I going?" he asked, moving swiftly along. He turned the key and watched the car come to life.

"Get on 95 and go until your hit Baltimore," Renee said.

"And what do we do once we get there?" he asked, easing the car into drive. The engine purred as he let his foot off the brake.

She was silent for a few seconds. "I haven't thought that far ahead, but I'm almost certain there's nothing we can do waiting around here," she said.

"We'll figure it out on the way then," Connor agreed, nodding.

He navigated through the parking lot, getting a feel for the car again. He had only driven it a handful of times, for oil changes and other maintenance. Kate beat it up; Connor took care of it.

They were on 95 within minutes, barreling southbound to Cornelia.

CHAPTER FIFTY FIVE
Present day, Fort Howard Neuro Clinic

Cornelia woke to a dim room. Everything was white, bathed in the single foggy overhead light. The rows of fluorescent lights above were dark.

She lay in a hospital bed, tucked under a crisp blue sheet and propped up on two way-too-fluffy pillows stacked underneath her head. Her neck screamed. She pushed herself to a sitting position, her bones cracking and creaking, and rolled her head in a circle a few times. She wore only a hospital gown.

A clock on the wall read 1:23am, but there were no windows in the room to verify. There was no phone, no computer, not even a medical chart at the foot of her bed. The hallway outside her room was dark. She pulled the IV out of her arm, hopeful it was only a saline drip. A droplet of blood rose in the needle's absence. She tensed and flexed; everything seemed to be in working order.

She swung her legs over the side of her bed. A long gash ran the length of her shin, from her knee down to her ankle, mirroring the car accident scar on her other leg. Part of it was sewn up with stitches. Her elbow had another ten.

She ran her hand over the tiny tender bumps. She couldn't have been there for more than a few hours. She breathed a sigh of relief, confident that she would remember the majority of this hospital stay.

Then again, maybe that's the way she felt last time.

She slid off the bed and padded over to the doorway. Scanning the room as she walked, she saw no other clothing, not even another hospital gown she could wear backwards. Across the room stood a mostly empty bookcase, aside from a few multiplayer games and empty manila folders.

As she neared the door, she realized she had seen this

room before, through the lens of a camera.

Down the long hallway to her right, two dim lights lit the space of 7-8 rooms, until the hallway turned. To her left, one light illuminated the rest of the shorter hallway, a lonely exit sign glowing haphazardly toward the very end.

She stepped out of her room and shuffled in that direction, holding the back of her hospital gown shut. She picked up speed as she went, gathering confidence in her body's ability to move and the growing proximity to an exit.

Someone coughed and Cornelia halted, turning toward the sound. A security guard, one who seemed to enjoy hiding in the shadows, manned the dark nurse's station. Cornelia could barely make out his face. "I wouldn't try to scale barbed wire in a hospital gown if I were you."

Cornelia walked toward him. "Well what *would* you have me do?"

"The doctor will be back in the morning. Go to sleep," he said.

She stared at him.

"You don't really have a choice," he pressed.

She pulled her gown extra tight and shuffled back into her room.

Now was not the time to push. She would gather information in the morning to plan her escape. If only Renee was there to help her like she had before.

CHAPTER FIFTY SIX
Present day, somewhere along I-95 S

"So what's our plan?" Connor asked. He put the car on cruise control and got into the middle lane. They had been driving for twenty minutes in silence.

"I don't know," Renee said flatly.

"We should probably figure one out." Connor paused as he thought of the throwing stars he had in his gym bag at home. "I uh, didn't know what to bring but I didn't bring any weapons."

Renee nodded. "I didn't either."

"So how are we going to get her out?" he prompted.

In his periphery, Connor saw Renee turn to him.

"How about I tell you what I know and then we can see if we can think of something together," she said.

"Okay." Connor nodded.

"So, we have a bunch of things working for us. The majority of the campus was abandoned, aside from the building I'm betting Cornelia is in now. It's where she lived for six months.

"Then there's the fact that the clinic was shut down, so there are no other patients or staff in the building. That also means the doctor's main source of income no longer exists. But I also think he's paying for the security guards out of his own pocket, meaning there's a chance that he's running out of money and might downsize," she considered. "But I'm also pretty sure he inherited some wealth, so that might not be a reliable conclusion."

"And there's also a chance that the security guards have a newfound fondness for he who was once a doctor and he who is now rainmaker," Connor added.

"Yes, that's also a concern," she said.

"How many guards do you think there are?" he asked. He could take a few, if they had skills similar to the one Cornelia fought off. And Renee looked scrappy, but he was sure she couldn't handle more than one at a time, if that. Cornelia, however, could take care of herself... if she was still Cornelia.

But Connor didn't want to think about that. She would be well and aware when they arrived.

"When I was at his hotel, there were two, though one of them let me go so I'm not sure where his loyalty lies," she said. "I just don't know. Maybe he thought all he needed were two to take a tiny girl like Cornelia. Or maybe that's all he could afford. Maybe he has a hundred waiting for us when we get there."

"Two, I think we can handle," Connor said. "But we're going to need an actual plan if we're looking at a hundred guards."

They drove in silence until they passed a sign for fireworks.

"I need a bathroom stop," Connor said, knowing another convenient opportunity would be unlikely on their trip.

CHAPTER FIFTY SEVEN
Present day, Fort Howard Neuro Clinic

Cornelia stayed in bed but couldn't sleep. She got up to pace aimlessly a few times, circling her room like a caged animal. She left her room once to walk down the hall and back, but the security guard followed on her heels until she went back to her room just to get away from him.

There was a large emergency exit sign to her right, at the end of the longer hall. To her left, in the distance, she could see a large board that looked like a hospital map, and she guessed that just beyond that corner was the entrance. All of the windows in the common areas were sealed shut, double-paned windows interlaced with wire. The rec room had a small outdoor area, but, like the security guard had warned her, it was lined with barbed wire. Nevertheless, she considered it an option.

The clock on the wall read 4:15. Sufficiently exhausted, she got back in bed and tried to sleep. If she wanted to find a way out, she would need all of her energy in the morning.

It felt like only minutes before she began hearing voices. They echoed, as if they were coming closer from down the hall.

Cornelia's eyes flipped open, and she listened as intently as she could. She slid out of bed and padded to the doorway. The security guard snored softly, his head tipped back, resting on his chair. She looked down both sides of the hallway but couldn't tell where the voices came from.

She heard footsteps. She ducked back into her room when she saw an elbow poke out from behind the corner at the end of the hall to her left. She shuffled back to bed quietly and dove under the sheets. The voices in the hallway grew louder, along with the approaching footsteps.

Liam and a man dressed in a military uniform rounded the corner into her room. Liam smiled, but the military man stayed expressionless. He had two guns holstered, one on each hip, and came to a stop in a wide stance with his hands held behind his back.

"Dr. Heltz, this is Cornelia," Liam said, motioning to her with an open palm. She raised his eyebrows at him. This was not what she was expecting.

The new doctor walked toward her and she recoiled, pushing herself up again the bed frame. Unphased, he continued his approach, so she rolled and slipped out of bed on the other side in one fluid motion. She knew better than to "wait and see" when a very large man with guns walks toward you with too much conviction.

"Corey, chill out," Liam said, eyes flashing back and forth between her and Dr. Heltz.

"Sorry, I didn't mean to alarm you," Dr. Heltz said, holding his hands up. He held his hand out to shake from across the bed. She glanced at Liam, who turned red. She limply shook Dr. Heltz's hand, and as he backed away from the bed, she wearily climbed back in.

"Dr. Heltz is here to see the remarkable progress we have made with Memories I and II," Liam explained to her, smiling.

"Again, I mean no harm. I'm just here to observe," Dr. Heltz said.

"So I'm just going to ask you a few questions, alright Cornelia?" Liam asked her, the smile still plastered to his face. He had so much pep in his voice she wanted to puke.

"Nah," she said. She couldn't resist, the anger bubbling so aggressibely on the tip of her tongue.

Liam brushed it off, giving her a very pointed look. He glanced to Dr. Heltz, who was still stolid. He scooched the arm chair closer to her bed, and she had a flashback to seeing him sit in that very position, quizzing her, through the screen of her laptop while she sat on Connor's couch and wondered if it could get any worse. She felt a burning sensation in her stomach.

"Alright. So Cornelia, let's start with your accident," he said, clearing his throat. He held a clipboard, a pen poised above it. Dr. Heltz stood by the foot of her bed, observing. "Can you tell me what you remember about the car crash and your recovery afterwards?"

"No," she said, shaking her head. It was technically correct; the best kind of correct.

"Alright, I understand you are a little uncomfortable, but the sooner we get through this process, the sooner we can make it a little more livable in here," he said, nodding as he spoke. The nape of his neck was bright red. "So let's start from the beginning. Go ahead and tell us what you remember."

She smiled, a true genuine smile. If she was going to be stuck in this hellhole, she was not going to make it easy for *anyone*.

"Cornelia," Liam warned.

"Yes?"

"Please cooperate," he sighed, like a sleep-deprived parent coaxing a toddler through the terrible twos.

"What are your intentions with me?" she started, including Dr. Heltz in her question.

"We want to see how your memory is functioning. If you are still doing well, we think you would be a marvelous candidate for the next treatment in this series," Liam explained. Dr. Heltz cleared his throat. "*I* think you would be a marvelous candidate for the next treatment."

She shook her head. "No, definitely not."

"Liam, why don't we talk outside?" Dr. Heltz prompted, nodding toward the door.

"No, she'll cooperate, just let her get it out of her system. She wants to help, she just gets *cranky* sometimes," Liam said, waving his hand at Dr. Heltz. Liam focused on Cornelia. Dr. Heltz pursed his lips. "Cornelia, please, just make it easier on all of us."

"Me, make it easier on you? After you pluck me up off

the street, drug me up and put me in some run down hospital just so you can show me off to your boss? No, you lost your chance at ease when I was dragged in here like a ragdoll at your behest. No! You lost easy when you tried to sleep with me. Or maybe when you were carrying a flash drive of medical interviews of me. Or, maybe when I was held captive here the first time. You can kiss *easy* goodbye," she said, crossing her arms and staring straight ahead.

"Liam," Dr. Heltz said sternly. Her heartbeat quickened, a mixture of fear and catharsis pumping through her veins.

Cornelia didn't look at either of them as they left the room. They wouldn't get that satisfaction.

"The trial is over, let her go home," Dr. Heltz said.

"But the treatments worked! She's a prime candidate for the third, it *will* work."

"Did she consent to being here?"

There was a long pause.

"Not yet, but if she would just let me explain what she's a part of, I'm sure she'll see why it's so important that she help us," Liam rushed. "She just doesn't understand, but she will once I have the chance to impress upon her the importance of these trials."

"She is *not interested.* I don't even want to know what she was talking about in there, because that has 'medical malpractice' and 'lawsuit' written all over it if one sliver of that becomes public. Get rid of her."

"Let me convince her," Liam insisted.

Dr. Heltz entered her room and took his spot by the foot of her bed. Liam poked his head in but didn't move further than the doorway.

"Cornelia, do you know why you're here?"

Unsure of the best answer, she shook her head, wide-eyed.

"You're part of an experimental drug trial for a series of treatments that will allow the military to manipulate and influence the memories of enemies of the United States. Liam assures me that this will be sufficient information for you to consent to further treatment. Is he correct?"

She shook her head again.

Dr. Heltz turned to Liam. "Liam, send her home. The trial is over, pack your things."

Dr. Heltz left the building, his footsteps steadily retreating down the hallway. His departure was punctuated by the resounding boom of the front door slamming shut.

CHAPTER FIFTY EIGHT
Present day, somewhere along I-95 S

The guy behind the counter had shaggy hair and a penchant for reggaeton. Connor thought he smelled a puff of weed, but he seemed to hide it well. He wondered how many customers came through at that time of night.

"Hey man, do you have a bathroom?" Connor asked. Renee leaned against the hood of the car, waiting.

"Customers only," the attendant said.

Connor grunted in disapproval.

"I'll buy something," Renee offered, stepping up to the counter next to him. She had been looking for an excuse to buy some fireworks now that they were legal in Pennsylvania.

The man behind the counter handed over the bathroom key and directed Connor around back to a ramshackle door labeled "HROOM," the first half missing. Meanwhile, Renee selected an assortment fireworks she had been itching to buy since they were legalized in Pennsylvania, the child in her excited despite the situation.

"Got enough fireworks?" Connor asked as he rounded the side of the building, taking stock of the four large boxes she had selected.

"Just enough, I think," she said.

They clambered back into the car, fireworks thrown into the backseat.

While Renee had waited for Connor to return, she realized all of her former patients would now be somewhere in the immediate area. She decided she'd ask Connor drop her off somewhere before he took Cornelia home so she could spend some time trying to find them.

Renee grabbed her bag and started ruffling through it, spilling the contents all over her seat and the floor beneath her. As Connor started moving, continuing on down 95, Renee found what she had been looking for – a notepad and a pen. Furiously, she started scribbling.

"What are you writing?" he asked her.

"Former patients were transferred to local hospitals," Renee explained. "After we find Cornelia, I'd like to check up on whomever I can."

"I thought Cornelia was the only patient to make it out alive?" he asked her. She stopped scribbling and turned to him.

"Alive in the sense that you and I are alive, yes. There were many patients who were *alive* in the clinic, but most of them were technically brain dead, others were very close, and several showed significant signs of activity." She tapped her pen against the notepad a few times. "In the beginning, the doctor actually did some really amazing work. It's a pity, how he changed."

They were silent for a few moments, watching distant taillights in front of them.

"I think we'll be there in about an hour," Renee said.

Connor nodded. "And then what?"

"Probably wait," Renee said. "He does all treatments at nine in the morning. That'll be our best opportunity to intercept. At the least it'll give us time to come up with a better plan."

"What if he's already given it to her? Memory III, or whatever it is?"

Renee clicked her pen against the paper again. "Then she was gone the second the car door closed."

CHAPTER FIFTY NINE
Present day, Fort Howard Neuro Clinic

Cornelia was antsy. Dr. Heltz had left the premises, and Liam had left the room, leaving a guard to bar her exit.

She asked if he had heard Dr. Heltz's orders to let her go.

He claimed Dr. Ingels held superiority. Cornelia claimed the guard was full of shit.

He claimed she needed to get back in her room, and then pushed her inside.

Maybe violence was finally the correct answer. She landed a punch to his cheekbone, and he to hers.

The guard wouldn't tell her anything after that. She wondered if he even *knew* anything else. He didn't seem overjoyed to be there, but he was at least a diligent watchman. He never left his post.

Cornelia paced, keeping her backside turned toward the inside of the room. Was Liam trying to keep her there regardless of Dr. Heltz's orders? If so, she needed to get out, *now*. Who knows how far he'll go? And she needed something else to wear – anything else. A bare ass wasn't a part of her exit plan.

She shuffled up to the doorway. "Can I get some scrubs?" she asked.

The guard looked up from his phone and held his arms out. "Does it look like I have any scrubs?"

"There's gotta be some around here somewhere," she said. She wrapped her hospital gown tight, and slipped around to the other side of the nurse's station.

"Go back to your room, I'll look," he grunted, guiding her back.

She watched him search from the doorway. He haphazardly pulled out drawers and opened cabinets, but found no spare clothing.

Defeated, she wandered back into her room. Shelves on one side of the room held a few board games and various card decks. She wandered over to look through the games, wondering if she could at least entertain herself for an hour or so. She told herself she was waiting for the doctor to finish up discharge paperwork.

"Why do you need scrubs?" he shouted, still rummaging through the nurse's station.

"I'm uncomfortable," she said, thumbing through the games.

"No one can see you," he said.

She rolled her eyes. "Doesn't mean I can't be uncomfortable."

She sighed and turned back towards her bed. From that angle, she noticed some red cloth poking out from underneath.

She ducked down and pulled on the fabric, revealing the tiny red dress from her date with Connor. She laid it out over her bed and inspected the damage. There were a few pulls in the fabric, but otherwise it still looked brand new. The metal clasp in back was broken, extended out in a funny direction, but it was nothing a pair of pliers and some willpower couldn't fix.

"I don't think there are any scrubs out here," the guard said.

"Oh well," she lamented. She unzipped the back of the red dress and stepped into it. It took a little bit of contortion but she was able to zip herself up, minus the locking metal clasp. At least her ass was covered.

"Where's the doctor?" she asked again, the minutes stretching longer as she waited.

Against her own better judgment, she had gotten excited. Someone in power knew of her struggle – someone, *finally*, with the power to stop it.

"Looks like he went home," the guard said as he sat back in his chair, checking his phone.

"He what?" Cornelia asked, pulling her hospital gown around her as she stomped to the nurse's station.

"He went home," the guard said, repeated. He didn't look at her as she came back to the doorway.

She shook her head and retreated into her room, sitting on her bed. "What a prick," she muttered.

She wondered what it would take to knock the guard out. Could she surprise him somehow? He was trained, smart. She'd have to be creative. What if it was the difference between life and death? Could she take him down then?

The clock on the wall read 3:30. It was going to be a long night.

Over time she heard his faint snores.

Cornelia slipped out of bed and tiptoed to the door. One of his arms fell off to his side, while the other rested on top of his phone and belly. His arm was surely falling asleep in that position; perhaps he wouldn't notice Cornelia sneaking away....

She padded out of her room and took a left down the hallway. It was dead silent, but she was quieter. She didn't worry about going fast – just that she was quiet. Turning the corner, she came upon the main entrance.

She took a moment to stare at the push bar doors. There was no way she would get out unnoticed with those things banging around, but *this was her shot.*

She glanced back down the hallway to the sleeping guard.

She took a deep breath, pushed open the door, and ran as fast as her legs would take her.

She was immediately disoriented, the darkness of the night effectively blinding her. She could barely see her own hands in front of her, and though she hoped she was running in the right direction, she had no clue how they had come. When she researched the complex, there were buildings surrounding the hospital on all sides, but she couldn't see any to help orient herself.

The gravel road dug into her feet. She could feel the skin splintering open and debris scrunching inside. As her eyes adjusted, she saw trees everywhere, interspersed with unlit, indecipherable, ramshackle buildings on either side. The roads were deserted. Where was she even going?

But she couldn't stop now. She couldn't go back now.

The road stretched on, but she refused to stop running. As she rounded a small corner, she came face to face with headlights, the car appearing as if from nowhere. Cornelia stopped, holding a hand above her blinded eyes. Behind her, she could see the dim outline of the building she had come from. She had barely made it a block, and if the road spanning beyond the red glow of the car's taillights was any indication, she had much further to go.

The driver's side door opened and Cornelia's heart caught in her throat. Liam stepped out.

"Cornelia," he warned, hovering in the space between the open door and leather interior. "What are you doing?"

"Nothing," she said, taking a few steps back.

He closed the car door and stalked toward her. "Just out for an evening jog, I see."

He was too close.

She backed away, but her heel connected with a large rock. She stumbled as she turned to run. He caught her by the arm, pulling her to the ground. She felt another pin prick in her neck, and she threw an elbow, connecting with his throat. He choked and flailed, struggling to keep hold of her. She pulled on his arm, bringing him head first to the pavement, but her grip slipped and she elbowed the ground instead.

Her searing feet went numb, and her eyelids felt heavy. She just couldn't hold them open any longer.

CHAPTER SIXTY
Present day, just outside Fort Howard Neuro Clinic

They drove up a narrow residential street, their right side lined with cookie cutter houses, the left with an abandoned park, overgrown grassland as far as the eye could see. Toward the end of the road, a swinging metal gate blocked their path. It was the entrance to Fort Howard Memorial Hospital, and guests were not welcome.

Renee hopped out of the car, pushing the gate out of the way and motioning for Connor to drive through. He stopped a few feet passed the gate and waited. As the car idled, Renee put everything back in place and hoisted herself back into the SUV. "You might want to turn the lights off," she said.

Connor obliged, and the night settled around them.

He let off the brake and the car inched along. He leaned forward, his nose nearly pressed against the window as he followed the dim line of the curb to the right of the car. "How far away are we?" he asked.

"About another block and a half. We have to go past this line of trees and make the next left. That should land us where we need to be," Renee said.

Connor squinted. "Those are trees?"

She paused. "Are you blind?"

Connor harrumphed. "I don't know the area like you do."

They inched forward, the mass on either side of the road fading to gray as the trees came to an end. Connor could see only distant outlines of a building looming ahead, four dimly lit windows on the bottom flow. He followed them, confident the only lit building in sight was the one they were after.

"Drive around to the back, I don't want anyone to see us," Renee said.

"Renee, I don't know my ass from my hand right now, you're going to have to direct me," he said. He felt like if he so much as blinked, they'd be tumbling down some unseen ravine just a misstep over the curb he followed.

"Go straight. Make a left after we pass the building. That's where the parking lot is. We should be able to get an idea of who's inside if we can get a look at the cars," she said. She repeated her directions as they passed. They stopped in the lot across the street from the small hospital, hidden behind the hump of a hill. Trees lined the edge of the parking lot behind them.

Some of the light from inside the building reflected outside, and Connor no longer needed to squint.

They peered out of Connor's window, their vantage point allowing them to see just over the hump and into the parking lot just below the lit building. There were three cars out front.

"I don't see the doctor's car," she said.

"That's good, right?" Connor asked.

"I mean, they probably came here in the SUV, I doubt he insisted on picking up his own car. It probably means nothing," Renee said. Connor stared into the parking lot, searching for movement.

"If there are three cars parked outside, we can assume there are at least three people inside, other than the doctor, right? Four, including Cornelia?" Connor asked.

Renee nodded.

"So we can guess it's the doctor, and three security guards?" he postulated.

"We could guess that," Renee said hesitantly. She watched the building intently.

Connor thought about their options. "If all of them have the same training that the one who attacked Cornelia had, I think I can take them," Connor said. Renee didn't say anything. "As long as you back me up," he joked, nudging her. She smiled.

"I don't think the doctor is here anyways," Renee mumbled. "He's usually strict about his schedule when it comes to experiments," Renee explained. "I don't think we have to worry about him right now. I think he'll be at home trying to get a good night's sleep. He'll arrive at exactly 8:15 in the morning."

Renee didn't know whether she was repeating herself for Connor's benefit or her own.

Connor nodded, and from the vehicle count outside the building, drew some conclusions. "So we're looking at three guards then," Connor concluded. "Plus Cornelia."

"Three against three sounds like a fair fight," Renee remarked.

"Will she be able to get out on her own, do you think?" Connor asked, scared to hear the answer. The question had been bothering him since they left Philadelphia.

"I don't think they knocked her out for long," Renee said. "Probably just a couple hours so they could get her here. She'd have to be awake for Memory III."

Then again, there were plenty of reasons they might have given her a stronger sedative, even if that pushed their experiment. "But, you're probably right. We shouldn't count on her much."

"So to be safe we can assume it's one and a half against three," he said. Renee scrunched her eyebrows together. "I'm counting Cornelia as a half person handicap if I have to carry her out."

Renee nodded. "I'm really hoping that will not be the case."

They were silent, the stillness of the night weighing down on them.

"I think we should wait until dawn," Renee said.

"So she has a better chance of walking out on her own?" Connor asked.

"So that I can see past my hand – I think it's too dark outside right now and we run the risk of screwing things up further if we try to go in blind."

CHAPTER SIXTY ONE
Present day, Fort Howard Neuro Clinic

Cornelia was back in bed. This time, handcuffed.

Her right wrist was in one link, the other around the railing of the bed.

She pulled at the handcuffs, feeling the metal strain against her wrist. She wouldn't be going anywhere soon – at least, not without carting her bed around with her. That would make for a noisy escape.

"Hello?" she shouted, wondering if the security guard was still outside her door. She heard footsteps.

"Ah, she's awake," Liam said, strolling into the room. He smiled, a big shit-eating grin that Cornelia wouldn't hesitate to smack off his face if she had the chance.

"Can you unlock me now please?" she asked, holding her locked wrist out to him.

"Not after that little run you took earlier," he said. He clasped his hands in front of him. "I'm afraid the handcuffs will have to stay on until further notice. You will be given a bathroom break every four hours."

"Are you serious? For the love of god just hire a guard that doesn't sleep on the job," she said.

"You'll be pleased to hear that Ben has been let go. Some more professional guards have been hired, and they will remain stationed and awake at all exits. Just in case."

He leaned down and kissed her forehead.

Just the scent of him triggered Cornelia's gag reflex. He inhaled as she dry heaved over the side of the bed.

"We'll be prepping you for treatment in the morning, so I suggest you get some sleep," he said, standing up straight.

"What treatment?" She already knew, but there was a small part of her that, despite everything, remained hopeful.

"We will be testing the third drug in our trial series. I think you are a fantastic candidate and after some consideration, Dr. Heltz agrees," he explained.

"What, did you kill him too?" Cornelia quipped. "Did he say, 'over my dead body'? Is that what you take as agreement?"

Liam paused and smiled, ignoring her question. "The procedure will begin with an injection at the base of your neck. It could take minutes or hours for the changes to be noticeable, but there is a high chance that we will need to induce a coma to make sure that the brain heals properly. Once you wake up, we can begin to ascertain effectiveness," the doctor explained. He wrung his hands together. "Get excited, Cornelia. You're about to become part of medical history. This could be the treatment that changes the world."

"No, I'm not doing this," Cornelia said, shaking her head. Her words were futile, but what else could she do? Words were all she had. "You need my consent to do this, and I do *not* consent."

Liam smiled. "If my memory serves me correct, as it would, you *did* consent to this procedure," he said, tapping his temple. "In fact, I seem to remember you *begging* me to administer it to you."

Cornelia was silent, wounded, realizing she had seen the aftermath on her videos.

"Maybe it would make a difference if Connor was here. If it was *his* turn to be my patient, would you be willing to cooperate? That seemed to work before," he questioned, taking a step closer to her head. She wiggled away from him, uncomfortable. "In fact, I'm sure he's on his way. Maybe we can see how the treatment works on him when he arrives."

Cornelia kept quiet and averted her eyes. The last thing she wanted to do was cause anyone else this pain.

The doctor stood by her side for a few more seconds, and then swiftly walked to the door. He paused for a moment before leaving. "We will begin promptly at 9am."

He walked out, tapping the frame of the door quickly as

he left. His footsteps echoed down the hallway.

She stared at the clock on the wall. The top left was faded, and it hung slightly lopsided, she noticed. Had she seen these things before?

The walls were white and bare, mind-numbingly boring. Had anything changed since the last time she was there? Did she have anyone to talk to, anyone who shared this unique experience? Who else had had something so precious as their own memory violated in such a barbaric way?

She pulled on the handcuffs again, thinking a low quality pair might just break under enough duress, but had no such luck. She developed a thick red ring around her right wrist, the skin there raw and sensitive. She slid out of bed to her right, and checked the wheels for a lock. The one closest to her had a small foot lever. Using her toe, she played with it until it popped open. Thus, she granted herself some minor freedom.

She resumed pacing, trailing her bed behind her as she moved. It was awkward, and the wheel kept flat-tiring her already beaten feet, but it was better than sitting around waiting for morning. She walked in small circles, increasing her radius as she adjusted to the cumbersome movement of her new caboose.

As her circles widened, her bed pushed up against the walls, clanging around the corners of her room. She realized why so many insane people are pictured in rooms with white walls, leaning. It wasn't that they were unsteady – they just wanted out, like the further they pushed from the center of the circle, the closer they were to going home.

She outlined the painted concrete blocks with her finger, feeling the smooth and then the rough. It calmed her, to focus on something so trivial.

Loop after loop, she dragged her bed around behind her.

She got careless, and the bed knocked into the sparsely used bookshelf. It landed with a thud on the floor that, on a normal day would be nothing more than a bang. But that night, in the quiet deadness of the hospital, the thump rang out like a gunshot or a sonic boom. Cornelia jumped, her breath catching in her chest.

"What was that?" the new guard asked, appearing at the door.

She adjusted her bed to her other side and tried to lift the bookshelf, but couldn't find the right angle for the leverage she needed.

"Nothing," Cornelia said, turning back to the bookcase. "I'm feng-shui-ing." When she glanced back, he had disappeared.

She shuffled around to the opposite side of the fallen shelf, and from that vantage point, noticed a manila folder poking out from the side. It must have been stuck behind the bookshelf before she knocked it over.

She picked it up, and as it turned in her hand, a small silver ring dropped out of the bottom. Cornelia froze, watching it spin to a rest.

She picked up the ring and slid it onto her finger, the metal loose and cold. She stared at it for a moment, recognition and Nate overwhelming her, and then took it right back off. Rather than risk losing it, she added it to the chain around her neck, right above her heart.

She opened the manila folder and found one sheet of paper – a marriage certificate, for Cornelia Winthorpe and Nathan Montgomery.

CHAPTER SIXTY TWO
Present day, Fort Howard Neuro Clinic

Dawn rose slowly, and Connor and Renee waited bleary-eyed until they had enough light to safely move from the car. They had a little less than an hour before Dr. Ingels would arrive, assuming he kept to his schedule.

They had spent hours thinking of the best way to get in and out quickly, without being noticed. After plenty of deliberation, they decided it was impossible, and they might as well use the front door. They would aim for speed, not stealth.

Connor would go in first and talk to the guard stationed just inside the door. He would get the guard turned around, keeping eyes on the intruder. While the guard's attention was on Connor, she would sneak down the hallway in the other direction, right to Cornelia's room.

If that didn't work... well, it had to.

They strode up to the front door and pulled. It was locked.

They looked at each other – that wasn't a problem they had planned for. Renee had never once before seen the hospital locked. It had always been fully staffed; there was never a need.

There was a numbered keypad to the right of the door, so Renee punched in her old employee number, but the pad was dark and unresponsive. The door was locked manually. She hadn't wanted to alert anyone that they were there by popping in through a window, but now she felt she had no choice. Peering through the small window in the door, she could see no guard stationed on the other side.

"I think this might be a good thing," Renee said, taking a step back.

"How is this a good thing? We have less than an hour before the doctor gets here. How do we get in now?" he asked.

"Well I don't know yet how we'll get in, but we will. And no guard at the front must mean they're scrimping. There might be even fewer people than we think," she said.

"It could also mean that they're all hanging out with Cornelia," Connor said.

"Yeah I suppose that's true," Renee murmured.

Connor stepped a few paces back, eyeing up the building. "Is there an emergency exit?" Connor asked.

"Yes, but it's always locked," Renee told him. "Patients were going out to smoke."

His eyebrows scrunched together. "Isn't that illegal, a locked emergency exit?"

"I mean yes, but is that really the only illegal thing you're worried about right now?" she asked.

Connor shrugged. "Well, we have to at least try it," he said.

They rounded the building, passing by a small recreation area surrounded by a 20 foot high, electrified chain link fence. "What are the chances that thing is on?" Connor asked, briefly veering off toward it. The top of the fence split out into a Y, serving as a base for a roll of barbed wire overhead.

"Good. For the love of god, do not touch it," Renee said, throwing an arm out in front of him so he couldn't get any closer.

The sole emergency exit opened to a small asphalt area, and also served as a trash area. She could tell by the smell that no trash service had been by in a long time.

Renee pulled on the door and then walked back toward Connor. "It's locked."

Connor started pacing. "We have to break a window then," he said.

"They're all double-paned and wired. They're impossible to break," Renee said, feeling her heart sink.

Connor nodded, widening his circle. He looked up at the building, scanning the exterior for any way in. "What about bathroom windows? Office windows? Kitchen windows or ventilation?" he asked.

"The vent thing only really works in movies," she said.

"Not if it's installed improperly. Do you know how many places will just cut a whole in the wall and call it a vent? This is an old building, there's a chance there's some shoddy work somewhere," he said, scanning he exterior.

Renee considered their options and checked the time.

"We have a good half hour before the doctor arrives. If you want to spend that time looking for another way in, I'm all for it," she said, knowing how painful it was to think of doing nothing. "But I'm wondering if, at this point, we should just wait for the doctor, restrain him, and steal his keys?"

Connor thought about it for a second. "I'd rather get Cornelia out of there before he's anywhere near here but that can be our backup plan. He's not much of a fighter, I could probably exhale in his direction and he'd drop his keys in fear."

"Whatever you do, don't let them stick you," she said, motioning like she had a syringe in her hand. "Alright. So we'll look for another way in for now, and when he gets here, you'll take care of him and I'll grab the keys."

"Look I really don't want to seriously disable the guy..." Connor started, but stopped after a piercing look from Renee.

"Let's just look for a way in," she said, and started walking around the building.

She had spent so much time in this hospital. It held that familiar air like going back to your old high school, but something about it still seemed distant. She hated the work she did there more with every passing day, and that feeling returned with a vengeance upon just looking at it. She felt like she needed to shower just standing outside.

They wandered around the side of the building, staring up the never-ending brickwork. There were small windows in the patient's rooms on the upper floor, but they were all covered in bars. The bottom floors only had patient rooms toward the inside, so those who lived there never even saw the light of day.

That was where Cornelia's room had been, and if Renee knew the doctor like she thought she did, he would have stuck her right back in the same place, even though the one above it was significantly nicer – and might have given her an opportunity to escape. Several of the rooms on the upper levels had faulty windows. Normally it wasn't a concern, since the metal bars would keep any flighty patients in, but when the metal bars started rusting, a few of them could be popped out. It took a lot of force, but it was possible.

Only one patient had ever escaped. The other patient who managed to open his window just wanted to smoke a cigarette.

Renee tried to remember which room it was the patient had escaped from. She knew it was the third floor, in the rear of the building, but as she stared up at the potentials, Renee was overwhelmed with the number of windows staring back at her. There was no way she'd be able to remember exactly which one it was.

"Maybe if we can get up to the second floor windows we can jiggle one loose," Renee said. Connor was bent over what looked like a drain, nestled in the ground next to the building.

He gave up on his search and backed away from the building, looking up to all of the identical windows. "Do they open?" he asked. He stood next to her as she racked her brain.

"Not by design but some of them were faulty. I just wish I could remember which," she said.

The escape happened when Renee had just started. She was new and while she was getting her feet wet, she worked mainly with patients on the lower level. She had fleeting interaction with other patients when needed, but she had talked to the escapee patient only once. She couldn't even remember the woman's name....

What kind of terrible nurse couldn't remember a patient's name? Renee felt a renewed need to help Cornelia, to prove she wasn't the terrible nurse Dr. Ingels insisted she was.

"What about the first floor windows?" he asked.

"Double-paned and wired. If we can get through the bars on one of the second floor windows, those will be a lot easier to break," she explained.

Connor nodded. "Bring the car around, I'll climb up and see if I can knock any free," he said, throwing the car keys at her.

She glanced over her shoulder as she ran back to the car, and watched as Connor scaled the dumpster and a nearby pipe that ran down the side of the building. He did it easily, almost catlike.

She started up the car and pulled around to the building, stopping underneath a window that looked extra shoddy. Connor, hanging from a set of bars on the second floor already, pulled on each one, crossing beneath the line of two close-set windows like a kid swinging from the monkey bars. He was able to cross between two windows that way, but needed to jump down on top of the car to get to the next set. Renee inched slowly, careful not to throw him off.

The thump of his body weight hitting the car's ceiling above her quick started her heart each time, but more so than the noise, the fewer windows of opportunity they had with every passing thump culled her anxiety.

Renee heard a clang, and a metal bar rolled down the windshield.

She froze, waiting for the thump.

Clang, bang, grunt, thump, thump, grunt, thump, crash...

"I'm in!"

He knocked one bar out and used it to break the two surrounding bars, creating just enough room for him to slide through. The window itself was harder to break, but luckily it wasn't wired. He hadn't broken cement in years, but used every trick he could remember for cement bricks, to break through glass.

He created a hole in the window that matched the size of the hole in the bars. The glass was shatter proof, but not incapable of doing some harm should he accidentally scrape it on his way in. He kicked out some more pieces before maneuvering through, using the bars on the outside to swing feet first inside the building.

He landed easily, and listened.

He was in an old patient room, set up almost like a dorm room. It was dark, illuminated only by a faint light from the hallway. Two single beds sat parallel to each other, stripped down to the mattresses, one with a large stain on it, and the other discolored, like it had been used far longer than it should have been. Fresh sheets were stacked at the foot of each, but they looked like they had been collecting dust for quite some time.

Connor walked to the door, and using the frame to hide his body, peeked each way down the hallway. It was quiet, seemingly deserted.

He stepped outside and searched for signs directing to a stairway.

Judging by the lack of life on the second floor, he guessed everyone was downstairs with Cornelia. He'd have to face three or more guards, and Cornelia might be a lifeless sack over his shoulder. He took note of his exits, planning his escape in advance.

He walked toward the farther end of the hallway, which opened to a nurse's station on his left. Beyond that, another hallway ran parallel to the one he had come from in front of the building. If Cornelia's room was in the middle like Renee said, she was likely right below him.

He passed the nurse's station as he walked the hallway at the front of the building, peeking out carefully first. To his right was a large EXIT sign, which he guessed would lead to the lower level and ultimately open to the locked emergency exit door. To his left was a sign for the elevator.

The emergency exit stairs were at the far end of the hallway and accessed through a large push bar door. He eased through slowly and quietly, hoping no one was waiting for him on the other side.

His footsteps echoed in the small space, but he heard no one else's. It was even darker here than it had been in the hallway upstairs. The stairwell was filled with a mild humming.

As he came to the first floor landing, he passed by an industrial generator, the source of the building's dim light. Wires splayed spider-like on the ground around it.

He peered through the tiny window of the first floor door.

He was sure opening it would alert someone. Straight ahead, he could see only a hallway that ran from the front to the back of the building. The second floor had been set up like a road, two parallel walkways with a nurse's station in the middle, connecting them. The first floor, if this hallway was any indication, was set up like a square, the patients contained in the belly of the building with hallways that wrapped around in a square.

If Renee was right, and Cornelia was in her old room, she was only half a hallway away.

Connor pushed through the door carefully, holding it until it closed noiselessly behind him.

He walked forward a few steps, listening.

He heard nothing, no one else coming or talking, like the entire floor was deserted. He had hoped not to run into anyone, but something didn't quite feel right. Was Cornelia even there?

He glanced into each room as he walked by, most of them empty patient rooms. The beds matched – all stripped down with a pile of dusty old sheets at the foot. As he got closer to the nurse's station, he passed a large rec room on his right, a cafeteria style room, and a TV room.

Twenty feet from the nurse's station, he heard a cough. Connor froze, taking a 360-degree snapshot of his situation.

He couldn't see anyone. He stayed still.

He heard a set of footsteps, but he couldn't tell where they were coming from. He looked in front of and behind himself, and as the panic bubbled up, a man dressed in a security uniform stepped out from behind the station, his attention fully invested in the magazine he carried.

Connor dipped into the closest room, hoping he hadn't been spotted. Luckily, it seemed the other cars in the parking lot had been a decoy – there was only one guard. Hopefully he wouldn't have to hurt the guy. After all, he knew what it was like to take a shitty job just for the paycheck.

He listened at the door for footsteps, but didn't hear any.

He turned to take stock of his situation, and came face to face with two other security guards with confused looks on their faces, sitting at a card table in the corner. An old table lamp plugged into one of the generator wires running under the door illuminated a small TV and a few bags of chips in the closest corner of the room.

The guards stood up. "Who are you?" the one on the left asked.

"I'm uh... just here visiting," he said.

"We don't really do visitor hours here," the same guard said.

"Well, shucks, I guess I'll just be going," Connor said, reaching back for the door. As his hand connected with the handle, the door opened up again and the third guard entered, the one Connor thought he had avoided.

The two inside guards advanced on Connor as the third stepped over the threshold. As he stepped inside, Connor sank a punch to his left cheekbone, knocking his head back against the doorframe, and then closed the door on him again. The guard grabbed his head, checking for blood, and slunk over next to the others. A few specks of blood popped out along his cheekbone.

Connor turned partially toward the two men advancing

on his left, and waited. The man whose head he bounced between the door and the wall came toward him faster, walking with a fist pulled back like he was waiting to shoot an
arrow. Connor grabbed it and twisted it around his back. He
screamed, and Connor pushed him to the ground with his
knee. He scrambled back up again, but backed up in line with
the other two guards.

They stared at each other, the tallest, beefiest one in the
middle, bleeding cheekbone with the mop hair on the right,
and buzz cut on the left.

"What do you say you just pretend you never saw me?"
Connor floated.

As much as he enjoyed practicing martial arts, he preferred to do it in a controlled, learning environment. To him,
it was an art form, a spiritual practice similar to that of yoga.

"Who are you?" Buzz Cut asked.

"No one," Connor answered. He widened his stance,
holding his hands behind his back.

"Why are you here?" the middle one asked.

"To see a friend," he answered.

The two men to the left glanced at each other, and took
a step forward. The man on the right followed, albeit hesitantly.

"We don't do that here," the middle man repeated.

"You will today," Connor countered. "So I can walk out
that door right now and you can go back to your TV show," he
said, nodding to the TV chattering in the background. "Or you
can try to stop me, but I will ultimately walk out that door.
It's up to you how much blood you retain."

The man to the right whispered something in the
other's ear.

"We will take you to Dr. Ingels," the tall one said.

"I don't think so," Connor said.

He nodded and turned toward the door, the guards hesitant. That was fine with him.

As his hand wrapped around the doorknob, the tall one

grabbed Connor by the shoulder, spinning him around. Connor hit him in the jaw and kicked him in the gut. He stumbled back and Buzz Cut stepped forward, aiming a fist for Connor's jaw. Connor sidestepped, caught his arm, and twisted.

The three men glanced at each other, and advanced on Connor simultaneously.

Connor inhaled deeply and braced himself.

CHAPTER SIXTY THREE
Present day, Fort Howard Neuro Clinic

Renee sat in the car with the door open, waiting for Connor to reappear from the second floor window. He had been gone a few minutes, and although she wanted to worry, she knew it would take longer than that to safely navigate to Cornelia and get her out, especially if she was hurt.

She heard a honk as she waited, a noise very out of place for a deserted medical campus.

Renee glanced at the clock; it was 8:15. That was the doctor.

Renee slipped out of the car and crept around the edge of the building, knowing that she needed to either get Cornelia out or create enough interference to throw the doctor off before he could start his routine. At best, she might trigger his OCD enough that he would feel it necessary to delay the procedure another day.

She watched as he shuffled through his bag for the keys to the building. Maybe she could sneak in after him, and as he went to his office, she could go the other direction to Cornelia's room. She wasn't sure what Connor was doing, but she could only hope he was diverting everyone else's attention. They hadn't discussed Renee entering the building, and she kicked herself for letting him go in alone.

She peered around the corner, watching as the doctor unlocked the door with an old-fashioned key. She grabbed a large stick off the ground, and as the door fell shut behind him, Renee sprinted over and threw it into the crack between the door and the frame before it could close all the way. She hadn't run that fast since high school track.

She waited a few seconds to catch her breath and make sure the doctor hadn't come back, and then pushed the door open.

He waited on the other side for her, a look of disdain on his face.

"Renee," he scolded, crossing his arms. "Go home. You don't work here anymore. I'll give you five seconds."

Her stomach churned as flashbacks ran through her head of being five and having adults talk down to her.

She pushed through the door, letting it swing shut behind her. "I never worked *here*. I worked for my patients, and one of them is in trouble," she said, standing her ground. The longer she kept him talking, the more likely Connor could get to Cornelia. Unless someone *else* got to *him...*

Renee was concerned by the lack of noise behind Dr. Ingels. Shouldn't she see Connor and Cornelia darting out of her room, making a break for the broken second floor window?

She thought of Connor as invincible, and it just dawned on her that he was just as human as her and Cornelia. She didn't know if she could save Cornelia, let alone Connor, too.

"Renee. This building is heavily guarded. I urge you, *leave*," the doctor said, and turned on his heel toward his office.

She didn't know anything better to do, so she ran after him and pounced on his back like the tiger she wished she was. *Go for the eyes,* she remembered Cornelia explaining to her one afternoon. *Go for the soft spots,* she heard in her mind.

She reached around his head and tried to put pressure on his eyes, but her hands couldn't bend that way. He thrashed, grabbing onto her arms and trying to throw her off, but she held on with all of her might. He stumbled backwards suddenly, the wall coming up on them fast. Renee ducked over his shoulder, and his head struck the wall instead of hers.

His legs gave out, and Renee tumbled to the ground on her side. He reached for the medical bag he had dropped. Renee didn't know what it contained, but she was sure it had several sedatives inside – he carried them "for protection."

He reached the bag before she did and rummaged through it. She slid forward on her butt, and used the momentum to swing her leg around, connecting with his arm just as he pulled a needle out of the bag. It went flying, shattering a ways down the hall.

"Renee, you know there's more where that came from. *Just go home,*" he urged. He spoke calmly, but she could see the veins at his temples beating red.

He reached for her, grabbing onto her wrist and pulling her toward him. She punched him in the cheek as hard as she could, but he just scowled. He reached for her other wrist, but she was fast enough to pull away. He grappled with her, grabbing any part of her that he could until he had both of her wrists in one hand. He held one knee on her stomach, and reached into his bag.

She twisted, and while he was distracted, landed an elbow in his groin. He grunted, but didn't let go. Instead, he held her wrists harder and put his weight into the knee on her stomach. She kicked, but couldn't land enough force at that angle.

He pulled out another needle. He popped the cap off with his teeth, and as he aimed, she twisted her body just enough that the needle went into her hip, the same exact place she injected her insulin.

He waited a few seconds as she struggled, and then loosened his hold and stood.

"Goodnight, Nurse."

CHAPTER SIXTY FOUR
Present day, Fort Howard Neuro Clinic

Renee had never been more thankful to be diabetic.

It might be a difference of two minutes, maybe ten. She might only have thirty seconds. The doctor disappeared down the hall as Renee clawed herself up the wall. It was all scar tissue where the needle entered her skin, preventing the absorption of medicine for, in extreme cases, up to two hours.

As a nurse she should have known better, especially given the near misses she had had with insulin injections and blood sugar in the past. Her career desensitized her, and as a patient, she continued on in life the same way she always had: hip injections. It was a routine similar to brushing your teeth in the morning.

She likely didn't have much time, so she moved as quickly as possible toward the car. She stuck the same branch in the front door, in case it locked automatically behind her, and she tripped over her own feet as she ran, barely catching herself as she reached the pavement behind the building.

She opened the backseat and grabbed the fireworks, but as she turned back to the building, she realized she didn't have a lighter.

She gave up. What use were fireworks without a way to light them? Perhaps she'd be better off curling up in the backseat and waiting for the sedative to wear off. It was 8:45, the time when Dr. Ingels should be taking vitals and preparing Cornelia for the procedure. Would Connor get to her in time?

Renee stared at the clock. Then she noticed the cigarette lighter below.

She turned the car on and punched the lighter in. She ripped open the box of fireworks and held a handful of sparklers to it. 8:28.

She was lightheaded, but she didn't know whether it was the sedative or the adrenaline.

A sparkler lit. Then another. Her heart beat faster.

She had a handful of sparklers spitting tiny flames from her hand as she grabbed the box and took off toward the front door.

She pushed inside, the door closing noisily behind her. She grabbed the chair from behind the guard station and pushed it into the center of the hallway, just underneath the sprinkler head. She climbed up, struggling to balance, and held the sparklers just underneath.

She waited, waited, waited....

A shower of water burst from the sprinkler, and she hastily removed the sparklers from the stream.

To her dismay, the fire alarm didn't go off. She was soaked within seconds, stale water streaming faster over her, but still, no alarm sounded.

She climbed down and stuffed the sparklers into the box of fireworks before they could fizzle out. She was flabbergasted. How much fire was enough for a building with oxygen tanks everywhere?

She threw the box into the entranceway and walked down the hall toward Cornelia's room, shadows dancing around her as she moved, little booms and pops drowning out her footsteps. She was disoriented, and soon realized she had walked the wrong direction. She turned to go back the way she came, but the fireworks exploded throughout the hallway, the sparks growing faster and louder with each passing second. She couldn't go that way.

On the far wall was a fire alarm. She walked toward it and pulled down, her body too heavy to support. The alarm blared and Renee succumbed to the light feeling flowing through her veins.

Cornelia!

CORNELIA!

CHAPTER SIXTY FIVE
Eight months and twelve days earlier, Fort Howard Neuro Clinic

Renee did a loop around the hospital. Whenever she had a morning shift, she made it a habit to check on all of the patients before the doctor did his normal rounds, just to make sure everything was taken care of as it should be. Her patients were the same as they always were, silent, still, sleeping.

As she passed Nate's room, she noticed a medical tray pulled up to his bed. It was 8:50, early for the doctor to be doing any of his regular work, but just about the right time to administer another drug in the Memory series. Dr. Ingels did them at 9 on the dot.

Nate was lying on his side facing the other wall. As she walked in, he didn't move. "Nate?" she asked. She turned him over, and he flopped onto his back. "Nate," she repeated, begging him to wake up.

"Ah good," the doctor's voice rang out behind her. "I could use your assistance." He walked right up to Nate and propped him back onto his side.

"Doctor, I understand how much you want this series to work, but Nate is still recovering not only from physical injuries, but also from the first dose you gave him of Memory II. I beg of you, please push this off at least for another week or two. Give him time to heal," she said, positioning herself between Dr. Ingels and Nate.

"I'm not giving him Memory II. He's going to be the first patient administered Memory III," he explained, sitting down on the swiveling stool next to his medical tray. Renee noticed one of the needles had already been injected. Nate wouldn't wake for at least 24 hours.

"We both know it's not ready yet. Please, don't do this.

He doesn't deserve this," she said.

"He's my patient, Nurse Cavallero. He deserves what I say he gets."

"I won't let you," she said.

"You don't have to," he said. He stood and elbowed her easily out of the way. She jumped on his back and grabbed for the needle, hoping she could at least destroy it. She just needed time, time to get Nate and Cornelia *out*.

"Renee?"

She whipped around, Cornelia's soft voice distracting her. While the two women looked at each other, the doctor quickly leaned forward, injecting the needle into the base of Nate's neck.

"No!" Renee shouted, whacking the needle out of his hand. It exploded on the floor, but it was no use. It was already empty.

"Renee?" Cornelia asked, stepping into the room and pushing past Dr. Ingels.

"Nate," she said, shaking his shoulder. "Nate." She turned back to Renee and the doctor. "What's wrong with him, why isn't he waking up?" Her voice was shaky.

Renee ran her hand over her face, the tears flowing freely. "Renee?" Cornelia asked. She could only shake her head.

"Your *husband* is the first patient to undergo the Memory III treatment," the doctor said.

Cornelia shook her head, looking to Renee for an explanation. "Renee, what does that mean?"

Renee shook her head. "He's not going to wake up," she said. "I'm sorry. I'm so sorry."

"No," Cornelia said. "He has to wake up," she said, unable to hold back the ugly crying any longer. "He *has* to wake up," she repeated, and squeezing his hand, touching his face, shaking him, shaking him, shaking him.

Renee left the room and leaned against the wall. She sank down to the floor and held her head in her hands. Cornelia's sobs echoed down the hallway as she screamed at Nate to wake up.

Wake up, please, I know you're there. Why not me, it should have been me, please, Nate, you have to wake up....

Eventually her cries turned to whimpers, and when Renee glanced into the room hours later, Cornelia laid next to Nate, holding on for dear life to someone who was already gone, gone, gone.

CHAPTER SIXTY SIX
Present day, Fort Howard Neuro Clinic

Cornelia couldn't sleep. Do people who know they have less than a day left to live sleep? It seemed like a waste. You should be doing something fun during the last 24 hours of your life. Eating anything you want, fucking everything in sight, indulging in time with your loved ones that you'll never see again... and Cornelia was stuck in a hospital bed.

It was fitting, really. She had no one left in her life, and she would rather eat a salad than a steak. She had stopped indulging in these things long ago. It just hadn't been worth it without Nate.

She couldn't help but think - he was here, at least six months after his supposed death date. He and Cornelia were married in Baltimore County, Maryland, according to the marriage license she had tucked into the cup of her red dress. The wedding ring she now wore, matched his, wherever it may be.

At least for a moment, she had thought she would spend forever with her one and only. However long forever might have been.

The clock read 8:33.

She had come to terms with her imminent death, or the equivalent of it. She knew she either wouldn't wake up, or wouldn't remember any of this. So much for spending the past year in hiding.

The front door of the hospital opened and slammed shut, and footsteps approached down the hallway.

Liam knocked before entering her room, poking his head around the doorway with a big grin on his face. His expression fell when he saw the downed bookshelf on the other side of the room.

"Got in a little fight with some furniture I see," he said,

walking up to her bedside.

He had a small medical bag with him that he placed at the foot of her bed. "We will begin the procedure in fifteen minutes. I'll start by taking your vitals," he said, holding his hand against Cornelia's forehead. He pulled out a thermometer forcefully under her tongue, and waited a few seconds to get a read.

He took her blood pressure, listened to her heartbeat, and finally, prepared the sedative that would be administered just after the final needle.

This is it.

He could take her memory, the love of her life, any semblance of recovery she thought she had attained, but she would not let him take her last few moments of happiness. Whatever he was planning to do, she would die in a good place, free of regret, contempt. She didn't want that to be the last thing she unleashed upon the world.

He asked Cornelia a series of questions, and she ignored them all. He could ask all the questions he wanted – she would be in her own dream world, imagining better days. She had never found it so easy to ignore an annoyance.

Three syringes sat on a small, wheeled medical tray between her and Liam. One was small, like the kind you'd see when you get a shot in the arm. The other two were large, intimidating.

Drawing her out of her end-of-life daze, an alarm blared and strobe lights flashed. Liam looked perplexed, glancing around the room. He shook his head, and continued the long-winded explanation he had been flapping about.

Then Cornelia smelled smoke, and Liam stopped talking mid-sentence. Cornelia, as much as she wanted to avoid the pain of another disappointment, felt her heart start. She couldn't hear him over the alarm.

Liam pursed his lips, his chest rising and falling for several breaths as Cornelia watched, waiting. He was a moving picture in the flashing lights.

He stood and ran out the door, his footsteps echoing in the hallway outside.

The smell of smoke grew stronger.

She sat up, sniffing. What on earth?

She slipped out of her bed and unlocked the wheels, dragging it to the doorway. Liam was gone, but billowing smoke moved toward her from the direction he had gone.

She wasn't quite ready to die by accident.

She ran the other way down the hallway, her bed inhibiting but not stopping her. She ran to the exit sign, and pushed through to a courtyard, her bed bouncing around as she pulled it across the threshold. The outdoor area was fenced in, barbed wire lining the top. A sign on the fence read WARNING! ELECTRIC FENCE!

She had thought this would be an exit. Why would there be an exit sign over a door you couldn't conceivably exit? She thought there would at least be a locked gate she could kick through.

There was only one way out: up and over.

The bed dragged on the unkempt grass. She needed to find a way to ditch it, *now*.

She looked around the yard for something metal, or some sort of leverage that could help her break free. The only thing in the yard was a decaying picnic table.

The railing of the bed was screwed into the bedframe, a separate addition held on by a metal plate with four screws. What were the chances of finding a screwdriver lying somewhere in the grass?

Smoke rose in a small stream from the far side of the building. How much time until Liam would come looking for her?

She stared up at the 20' high chain link fence. She would take some scrapes if it was that or her life. She noticed that no wires form the generator ran under the outside door.

She slipped her hospital gown off, and pulled as hard as she could on the strap of her dress, breaking it so she could take it off around her cuffed hand. She slipped the left side off and pulled the back of her dress around to her front, unzipping it and stepping out. She held her marriage certificate between her teeth.

The clasp in the back of her dress was broken, one side of the clasp consisting of a bent piece of metal about half a centimeter wide. She held it between two fingernails, fit it into the head of the top right screw, and twisted to the left. It worked.

Her fingers were bleeding by the time she got to the fourth screw, the thin metal edge of the clasp digging into her skin. The last screw was older than the others, as if the first three had been replaced but this one *just* managed to hold up. It had spots of rust on the head, and refused to cooperate with Cornelia's makeshift screwdriver.

She dug the clasp into the rusted head but stripped both the screw and her finger. She needed to be spending her time getting over the fence, not unscrewing herself from her bed.

Finally, she tipped the bed over and jumped on the angled underside. She slipped, twisting her arm as the railing pulled her handcuff to the ground.

The head of the screw popped off, and triumphantly, Cornelia held the 10-pound railing up above her head, disconnected.

A ring of blood wrapped her wrist like a bracelet, so she stuffed her hospital gown down between the metal and her skin. She stepped back into her dress and looped the remaining strap over her shoulder. She zipped what she could in the moment, but didn't do the contortionist routine to fully close the back.

She wanted at least some protection from the barbed wire, but it wasn't like she was about to take prom pictures.

She reached out hesitantly, tapping the fence with a fingernail. Feeling no shock, she palmed the metal. As she'd hoped, the fence was not connected.

She looped the railing around her right arm and scaled the chain link fence. At the very top, the fence angled in at about 45 degrees. She climbed towards the Y joint.

When she got to the top, she reached through the barbed wire to the other side, hoisting herself up so her waist was level with the very top of the fence. Holding onto the joint in front of her, she hooked her bed railing to the opposite side of the Y joint. She pushed herself up further, using one foot to balance on top of the fence between the barbs, the railing hooked to the opposite joint, holding her steady.

She braced herself, both hands pulling on the railing, both feet balanced on the top of the fence.

She held her breath, closed her eyes, and dove.

A barb dug into her shin, but the railing did exactly what she wanted it to. She swung, the railing hanging from the outside half of the Y-joint, in disbelief that she hadn't hit the ground headfirst.

She pulsed her legs forward, grabbing hold of the fence first with her toes and then her non-railing hand. She unhooked the railing from the joint and climbed down slowly.

As she stood back on solid ground, she took stock of any injuries, and aside from the gash on her shin, deemed herself perfectly fine. She released a sigh of relief and *ran*.

CHAPTER SIXTY SEVEN
Present day, Fort Howard Neuro Clinic

Connor wiped blood from his lip. Mop head was down after three blows to the head. Buzz cut was slumped against the wall, a kick to the gut sufficient for him.

Connor had taken more hits that day than he had in years. He fought fair, trained people one on one. He had never taken on a trio by himself.

The first two were easy enough, relatively untrained as they were.

But the tall one in the middle... he had at least a modicum of training. He was about Connor's height, and as Connor could usually rely on his own wingspan to land a few punches that would prove impossible for a shorter man, he could barely focus on his own movements for fear of Cornelia's safety.

The first two showed what they were going to do next in their eyes and their movements. The tall one, like Connor, liked to wait to see what his opponent was planning before deciding on anything. The only thing that played to Connor's advantage was his speed. Over years of training, he had increased his speed even though his body frame was characteristic of a slower fighter.

He tasted blood, and he desperately wanted to run and find Cornelia. He could feel time running out for every second he calculated his opponent's next move.

A noise startled both men. The fire alarm blared throughout the hallways, the strobe light illuminating the building in a hazy rave. Both men looked at each other, realizing the urgency of their situation.

Against his better instincts, Connor made the first move. He faked like he was going for a punch, grabbed the man's arm, and pulled it around his own shoulder, flipping him onto his back. The alarm drowned out the sound of his body hitting the floor and the groan that accompanied it.

Connor didn't wait to see if he was down before whipping out into the hallway. Smoke trailed from the far end.

"Cornelia!" he shouted. There was no time to waste being quiet. "CORNELIA!"

He ran down the hallway, checking each room as he went. Patient rooms, rec room, game room.

He passed a room with sheets on the bed and doubled back. A medical tray sat next to it, with three syringes. This was the location where Renee had indicated Cornelia's room would be, but she was nowhere in sight. Connor checked the syringes – all three looked unused.

She must have gotten out.

Connor ran down the hallway toward the smoke.

"Cornelia!" he shouted, a vain attempt.

He held his breath as he rounded the corner, and saw Renee on the far side of the hallway, slumped underneath the fire alarm, unconscious. The box of fireworks lay between them, rocking and exploding. One of the larger fireworks exploded out of the box, shooting to the wall only a foot or so past Connor's head.

Connor pulled his shirt up over his mouth and covered his face with his arm as he ran past the hazard to Renee. He scooped her up, accidentally knocking her head off the doorframe as they ran out of the building. He cursed himself as he placed Renee gently in the backseat of their SUV.

He closed the door on her and turned back to the hospital. He ran for the emergency exit on the other side, but pulling on the handle, realized it was still locked. He came back around to the front entrance, but saw no sign of Cornelia.

What were the chances she was still inside? Connor didn't know if he could weather the smoke if he went back in. Would Renee be able to get herself back home if he didn't come back out?

He stood out front, watching as the entrance to the building erupts, fireworks creating a barrage of angry colors threatening to blow the front doors right off. Smoke bellowed out in streams. The only thing louder than the booming fireworks was the alarm blaring on top.

He bit his lip. He couldn't chance it. Damned if he did, damned if he didn't.

He looked back to the car. Renee wasn't sitting up yet.

He glanced toward the street, searching for any sign of emergency personnel, but saw none.

He was at a loss, unsure what to do or where to go, when he saw something.

Out of the corner of his eye, a blaze of red sprinted away from the hospital. He would recognize that dress anywhere.

"Cornelia!" he bellowed, and she looked over her shoulder.

She stopped, smiling, and redirected toward him.

She got about twenty feet before a blaze of hunter green and khaki blew by Connor, running straight for Cornelia. But she didn't slow down. She scowled, running straight for him.

Before he could grab her, she ducked and tackled him with the ease and grace of a pro-football player, throwing him right over her shoulder. She ran for Connor, never missing a beat.

He couldn't squeeze her tight enough. He kissed her and ushered her into the car.

CHAPTER SIXTY EIGHT
Present day, Johns Hopkins Bayview

Cornelia didn't want to go to the hospital, but Renee presented a convincing argument.

"How else are you going to get those handcuffs off?" she reasoned, while directing Connor first to the nearest Wawa to clean up a bit. "Besides, you really need to get a tetanus shot for your leg. There's no knowing what grime was coating that barbed wire."

"I suppose you're right," Cornelia lamented.

"I can't believe you scaled an electric fence, *and* barbed wire," Renee said, shaking her head.

Cornelia laughed, the weight of her night lifting. "You and me both."

Cornelia checked on Renee in the side mirror. They spent a few minutes outside Fort Howard waiting for Renee to come to, and though she talked and rationalized fine, she sat still slumped in the backseat with her eyes closed.

As Cornelia watched her, she opened one eye, taking in their location. "Wawa's your next right," she said, and closed her eyes again.

Renee and Cornelia ducked into the women's bathroom, Connor to the men's. Cornelia tucked the railing into her over-sized coat in an effort to draw less attention as they walked through the store.

She was thankful Renee and Connor had had the fore-sight to bring the coat and some extra clothing for her. Unfor-tunately, the clothes would have to wait until she was discon-nected from the railing.

"Wow, I look like *crap*," Cornelia remarked, tracing the dark marks underneath her eye. She had a new red blotch on her neck, and one in her shoulder. She flexed her muscles, searching for other injuries, and felt a ripe one forming across her abdomen.

"Don't we all," Renee said, wiggling her eyebrows.

Renee splashed water on her face, and Cornelia followed suit, using a moist paper towel to remove the random splotches of dirt from her body. There were a few dark lines on the back of her knees that she guessed were from the lip of the van as she was pulled inside. Dirt covered one of her knees, stretching down into the gash in her leg. It was still bleeding, even more so now that she was standing.

Cornelia wiped down the dirt and blood as Renee covered their bruises and cuts with makeup. Unfortunately nothing could be done with the tears in Cornelia's dress.

They met Connor outside. He had picked up food while he waited, but seemed stunned when they climbed inside the car.

"What did you guys do?" he asked. He had a power bar in his hand that he was about to take a bite of, but rested in his lap when the girls clambered in.

"Just cleaned up a bit. We looked like something out of Mad Max," Cornelia said.

"But we have to go to the police, that was evidence," Connor said. He had cleaned the soot off of his face, but the scrapes and bruises on his face and knuckles were unchanged.

Renee and Cornelia locked eyes in the mirror.

"I don't think we were really planning on police," Renee said.

He turned in his seat so he was facing both women. "How do you expect anything to change if you don't take the first step? Getting police involved helps you build a case so he can't do this again," Connor explained.

"Connor, we've tried to many times. I know Corey doesn't remember, but we went to the police already. They can't and won't touch something like this," Renee reasoned. "And at least we destroyed a good amount of his work. I'm pretty sure some fireworks went directly into his office. He's done. He lost everything."

"He's tried so many times, in so many different ways. It just doesn't make sense to drag things on when we could be done with it now," Cornelia said, catching Renee's eye in the mirror again.

She felt strange saying it. Part of her wanted vengeance, but at what cost? Renee had told her about the last time they tried contacting the police – it wasn't something a local precinct could deal with, and it wasn't something a higher bureau would.

Not to mention, who would believe her?

"Cornelia," Connor said, enunciating each syllable like it might make her listen harder. He looked her right in the eye. "You don't get to decide what his next move is. *You* know that."

She nodded. She understood; she just disagreed. "Maybe we should talk about it later," she said, motioning to her bleeding leg. She had grabbed a few paper towels from the bathroom, but they were nearly soaked through.

"Yeah let's get that stitched up," Renee suggested.

Connor shook his head, but drove on regardless.

They arrived at the local public hospital within five minutes and rushed through the cold air into a moderately busy emergency room. Cornelia was pulled into a triage area right away, where she was given a series of shots and her wrist was finally freed.

She rolled her joints, marveling at the freedom of movement. The red ring would take some time to heal.

"Feel better?" Renee asked, squeezing her shoulder.

Cornelia nodded, grinning.

"Good."

They gave her a bed with a flimsy wrap around curtain, as the doctor on duty was running a bit behind. Another thirty minutes, a nurse said, and someone would be over to stitch Cornelia right up.

She asked for the curtain to be left open, so she could watch all of the other patients and nurses and doctors while she waited. For once, the bustle felt homey, comfortable.

"Will you be okay if I duck out for a little while?" Renee asked.

She nodded. "Where are you going?"

Renee held up a notepad, a list of names about twenty long. "I think some of my previous patients might have ended up here. If they are, I'd like to check in on them," she explained. "As long as you're okay."

Cornelia nodded. "As long as I'm not chained to anything, I'll be just fine," Cornelia said.

Renee smiled and patted Connor's arm as she walked away.

Connor motioned for Cornelia to scooch over and sat down next to her, wrapping both arms around her as tight as he could. Cornelia closed her eyes, resting her head against his shoulder. "That was quite an adventure," he said.

"Thank you for coming to my rescue," she said.

"I think you rescued yourself," he said, his breath warm on her ear.

"Well, thanks for driving the getaway car then," she said.

"For you, anytime."

CHAPTER SIXTY NINE
Present day, Johns Hopkins Bayview

Renee had been in this hospital several times before. After all, she used to live just down the street. She had applied for a nursing position there before the one at Fort Howard.

How different things could have been....

She had a general idea of the direction she wanted to go – she knew the coma ward was on the west side, emergency care on the north – but she hadn't been there in so long, she needed to follow those ridiculous foot paths that wind around the hospital. Those were one of her greatest peeves, considering a blind donkey could probably find an easier route.

After a few minutes of wandering and a few sideways glances from fellow nurses, she began to recognize the hallways again. This, she knew she had seen before. She was getting close.

Notepad in hand, she ran down her list of names again. There were one or two people she might be forgetting, but she cared most about the patients she had had direct interaction with. *Ideally*, she wanted to check in on every patient that Dr. Ingels had ever laid eyes on, but she knew only a handful would have been transferred here, and the ones who were, were probably brain dead.

She wondered again what she might gain from seeing her old patients. Would she suddenly feel like a better nurse, checking on them one last time after abandoning them, again?

She was reminded of that moral test they ask you in college: a train is heading toward five people, but you can control the switch so that it only hits one person instead. Do you intentionally kill one to save the accidental five?

Should she have stayed? Could she have made a difference in more than one life?

It seemed clear at the time. Cornelia was the only patient that showed potential for a real life after release. Maybe if she had stayed, her patients would have gotten slightly better quality of life care, maybe not. But if she hadn't focused on Cornelia, *no* patient would have had the opportunity to live a full life. Is that how the moral test was supposed to work?

She followed the blue line around a corner and nearly walked into a thin man with shaggy hair, dressed in blue scrubs.

"Pardon me," Renee said, pushing by.

"Renee!" he said, touching her elbow and bringing her out of her trance.

It took her a moment to recognize him, as the last time she had seen him, they were both more concerned with loading Cornelia into the back of an ambulance.

"Dan!" she said, and hugged him.

"What are you doing back here? I thought you moved to Philadelphia," he asked.

"I did. It's a long story. And hey, you're a nurse now, congratulations!" she said, remembering how he yearned to move on from driving the ambulance.

"Thanks," he smiled, pinching his scrubs. "I'm finally moving on up."

A thought dawned on her. "I'm actually looking to reconnect with some of my former patients. I think a few of them might have been transferred here?" She gauged his reaction. "Would you be able to help me find them?"

He shrugged. "I can try," he said.

Renee wasn't daring enough to ask for medical records, knowing that would overstep boundaries, but she was happy to have an escort for visiting her patients. The last thing she wanted was to alarm the nurses and get herself kicked out.

"So you're looking for the Fort Howard patients, right?" he asked as they walked toward the coma ward.

"Yes, I didn't realize until recently they had been transferred," she explained.

Dan nodded. "Some of them were brought here, a couple of them were transferred to hospitals near family, and a few were taken to long term care facilities," he said. He glanced at her out the corner of his eye. "Do you know what happened to them?"

"What do you mean?" she asked. "They were all in comas."

"Yeah, we know that, but they were transferred without any medical paperwork. Like some of them have medical information from as long as ten years ago, but nothing entailing the time they were at Fort Howard," Dan explained, gesticulating with his hands. "The doctors can't figure out how to treat them or why some show brain activity when we wouldn't expect it and others are the complete opposite."

"And I don't know what you can tell me, but I know your friend came from there, and I know you told me it was a no-questions-asked pick up, but I just... can't help but wonder," he said, shaking his head. He was waiting on answers she'd never be able to give him.

Renee nodded. She wondered how far Dan would spread the information if Renee let him in on it. She understood the wonder, a deep yearning to know and help, because that tidbit of information might be the *one thing* you need to help a patient.

She bought herself some time instead. "How about we meet for a coffee when you're done your shift, and I'll tell you what I can," Renee suggested.

"Absolutely," he said, as they came upon the nurse's station of the coma ward. "Hey, let me see that list, I'll point you in the right direction."

She passed over her notepad and he read through the names, nodding.

"Looks like we have six of your patients," he said.

"Great," Renee said, her heart swelling.

He smiled. "Della and Rose are down that hallway," he

said, motioning over his right shoulder. "And Jerry, Alyson, Peter, and Karen are down the hallway behind you." He nodded toward the hallway behind her.

"Thank you," she said. Dan rounded the nurse's station to talk to the coma ward staff, careful to say goodbye so they would see that she was good.

She chose to visit Alyson first.

She was a young mother, blonde, with a heart-shaped face. She, like Nate, was an orphan, and her husband had died only weeks earlier, right around when she had her second child. Both kids were adopted out several months after Alyson fell into a coma. One was two years old and the second was three months. Alyson had drunk herself incoherent, fell, and hit her head on the sidewalk.

She was just as Renee remembered. She held the woman's hand, willing her to wake up, just like she did when she worked at Fort Howard. They never did, but Renee couldn't shake the belief that just maybe, that innocent touch, a "hello," the electricity that exists between two people, might be enough to make some magic happen.

As usual, it wasn't.

"Nice to see you again, Alyson," she said, as she left the room.

She wasn't sure what she was expecting to feel. She thought that maybe after all this time, checking up on her patients might make her feel better about leaving them behind, but she felt the same helplessness for them she always had.

She continued down the hallway, peeking inside each room in case she missed someone.

Halfway down the hallway, she came to a halt, recognizing the patient inside room 317.

He was alive.

CHAPTER SEVENTY
Present day, Johns Hopkins Bayview

Cornelia and Connor were silent, listening to the noises of the busy emergency room. From the connected waiting room, they could hear the low murmur of a news station. Somewhere a toddler cried. A few beds over, two teenage girls chatted.

"Hey," a hand on her shoulder aroused her. Renee stood above her. "Hey, how you doing?" she whispered.

"I'm alright," Cornelia said. "What's up?"

Cornelia pushed herself to a seated position, gently untangling herself from Connor. He had fallen asleep, his head rested against the wall behind the bed. He sniffled awake as Cornelia shifted.

"There's someone I'd like you to see," Renee said. Her face was somber, cold.

"Right now?" Cornelia asked.

Renee nodded. "Yeah, come on."

"Hey, we'll be right back," Cornelia said to Connor. He nodded, crossing his arms and leaning his head back against the wall again. "Let me know if you need anything," he said, his eyes already closed.

They walked through two wards, following a thick blue line that criss-crossed itself at some point. Cornelia was lost, but Renee knew where she was going. They ended up in the coma ward.

"Why are we here?" she asked. It gave her a strange feeling, being there. She felt flighty, like she needed to be anywhere else. Renee had told her previously that the Memory trials erased memory, but not emotion. She wondered what her subconscious perceived.

Renee said a quick hello to a nurse doing paperwork.

Judging by their friendly interaction, Cornelia guessed they knew each other outside of the hospital.

"Renee," he greeted. "Cornelia," he said, nodding and smiling. Cornelia's eyebrows furrowed.

They entered room 317.

He was paler than she remembered, gaunt, with dark circles under his eyes. He laid in bed on his back, arms by his side, with a breathing machine over his mouth and nose. Two machines to his right monitored brain activity and heartbeat. His hair was shaggier than he liked, and a little too long on the sides.

Cornelia walked to the side of his bed, the lump in her throat threatening to explode.

"I'll give you a moment," Renee said, squeezing her hand before leaving the room. She shut the door, and Cornelia burst into tears.

She had imagined meeting Nate again so many times, but never like this. *Never like this.*

She grabbed his hand. It was colder than hers, but not ice cold. With every second that passed, she expected him to wake up and hug her, tell her how much he missed her. What kind of cruel joke it is, to give you back everything you ever wanted without the *essence* of the thing.

"Nate," she whispered, willing him to wake up. "Nathan."

She wasn't sure how to read brain waves but she was fairly sure flat was bad. She didn't need a doctor to tell her that Nate wasn't there anymore – she couldn't feel him.

"I love you and I miss you so much," she said.

There was a sharp knock at the door and an unfamiliar doctor poked his head in.

"Ms. Winthorp," he greeted her, shaking her hand. He glanced down at her battered clothing and body, but covered his reaction well. "I'm Dr. Gupta, I've been in charge of Nathan's care these past few months. I understand you are his wife?"

"I am," she said. How bittersweet.

"It's nice to finally meet you," he said, shaking her hand. He had kind eyes, an inviting smile.

"Let's take a seat," he said, motioning to the table and chairs on the other side of the room.

He didn't tell her anything she didn't already know. Nathan was not there, and as far as the doctor knew, he never was. Medical records from his previous hospital "disappeared," when it closed, leading to blind treatments for their transferred coma patients. Cornelia didn't tell him she was there too, or about the treatments they received. It wouldn't help anyone.

"We've been trying to track down the loved ones of some of these patients for some time now. It's strange that so many of them are alone in the world," the doctor said, making conversation. "I'm very happy you were able to be here today."

He took a deep breath. "But unfortunately we have some difficult choices ahead," he continued. He studied Cornelia's face. "With this type of brain activity, it would be impossible for Nathan to wake up and experience a normal life."

Cornelia nodded. She knew where the doctor was going from the second they sat down. "You want me to take him off life support," Cornelia said.

"The decision is yours, but in these situations, I do suggest letting the patient pass nobly," the doctor said. He let her digest the information. "You can take as much time as you need."

Cornelia nodded. "Walk me through it."

CHAPTER SEVENTY ONE
Present day, Johns Hopkins Bayview

Cornelia sat on an uncomfortable bench situated across from the nurse's station. The entire area was quiet, the only noise cutting through the silence that of the nurse behind the counter, typing, whispering.

Renee kept herself busy talking to Dr. Gupta, Dan hovering only feet away. They discussed typical treatments for coma patients, having wormed her way into a hesitant friendship with Dr. Gupta through Dan. Cornelia listened as he hedged, Renee having asked one too many pointed questions.

She held Connor's phone in her hand, her own having been lost somewhere between Philadelphia and Baltimore, potentially on roadway or possibly buried beneath the wreckage leftover at Fort Howard.

She had his phone number memorized, yet found herself screwing up the numbers, mirroring the jumbled mess inside her head. She pressed 'end,' and started again.

The phone rang.

"Luca Hotchkin," he said brashly.

"Luca, it's Cornelia," she said.

"Coreeey," he said, drawing out the vowel. She heard him typing. "How is the weather in Nicaragua this fine day?"

"79 degrees and sunny," she said, exiting the weather app and handing Renee's phone back to her.

"Good to hear from you, Corey. What can I help you with today?" he asked.

She stuttered, the words refusing to come out on their own. "I just wanted to see how the investigation is going. Into Petyr's death," she said, punting.

"I am happy to inform you that a good deal of progress has been made, but it's nothing for you to worry about, we have everything covered," he assured her. "And if all goes well, someone else will be able to continue your disbursements within a month or so. In fact, it might be me."

"You?" she asked, pleasantly surprised. "I thought you lived in Italy?"

He sighed. "Yes, I do now. But a lot has changed in my life and I think it's the right time to make the move to the US. I'll be retiring in June, actually," he explained.

Cornelia was stunned. "Well, Luca that's great. Congratulations."

"Thank you," he said. "But I wanted to make sure we stayed true to our agreement, so I'll be in and out of the US over the next few months and I'll make sure we find some time to meet while I'm there."

She could hear the smile in his voice. She should have gotten the bad news out of the way first.

"That's great, Luca. I uh... well, I'm not sure I'll be needing to take such extreme measures anymore," she said. "I think it's time to do everything on the books again."

Luca hmmed. "Did something happen?"

"It turns out I didn't have as much to fear as I had thought," she told him, playing with the hem on her torn dress.

"Well I'm very glad to hear," he said softly. "Let me know if any changes are necessary in your accounts."

Cornelia nodded. The line was silent.

"Is there anything else you need, Corey?" he asked her.

Spit. It. Out.

"Nathan is in a coma," she blurted. The line was silent for so long she felt the need to ask, "Are you there?"

"Yes, yes I'm here," he said, his voice lower. "He's... alive?"

She nodded. "He's alive, but he's not present. They've been waiting for a family member to consent to taking him off life support," she explained. She tried so hard to keep her voice from wavering. Maybe Luca wouldn't notice. "I just wanted to let you know, in case you wanted to be here."

"Yes, of course I'll be there. When?" he asked.

"We're scheduled for tomorrow at noon, but we can move it if you need more time," she said.

"No, no, that's just fine," he said. "Where?"

"Johns Hopkins Bayview, in Maryland."

"That works out well, I actually have some business in the area. I'll see you at noon," he said. He paused. "Thank you Cornelia, for including me."

"Of course," she said.

They hung up, and Cornelia sat alone on the uncomfortable, pristine couch. She hoped Nathan, if there was anything left to feel, at least felt comfort, or peace, or whatever makes being in a coma a smidgeon better than death.

CHAPTER SEVENTY TWO
Present day, Johns Hopkins Bayview

Renee and Connor trekked down the street to a local bed and breakfast, leaving Cornelia alone with Nathan and her thoughts.

Nate's room looked like it had been set up for two patients, most of the furniture arranged in an unbalanced way on his side of the room. The table and four chairs were directly underneath the window, and a couch lined the wall between his bed and the door.

The sun set early, trails of pink dashed through the sky. She opened the blinds so she could watch, and pulled the couch parallel to his bed, so they laid next to each other. The neon sky framed Nathan's profile.

She didn't know how long she watched the gentle, controlled breathing in his chest, but by the time she moved, the sky outside, as well as Nathan's room, was dark.

She was wide awake, recognizing the urgency of the night as well as how little a difference it ultimately made.

Nate wasn't there.

This night was for Cornelia, but she couldn't help but wonder what the point was.

She had accepted a long time ago that Nate was dead, and she was confident that if Nate was truly *alive*, she would feel *something*. Renee said that patients forgot what happened, but their emotions held strong. She had felt the compounded pain of death from the moment she woke from her own coma.

She supposed it was closure, a way for her to finally say goodbye to someone who had already been gone for months. She didn't feel any different, knowing she only had a few hours until The End was official.

Yet when she held his hand and felt his heartbeat, she

was sure he would wake up. The discrepancy between a heartbeat and consciousness made her stomach broil. When she felt his heartbeat, she was sure that he was in there somewhere, *buried* so deep that machines just couldn't sense it. *Before,* she had always thought that as long as something was happening somewhere in your body, there must be a little part of you left – just the tiniest bit – and life would find a way.

But she couldn't feel him.

Anger bubbled in her chest. If it weren't for Liam, she would be home, in their little house, maybe with a dog or a cat or who knows, maybe even a kid. She had a life planned, one that was happy and full of love and family. No one could have saved her parents or her sister, but Nate could have survived.

She thought about the last two years of her life. She thought of her mom, with that frizzy hair that perfectly matched Aunt Tanya's, her dad, the stoic yet loving father figure that so many kids yearned for, and her little sister, her very best friend in the whole wide world.

She felt the tears she had been missing, without a twinge of guilt that they weren't wholly for Nathan. He was in front of her now, in his deathbed, and he now represented of all the loss that she had never gotten "closure" for, whatever that may mean. Nathan filled the bed, but it was her family that filled the room.

She was deep in a coma during their funerals. They had had a joint funeral for her mom and dad, several days after the accident, and a separate one for her sister and future brother-in-law. Tanya kept the programs so Cornelia could experience it later on, but she could never bear to look. They sat on a dusty shelf in a manila folder, buried by fabric swatches she used to reupholster a rocking chair she bought off Craigslist.

She wanted to climb in bed with Nate one last time, but all of the wires and monitors were in her way, and the last thing she wanted to do was prematurely kill him before his family was even there to say goodbye. She settled for holding his hand.

As she stared at his monitors and crisp bed sheets, it was the simple things that made her smile.

The glass of champagne when they finished moving into their first apartment, a trip to the beach on one of those perfect end-of-summer days where the wind is just right and the sun doesn't burn, waking up for work in the morning and asking for another five minutes not because she was tired, but because she liked the feeling of his arms around her....

Bonfires with old friends, families coming together, meaningless tiffs, dishes after a TV dinner, not-so-surprise chocolates on her birthday, arts festivals in the city, how was your day?, lazy Saturdays, drunk brunches, holiday work parties, how much do we tip?, walks without destinations, a world without devastation....

The sun rose anticlimactically, light seeping into the horizon little by little until they were met with a clear, bright blue day.

Connor and Renee arrived early in the morning, two shopping bags in tow.

"Hey," Renee said, knocking on the door as she tiptoed inside. Cornelia sat up, pushing her hair from her face and wiping stale tears from her cheeks. "How are you doing?"

"I'm okay," Cornelia said. *Numb, but okay.*

"We brought you a change of clothes and some shower stuff, in case you wanted to freshen up," she said, motioning to the bag in her hand. "Actually, Connor did. I never would have thought of it," she continued, motioning for Connor to come closer.

"I didn't know what you needed but I know you get uncomfortable in jeans and dresses and stuff so I got you some sweats, but I wasn't sure what you want to wear for... today, so Renee helped me find something else that might work," Connor rambled, holding up the bags in his hands.

He sat down next to Cornelia, his eyebrows scrunched together. "Can I do anything?" he asked. He was dressed nice, a pair of slacks and a nice sweater. *How sweet.*

Cornelia shook her head. "Thank you."

"And I wasn't sure what you wanted, but I can wait outside or I can be here or you can let me know as the whim strikes you," he said.

Cornelia smiled. "I'd really like it if you were here," she said, patting his knee.

He nodded enthusiastically. "Okay. I'll be here then."

Cornelia stood and picked up the less squishy bag. "Is this the shower stuff?" she asked.

Renee nodded. "Here, let me help you find one. I think there's a locker room just down the hall," she said. She was also dressed in black, a long dress that cinched at the waist and fluttered above her feet as she walked.

She led Cornelia down the hall and guided her toward the stalls. "Just through there. I'll wait here and make sure no one gives you any trouble," Renee said, urging her on.

Cornelia shampooed and conditioned and soaped, and then did it all over again because she forgot what stage of the process she was in. She forgot to wash her face, but accidentally washed it twice. Just when she was about to turn off the water, she realized she shampooed after conditioning and had to start all over again. She only brushed her teeth once, because the minty taste lingered long enough to remind her she already had.

She pulled on the dress that Connor had picked for her – a smart, classy cut with a high neck that ended just above her knee. If she didn't know any better, she could have been on her way to work.

She ran her hands through her dripping hair as Renee struggled to apply makeup over her bruises. The back of her dress was damp, and Renee haphazardly stuck a towel over her shoulders.

By the time they returned, Luca had arrived. He stood just outside Nate's room, chatting in a friendly yet somber way with Connor.

"Cornelia," he said, smiling when he saw her.

He looked the same as the last time she had seen him – tan, with a head full of salt and pepper hair. He was a stocky, jaunty man, who always smiled when he saw her.

"It's so good to see you," she said, pulling him in for a tight hug. They didn't know each other well, but Cornelia felt safe around Luca. He felt like a protector, or even just another dad.

"You look beautiful!" he said, but she could feel him eyeing the dark spot under her eye that Renee hadn't been able to totally cover.

"Thank you."

Dr. Gupta hovered behind the nurse's station, watching them out of the corner of his eye. Cornelia hadn't looked at the time since calling Luca the day before, but she guessed it was close to noon.

"Would you like a few moments?" Cornelia asked Luca, motioning to Nate's room.

He looked toward the door and took a deep breath. "Yes, I would. Thank you," he said.

He squeezed her hand and walked hesitantly into the room. Cornelia pulled the door closed behind him and sat down on the bench lining the wall.

"How are you doing?" Connor asked, sitting down beside her.

"I'm fine," she said, but she was starting to wish people would stop asking.

He nodded, resting a hand on her knee.

Luca returned a few minutes later, gingerly dabbing his eyes with a handkerchief.

"You know, if I could do it all again, I would be here so I could have seen him grow up," Luca said. Cornelia looped her arm around his waist, pulling him in for a quick hug before they filed in.

From noon until 12:03, they listened to Nate's favorite song. At 12:04, he was declared dead.

CHAPTER SEVENTY THREE
Present day, Johns Hopkins Bayview

Cornelia and Connor sat on the bench outside Nate's room. They hadn't spoken in minutes. Renee chatted in hushed tones with Dan behind the nurse's station.

Cornelia wasn't sure what to feel. One second she felt like crying, the next a burning rage in her stomach, and the next an odd calmness, like this was just another day in Baltimore.

Renee finished her conversation. She stood by Cornelia, and squeezed her shoulder. "How are you doing?" she asked.

Cornelia nodded. "I'm fine." It was becoming her mantra, just like Connor's words in her head that Liam would come back for her.

"Can I get you anything?" Renee asked.

Cornelia shook her head. "No, I'm fine. Thank you."

Her thoughts felt raw, saying the same thing over and over again. *I'm fine, I'm okay, yes fine.*

But really, when does it end? When does the nightmare end?

On one hand, Cornelia already knew Liam's tricks. She knew what she was up against, and she was confident she could take it. She would keep training, keep her guard up, always have that watchful eye in the back of her head. Sure, Liam fought dirty, but she just wouldn't ever give him time to get a needle out. Being outside alone on a Saturday night was poor planning on her part – she should have known better.

So she would just have to keep doing what she was doing: stay inside, keep a low profile, and train until a needle was no match for her fist.

Her heart sank, realizing she would have to tell Luca, "hey never mind, let's keep those ridiculous foreign accounts,

I've decided I'm still a hermit house rat."

For a long time, the hermit house rat was all she wanted. She wanted to be alone, undisturbed, allowed to keep whatever strange schedule she wanted, permitting it allowed her to meet her ATM every third Thursday of the month.

But Cornelia didn't want that anymore. Maybe she never wanted it in the first place. Maybe it was just the easiest way to combat a threat she didn't even know existed.

She had begun to enjoy her new life with Connor, laughing, drinking, eating, loving. How could she go back now?

"Actually," Cornelia said. Connor and Renee snapped to attention. "I could really go for a chai latte," Cornelia said, looking to Renee. "Would you mind grabbing me one? I think I saw a machine down the hall."

"Absolutely," Renee said, rummaging through her purse to grab her wallet. She skittered down the hall.

Connor rubbed her knee, smiling. "Stealing my order, are you?" he asked her.

She furrowed her eyebrows. "What do you mean?"

"That's the order I always get. I was under the impression you disliked anything chai," he said.

"What did I ask for?" she asked.

Connor glanced down the hall, as if Renee, from her distant run to the coffee machine, could tell him the answer he was looking for. "You ordered a chai latte?" he said.

She palmed her forehead. "Shit, I must have been thinking of what you usually get and I just got them mixed up," she said. "I'm sorry, do you mind grabbing her?"

Connor ran down the hallway after Renee, leaving Cornelia alone. She glanced to the pile of stuff they had accumulated over only the past day – a variety of snacks and sodas, clothing of all types and sizes. On top of the bag sat Connor's car keys, taunting her.

Connor and Renee had disappeared around the bend in the hallway.

She grabbed the keys and bee-lined to the nearest exit.

They were parked in a garage about equidistant to the coma ward and the emergency room, and thanks to the panic button, she found the car right away. Parking levels and numbered spaces had been the least of her concern when they checked in.

She didn't realize she had forgotten a coat until the bitter wind whipped through the damp concrete walls of the garage. It howled in discord with the panic alarm on Connor's car.

She sat in the driver's seat, and despite not having driven for about two years, she could tell this an off-roading kind of SUV. She could see over everyone else, suddenly the hunter on a highway of prey. She wondered if it had a roll bar.

She inched out of the parking spot, getting used to the feel of a car around her.

As she pulled out onto the highway, she settled into her regular old routine. She turned the radio on and something too poppy blasted through the stereo. She turned it off again, preferring the cold silence.

She shivered, goose bumps covering her entire body. She flipped on the heated seats.

She wasn't sure what way she was supposed to be driving, but she was pretty sure about the general direction. When she came upon residential houses to her right, a long, unmaintained park on her left, her memory came back to her. She wasn't sure which memory, but she knew where she was.

She drove right through the metal gate barring her way, mentally tipping her hat to Connor's ex-wife.

Trees lined her drive into the deserted medical complex. It was bright now, the sun shining overhead as she parked the car by the main entrance.

She wasn't sure what she was planning on doing, just that something had to be done.

She slammed the door shut and walked up to the building. It looked like the fireworks had done some damage, the door swaying slightly with the wind. Cornelia strolled right in.

The entryway was littered with the remnants of burnt

up fireworks. A few ceiling panels hung down, having been blasted away. The elevator door looked like it had been under gunfire, the metal door decorated with small black splotches. The majority of the fireworks had gone off in that direction.

She let the door fall shut behind her and listened, taking stock of her surroundings. It was then that she heard muttering from her right, originating behind a door just a few feet past the security station and front doors.

Cornelia crept closer.

"Can't believe this, everything destroyed!" he said angrily, and she heard a swish of papers being thrown or dropped. Liam.

She took a step forward, in full view of the open door. He knelt on the floor, going through a stack of blackened papers. A few fireworks had made their way into his office and started a nice billowing fire. The damage in the hallway consisted of pings and quick fires easily snuffed out by the sprinkler and industrial grade fire resistant building materials, but inside the office, thousands of precious documents waited for the hungry fire to consume them.

He felt her presence, and turned to her just as she blocked his doorway.

"Cornelia," he said, and his face brightened.

"Liam," she mimicked.

He stood, and the stack of papers in his lap fell to the ground. "You came back," he said. He took another step forward. "I knew you would, I knew you would come around!"

He took another step toward her, reaching out as if to pull her into a hug. She punched him in the nose, feeling a crack. Blood splattered, dripping, as his hands flew to his face.

"I understand you might be a little upset, but that's no reason to resort to violence," he reasoned. She kicked him in the gut, and he fell back against the desk behind him.

He scrambled to reach something behind the desk, and Cornelia didn't need to see the medical bag to figure out he was looking for a sedative. She grabbed him by the arm while he wasn't looking, and spun him head first into the opposing wall.

"Cornelia please, let's just talk," he begged, backing further into the office. He hit the bookshelf behind him and stopped.

He made no move to stop her as she walked up to him, close enough they could have kissed. She kneed him in the groin. He crouched down but didn't fall.

She punched him again. And again.

Again, again, again....

She stopped when he fell to the ground, unmoving.

Fear coursed through her veins as she realized what she had done, followed by a sense of calmness. Blood dribbled from his head onto a scattered pile of papers on the floor, seeping in and staining them red.

She walked back into the hallway, heading to the shower in her old room. She had blood on her hands that she would rather not take with her.

As she crossed the threshold of the room, she heard a cough from behind.

Cornelia whipped around and saw a man in a suit standing quietly behind the nurse's station. He wore a hat and dark sunglasses that covered most of his face.

"Who are you?" she asked.

He turned to the cabinets on his left and retrieved a bottle of bleach. He rounded the nurse's desk and held it out to Cornelia. "For your dress," he said, motioning to the red glow her black dress had taken on.

"Who-"

"Luca sends his regards."

She nodded, accepting the bottle of bleach, and entered her room. The medical tray still sat next to where her bed had been, the three syringes untouched, pristine. She threw them to the ground and stomped on them as she passed.

She stripped off her dress and underwear into a small pile on the shower floor, letting the bleach soak through. She washed the blood off her body, the hot water scalding and tightening her skin. She had no towel, so she squeezed out as much of the water from her clothes as she could and pulled them back on, wet and loose.

When she walked out of the shower, the man in the suit had gone. There was a small yellow envelope on the counter of the nurse's station, labeled "CW."

She picked it up and peered inside to find what she estimated to be about $50,000 in cash. Luca's unwillingness to talk about the conclusion of the investigation suddenly made sense.

She walked down the quiet hallway, her footsteps echoing. As she neared the front doors, she passed Liam's office. It was neat, organized, seemingly untouched. The acrid stench of bleach hung in the air.

Water from her dress dripped down her legs as she pushed through the front door, into the frigid sunshine.

May this be my new beginning.

ACKNOWLEDGEMENT

First and foremost - thank YOU, for taking a chance on a self-published author. The landscape of publishing is constantly changing and evolving, and without curious, open-minded readers like you, self-published authors would have no chance.

If you enjoyed reading The Girl in Apartment 19, I would be sincerely grateful to see your feedback and/or your review on Amazon or Goodreads. An author, self-published or not, is always learning - I take your feedback seriously, and consider every last bit of it.

I'd like to thank everyone who has been a part of this journey with me - first and foremost, the ladies of my writing group who picked up apart and helped me re-imagine this story, chapter by chapter. Caroline Schley, Rosa Castellano, and Becky Randel - the three of you have made me a better writer with every ounce of critique you've given me.

And lastly, to my wonderful friends and family, and especially my boyfriend, for the encouragement and excitement you have given me over seeing this book published. There is no greater motivator than love.

ABOUT THE AUTHOR

ALEXANDRA WILLIAMS

ALEXANDRA WILLIAMS is the author of THE GIRL IN APART-
MENT 19. She grew up just outside of Philadelphia and spent
her formative years gallivanting around the city, before moving to Pine Hill with her boyfriend and cat. She spends her
time writing, crafting, and drinking hard seltzers.

For new releases, sign up for her mailing list at : alexandrawil-
liamsbooks.com

Just want to chat? Shoot her an email at: awilliams@tem-
ple.edu

Made in the USA
Columbia, SC
15 July 2021